The
Village
Hall
Vendetta

JONATHAN WHITELAW

Harper
North

HarperNorth
Windmill Green
24 Mount Street
Manchester M2 3NX

A division of
HarperCollins*Publishers*
1 London Bridge Street
London SE1 9GF

www.harpercollins.co.uk

HarperCollins*Publishers*
Macken House
39/40 Mayor Street Upper
Dublin 1
D01 C9W8

First published by HarperNorth in 2023

1 3 5 7 9 10 8 6 4 2

A catalogue record for this book
is available from the British Library

ISBN: 978-0-00-852054-0
TPB ISBN: 978-0-00-861818-6

Printed and bound in Great Britain by
CPI Group (UK) Ltd, Croydon

MIX
Paper | Supporting
responsible forestry
FSC™ C007454

This book is produced from independently certified FSC™ paper
to ensure responsible forest management.

For more information visit: www.harpercollins.co.uk/green

For Anne-Marie and Henry, the eternal loves of my life
And to art – for always illuminating me.

PROLOGUE

To the trained eye, *Buttermere at Dawn* is a modern master-piece. Subtle in its colour, its tones, even its brushstrokes seem minimal, barely caressing the canvas. It captures so much of an often overlooked wonder of the Lake District in next to nothing. And even the experts are left wanting more.

For everyone else, it's a part of the cultural zeitgeist. A titan of modern British minimalism, the painting can be found on everything from calendars, T-shirts and tote bags to postcards and tea towels. Not bad for a painting that's been in the hands of private collectors for most of its existence.

The art world is in mourning this week after the sudden death of *Buttermere at Dawn*'s creator. The enigmatic and elusive Elvira was as inscrutable as the masterpiece that made her a household name in the late seventies. But who was the woman behind this legend? And has the fabled curse of *Buttermere at Dawn* claimed another victim?

Like everything else that surrounds Elvira, her own past is even up for debate. Most profilers of the artist agree that she was born Mae Anne Armstrong sometime in 1951, although years have varied depending on who you read. Her mother was a housewife and her father a farmhand who worked the dales of Cumbria after the war. A loner at school, she had always shown a keen interest in nature and the surrounding splendour of the countryside. One biographer in the 1990s noted that the young Mae Armstrong had shown an eye for detail in her art classes from as young an age as five. And friends who were interviewed over the years always said she spent most of her time on her own, wandering the fields and exploring the Lakes.

Although Armstrong was noted as having enrolled in the prestigious Manchester School of Art in the autumn of 1969, when she was eighteen, no further academic notes have been discovered. And there are no records of any student sales by the woman who would go on to be dubbed the 'monumental talent of her generation.'

Very little of what Armstrong worked on during these years is evident now. Lost to history, her formative experiences and evidence of being a working artist are tragically scant. It's not until *Buttermere at Dawn* first sold at public auction that the public learned of this enigmatic talent. But almost as quickly as it was sold, it was sold again. It had already been privately bought and sold before it came under the auctioneer's hammer, and soon after, the rumours of a curse began to rear their heads. Tabloid tales abounded of ill-fated accidents and the untimely deaths of those connected to the picture. There were even tales of financial ruin brought on by merely being in the *presence* of the painting.

By the end of the decade, young Armstrong, who had adopted her moniker 'Elvira' soon after graduation, was making huge waves, not just in the art world, but the wider cultural sphere. While the likes of Damien Hurst and Banksy are household names now, Elvira was paving the way decades earlier. Interviewed in 1977 ahead of her first major exhibition, a celebration of minimalism at the National Gallery in London, she was asked about her new guise.

'Vira is a Sanskrit word. It means a brave person or hero,' said the artist. 'I'm neither of those things, the opposite in fact. But it's a mask I wear, like you read in the comic books, or the Lone Ranger. When I paint, when I talk to people, I'm wearing this mask. Elvira, she's the one who does the painting. She's a creation, like my work. I'm just the vessel where she lives.'

The exhibition was a huge success. And Elvira very quickly became the hottest name; the must-have artist to hang on the walls of the great and good. That success carried over into the new decade, when a whole new generation of wealthy, art- and asset-hungry fans were gobbling up everything she did – from huge landscapes and distorted portraits to sketches, drawings and signatures on napkins. And yet, the woman behind the brand stayed well away from the limelight. Happy to smile sadly for the cameras at an unveiling or a multi-million-pound sale of one of her works, but the real Mae Armstrong remained an enigma that hid away when she wasn't needed. No boyfriend, no family, no known fixed abode even. The world knew nothing of her beyond her Elvira act – something that many believed was exactly what Armstrong wanted all along.

The painting that would go on to define Elvira's career has a chequered history. *Buttermere at Dawn* had almost no public showings, except for a brief stint in the late 1980s to celebrate Elvira's much heralded *Next to Nothing* exhibition in New York before an unfortunate accident ended the show early.

In the ensuing years, Elvira continued to produce work. But it was the same question at every exhibition – what about *Buttermere at Dawn*? The painting itself retreated into privacy, much like its creator. She even owned it and sold it herself at one point. It even went missing for a few years – nobody knew where it had gone, only for it to appear again in 1996 in a private collection.

Interest waned as tastes changed. And while *Buttermere at Dawn* was still lauded, it came to be regarded as a piece of art history, rather than at the cutting edge.

Like every great piece of culture, *Buttermere at Dawn* is steeped in its own myth. And its curse has become the stuff of legend, a piece of melodrama lurid enough to make the painting famous way beyond the art world. One incredible story even proposes that *Buttermere at Dawn* doesn't, in fact, show the mile-long Cumbrian lake, but instead is a hellish landscape that foretells the end of the world. Perhaps it is this mystery that has kept us enthralled for so long: the dark hues, the angry hills and yet strangely calm water and sky all allude to something otherworldly, yet grounded very much in reality.

It should be stated that no former owner has ever gone on record to talk about the curse. And yet, with every passing year, not to mention the dawn of the digital age, more and more theories, rumours and whispers are created around it.

With Elvira's death there has been a renewed interest in her work and, in particular, *Buttermere at Dawn*. In the past few days campaigns have been launched to have Elvira permanently remembered in her home county, with Carlisle and Penrith councils both flooded with requests for statues, museums and monuments.

Elvira's legacy will be that of stellar success. And yet the brighter her star shone, the more unknowable Mae Armstrong became. She made no public appearances in her final years and gave next to no interviews since the dawn of the new century.

That reclusiveness merely fuelled her legend. Some claimed that Elvira's seclusion was a publicity stunt designed to drum up intrigue and raise the price of her work. She was even accused of cooking up the curse as a way of bumping the price tag. As was always with Elvira, she didn't rise to the taunts, the accusations, or even the plaudits. Instead she stayed quiet and worked. And that work should be a fitting epitaph to a woman who shaped popular culture in her own way, either by design or accident. Who was she really? We'll never know.

Elvira, artist. 1951–2018

Chapter 1

LUNCHEON OF THE BOATING PARTY

'What do you mean there's no stew?' asked Amita.

'Stew? Why would we serve stew?' The question almost sounded like an insult.

'Why *wouldn't* you serve stew? This is a restaurant, isn't it? People come in here, sit down, eat a meal and pay good money for it.'

'Amita,' said Jason.

'Why would you not have something as staple as stew on the menu?' she said angrily.

'Menu?'

'Amita.'

A long queue was forming behind them now. The whispers of unrest and disgruntlement were beginning to gain in strength. Whispers became murmurs. Soon there was an air of unhappiness hanging over the stifled, stale air of the *Emperor Burger* chain that was the pride of the company's presence in Cumbria. Awards adorned the walls: certificates of excellence and congratulations for passing basic health inspections. There was even a team photo, faded from the dappled sunlight bursting in through the huge windows that looked out onto the motorway service area.

Jason knew there was trouble brewing. As a journalist he was never too far away from thinking with his stomach. This was one of the busiest rest areas on the already log-jammed M6. People were, in general, in lousy form when they stumbled and hobbled through the doors of *Emperor Burger*'s flagship fast food restaurant in Cumbria. The last thing they needed was a seventy-year-old grandmother kicking off at the baffled staff.

'Couldn't you just have something else?' he said quietly, hoping a gentle touch might give Amita something to think about.

'What? No!' she shouted. 'I want a bowl of stew. I haven't eaten anything since breakfast, I've been folded up in the car like an accordion for three hours and I think, being a woman of my age, I've earned the right to choose what I have for dinner.'

'Stew?' the gormless teenager behind the service desk asked again. 'But we're a burger place. Why would we serve stew in a burger place? That doesn't make any sense.'

Amita gritted her teeth. She wasn't exaggerating when she said she was in a bad mood. The whole day had been a total washout from the moment she got up. Why they had to travel all the way to Carlisle to pick up a pair of her new running shoes she would never understand. This was supposed to be the twenty-first century, everything was meant to be no further away than a click of a button. And now this.

'Let me speak to the manager,' she demanded.

'What?'

'Young man, if you're going to keep asking questions then it's clear that you're not qualified to be dealing with my complaint,' she said, 'I'd like to speak to somebody in charge before I *really* lose my temper.'

'Amita,' said Jason again, feeling the heat of anger from the crowd begin to singe the hairs on the back of his neck. 'I really think you should just order something else and we can get back on the road.'

'The manager please,' she said, ignoring her son-in-law. 'Right now.'

The feckless server shrugged. He turned in a long, slow arc and shuffled away into the back of the kitchens, dragging his feet as he went.

'Couldn't you just have chips or something?' Jason pleaded. 'Or a milkshake?'

'A milkshake?' Amita's voice almost broke it went so high. 'What age do you think I am Jason?'

'Something, anything Amita, please,' he said.

'I want stew.'

'They don't have any stew.'

'Well I want to know why.'

'They're a burger joint, Amita. They serve burgers and chips and half-arsed attempts at salad that taste strangely like burgers and chips.'

'Why would you have a place like this in a motorway service station? Especially here.'

'Because people don't want to think about what they're eating when they're driving the length of the country.'

'Yes, but I'll bet there are plenty of the elderly community who come through here. Coach trips, folk heading south. I'm sure none of them want to be putting whatever that is into their bodies.'

She pointed at the next till over as a woman took her tray, a mountain of greasy meat and melting cheese dribbling all over the place. Jason silently admitted that even he didn't fancy it that much. But that wasn't the point.

'Look Amita, I get what you're saying, really I do,' he said. 'It's not perfect, it's not even ideal. But could you please, just this once, try to play with the cards that are in front of you rather than make a whole big song and dance about changing the world? Because there is a *very* long queue behind us and they're not going to stay patient for–'

'Oi!' came an angry shout from down the line.

Jason and Amita both turned to face the gruff voice in unison. A tall, sour-faced man with tattoos on his neck and bald head was scowling at them. He looked like a Hells Angel, if Hells Angels wore tartan headbands and spoke with sharp Scottish accents.

'What's the hold up here, eh?' he barked. 'We're all starving here and you're hogging the till.'

A low ripple of agreements went up and down the line, faces frowning.

'They don't have any stew,' shouted Amita loudly.

'What?' barked the Scottish biker.

'Oh don't you start as well,' she rolled her eyes.

'They don't have any stew?' the biker asked.

'I know!' Amita fired back.

This was getting ridiculous. Jason was about to have his face punched in by a very angry Scotsman all over a lack of well-cooked brisket. Even he couldn't have written that one.

'Just get on with it!' someone else cried from the crowd.

'No, I want stew,' said Amita. 'If a pensioner wants a bowl of stew she should be able to order it.'

'Order something else!' cried another faceless voice from the mob.

'You might want to settle for something else, whoever said that, but I'm not. I was raised in a single room and kitchen in Sheffield, we didn't have any shoes on our feet. I brought up a family and even caught a murderer once. I shouldn't have to settle.'

That was it. Jason clapped his hand to his forehead. The 'I was raised in a single room' speech had been rolled out. There was no going back now. The whole of *Emperor Burger*'s chief operating staff could come marching out, wielding the biggest pot of gourmet beef bourguignon ever created and Amita wouldn't be appeased.

More importantly, the crowd had lost its patience. Amita was fielding arguments left, right and centre. The queue's neat line had broken down and she was pinned in. Jason had had enough. Thankfully, his phone began to vibrate in his pocket. He pulled it out, half hoping it was the police telling him they were coming to end the siege. Instead it was a mobile number he didn't recognise. Caught between an angry mob, his rabid mother-in-law and the unknown, the choice was simple.

'I need to take this,' he said.

But Amita couldn't hear him. She was bellowing orders and instructions, arguments and counterarguments and the latest statistics she'd allegedly read from the National Federation of Retired Persons to be bothered with him.

Jason slipped through the crowd. They were beginning to argue amongst themselves now. Maybe it was the hunger getting to them. Or the incessant, indecipherable music that always seemed to be playing in these places. Tempers were frayed, straws had broken camels' backs. Irritation and disobedience were starting to take over.

Jason hurried towards the front door, keeping his head down. His phone was still ringing but he didn't want to answer with the fall of Sodom and Gomorrah unfolding around him. A cool, early summer breeze hit him as he stepped onto the forecourt, blowing away the fast food cobwebs. He answered the phone and tried to breathe in some proper air.

'Hello?' he asked.

'Oh, hi there,' said the voice on the other end. 'Is that Jason Brazel, the journalist?'

'Yes, it is,' he said cautiously. Jason had found that journalists were rarely called for friendly chats. 'And who might this be?'

'Good,' said the man. 'It's sometimes pot bloody luck if you get the right number with these companies. I once tried to reach the British consulate in Bermuda and ended up buying a vintage Ford Consul from a bloke in Walsall instead.'

Jason blinked, his head swimming. Images of golden beaches and crystal clear waters interrupted by the theme music for *The Sweeney* was causing him no end of confusion.

'Eh... okay,' he said. 'Who did you say you were again?'

'Oh aye, sorry,' said the man. 'Forgive me. My name's Mulberry, Hal Mulberry, I got your number from a friend of a friend of a friend who has access to these sorts of things. Say no more eh.'

'Hal Mulberry?' asked Jason.

'That's right.'

The name sounded familiar but Jason couldn't pinpoint it. The shouting from Amita and the mob was getting louder, echoing out from the service station behind him. A full-blown riot wasn't far off and it was distracting him from nailing down the name.

'Eh... okay, what can I do for you Mr Mulberry?'

'Well actually, it's more what I can do for *you*, young man,' he said.

There was a clatter from behind him. Something smashed and there was a large commotion. Like it or not, he should probably head back inside to rescue the biker and mob from his mother-in-law.

'Right, I see,' he said. 'And how do you suppose you can do that then?'

'Ever heard of a painting called *Buttermere at Dawn*?'

'The what?'

'*Buttermere at Dawn*, it's by the world-renowned Elvira.'

'Elvira? I've never heard of him.'

'*Her*, young man, her. Elvira is a she, or she was.'

'Elvira what?'

'Just Elvira,' said Hal. 'That's all.'

Jason rubbed his forehead. He was hardly a leading art expert but he thought that if there was an artist out there famous enough only to have one name, he probably should have heard of them. He made a mental note to be more culturally cognisant.

'She was the Banksy of her day – very elusive, very mysterious,' said Hal. 'Her stuff goes for a fortune now, serious money. But we're talking about her masterpiece here. It was done when she was a nobody, fifty years ago.

It's going up for sale and I'm going to buy it and bring it back to its spiritual home here in Penrith.'

An alarm was going off now. Through the sliding doors Jason could see the bodies all pushing around, chairs hoisted in the air, voices raised almost as high.

'Right, okay,' he said. 'Look, Mr Mulberry, I'm sorry, I'm going to have to go as something is unfolding right in front of me that I think the police are going to have a field day with. You're going to buy a painting?'

'That's right.'

'And bring it home to Penrith, yes?'

'Correct.'

'Is it worth anything?'

'I should say. Sotheby's have a reserve of two million quid on the bloody thing!'

Jason felt the air leave him like he'd been punched in the chest. Which was convenient as a little old woman did exactly that to the Scottish biker right in front of him as they spilled out from inside the service station.

'Two million pounds,' he gasped. 'You're paying two *million* pounds for a tatty old painting?'

'It's a masterpiece from a genius at the start of her career. It's priceless to me Jason and I want *you* to come with me to London to write the story. Exclusive, nobody else is getting it. You and me, down in the big smoke at the end of the week. I'll give you everything you need.'

Jason was gobsmacked. He was genuinely speechless. Life, it seemed, had a strange way of pulling the rug from under his feet. Just then Amita appeared, gasping for air and thumbing back at the full blown rammy unfolding inside.

'That's it, Jason,' she panted. 'I'm never eating in one of these places again. You can't even begin to have a civil conversation with those people. All I wanted was a bowl of stew. Can you believe that they didn't serve stew. It's outrageous. A restaurant that doesn't serve stew, I've never heard of anything so downright preposterous.'

Jason's mind was made up.

'When does the train leave Mr Mulberry?'

Chapter 2

THE BLUE WINDOW

The champagne cork popped and the frothy fizz spilled over onto the little table between them. Jason had only ever heard that sound for his own enjoyment a handful of times. More often than not, the bubbly was broken out by the big shots he was reporting on. He was left with the machine Bovril that always had a shimmering film on its surface.

'There you are my boy! Bollinger! Drink up, drink up, nothing but the best will do! *Nil satis nisi optimum* as they said in the ancient world.'

Hal Mulberry emptied half the bottle into two plastic flutes. He then took a long gulp from the bottle itself and laughed loudly. He was the type of man who when he laughed, everyone around knew it was happening. Big, boisterous but still strangely likeable, his open, ruddy face lit up the first-class cabin of the train as it sped from Euston Station.

'Do you know why I drink Bollinger, Jason?' he asked.

'Because it's the most expensive?' Jason asked back.

'No, no, no, it's not. Not by a long shot. It's because James Bond drinks it. I remember watching Roger Moore in the cinema and he asked for Bollinger and that was it. I was sold. I told myself, as I scoffed down my cheap crisps, that when I grew up that's what I was going to drink, just like him. And here we are.'

'Here we are,' said Jason with a smile.

This wasn't the first bottle that Hal had loosened off today. It wasn't even the first in the last hour. A celebratory mood was in the air. The local boy had done good and he was returning home with his prize. He had bought *Buttermere at Dawn* and was feeling pretty pleased with himself.

Jason, on the other hand, was trying to feel professional. He was, after all, still working. And no amount of expensive champagne and guffawing businessmen were going to distract him from doing his job. Unfortunately, Hal Mulberry was the type of man who made it very difficult to say 'no' to. Over six feet tall with a sparkly cheekiness and wicked good fun in his hazel eyes, he seemed to weave a sort of magic wherever he went. Jason liked him. He liked him a lot. Especially when he was picking up the bar tab.

'I've got her Jason. I've *got* her!' he said, loosening his top button and tugging at his polka dot tie. 'Do you know how long I've been waiting for this moment? Have you any idea?'

'I'd need to check my notes Hal, but you might have mentioned that it's been a dream forty years in the making.'

'Forty-two.' He drained his plastic glass and went back to the bottle. 'Forty-two long, hard years of graft, ducking, diving and every-bloody-thing else it takes to scrounge up enough money to buy a masterpiece. But I'll tell you this, and I want this in your article, it's been worth every second. Every single second Jason, to be able to call that painting my own.'

Jason politely and subtly pushed his flute away from him, pulling out his tatty notepad and the third pen of the day. He'd been charting their journey since six this morning. Down the spine of the country, through the bustling streets of London and every nerve-shredding, anxiety-inducing moment of the auction itself. Hal Mulberry had regaled him with stories of his meteoric rise in business, a rags to riches story from potless school leaver in the 1980s to a thriving entrepreneur of the dot com bubble in the 90s. Every love, laugh and leer had been described in great detail. Yes, his family had historically had wealth, the Mulberry's had been generous philanthropists in Cumbria in their day but most of it had been gone by the time Hal was born. So Hal had made his own pot of gold, through hard work and intuition. And as the clock struck six in the evening, Jason felt like he'd lived all of Hal's fifty-odd years with him. The arts story he had been reeled in with had now turned into an elaborate profile, a look at the ways and wonders of Hal Mulberry in his entirety.

What he still didn't know, however, was why. Why would a successful businessman, the owner of an international import and export firm, drop two million pounds on a work of art? That's what he was going to find out.

'I still can't believe it,' said Hal, resting his head on the plush cushion of his first-class seat. 'The moment the gavel came down and those Sotheby snobs told me it was mine.

It was like something out of a film. I can still hear the sound in my head. Can you hear it?'

'I'm surprised you heard anything,' said Jason. 'The amount of shouting and hollering you were doing in that auction room. I thought they were going to throw you out.'

'They wouldn't *dare*,' Hal grinned. 'I'd just given them a nice big chunk of change for commission. If they threw me out their bean counters upstairs would have a fit. A positive fit!'

Jason laughed at the thought. He had rarely ever seen such joy on a person before. When the auctioneer had stiffly closed on the sale and Hal's bid was victorious, he had almost jumped out of his skin from the tycoon's outburst. The room had been busy, just as Jason had imagined it would be. And there had been plenty of interested parties. This, however, felt like it was destiny. Hal Mulberry was destined to own *Buttermere at Dawn*, despite it being a little drab and conceptual for Jason's taste. It all looked more like ink blots and smudges to him, as opposed to the Buttermere he knew. Even the sky, to his mind, should have been at least blue, instead of the grey and charcoal sweeps of the paintbrush.

Now they were winging their way back up to Cumbria on one of the early evening trains. The painting would be waiting for them, specially couriered that very afternoon at no expense spared, Hal had boasted. Jason was glad not to be sat beside it. He didn't imagine Hal Mulberry carried his own luggage very often. That would have left him holding the very expensive cargo. If his nerves had been shredded by the auction, just holding the painting probably would have finished him off.

'What is it about this particular painting Hal?' Jason asked bluntly.

The businessman finished the last of the bottle. He wiped his lips and put it down hard on the table, smiling. The train whizzed through a tunnel and when it emerged again, Hal looked different. He was staring away into nothing, a haze of nostalgia now over him.

'I told you about Bond and Bollinger,' he said. 'Well, *Buttermere at Dawn* is almost the very same. Almost, mind you, not exactly.'

'No?' Jason prodded. 'Tell me about it.'

Hal steepled his fingers. He was still smiling, although there was sadness there now too. He wrestled his own thumbs, watching them rub back and forth against each other.

'When I was a young boy, we didn't have a lot,' he said. 'My father worked the land for one of those big houses down near Windermere. Six days a week shovelling horse dung for a pittance. You know the old routine, abject poverty, kids starving, not enough hours et cetera. Funnily enough, Elvira's dad was the same. We had that in common, me and the artist. Then he got to thinking that he wanted to be his own boss. He quit then and there, did what he could to stand on his own two feet and made a fortune. Lost a lot of it too, mind you. Loved a flutter he did, horses, dogs, you name it. A lot of his money went to pay off his debt when he died. My mum didn't know anything about it. I might have been born with a silver spoon, Jason, but I didn't live like it, not when I was old enough to make my own decisions. Every penny I own, I've earned it. I'm a rags to riches boy, in a way. But I don't talk about it.'

Jason held in a scoff at that.

'The telly was my out, that and the movies. Film stars, TV stars, amazing worlds in your living room, in the cinema, all just there for the price of a ticket. Or free when you're at home. I watched everything, from *Thunderbirds* to *Wildlife on One*, I was hooked. I could sit for hours in front of that box. And when I wasn't watching it, I'd be wanting to go see the latest big film at the old Odeon. Do you remember it?'

'Can't say I was much of a film buff growing up,' said Jason meekly. 'I used to be down the side of the sofa writing my own stories while my folks watched the box. Or if they went to the Odeon I'd go to my gran's. There's just something about a big, dark room, loud noises and a giant screen that's never done it for me, I'm afraid.'

'You missed out. Worlds of wonder waiting for you. They could take you all over the galaxy and have you back in time for tea. And they were a refuge Jason, a real refuge, especially when my old man had had a few too many. Do you know what I mean?'

He softly punched his hand with a curled up fist. It was gentle and he shook his head.

'I'm afraid so,' said Jason. 'Absolutely no excuse for that that. Not then, not now, not ever.'

'You'd like to think so,' said Hal. 'Although there's still too much of that about. I do a lot of campaigning for domestic abuse survivors Jason, in memory of my old mum and everyone my dad hurt. You should do a story about that one day, I'll show you. I hate violence – it's never the answer. Anyway, where was I?'

'The painting,' said Jason.

'Oh aye,' Hal snapped his fingers. 'That painting, *the* painting. It was the most beautiful thing I had ever seen.

I was six, maybe seven, or thereabouts, still in shorts, and I don't mind saying, I was a sad little mite at that time. I'd just lost my dad, Mum was trying to run his business and leaving me in front of the gogglebox alone. Then it comes on the telly. It was a programme about the art scene, all very high brow, BBC Two, that sort of thing, so you knew it was kosher. I was waiting for something else to come on and I flick over to see this painting – *Buttermere at Dawn*. My heart leapt Jason, it really did. I couldn't take my eyes off it. Everything else melted away around me. There was nothing but me and the painting on the screen. And for some reason, it just felt familiar. Like it was already a part of me, like I'd already seen it somewhere before, somewhere close. The colours, the shapes, the majesty, the wonder. It was like Cupid had shot me with an arrow. I was dumbfounded.'

Jason was jotting down notes. He wasn't sure if it was the champagne talking or Hal was growing misty-eyed for the past. Either way it would make good quotes for his piece.

'Then the camera cut away. It felt like I'd been woken from a deep sleep, a dream,' he went on. 'And standing beside it is Elvira. Tall, as fat as a match, as my old mum used to say, dressed in this long, shimmering gown that hung on her shoulders like her hair down either side of her gaunt face. She was being interviewed, as part of this look at young artists.'

'And what did she say?' asked Jason.

'Nothing.'

Jason's pen stopped, like it had been told to. He waited a moment then looked back up at Hal.

'Nothing?'

'Nope,' he laughed. 'Not a single word.'

'So, what, she just stood there?'

'Yup.'

'And didn't say anything?'

'She was completely mute,' Hal chuckled. 'The journalist interviewing her did a fair job I suppose. He kept trying to coax some answers from her but she just smiled at him, standing there beside *Buttermere at Dawn*. He was full of praise, flattery gets you everywhere, my boy. He said, and I still remember to this day, that she was fast becoming one of the greatest talents to come out of the Lake District, right up there with William Wordsworth. And that was it. I was hooked. That someone alive, from my neck of the woods, could be so good at something, so revered to be spoken about with the greats, it was astounding, thrilling. There she was, just standing there, like she'd stepped off the *Starship Enterprise*. And she was from Cumbria. From that moment on I was an art lover. Or at least, I loved everything Elvira would do. You see Jason, when you're that age, you're very impressionable. When somebody does something that is the most hilarious or shocking thing in the world, it leaves an impression on you, like a fingerprint. And I knew, I bloody well *knew* that I had to own that painting. One day. Some day.'

He opened his hands out wide towards Jason.

'Here we are,' he said, his bottom lip starting to tremble. 'Here we are, my boy. I've made it. I should know that money doesn't make you happy, and that status can be a trap as much as people chase it. No, forget all that showy stuff. This picture is what tells me I've done good.'

At that, Hal began to well up. He blubbed a little before his eyes turned red and he scrambled about the big pockets of his suit for a handkerchief. Jason, thankfully, was able to spring to his aid quicker and offered him a packet of disposable ones he'd had mashed in his back pocket for months.

Hal thanked him as he blew his nose, the whole carriage filled with the snorting. A few of the other passengers looked up then quickly back down again in disgust. Jason didn't exactly blame them.

'You should be very proud of yourself,' he said, feebly trying to offer some encouragement to a man who had spent more money than he could ever earn. 'You've done something very special today. And you're doing something truly wonderful for your hometown community. Can you tell me some more about what you intend to do with the painting?'

That seemed to snap the tycoon from his funk. He sniffed again and wiped his face.

'Yes,' he said. 'The painting is going on public display in a brand new, state-of-the art facility in the heart of Penrith. I want everyone to be able to enjoy this master-piece by one of our forgotten local heroes. I want kids to come with their granny and grandad and be as inspired as I was watching it on TV all those years ago. Good art, Jason, should be enjoyed by the masses, by the people. Not locked away in a damp, dusty cellar where the mega rich show it to their equally mega rich pals.'

'And where is the facility going to be?' he asked.

'The old Penrith Village Hall.'

Jason almost punctured his notepad. He swallowed and looked across at Hal Mulberry. 'The village hall?' he said. 'The one close to the castle, beside the train station?'

'That's right,' said Hal, looking around for somebody to serve him.

'But… but it's falling apart, isn't it? I thought it was only a bunch of local community groups that use that place now, don't they, because it's cheap and they don't mind the fact it's freezing and looks like something from a "before" on a DIY makeover show? And I'm pretty sure some unruly teenagers use the car park as a place to smoke and drink without fear of getting caught at night.'

'I know,' he leaned over the chair and waved at a member of the train crew in the next carriage, breezily unbothered by Jason's alarm.

'But… but it's practically a ruin, Hal,' Jason pressed on. 'I mean, I would bet that there isn't even an intact *roof* on the thing. How can you leave a two-million-quid painting in what's essentially a hut across the road from some tatty medieval boulders and bricks?'

'It's alright Jason lad, don't panic,' said Hal as the crewmember arrived, ready to take his order. 'We'll get a new roof on it and everything, you'll see. I've bought it.'

'You've *what*?' he gulped.

'It's not just this painting, I've bought the village hall too.'

The train barrelled through another tunnel. And this time it was Jason's turn to come out the other end another man. This was how the other half lived. Although if he came into untold riches, he wasn't sure a crumbling village hall would be top of his personal shopping list.

'And for you, sir?' asked the crewmember.

Jason gathered his thoughts. Sure, he'd had a run of bigger stories to report on – ever since Amita put him onto some dark goings-on at the bingo club. But recently it was all small fry compared to this. Million-pound painting sales, heartfelt outpourings from one of the region's top entrepreneurs and now a beloved, if decrepit, village hall becoming a gleaming centre of public art. It was all a bit much.

'Lager please,' he said, all thoughts of professionalism now out of the window. 'Better make that two.'

Chapter 3

THE KISS

Jason was never drinking again. And he meant it this time. The combination of a young family, an ambitious lawyer for a wife and a mother-in-law who had no volume control conspired against him time and time again. He should always listen to that little voice in the back of his head telling him to quit the sauce long before it's too late. Otherwise suffer the wrath of some very large, very loud voices outside of his head making his life a misery.

He was sitting on the edge of the sofa, face resting in his hands, elbows balanced on his knees. If he could just stay there, perfectly still, and never move again, he might be alright. The living room door opened and Radha came billowing in like a tornado. Dirty clothes in one hand, briefcase and laptop bag in the other, her efficiency put Jason to shame on a daily basis – doubly so when he was hungover.

'Good grief,' she said, spotting him. 'Godzilla has awoken and is looking as rough as the floor of a taxi cab.'

'Please stop,' he moaned. 'I know you haven't started yet but please stop beforehand. I don't think I can handle it.'

'I'm sorry Jason, I had no idea that reality could be so painful for you,' she smiled. 'I mean, we can't all be zooming up and down to London every day, sipping champagne and buying up oil paintings, can we?'

'Please don't mention booze,' he said. 'I think I may have drunk my own bodyweight on that train last night. How is that even possible in just three hours. I mean, isn't there some sort of biological law against that kind of thing. Help me out here Radha, you're a solicitor.'

'I am,' she said. 'And it's a good job I am too. Because if you and your new bestie, Hal Mulberry, had got further than the station when the train came in last night, there's no telling what trouble you could have gotten yourselves into. Remind me to run a background check on him, he's a bad influence on you, Jason Brazel.'

She continued to tidy up around him, piling even more toys, towels and stray socks into her arms. Jason sat perfectly still, hoping that the misery would end soon and everyone would leave him to wallow. He felt dreadfully guilty of course. Radha was so busy at work, the least he could do was look after things at home when she wasn't there. Instead of gallivanting around on trains with multi-millionaires.

'Thank you for making sure I got home safe and sound,' he said. 'I tell you something, there's something to this lives of the rich and famous thing. Hal runs into a problem – and snap, buys his way out of it.'

'Is that a fact?' she said, turning her attention to the kids' toybox in the far corner.

'Did I say he's bought the old village hall?'

'The village hall!?'

'I know,' said Jason. 'He's going to turn it into an exhibition centre for this bloody painting. Honestly Radha, I think he's got more money than sense. He's got all these noble notions of philanthropy, but why the hell would you spend even more cash on a folly like that.'

'It's a legacy, a temple to the self, that's what this is about, Jason. Ever heard of the Pyramids?'

She made a good point. Although he'd never exactly thought of Penrith and Luxor in the same breath before.

'I don't think he really cares what happens next – men like that, it's all in the chase,' she continued. 'And I bet he's the kind of man who likes the sound of his own voice above all else – I bet he won't care if you write a good story about him. Which you're going to do right?'

'Oh yeah,' said Jason. 'It's all there. Great quotes, the Cinderella of a working-class hero. Even the breaking down in tears to show a human side of capitalism, it's got the lot.'

'He cried in front of you?' asked Radha, stopping her cleaning crusade.

'He did,' winced Jason. 'You know I reckon there might be more to Hal than the kind of cartoon tycoon you're painting him as. He's a blubberer.'

'Aww, bless, like a big bairn.'

'A big bairn with a *lot* of money to burn, it would seem.'

'Well good on him,' said Radha. 'If you say he's a good egg, I'll take your word for it. Buying the painting and the village hall, turning it into something that the community will actually be able to use. When's the piece due?'

'I need to find an editor who'll run it first,' he rubbed his face and instantly regretted the sudden movement.

'Hal mentioned something about having the ear of a business bod down in London but I can't remember. I'll write it up today and take it from there. It's a total puff piece Radha, but somebody will buy it.'

Radha finished her morning sweep of the living room. Her arms bulging with all the clutter and chaos of family life. She stopped in front of him on her way to the kitchen. It took all of Jason's effort to raise his head, his brain rattling around in his skull like a dried-up walnut.

She leaned down and kissed him over the pile of dirty laundry and squeaking teddies and diggers.

'I'm very proud of you Jason Brazel,' she said, smiling at him. 'You're back in the game and doing what you love.'

'Doing what I love? Drinking too much and hanging around with captains of commerce?'

'Being a journalist,' she said, kissing him again. 'It's what you were born to do and you do it so well. And I'm always, *always*, immensely proud of you. Don't forget that.'

Jason felt a lump form in his throat. For an all too fleeting moment his headache vanished and he felt alive again. Then two screams from the kitchen as Clara and Josh tried to outdo each other on the decibel level brought him back down to Earth with a thump.

Radha glanced over at the door and closed her eyes. She leaned back in and rested her forehead on his.

'Remember those Saturday mornings where we'd lie in bed until noon, get up and go to the pub just in time for lunch and a night out?' she asked.

'No,' sighed Jason. 'You're getting me mistaken with another man, Mrs Brazel. I was never that fun.'

'True,' she opened her eyes. 'And you're even less fun now.'

He kissed her and she glided away into the kitchen, ready to corral their children. Jason watched her go. He was lucky, so lucky, to have Radha, and the kids. While it didn't feel much like it right now, his hangover would evaporate. But the love from his family wouldn't go. He cherished each and every one of them dearly. He would be lost without them. In fact he had been lost, not so long ago, and even then they'd stuck by him.

The wholesomeness of his thoughts gave him a glimmer of hope. He slowly, steadily lowered himself backwards until the sofa provided a much-needed rest. Staring blankly ahead, he let his head settle of its own accord. Maybe he was going to outpace the hangover stalking him. He had gotten lucky.

Luck, however, vanished as easily as it materialised for Jason Brazel. He had no sooner recovered from the taxing order of sitting back when Amita came storming into the living room.

'Have you seen my keys?' she asked. 'My keys, where are they Jason? Have you seen them? Please tell me you've seen them.'

The vibrations on the floor, the voice bouncing off the walls, and the day-glo colours of Amita's outfit were enough to make his stomach churn. His mother-in-law was the very last person to be around while hungover. She should have come with a government warning.

'My keys, Jason, have you seen them?' she asked again.

'Please stop speaking so loudly, Amita,' he groaned.

'Why? What's wrong with you?' she started pulling the comfy chair by the TV apart, searching.

'Because I had far too much to drink on the way home last night and now my head is about to pop like an over-filled balloon. That's why.'

'It's your own fault as usual,' she said, moving on to the flat surfaces. 'You won't be told Jason, you can't be. And the rest of us all have to suffer you suffering because of your foolishness. Behave yourself now.'

Amita bumped into the coal scuttle by the fireplace. It rattled and scraped before finally tipping over. Jason thought it was the end. He keeled over onto the sofa and tugged at his hair.

'Please stop,' he begged. 'I'll do my penance later, just give me some mercy now.'

'I assume you had a good time in London. You got enough for your story?' she said, replacing the scuttle.

'Yes,' he said, hiding beneath a cushion. 'It turns out Hal Mulberry's wealth is only matched by his generosity, especially when it comes to booze.'

'Yes, he's a very generous man,' she smiled. 'Always has been.'

Jason took a moment to process what she was saying. He pulled the cushion back and stared at her.

'You know him?' he asked. If the fug of alcohol clouding his thoughts had lifted for even a few moments he should have known Amita would know Hal Mulberry. Or know someone who knew someone who knew Hal at least. They didn't call her the Sheriff of Penrith for nothing.

'Oh yes,' she smiled. 'I've met him a few times. He's helped out with a few groups I'm a part of.'

'A *few* groups, Amita? That's like saying Venice has a *few* canals.'

'Yes, well, that's what happens when you're an upstanding pillar of the community Jason. You should try it sometime, instead of staggering in at all hours having been out on a booze cruise all day, or whatever they call it.'

'I'll have you know that Frank Sinatra once said he didn't trust people who didn't drink, because when they wake up that's the best they feel all day.'

'You're not Frank Sinatra, Jason,' she said bluntly.

'No, I'm not.'

He kicked his feet off the couch. With a deep breath he hauled himself to his feet and shambled over to help his mother-in-law with her search for her keys.

'What did Hal do to help exactly?' he said, rummaging about near the door.

'I can't remember it all off the top of my head,' said Amita. 'He's donated various cash prizes and things from his business to raffles for the WI and other places, I know that much. He's always happy to help.'

'He seems that way,' Jason agreed. 'He was telling me he does a lot for all sorts of charity. Domestic violence survivors and the like.'

'Yes, that rings a bell,' said Amita.

'Now he's bought the village hall and he's doing it up.'

Amita stopped dead. Jason searched beneath the couch and the comfy chair for her keys but couldn't find anything.

'He's what?' she asked.

'He's bought the village hall, across from Penrith Castle,' he said again, wincing as he got back to his feet. 'He's turning it into an exhibition place and a kind of shrine to Elvira, the artist behind that painting he's just got.'

'He can't do that,' she said.

'Well he's done it.'

'But it's a place for the community.'

'Don't kid yourself, Amita, it's a wreck.'

'A historical wreck.'

'And it'll still be historical, only in a slightly less ruinous state when he's finished with it.'

'Oh no, this won't do,' she said, fishing her phone out.

'What are you doing?'

'I have to tell people,' she said, scrolling through her endless list of contacts. 'We have to make some sort of stand against this. You can't just waltz in and buy up a place of local importance. It's barbaric.'

'It's not Amita, it really isn't,' said Jason. 'It's the opposite of that. He's going to turn an eyesore into something the whole community can enjoy again, not just the WI and a few other hangers-on who don't mind putting up with the damp. The council has been trying to offload that place for as long as I've been a reporter here. Personally, I think it's a great idea.'

'You would though,' she said.

'Yes, I would, and I do.'

Something jingled as he stepped on the rug. Bending down, he pulled back the corner and found Amita's keys. He picked them up and spun them around his finger in front of her face.

'You're worse than the kids,' he said.

'This is awful, I can't believe Mulberry. The gall of the man. I mean, does he have no shame? That village hall has been there forever, it's for the people, by the people. And what about the area as a whole? That castle has been there since the fourteenth century. Think about what it's seen, what it's lived through. And now it's going to be bombarded with traffic and people who come to leer at that silly painting of his. How are we going to have book groups, or Spanish for Beginners, or chair yoga while people are queuing up to talk modern art, or worse. It'll be abstract this and life drawing that. All kinds of obscenity before you know it, I bet.'

'Art is hardly a peep show, Amita, please,' said Jason. 'And I'd like to remind you that the whole area has seen better days. I mean I know the castle is a piece of local heritage, but it's barely a castle these days. More like a load of crumbling walls that will only continue to crumble until there's nothing left. Who knows, he might even end up buying that too.'

Amita let out a laugh. She started typing away on her phone, sending message after message to the far-reaching corners of the busybody community of Penrith and beyond. Her thumbs were just cooling off when her phone started to vibrate with numerous notes of consternation from people equally appalled.

Jason stopped jangling the keys. Only then did he remember what day it was.

'Hold on,' he said. 'It's Saturday.'

'It is,' said Amita, head buried in her phone. 'Well done, I can see there's been no lasting damage from your Oliver Reed impression last night.'

'It's a Saturday and you're looking for your keys,' said Jason, suspiciously. 'What do you want with your keys on a Saturday? You never do anything on a Saturday. The Sheriff of Penrith *famously* does nothing on a Saturday.'

She didn't answer him. He took a step back and properly looked at her for the first time. The dread of his hangover was lifting and he could start to think properly again.

'Wait a second,' he said. 'Are you... are you wearing a skirt?'

Again, Amita didn't answer him. She was purposely busying herself on her phone.

'You are!' he said, a little too loudly. 'Amita, are you feeling alright? You do know you're wearing a skirt don't you? This isn't some sort of sign that we should be getting you to the hospital or something is it? Because I'm pretty sure I'm still over the limit and–'

'Would you stop it Jason,' she said, finishing on her phone. 'Yes, I'm wearing a skirt and yes, I'm going out on a Saturday. Is it such a terrible thing to break with tradition? You should be pleased for me. Women my age should stay active, the same could be said for you.?

'What's that supposed to mean?'

'It means you could stand to get up off the sofa a little more.'

Jason looked down at his growing gut. He prodded it gently. Almost fondly.

'And we *are* allowed to wear what we want, when we want to. Despite your best efforts.' She stormed out into the hallway and started pulling on a pair of shoes.

'On a Saturday though Amita,' he said. 'I don't think I've ever known you to cross the door on a Saturday. For as long as we've known each other. Where are you going?'

Amita pulled her shoes on and snatched her keys from him. 'If you must know, I'm going to a football match.'

Jason blinked. He shook his head, feeling his walnut brain rattle around inside. 'I'm sorry, what did you just say? Because for a moment I thought you just told me you are going to a football match.'

'That's right,' she said, pulling a jacket from the cupboard by the front door.

'You, Amita Khatri, at a game of football? I don't think a stranger thing has happened in the annals of Penrith history.'

'Well, strange things tend to happen Jason. You and I know that all too well, don't we.'

She had him there. His mother-in-law had him so much that he had no comeback. Jason put it down to him not firing on all cylinders yet. Or any cylinders for that matter.

He was about to continue with his inquisition when the doorbell rang. Amita hurriedly pulled on her jacket and bag and made for the door.

'That's me off now love!' she shouted down the hallway to Radha. 'I'll be home for dinner.'

'Wait, hold on,' said Jason. 'You can't just leave me here wondering what's going on. You're going to the football? Who are you going to see? And who are you going with? Who could possibly be taking *you* to the football?'

Amita opened the door. On the other side, waiting and smiling, was Irvine Carruthers and his little dog. Jason still could only think of him as 'The Ghost', and as he greeted Irvine, had to make his usual attempt not to say the nickname out loud. He and Irvine had first met under strange circumstances, and it was hard to get back to normal pleasantries, even if he was courting Amita under the guise of a genteel friendship.

'Oh,' said Jason. 'I get it.'

'Hello Jason,' said The Ghost, tipping his cap back and staring at him with his big, deep eyes. 'How are you today?'

'I'm fine,' said Jason weakly. 'I hear you and my mother-in-law are for the footie.'

'That's right,' he said, laughing. 'Penrith. We're playing Newton Aycliffe in the lunchtime kick off. Should be a cracker.'

'I'll bet. Sky Sports were just showing a glossy build-up video there before you arrived. Graeme Souness reckons it'll be close.'

'Eh?' The Ghost choked.

'He's teasing you Irvine,' Amita tutted. 'Don't listen to him. He's hungover. Was drinking last night with local dignitaries and now he feels awful.'

'Oh, I see,' said the old man. 'Well, I hope you feel better soon Jason.'

'Thank you, Irvine,' he nodded.

The Ghost turned back down the path, pulling his little dog along with him. Amita gave Jason a dirty stare as she went to follow him.

'I know what you're thinking Jason Brazel,' she said. 'And it's just for a bit of company, that's all.'

'Company for him or you?' Jason sniggered.

She didn't reply. He watched them head down the path and out into the street, passing the postman on the way. Jason laughed.

'They look happy,' said the postie in his broad Welsh accent.

'Don't they just,' replied Jason. 'Anything good Bill? Any uncashed million-quid cheques or news of some gold bullion that's been lost for a hundred years?'

'Nope, nothing like that,' said Bill. 'Oh actually, there is one thing. Addressed to you, looks expensive.'

He rummaged about in his big bag and pulled out a jet black A4 envelope. Jason got a chill when he saw it. He wasn't sure why. Most of his post came in brown envelopes, occasionally with a flash of angry red type. Certainly not this kind of expensive affair. His name was on the front, printed in faux gold handwriting.

'Very mysterious, eh?' said Bill. 'We had a whole load of these land in the early hours this morning. Special delivery, going to folk all over town.'

'Really?' asked Jason. 'What kind of folk? Gangsters? Police?'

'Don't know mate,' sniffed Bill. 'Well go on then, aren't you going to open it?'

'Why? You got a bet on what it might be or something?'

'How'd you guess?'

'Intuition,' Jason rolled his eyes.

He flipped the glossy envelope over and broke the little seal on the back. The whole thing unfolded like a house of cards collapsing, paper spilled out, and a beautiful scroll unfurled from within. Bill took a step back.

'Blimey,' he said. 'Wasn't expecting that.'

Jason scanned the elegant text written on the scroll and raised his eyebrows.

'So?' asked the postie eagerly. 'What is it then, Jason? I could be on to win fifty quid here.'

'It's an invitation,' he said. 'To see a preview unveiling of *Buttermere at Dawn*.'

Chapter 4

FOXES

The church hall was filling up, although it wasn't as busy as usual. While the lighter nights and warmer weather was mostly seen as a blessing, Father Ford couldn't help but secretly regard them as curses. Attendance from Spring to Autumn for the Penrith Bingo Club was normally bleak. And that meant drawing on the reserves.

He stood at the door, smiling and nodding, greeting the faithful as they arrived. In the short time he had been in this parish, Wednesday nights had never quite been the same. Bingo was taken *very* seriously in these parts. One mispronounced number, one second's hesitation over the next call and he'd be hearing about it for the next week.

Not complaints as such, more little niggles, quiet jibes from the more flippant of the flock. When he first took over from the previous vicar, the whole notion of bingo calling had been quite foreign to him. He'd even had to ask the archdeacon if gambling was strictly allowed. But the cleric had muttered something about community outreach and he'd left it at that, assuming it was a simple bit of fun. Foolishly he hadn't taken any advice on the serious matter of hosting the evening before his first session. It had been a disaster of quite biblical proportions. No nicknames for the numbers, no tea for half time. Only crumbs where there should have been biscuits. He had been lucky to get out of the hall alive without a full-blown riot erupting in the aisles. The mild-mannered pastor spent the following week thoroughly researching the ins and outs of the game and what was to be expected. He even bulk-bought extra tea bags should the standard amount run out.

This, Father Ford imagined, was what being a famous actor or politician must be like. A single lapse of concentration and boom, the crowds, the media, everyone would be all over you. The thought made him break out in a cold sweat.

'Good evening, Father,' said Amita.

Father Ford jumped. He was stirred from his panicking daydream to greet her as she came up the steps of the hall.

'Oh, hello Amita,' he said. 'What a lovely surprise.'

'Is it?' she smiled warmly. 'Why so?'

'Why so what?'

'A surprise? I'm here every week.'

'I know you are.'

'Well... why is it a surprise then?'

'Did I say surprise, oh my, sorry, I meant... not a surprise. Sorry, I was miles away there, lost in a daydream as I admired the sunset.'

Amita cocked an eyebrow. The whole of the street was steeped in shadow, the sun long gone behind the rooftops.

'Are you feeling alright Father?' she asked. 'You look a little peaky.'

'What? Me? No, I'm fine, yes fine, very fine in fact,' he pulled a handkerchief from the pocket of his cardigan and patted his forehead. 'Yes, never been fitter. I'm thinking about taking up running, first thing in the mornings, just to make good use of all this fitness.'

'I'd highly recommend it,' she said, stopping at the door. 'I've run three times a week for the past fifty years. Nothing beats it, gets you outdoors, lets you see the world. Particularly handy that we live in, what I happen to think is, the most beautiful corner of the world, too. And it helps you clear away the cobwebs. We can't have you not performing at your best for the numbers, can we?'

Father Ford's throat suddenly became very dry. Amita patted him gently on the arm and headed into the hall. He didn't follow her.

Amita had the choice of seats tonight. There were plenty of gaps, barely any of the long, thin tables taken up by players yet. The nice weather was evidently keeping them away, which made her sad – and it cut off one her prime routes of knowledge about what was really going on in Penrith, and she always prided herself on keeping a finger on the pulse. But there was a selfish reason for Amita's disappointment, too. The emptier the hall, the less excuse she had to not sit with Georgie Littlejohn, the self-anointed Queen of Bingo.

'Amita! I must have a word with you.' Georgie's piercing tones rang in the air.

Amita could swear that Georgie was psychic. No sooner had she thought of her when she appeared out of nowhere at her side. She took Amita's arm and walked her conspiratorially towards Georgie's usual table near the back of the hall.

'Evening Georgie,' said Amita. 'How are you?'

'Never mind how I am, what are we going to do about the village hall?' she asked. 'I've been trying to raise you all week. I almost died when you messaged us all on Saturday. We're letting precious time slip through our fingers.'

'Yes, sorry, I've been busy,' Amita lied.

'I see. Busy with Irvine Carruthers I'll bet, eh?' she jabbed Amita playfully in the ribs. 'I heard he took you to the football, how romantic of him.'

'Stop it Georgie, there's nothing in it,' said Amita, trying not to get flustered, or embarrassed. 'He's a lonely old man, I can't very well turn him down when he's looking for a bit of company, can I?'

'I would,' she said.

Amita bit her tongue. She was about to say there weren't an awful lot of social occasions Georgie Littlejohn *would* turn down. She'd turn up at the opening of an envelope if she could guarantee she'd get her picture in the paper or splashed all over the parish Facebook page.

'And there's been family things too,' said Amita. 'Then there's the big summer fundraiser for the WI on the horizon. You know about that of course.'

'Of course.' Georgie gave a curt nod.

'I'm trying to clear my schedule so I can give it and Violet my full attention this year.'

'Very noble of you,' said Georgie, a hint of venom in her voice although expertly disguised. 'Violet is a lovely woman but she's a bit scatter-brained at times. I'll be glad when she signs off from her presidency at the fete.'

'We can't all be Georgie Littlejohns,' said Amita.

They reached the table. Their friend Sandy was already there. He stood up as the ladies approached and smiled at Amita.

'Evening,' he said, bowing a little.

'Evening Sandy,' said Amita, desperate to sit down and unhitch herself from Georgie's claw-like grip. 'How are you on this lovely evening?'

'I'm well Amita, thank you,' he said. 'Back is giving me a bit of aggro though. Think I tweaked it this morning when I went fishing.'

'How many times do you have to be told that standing up to your waist in freezing cold river water is bad for your health,' Georgie scolded him.

'It's either that or sit and stare at the four walls Georgie,' he fired back. 'And besides, it's my one vice these days. Unless you want me to take up smoking again.'

'I wouldn't recommend that,' said Amita.

'Then I appreciate your worries but I'll be fine, thank you.'

'He'll be fine,' said Ethel. 'He'll be fine.'

'And how are you this evening Ethel, keeping well?' asked Amita, in a louder voice.

The older woman, the oldest woman there by a long chalk, in the wheelchair down the end of the table gave her a long, hard stare. She raised a bony finger and pointed it directly at Amita. 'You've been out with a man,' she said. 'You've been out with a man, Amita Khatri.'

Sandy muffled a laugh. Georgie sniffed the air, as if to stifle a chuckle. Amita wished the ground would just open up and swallow her there and then.

'Yes Ethel, I have,' she said, resigned to the fact she was the talk of the town. 'Thank you for asking.'

'I didn't ask,' Ethel cackled.

'We're not late are we, oh dear.'

Amita had never been so glad of a distraction as Violet Heatherington and Judy Moskowitz came barrelling up to the table like twin tornadoes. Bags slammed down hard, change jingled and fell out of pockets. There was even a brief scramble for the bingo pens now rolling away on the floor. As Sandy and Georgie scrambled around to bring order back to the table, the two women fanned their flushed faces.

'That's it, Violet, never again,' said Judy. 'Next time we're late, I'm doing the driving.'

'I'm sorry Judy, I wasn't comfortable driving in the dark, you know that,' came the reply.

'The dark? It's broad daylight outside Judy! One of the nicest evenings of the year. You could get dressed in the twilight it's so bright out there.'

'It's after six o'clock Judy, you know I don't like to drive after six o'clock.'

'Give me strength.'

Amita could be sure that she had never met two women so opposite in all of her life. Violet and Judy weren't just chalk and cheese – they were chalk and cheese extreme. How they were ever able to manage the local WI had always been beyond everyone. Especially when they were fighting, which felt like all of the time.

'Good evening, ladies,' said Amita, grateful for the whirlwind of chaos. 'You made it on time.'

'Yeah, just,' grunted Judy.

'Please Judy, I said I was sorry,' Violet said weakly. 'We're very well Amita, thank you for asking. Judy was over at my house for tea to discuss this summer's fete and festival and the time got away from us.'

'Got away from *you* more like,' said Judy. 'I was all ready to go at five when you just had to stick that leg of lamb in the oven. Which, by the way, was tasteless.'

'That leg of lamb came from the butcher's in Kendall I'll have you know,' Violet fired back. 'I doubt it was the lamb's fault. More likely your taste buds are shot from all of those ghastly Mint Imperials you choke down.'

'You've got a problem with my mints now, is that it? Surprise, surprise,' said Judy, pulling a fresh packet from her bag. 'I'd offer you one Amita but I'm afraid I'd offend Her Nibs here.'

'That's okay,' laughed Amita.

Despite the bickering, she was sure Violet and Judy quite liked each other. How else would you explain a near twenty-year reign as the queens of the local Women's Institute. Amita had gotten to know them both quite well down the years and she'd always found they were never quite the same when the other wasn't around. Both widows, both deeply passionate about the cause, they were the perfect double act – if you kept them at a safe distance from each other.

'How are preparations going anyway?' she asked. 'This will be your last as president, am I right Violet?'

'You are right Amita,' she said. 'I'll be sad to go. But nothing lasts forever, not even my stewardship of the committee. I'll be leaving on the best of terms and it's more than time somebody else had a go. If for nothing else I won't have to put up with that draughty village hall every month. I think it's given me rheumatism.'

'Well put,' snorted Judy.

Violet ignored her.

'And will you be putting yourself forward as a candidate?' asked Amita.

'Me? Hell no,' Judy shook her head, long, gaudy earrings slapping her cheeks as she did so. 'I've spent long enough in this one's company to know that it's not worth the effort Amita. My husband was a bank manager for twenty-seven years and he spent twenty-six of them snivelling, grovelling and wiping the backsides of every snooty superior he could find. If I wanted lickspittles I would have told him not to kick the bucket.'

Amita wasn't sure what she could say to that. As damning an insight into Judy's marriage as she could have hoped for. But that was Judy Moskowitz all over – as blunt as a scimitar.

'Besides, we've got bigger fish to fry than some silly WI fete,' said Judy, leaning in closer. 'What the hell are we going to do about this bloody village hall fiasco? Doesn't Mr Industry know that's where we've held our meetings and everything else for decades? It's the life and soul of the community. Sure, it's a bit run-down and those bloomin' teenagers keep breaking in. But it's *our* village hall, the people of Penrith. He can't just come in and buy it up like he's playing Monopoly. Where are we going to go?'

'I've heard some people are quite happy about the plans,' said Georgie, stirring the pot. 'You know Barbara McLemore?'

The group all turned to face the rakishly thin woman in athleisure wear sitting by a table close to the door.

'She uses the hall for her Yoga for Oldies class every Monday morning. She says it's been an absolute pain to put up with for years but now it'll be renovated and turned into something that's halfway useable.'

'But she'd lose her class,' said Judy. 'Doesn't she know that all of that stuff will be binned to make room for Mulberry's latest pet project.'

'She doesn't care,' said Georgie. 'And she's not the only one. Albert Chamberlin is all for the changes too, he told me as much. He says that the exposed girders in the roof play havoc with his metal detector club when they gather to fine tune their instruments.'

Amita shook her head. 'Ghastly,' she said.

'It's dreadful isn't it,' said Violet. 'Absolutely awful. I'm so surprised that Mr Mulberry would behave like this. He's always been such a kind-hearted man, so generous.'

'Oh please,' Georgie interrupted her, her pens and change returned to a neat and fashionable order in front of her. 'Hal Mulberry likes to paint himself as a great philanthropist but it's all for show. The man is a walking PR machine. He even had Amita's Jason follow him down to London to buy the silly painting that's caused this monstrosity to be built at the village hall, *our* village hall.'

Violet and Judy both stared at Amita. She shifted a little uncomfortably in her seat, as if it was her fault.

'That right?' asked Judy.

'Yes, well, it's a job isn't it,' said Amita. 'Since that awful business last year Jason has been in demand. He's freelance, it's just another story for him and it puts food on the table.'

'And an invite to the unveiling too I heard,' said Georgie.

Violet and Judy's eyes widened. Amita hadn't planned on making it public that Jason was taking his family to the black-tie affair. She knew that it may come across as hypocritical, if not outright brazen. She should have known better than to expect Georgie to keep her mouth shut. Prized gossip like that was too good to be kept in that buffooned head of hers.

'Yes, that's right,' said Amita.

She could feel the chill of resentment coming from the WI pair. Georgie, on the other hand, was relishing it all.

'I've seen the guestlist, it's quite impressive,' she said, casually examining her talons. 'The mayor is going, and the chief of Cumbria Police. A couple of the names from local radio are there too, you know them, young things, they make all those honking noises in the morning. I believe there are even whispers that our elusive local MP will be making a rare appearance, not only at the unveiling but in the constituency.'

'Rubbing shoulders with the top brass then Amita,' Sandy winked. 'Exactly where you belong, don't listen to them.'

That made her feel better. Georgie was quiet after that. Violet and Judy joined her in silence, although Amita could sense they were stewing already. The consensus on Hal Mulberry's plans for the village hall was wholly negative. Now she was going to be fraternising with the enemy. But she suspected there was more at play here. Call her cynical, and Jason often did, but Amita believed that jealousy was rife among her bingo colleagues. She was, after all, going to the civic occasion of the year. And they weren't. She would be lying if that didn't make her feel just a little bit good about herself. She made a mental note to thank Jason later.

'Good… good evening ladies and… ladies and gentlemen,' said Father Ford, taking up his usual place at the front of the hall. 'Now before we begin tonight, I'd just like to reassure everyone that I'm in peak physical and psychological condition. I'm as fit as a flea and twice as smart as they say. And I can promise you my performances and standards here, every Wednesday night, will *not* be slipping, contrary to popular belief.'

The club didn't know what to say to that. So some clapped a little, most were just confused.

'If that's settled then,' said the pastor, pale and jittery. 'Shall we begin? Stuck in a tree, fifty-three.'

Chapter 5

RED BALLOON

Jason tugged on his shirt collar. It was too tight, he was sure of that. No matter what the man in the shop had told him. He was sure he wasn't a sixteen in collar size. He hadn't been that size since he was sixteen himself. But the shop assistant had insisted that's what the tape measure had said.

Now it was too late. He was choking. As if being trussed up in a rented tuxedo wasn't bad enough. Now he'd have to spend the evening worrying he'd pass out from a lack of oxygen.

'This shirt is too tight,' he said for the umpteenth time since they'd left the house.

'It's made to measure,' said Amita. 'I watched them wrap the tape measure around your throat.'

'Like a noose,' he said.

'Well, we'll say no more about that shall we.'

Jason lingered a little as Amita and Radha went on. They'd managed to find a babysitter for the kids, one that didn't mind being subjected to five hours of *Ring-a-ring-a-roses* on repeat. He thought she must have the patience of a saint. Or she was desperate for the cash. The invitation to the unveiling of *Buttermere at Dawn* in its new home had sat on their mantlepiece all week, out of place among the takeaway leaflets and kids' art projects. Jason had read it at least five thousand times. Yet nobody else seemed to be as enthusiastic as he was. The sour taste of Hal Mulberry purchasing the local village hall still lingered in the air.

He was very much on board for what Hal was planning. And he'd said so plenty of times in the interim week. He'd even managed to get it into the article he'd filed through the contact Hal had provided. It wasn't his best work, not by a long shot. But it was good, a proper piece of long-form profile journalism that would sit well in the Sundays. People liked to read about the expensive tastes of the rich, famous and infamous. Splurging a couple of million pounds on a painting and buying somewhere to house it ticked all of the boxes.

The editor had been a bit rough though. A proper hack, all smoke-laden voice and every second word a swear. Jason had bitten his tongue plenty of times over the years to superiors who didn't have a clue. He thought they'd all gone out with the ark. Instead, they were hiding away in London, ready and waiting for freelancers to paddle into the waters to take a bite.

He had filed it on time and was now looking forward to an evening of hobnobbing with Penrith and Cumbria's finest. That was until he'd buttoned up his shirt and found it was, as he had insisted, too tight.

'Sod this,' he said, unfastening the top button.

He retightened his bowtie enough to make himself look at least partly presentable and raced to catch up with his wife and mother-in-law. There was no fear of those two appearing scruffy. Both looked dazzling in their respective frocks, hair done and makeup worthy of the pages of *Cumbria Life*, as they'd no doubt be gracing. Though he'd surely be cut out of shot by any decent photographer. He decided to cheer things up a little.

'Did I mention how beautiful you two look this evening?' he said, slipping between them. 'I'm indeed very lucky to be attending this art show with the two most gorgeous women in Cumbria.'

'Oh, stop it,' said Radha, giggling. 'I'm not that kind of girl Mr Brazel.'

'And I'm not a girl, full stop,' Amita chimed.

He laughed as they rounded the corner that led to the venue. Although, there was nothing ruinous about the village hall tonight. The tall, decrepit walls had been lit up from below, turning amber to gold to purple in sequence. Large spotlights glided back and forth, their beams reaching high up into the night air. Projections of *Buttermere at Dawn* were being beamed onto the remains of nearby Penrith Castle, changing in time with the lights.

Everyone was in their finery. Jason had never seen so many expensive, well-polished cars in the hall's car park, the overspill taking over the station facilities across the road. Security personnel were checking invitations at the small makeshift archway that led to the site, checking luxury handbags and patting down tuxedos and dinner jackets with suitable subtlety.

The village hall was the last place Jason expected to see security. Nobody normally threatened to steal the giant veg from the local produce show or heckle the Cub Scout Christmas panto. Jason started to feel a little nervous. He wondered what kind of trouble Hal was expecting at this lavish gala. Penrith was hardly the art crime capital of Europe. He doubted any self-respecting thief would be in town. Or at least, he thought not.

'Wow, looks like all the great and good have come out for this,' said Radha as they joined the loose queue for the entrance. 'Is that...'

'Yes, it is,' said Jason as his wife pointed at a dazzling couple up ahead.

'And there's–'

'Yes, them too.'

This went on and on as Radha checked off the local celebrities and dignitaries who were gracing the unveiling with their presence. Jason was secretly chuffed. When he had first met his wife he had hoped for nights like this. The glamour of journalism was often low grade and kept to the shadows. But he had always prayed for banquets and black-tie affairs that would let him show Radha that he wasn't just some hack from a local rag. When the old paper had shut down he'd assumed that was it, but now here they were, rubbing shoulders with the bold and beautiful of the county. Life could be funny that way.

They passed through security with no problems. Although Jason almost took one of the security men out as he produced their invitation with a magnificent flourish. He had half feared there would be some additional, ultra-hi-tech add-on he'd missed. But the guards let them through without question – no retinal scans at the coat-check where normally the playgroup hung up their potato print art.

Outside of the village hall was a huge, temporary gazebo. Plexiglass windows reflected the dazzling lights, giving delegates a glimpse into the painting's temporary new home. Hal had told Jason that this would all be replaced with something that would last ten lifetimes, but he was clearly a man who wasn't used to waiting patiently for what he wanted. The marquee would do for now to show off his pride and joy.

The guests were milling around outside. Waiting staff moved silently like sharks between them, effortlessly collecting empty champagne flutes and replacing them in one motion. Jason helped himself to three as the nearest one passed by.

'I don't drink champagne,' said Amita.

'Come on mum, just a sip, it's a special occasion,' Radha coaxed.

'Fine,' Amita pretended to sip but she took nothing.

Jason detected something off with her. She had been on edge, wary, glancing about wherever they went all evening.

'Are you having a nice time, Amita?' he asked her outright.

'Yes, fine thank you,' came her curt response.

'You don't seem to be,' he said. 'You're casing the place like you're going to steal the painting.'

'I don't know what you mean.'

'He's right, mum, you don't seem yourself,' said Radha. 'You're just a bit, I don't know, angsty.'

'I'm fine, would you please stop asking how I am,' she said. 'I'm trying to soak up the ambiance of this farce. I mean look at everyone, trussed up like mutton dressed as lamb.'

'That mutton is among the richest and most influential of Cumbria, Amita,' said Jason. 'It's a great honour to be here.'

'Oh yes, of course, I forgot how humble and beholding we should all be to the great Hal Mulberry for this invite,' she said. 'Have you seen that monstrosity he's erected over there outside the hall, *our* hall? And that's just a gazebo. What's it going to be like when his permanent shrine to this Elisa woman is complete.'

'Elvira,' said Jason.

'Elvira, sorry, I should remember that. It's all this town is going to be able to talk about when Hal Mulberry is finished.'

Jason rolled his eyes. Sometimes there was no pleasing his mother-in-law. And he was sure that the bingo club and her cronies were making it worse. As far as he was concerned, Mulberry was doing a good thing. Rejuvenation, regeneration and a lasting legacy for one of the area's most famous, oft forgotten daughters. Not that Amita would listen to a word of that.

'I say, excuse me,' came a gruff voice from behind them.

The three of them turned in unison to be greeted by a tall, bald man wearing a kilt. His huge, bushy handlebar moustache dripped over his lip like white walrus tusks, and the medals pinned to his chest jingled a little as he bowed at them.

'Colonel Alastair Hector McKenzie-Stewart, retired, at your service,' he said as he came back up from his bow. 'I have to say, I saw you all coming in, you look resplendent, every one of you.'

Jason wasn't sure what was going on. Radha was smiling. Amita not so much.

'A pleasure to meet you, Colonel,' said Radha, offering her hand. 'Radha Kahtri-Brazel. And what a terrific kilt.'

'Oh, this old thing,' he said, taking her hand and kissing it. 'One has to scrub up every now and then for the right occasion. Doesn't one?'

'One certainly does, doesn't one?' Jason said, unable to keep a straight face. He'd never been one for calling rank.

'And what brings you to this evening's unveiling Colonel McKenzie-Stewart?' Radha pressed on.

The old soldier flexed his eyebrows, looking about the lawn. 'I'm rolled out for these sorts of things every now and then,' he said. 'The shrapnel on my chest seems to act like a magnet if someone is looking for a rent a crowd with a dash of respectability. Few war stories, a dash of derring-do.'

'I'll bet,' said Jason, snorting into his champagne flute.

'And are you having a nice time?' Radha ignored him.

'Perfectly pleasant. I think I've been to more black-tie functions since I retired than over the rest of my career put together. You get to a certain age where it's less about leading men and more about leading a good example.' The colonel tucked his hands behind his back. He puffed out his chest so his medals jangled again. Jason had a feeling where this might be going.

'I'm feeling a little thirsty,' he said. 'Radha, would you like to join me in stalking one of the nice waiting staff with the champagne.'

Amita's eyes opened until they were almost as wide as dinner plates, clearly not thrilled about being abandoned with the old guard.

'Can we get you and the colonel something, Amita?' Jason asked.

'Amita, what an enchanting name,' said the old soldier. 'You know I haven't heard that name since I was stationed in India. And I remember hearing it then and thinking how utterly wonderful it was.'

Amita nodded curtly in acknowledgement then turned back to her son-in-law. 'Couldn't I give you two a hand at all?'

'No, no, we're perfectly capable,' said Jason, leading Radha away. 'You keep Colonel McKenzie-Stewart company until we come back.'

'But I really think–'

'Bye mum,' said Radha.

'Brutus,' Amita cursed under her breath.

'Shall we take a stroll Amita?' asked the colonel.

He gestured towards the makeshift gazebo. Amita was still cursing. She had been set up, left high and dry. If anyone here knew Georgie Littlejohn or the others at the bingo club and saw her with *another* man, there'd be no living it down. She tried to keep as far a distance between herself and the colonel as was polite. Clutching her bag, she remembered all she could about negative body language and tried to put it into action.

'So, I got back from India in about seventy-nine I think,' he was droning on. 'Or was it eighty? Of course, by that time I was like a stranger in a strange land. Then the Falklands happened and they thought they still had some use for me.'

'Yes, that sounds fascinating,' Amita was tuning in and out as she combed the attendees for familiar faces.

They walked around the perimeter of the gazebo. Security staff were standing either side of the door. Inside was lit up and she could see the outline of the painting, a long, luxurious velvet sheet draped over it, row after row of seats set up for the audience's admiration. They were about to start on another lap, Amita's feet beginning to burn from her sensible heels, when the tinkle of a small bell stopped them.

Every set of eyes fell on a tall, slender, young woman with her short, prim hair combed stylishly back behind her ears. She wore a smart suit and was brandishing a tablet in a show of efficiency. Two of the swaying spotlights fell on her, making her bright blue eyes dazzle.

'Ladies and gentlemen, *mesdames et messieurs*, it's my great honour to welcome you on behalf of the Hal Mulberry Foundation to this, the unveiling of Penrith's newest, most exquisite masterpiece.'

Her voice echoed out across the crowd, amplified through speakers hidden somewhere among the lights and gazebo. Elgar's *Nimrod* was playing quietly in the background, adding weight to the ceremony. Amita was relieved, it was the only thing that had shut the colonel up in the ten minutes she had known him.

'I would like to thank you all on behalf of Mr and Mrs Mulberry for attending this evening,' said the host, standing in the pools of light like a supermodel. 'We know this has all been hastily put together and you all have such important and busy schedules. So it's a great privilege to have so many wonderful people here for the unveiling. Mr Mulberry said to me just this morning that if everyone on the guestlist attended tonight's function, then who would be running Cumbria?'

A ripple of subdued laughter trickled around the crowd who were now slowly moving towards the entrance of the gazebo. Amita scanned the crowd now they were closer, trying to work out who might be snitching her to Georgie and the others.

'As you'll all know, *Buttermere at Dawn* is a hugely significant painting to this area's cultural heritage,' said the host. 'Painted in the 1970s, it has passed through many hands until now, finally, it has returned home to its birthplace. I don't need to tell you how important the painting is to Mr and Mrs Mulberry either. To quote a recent article charting the journey back to Penrith, Mr Mulberry's lifelong childhood fantasy has now become a reality. And *everyone* in Penrith and beyond can enjoy the rewards for generations to come.'

Amita looked about for Jason. She spied him, braced for a namecheck. When none was forthcoming he scowled into his champagne flute. The music was beginning to build to its spectacular crescendo. And with it the host's speech.

'The return of *Buttermere at Dawn* is a gift from Hal Mulberry and his foundation to the people of this town and this county,' she went on. 'In time there will be a permanent memorial and tribute to Elvira's memory and legacy on this very spot. And with it a new "home at home" for the painting that has formed so much of what Mr Mulberry has done in his life. So, without further ado, before we take our seats for the official unveiling, I would like you to join me in a toast and round of applause for the man himself. Please, ladies and gentlemen, Mr and Mrs Mulberry.'

The crowd began to applaud as the hostess beckoned towards the back. Everyone turned around, an aisle forming in the audience as they split in two. The search-lights zoomed from the hostess to the rear of the crowd and settled on an empty space. The applause stopped.

There was a brief moment of silence as everyone waited for something to happen. But there was nothing. Only the blazing circle of light on the tarmac.

Amita felt a sudden chill run up her back and across her shoulders. She shivered, the colonel immediately springing into action.

'Are you cold my dear?' he whispered. 'You could have my jacket and–'

'I'm fine,' she batted him away.

The crowd started to get restless. They sensed there was something wrong. Faces turned to the hostess in expectation. She remained calm and collected, her hand delicately pressed to her earpiece.

'Ladies and gentlemen, my apologies,' she said. 'It appears we are having some technical problems and–' She was cut off by a hideous scream.

Amita stepped forward, a feeling of dread enveloping her. There was another scream, this time louder, more pained.

Some screams send crowds fleeing – turning on their heels and scarpering from danger. But there was a plaintiff note to this scream – a cry for help in the dark, and almost as one, the audience murmured and turned towards the source. It came from beyond the hall's car park, somewhere in the darkness towards the main street.

The crowd surged forward, panicked stilettos and well-polished shoes scuffing hurriedly across the ground. Those at the front were running now, pulling the others with them. The group funnelled out through the makeshift archway, Amita dragged along with them. People were shouting, calling for order, the security staff unable to corral the chaos. The audience spilled onto the street and towards the railway station car park across the road.

Almost as abruptly as the stampede had started, it scattered and broke up, people coming to a stop as they saw who it was who had summoned them. Amita, jostled and bedraggled, stumbled to a halt with the others, straining to see. A figure stood in silhouette, in front of them all, a woman who as she took a step forward was cast in a strange, sickly orange glow from the streetlights that just flickered on above them all.

She was crying, her shoulders bobbing up and down as she gasped for air. As she lifted her face to the crowd, Amita spotted her hands, covered in blood, quivering as she held them out in front of her. Nobody spoke, they just stood there, watching the woman, her faux fur coat caked in gore, expensive jewels glistening in the haze of the streetlight.

'Mrs Mulberry?' gasped the hostess, pushing her way to the front of the crowd. 'What... what on earth has–'

'He's dead!' Mrs Mulberry screamed at the top of her voice. 'Hal is *dead*! He's been murdered!' She sank to her knees, face contorted as she sobbed loudly.

It took a moment for the crowd to react, almost as if they were expecting some grand reveal – one more twist in the night of theatrics. Then reality began to bite and the hostess and a few others, close friends, colleagues, hangers-on, raced forward and tried to console the heart-broken Mrs Mulberry.

Amita felt Jason and Radha arrive beside her.

'Bloody hell,' he said, still holding his champagne flute, the contents sloshing onto his rented tuxedo. 'Did she say Hal was dead?'

'No,' said Amita gravely. 'She said he's been murdered.'

Chapter 6

WATER LILIES

There was a chilling feeling of familiarity that Jason and Amita couldn't shake. Maybe it was because they were tired, hungry and altogether traumatised. Or maybe it was because they hadn't quite gotten over the shock of what had unfolded in front of them.

They had all returned home as soon as the police and ambulance had arrived. Mulberry's people did their best to contain everyone for the detectives, but it had been like herding cats. These were powerful people, with reputations to uphold. They couldn't be seen gawking at the site of a potential murder. What would the press think?

The press, for Jason's part, was too knackered to think straight. He sunk into the couch while Radha paid the babysitter and went to check on the kids. He kicked off his shoes, letting his feet breathe, as Amita sat down beside him and did the same.

'Jason, I–'

'Don't say another word Amita,' he said, rubbing his face.

'But I–'

'I know what you're going to say.'

'How could you know that?'

'Because I know *you*. Too soon, Amita, too soon.'

She started rubbing her feet. 'All I was going to say was–'

'Nope, I'm not listening,' he pushed himself off the couch and started for the kitchen.

'I don't know why you're being so difficult Jason,' she said, following him. 'I was simply going to say that I have a dreadful feeling–'

'No, stop right there,' he said, flipping the kettle on. 'I know *exactly* what you're going to say next and I'm not being sucked down that rabbit hole again Amita. No chance.'

'Alright,' she pouted, folding her arms. 'What was I about to say?'

He watched her, sensing a trap.

'Well, I'm waiting,' she said. 'Let's be having it. I had no idea you were psychic, another accolade to add to your long list of enviable attributes. I really am a very lucky woman to have such a multi-talented son-in-law.'

'Steady,' he said, fetching the mugs. 'Sarcasm is my department, remember.'

'I'm waiting Jason. Out with it.'

He sighed loudly. The water boiled and he poured the kettle into the waiting teapot. He watched the steam rise gently out of the spout for a moment. He didn't like what he was about to say. He didn't like cutting Amita off so sharply. But a terrible, foreboding feeling was gripping him ever tighter.

'You were going to say that all of this feels a little familiar,' he said, voice low. 'You were going to say that there's a sense of deja vu about what happened tonight and what we've gone through before. And ultimately you were going to get us involved again, right up to our necks in trouble. That's what you were going to say.'

Amita pursed her lips. She shook her head, eyebrows arched. 'Rubbish,' she said.

'Aha!' he said triumphantly, pointing at her. 'I was right. I *am* right!'

'I have no idea what you're talking about.'

'I was spot on Amita, come on, admit it. I mean, I knew I was in the right ballpark. But I was pinpoint accurate, wasn't I? Wasn't I?'

'Would you keep your voice down please, your children are trying to sleep,' Radha scolded him as she came in. 'What were you right about?'

Jason and Amita exchanged a mistrusting look. It was his turn to fold his arms and look smug.

'Ask your mother,' he said.

'Oh no, are you two fighting again?' Radha asked with a groan. 'I think we've all been through enough tonight without you going at it hammer and tongs.'

'We're not fighting Radha,' said Amita. 'We're having a friendly exchange of ideas. And you're right, he shouldn't be shouting when the bairns are in bed.'

'I wasn't shouting. I was celebrating,' he said.

'Well regardless of what it was, it was too loud so turn it down a bit, please and thank you,' said Radha, pouring them tea.

Amita took her mug and felt the warmth charge up her arms. She sipped at it gently, Earl Grey, delicious. She was in need of something, anything, to focus her mind. All she could see was the lone figure of Hal Mulberry's wife, standing under the streetlight, covered in blood, sobbing. She shivered again.

'Bloody dreadful what happened tonight, wasn't it,' said Radha.

Jason and Amita said nothing. They were staring at each other across the kitchen.

'I mean, it's like something you see on *Crimewatch*.'

'Or *CSI*,' Jason chimed in. This kind of stuff wasn't meant to happen round here. There was a reason why American cop shows were set on the mean streets of Detroit or Baltimore. Even the glitzy, glamorous avenues of LA and New York were liable to have a body or two every now and then. But he liked to think people were more at risk from twisting their ankles hiking the fells than being felled in their prime round here. Yes, there had been that unfortunate event last year – but that was a one-off wasn't it. Wasn't it?

'Yeah,' said Radha. 'Are you okay?' She rubbed his arm. He nodded.

'I haven't really let it sink in yet,' he said. 'I'll probably be more upset in the morning. Hal seemed like a really lovely guy. Too full of life to be... well, dead. I mean, completely mad, boisterous and brash, but a nice bloke. And very generous. I can't imagine who would want to do that to him.'

'I can think of a few,' Amita snorted.

'Mum,' said Radha, disapprovingly.

'Come on Amita, don't be like that, the guy isn't even cold yet,' said Jason.

'No, he's not. That's why we should act quickly, while things are still in flux.'

'Here we go,' he threw his arms up.

'Mum, don't,' said Radha.

'Oh, don't you start too Radha,' she said. 'Can you think of anyone better to try to get to the bottom of this than Jason and I? Look what we did last year, does that count for nothing?'

'No, it doesn't count for nothing,' she answered her mum, 'but you were both warned by the police that it was up to them to sort these things out. You can't go running around all over Cumbria solving mysteries like Scooby-Doo and Shaggy. There are consequences, legal ramifications at the very least. Not to mention it's bloody dangerous!'

'She's right,' said Jason. 'We got lucky last time Amita, really lucky. I don't fancy hunting down *another* murderer.'

'It was a good story though, Jason,' said Amita, putting her mug down. 'It rejuvenated your career.'

'It did,' he said. 'But it's done, it's over. We're not coppers, we're not even traffic wardens. Something like this, high-profile businessman, murdered, that's top-end stuff Amita. CID will be all over it, major crimes too. What happened last year, well it was because the police had missed something. There'll be no such slip-up this time, I can tell you that. They don't stint on investigating the deaths of millionaires, that much I'm sure of. I'll bet his mansion is being torn apart right now by police officers, every minute detail of Hal Mulberry's life picked apart and analysed by professionals who specialise in this. There's probably even a countywide manhunt operation on the go too, right now as we speak. The killer could be caught before we get up for our breakfast in the morning. It's probably a dreadful case of him just being in the wrong place at the wrong time.'

Amita wasn't convinced. She had the same burning, churning discomfort in the pit of her stomach that told her there was something more to all of this.

'Businessmen, good people like you said, Jason, they're not just targeted at random,' she said. 'You know that, we *all* know that. Don't you want to know what happened to your friend?'

That caught Jason a little short. He went a little paler, like the reality of the evening's events had just dawned on him.

'He wasn't really a friend Amita,' he said. 'Just an acquaintance, a job.'

'Nonsense,' she said. 'He's all you've talked about for the past week. Hal this and Hal that.'

'So? What's wrong with that?'

'Nothing! Absolutely nothing. Radha and I have found it actually quite sweet, haven't we?'

'I'm staying out of this,' she held her hands up and made for the door. 'You two fight it out as to who gets to be Morse and who is Lewis. I'm going to bed.' She escaped without further questioning.

Amita rounded the kitchen table so she was close to Jason. He rubbed his arms, suddenly cold.

'All I'm saying Jason is that we made a good team last time,' she said quietly, smiling gently. 'You're probably right, they'll have the murderer by morning. But if they don't, what's the harm in us doing a little digging around to see what we can do to help?'

'Is this because of the hall?' he asked her.

'What?'

'The village hall,' he said pointedly. 'You and the rest of the bingo club, Georgie and all of that lot, you've been in a surly mood since you found out Hal bought it over. Are you trying to turn up some dirt on him or something?'

'Absolute rubbish,' she said. 'And I'm offended you'd think I'd do something as low, as scurrilous, as to try to defame a dead man's reputation.'

He looked at her like he didn't believe her. Amita was genuinely a little hurt. Although the thought had crossed her mind. She decided to keep that to herself.

'I'm only saying that we did a very good job the last time something like this happened,' she said. 'We saved a reputation and brought her killer to justice. Any police force would be *lucky* to have us helping them.'

'I doubt they would see it that way Amita,' he yawned. 'Anyway, I'm going to bed. I don't want to talk about it anymore tonight. This whole business is awful, we'll probably be cited as witnesses at some point and a good man is dead. Not the evening of fraternising with the high and mighty that I had planned.'

'Best laid plans of mice and men and all that,' she said.

'I've heard *that* before.' He started for the door.

'Just think about it Jason,' she called after him. 'That's all I'm asking.'

'Yeah, yeah,' he waved her away. 'Goodnight Amita.'

'Goodnight,' she said as the door closed.

Jason started up the stairs. He weaved between the overturned toy trucks and beheaded Barbie dolls, making sure he didn't trip and fall. He'd clear it all up in the morning. As he conquered the hazardous climb, his phone began to vibrate in his pocket. He thought about ignoring it. Nothing good could come of a call this late at night.

Then the bug bit him. He was a journalist, and journalists' curiosities were like itches that *had* to be scratched. The call, whatever it was, might be the *big* one, the Pulitzer Prize, the job offer of a lifetime, or lunchtime, depending on how skint he was. Jason blew out his lips and pulled his phone out with a defeated sigh and answered.

'Brazil!' barked an already angry voice from the other end.

'It's Brazel, Arnold,' he said.

'Oh yeah, of course it is. You awake?'

'I am now,' he said.

Arnold Beeston was a tabloid newspaper editor from roughly the Jurassic period. Jason had been introduced to him through Hal's foundation and was the go-to contact for the puff piece on the tycoon. He was infamous in the industry as a no-nonsense, cut-throat sort of editor. His methods may have been blunt and forceful but they got results. Now he was calling late at night. That spelled trouble.

'What's this about Hal Mulberry being murdered?' asked Beeston.

'How did you... how did you know about that?'

'Never mind all that, is it true?' he rasped.

'He's dead, I know that much.'

'And the murder part? Can you stand that up?'

'That's what his wife was saying as she broke down in front of us.'

'Crikey,' said Beeston, sounding genuinely shocked. 'Did you get pictures? Our late reporter is hopeless. He once asked me where a comma was on a Qwerty keyboard, I don't trust him as far as I can throw him and he's messing around with the cops.'

Jason stifled a laugh. The first time he'd cracked a smile since he'd heard the news. A dark sense of humour had been his shield plenty of times before. Sometimes, laughter was the only thing you had left…

'I want you to be my eyes and ears on the ground for this Brazel,' said Beeston. 'We'll cover your expenses and all of that. This is a big story. I want you to find out as much as you can and stay in touch with me at *all* times. We'll get a spread on the life and times of Mulberry for the first edition and online, there's plenty of background in that big profile piece you did of him when he bought that picture. But we'll hold off on the suspicious line until the dibble have come up trumps. That work for you?'

'I… I don't know…'

'Come on Brazel, I've got the cheque burning a hole in my pocket. You knew Mulberry, you know the patch. If I send my man up there he'll get lost on the train, probably end up in Penzance or Pentonville rather than Penrith. Take the job, file the story, then treat the kids or take the wife dancing.'

Jason couldn't imagine Radha's reaction if she heard anyone called her 'the wife'. 'I… I…'

'Good. Stay in touch Brazel, keep me posted on every move, every announcement, every whisper that's going about the town,' said Beeston. 'I want to know *everything* right up until there's an arrest. Speak to you tomorrow.'

Arnold hung up. Jason stood at the top of the stairs, peering down at the glow coming from the kitchen and living room. Was this how newspapers behaved now? It had always been a pretty fast-paced industry, he wasn't naive enough to think otherwise. Only he'd not really been given the chance to say 'no'. Arnold Beeston, Jason suspected, wasn't the type of man who took 'no' easily. If at all.

Strange, he thought, starting back down the stairs, how life could change in a matter of moments. He really shouldn't still be so surprised. There was absolutely *no* chance he was getting away with saying 'no' to Amita. The universe liked to conspire against him and with his mother-in-law. The Sheriff of Penrith always got her man. And this was going to be no different.

'Amita,' he said, defeated, 'about what you were saying earlier.'

Chapter 7

WILLOWS, GIVERNY

'There is absolutely nothing I loathe more than an early morning at a police station,' said Jason.

He was still in a bad mood from the night before: from his orders, from going back grovelling to Amita. In her defence, she hadn't made a big deal out of things. She had humbly and quietly accepted his news that he would be covering the story with a dignity befitting the Sheriff of Penrith's office. Jason, however, was certain she was just storing up her 'told you so' speech for a later date. Usually when he least expected it and it would have the most impact.

The streets were quiet around Penrith Police Station. They usually were, especially this early in the morning. Off the beaten track and surrounded by terraced houses, the station house itself could easily be mistaken for the Salvation Army Hall that sat across the street. Only the occasional police car thumping in and out of the narrow car park beside it gave any indication that this was where Jason and Amita had to be.

'Right, let's get a few things straight before we go in here,' he said, stopping her just shy of the main door.

'Okay,' she said. 'I'm listening.'

'One, we're here in an official capacity, or at least I am,' he said. 'I'm a freelance journalist who has been commissioned by a newspaper to cover this story. There's no subterfuge, no going off on tangents and spinning lies, is that understood? I could get into some serious trouble if I obtain information through the wrong channels.'

'But—'

'Number two, same as number one. We play this by the book Amita. Nothing dodgy. Is that clear?'

'Jason, you really shouldn't speak to me like one of my grandchildren, it's so unbecoming,' she tutted.

'Am I making myself clear Amita, I'm serious!' he said.

'Yes, of course. Do you really think I would do anything to jeopardise this opportunity for you,' she said. 'You've been given the task of covering a major news event. It's all over the internet this morning.'

'I'm sure it is,' he said, starting towards the door of the police station. 'Just let me do the talking in here and we should be okay.'

'Fine,' she shrugged.

They stepped inside the police station. It was dark, dingy, like some of the lights weren't working. The early summer's day seemed a long way away from this place. The reception area had a sorrowful air – chipped lino and a flickering fluorescent light greeted him. Jason walked as confidently as he could up to the desk, a sergeant sitting at her computer behind it, doing a sterling job of refusing to look up at whoever had walked in to disturb her morning.

'Good morning, I'm Jason Brazel and I'm–'

'Sshhh,' said the cop. Still no eye-contact.

He stopped abruptly as she stared at the screen for another moment. Then she started to laugh, a cheeriness brightening her up.

'Sorry,' she said. 'My nephew, he's only a year old, my brother keeps sending me clips of him through to brighten up my nightshift.'

'Sounds lovely, may we see?' asked Amita.

'Eh...' The officer was taken aback but Amita was leaning over the reception counter before Jason could do anything. The desk sergeant turned her screen around and played the video. The little baby was banging pots and pans together and ended up with one on his head. They both laughed as the clip ended.

'They're adorable at that age, aren't they?' asked Amita.

'They are. Kids are adorable anyway,' agreed the sergeant. 'Until they become teenagers. Then it's all down-hill from there.'

'Thankfully we're still a few years away from that with my grandchildren,' said Amita.

'It'll come fast,' said the cop, pulling her screen back around. 'Time makes fools of us all, and all of that. Now, how can I help you guys?' She was all sweetness and light now. Jason hardly wanted to sour the mood by flashing his Press ID.

'Yes, my name is Jason Brazel, I'm a reporter for–'

'Who is leading the Hal Mulberry case please?' said Amita.

The desk sergeant leaned back a little in her chair. 'Hal Mulberry case?' she asked. '*You* want to know who is leading that case?'

'Yes, if you wouldn't mind,' said Amita. 'You see, my son-in-law and I were at the event last night, we saw what happened with Mrs Mulberry. It was a terrible thing and we've spent the whole night tossing and turning, just unable to settle, haven't we Jason.'

'Amita,' he said, low and deep.

'We just can't get the image of that poor woman out of our heads, what she must be going through,' Amita went on. 'And we want to help as much as we can. So we thought we'd come down here first thing and offer to give statements, accounts of what happened, anything that might aid your investigation.'

The desk sergeant took a moment to compute everything Amita had bombarded her with. She puffed out her cheeks and started clicking her mouse as she brought up her filing system.

'That's very honest and kind of you both,' she said. 'Truth is we've had a bit of bother with this overnight.'

'Oh really?' asked Amita innocently. 'How so?'

'It was a black-tie event,' said the policewoman. 'And the guests were keen to make their exit when it was clear that there might be questions to answer. Guests, I should say, who have PR machines and press people to answer enquiries before we can actually get to them.'

'I can imagine,' said Amita, rocking back and forth on her heels. 'Well, you'll be glad to hear they weren't *all* like that. We are distinctly normal, isn't that right Jason?'

He chose very deliberately not to answer her. The desk sergeant clicked her fingers.

'Okay, here we go,' she picked up a phone. 'It's our new kid on the block, Detective Inspector Arendonk.'

'Ah, is that DI Alby's replacement?' asked Amita.

'It is,' said the policewoman. 'Did you know him?'

'We had our run-ins,' said Jason.

'She's lovely, very down to earth,' said the cop. 'I'll call her and let her know you're here if you both want to take a seat.'

Jason and Amita did as they were told. They sat down beneath a huge noticeboard that was covered by posters and notes encouraging them to do everything from lock their back doors to report any online trolling. When he was sure the desk sergeant wasn't listening, he let Amita have it.

'What did we talk about ten seconds before coming in here?' he said, voice muffled. 'We're here to ask questions as press, not as witnesses.'

'She wasn't going to give you any answers, Jason, you know that,' said Amita. 'They have whole teams of press people trained to say nothing juicy. This way we're getting to the source, straight away. And also, isn't it interesting about the other guests?'

'I'm not surprised by them,' he said. 'The mayor, politicians, even that old colonel boyfriend of yours, he'll not want to have his reputation sullied by being part of a murder investigation. If that's what this turns out to be.'

'He's not my boyfriend,' said Amita. 'Quite far from it in fact. The man was an insufferable bore. He spent twenty minutes telling me about how wonderful a soldier he was and how nobody could lace his boots, or whatever it is they do in the army. When that lovely hostess started her presentation, I could have kissed her.'

'She was rather beautiful wasn't she,' he said wistfully.

'I said *lovely* Jason, not beautiful. You're a married man,' she sniped.

'I know but I was just saying.'

'Well don't just say,' she said. 'And remind me to have a word with you and Radha about leaving me with that McKenzie-Stewart character. I've never been more mortified in my whole life.'

The doors of the police station opened with a flurry. In walked a woman, head cocked as she balanced a phone between her ear and her shoulder. Her hands were full, a tray of coffees in one and a large box of expensive doughnuts in the other. A small whirlwind followed her as she marched up to the front desk, Jason and Amita's eyes were glued to her every move.

'Morning, morning, sorry I'm late,' she said, letting the phone expertly slide down to the desk. 'I got your call there, you said somebody wanted to see me.'

The desk sergeant pointed over towards Amita and Jason. The woman nodded and walked towards them. She was young, fresh faced, her hair cut short and practical, cheek bones drawing her face towards a sharp-pointed chin. She juggled her coffees and doughnuts around with a well-rehearsed ease and made sure she had a free hand as she arrived at the duo.

'Sally Arendonk,' she said. 'Pleased to meet you.'

'And you,' said Amita. 'My name is Amita Khatri and this is my son-in-law Jason Brazel.'

'Lovely to meet you too,' said Arendonk. 'My colleague tells me you were both at the Elvira unveiling last night and you want to make statements.'

'That's right,' said Amita. 'If now's not a bad time?'

'Not at all,' the DI smiled. 'Actually, you'd be doing me a favour. I'm sure you'll have heard about how hard we're finding it taking witness statements. Swanky bash, lots of important people. They don't want to spend their evenings and mornings in CID with me.'

She led them through the bowels of the police station. It was still quiet, only the odd uniformed officers milling around before their shifts ended. Arendonk took them to the main squad room, a place Jason and Amita had never seen before, and pulled a pair of chairs up to her desk. She pushed the box of doughnuts to the end of the desk and pulled one of the coffees from the little cardboard carrier. Blowing down the lid, she drank a huge gulp and let out a satisfied sigh.

'Ah, that's the good stuff,' she said. 'You know, when I got this transfer, I thought that was it for my wonderful coffee days. Liverpool has all these brilliant little cafes and bistros who all serve up the most amazing roasts. But actually, Penrith is just as good. Better even. Do you guys know a place called *Murphy's?*'

'Yes, we know it,' said Jason, giving Amita a sly look.

'It's wonderful, it's got everything. This is their new Guatemalan blend, it's the best coffee I've tasted this side of the Atlantic Ocean. Really superb.'

The whirlwind was continuing to rage. Everything Sally Arendonk did seemed to involve huge amounts of movement. She was fizzing with energy, not to mention caffeine. Jason suspected this wasn't her first coffee of the morning. Or the hour.

'So, you guys were at the party last night?' she asked, finally settling.

'We were, yes,' said Amita.

'Sally, if I may,' Jason interjected.

The DI looked at him over the rim of her cup as she sank another huge gulp.

'I'm afraid my mother-in-law wasn't being entirely truthful to your desk sergeant out front,' he said.

'Okay,' said the detective.

'You see, I'm a journalist…'

He paused. Usually when Jason said he was a journalist, especially to the police, there was an inevitable sharp intake of breath. He would then have to follow that up with a quick explanation as to why they should still talk to him. Only this time the DI said nothing. She sat watching him patiently.

'And I've been commissioned by a national newspaper to cover this Hal Mulberry death,' he said, still waiting to be stopped. 'My mother-in-law, she doesn't mean any harm. She just wants to get to the bottom of things and can sometimes be a little, how should I put it, overeager.'

'I'm sitting right here, Jason,' said Amita.

'What I'm trying to say is I don't want us to get off on the wrong foot,' he said. 'Yes, we were at the event, and of course, are more than happy to give statements. But I'm here to ask questions as well as answer them. Any information you give me needs to be official or clearly marked as off the record. I'm not a hack, Detective Inspector. And I certainly don't want to cause trouble when we've only met each other for three and a half minutes.'

Arendonk nodded.

'It's a murder, by the way,' she said, after a moment's consideration.

'Pardon me?' he asked.

'You called it the Hal Mulberry death, just there,' said the detective. 'It's not a death, it's a murder case. Hal Mulberry was murdered.'

'I *told* you!' Amita clapped her hands, bouncing up and down in her seat. 'Didn't I tell you Jason. I told you, I told you.'

'Definitely a murder,' he gulped. The last shreds of hope that Hal's wife had got it tragically wrong, and actually the poor chap's death had just been a nasty accident, faded. 'And you're happy to just tell me that's the case?'

'I don't see what the issue would be with the press knowing,' Arendonk shrugged. 'After all, Mrs Mulberry did scream that to the onlookers. It's hardly a secret. If you've lived round here for long you'll know news travels fast – and gory news even faster. The victim was found dead by his wife in his car, his throat sliced wide open and blood everywhere. It's hardly a shaving cut. She doesn't know what happened to him and he's dead. That's murder in my book and my team are treating it as such. In fact, Mrs Mulberry is having some precautionary checks at the infirmary as a result of her trauma and shock.'

This was it, Jason thought. He realised he'd been half hoping that the police would say it had all been a dreadful error – mistaken identity, or a road traffic accident. But, despite his best intentions, here he was, first reporter on the scene of what was now a confirmed murder. At least this exclusive reveal would keep Beeston off his back, until the first edition anyway.

'So let me get this straight,' he said, feeling a little giddy. 'If Hal Mulberry was murdered, you're telling me that you're conducting a search, no, sorry, a *hunt* for his killer right now.'

'That's correct,' said Arendonk.

'And you know I'm a journalist, right?'

'I do now,' she said with a wry smile.

Jason had a sinking feeling. Nothing was ever this easy, especially for reporters. There was bound to be a catch.

'What's the catch?' asked Amita, as if reading his mind.

Arendonk drew in a long breath through her nose. She went to take another sip from her coffee but it was empty. Casting it to one side, she leaned in closer to Jason and Amita.

'This is all off the record,' she said.

That wasn't ideal, Jason thought, but it wasn't a disaster. The murder probe was true, he just couldn't credit the police for telling him so.

'And you won't be able to report it, not until it's cleared with our communications division,' she added.

That *was* a problem. Although he imagined they would work quite quickly.

'Oh, and if it gets out that we're treating this as murder before any statement from us, I'll know exactly who to collar,' she nodded at them. 'Because you two are the only ones other than me and my team who know.'

Now that *really* was a problem. She had them, hook, line and sinker. Arendonk was clever, Jason could clearly see that. But unlike most clever coppers, he didn't really have a problem with her. In fact, he actually quite *liked* her.

'Damn,' he said, trying to sound disappointed. 'Very smart, Detective Inspector.'

Arendonk laughed a little. She shrugged and sat back. 'This isn't my first lap of the racetrack Jason. And unfortunately, you're not my first journalist who thought he could wriggle a juicy scoop out of me either.'

'I'm confused,' said Amita. 'You see, I'm *not* a journalist DI Arendonk. I'm a concerned private citizen who saw a woman covered in her husband's blood break down in tears a few yards away from me last night. Now what exactly is it you and your officers are doing to catch Hal Mulberry's killer?'

'Tenacious, isn't she?' said the policewoman to Jason.

'Oh, like you wouldn't believe,' he replied.

Amita cleared her throat. The joking was over. They'd had their fun. She wanted answers now that she was here, in the squad room, with the investigating officer right in front of her.

'Ms Khatri...'

'Mrs Khatri,' said Amita. 'I was married for forty years.'

'Apologies, *Mrs* Khatri, I'm not at liberty to discuss the details of a murder investigation with a member of the public,' she said calmly.

'But I'm not just any old member of the public, I'm a witness.'

'Yes, and I'll take your statement shortly,' she said. 'That doesn't mean I can start filling you in on the gaps in your memory. In fact, that's the opposite of what I should do. I need you to have a clear and untampered memory of what you saw. That way we'll be able to carry on with the investigation and hopefully bring whoever did this to justice.'

'But—'

'Mrs Khatri, please.' The inspector was starting to get annoyed.

For all her playfulness, her pleasant smile, and energetic demeanour, Jason suspected that Sally Arendonk did not suffer fools gladly. And that when the chips were down, she was every bit a hardened homicide police detective as anyone else who might breeze in through the doors.

Amita, thankfully, took the hint from her still pleasant but much firmer tone. She piped down. Arendonk logged into her computer.

'Now, regardless of our little dalliance with the fourth estate,' she said. 'You're both happy to give statements about what you saw at the event last night?'

'Yes,' said Amita, huffing.

'I suppose so,' said Jason.

'Good,' the policewoman cracked her knuckles. 'Then let's begin.'

Chapter 8

THE HIRELING SHEPHERD

It was almost lunchtime when Jason and Amita were let go. Giving official statements to the police to help with murder investigations was a lot harder work than both of them had been expecting.

'Blimey, I'm knackered,' said Jason, stretching as they walked down the road and out towards the main street. 'That was a bit more brutal than I thought it would be.'

'You had to go and open your big mouth, didn't you,' said Amita.

'Wow, that's a bit sudden,' he said. 'What do you mean?'

'Back there, speaking to the new detective inspector, who is lovely by the way. You had to go and tell her you were a journalist right off the bat.'

'Amita, we discussed this before we went in,' he said. 'You can't mess around with the police, and you can't mess around when you're writing for big newspapers. You can't mess around with *any* newspaper for that matter.'

'I know, I know,' she said, flustered. 'I'm sorry. I'm just... I think she would have been more help if you hadn't gone wading in so early.'

'I didn't have a choice, you know, I am a professional and I don't want to be prosecuted,' he said.

Amita nodded begrudgingly. She was frustrated and she was taking it out on him. She didn't mean to. He was, as always, just the closest person in range.

Not that she was ready to admit it of course, but reliving the night's events had been rather difficult for her too. She could still hear Sheila Mulberry sobbing, her hands lifted out in front of her, her husband's blood coating her expensive clothes. Going over the whole incident again hadn't been fun. She thought, after everything she had been through, she might have been tougher, better at handling this kind of thing. Evidently there was still work to do.

'I'm sorry Jason,' she said.

'You're sorry?' he sounded surprised.

'Yes, I'm sorry. You're right of course. You were a complete professional. And you did the right thing. I'm proud of you.'

'Gee, thanks Amita,' he said. 'I mean... are you feeling okay?'

'What? Yes, of course,' she walked onto the main street, busy with lunchtime shoppers and workers. 'We need to work out what the next move is.'

'The next move is me going home to write up some copy for Arnold Beeston,' said Jason. 'If I file the copy and tell them to wait until the official announcement goes out, that should keep him ticking over and I can file today under expenses.'

'I mean what's *our* next move,' she said.

'I just told you Amita. There's no next move for *us*, just *me* writing some words.'

'Yes, yes, you can do that any time. What are *we* going to do next?'

'Get something to eat.'

'Don't be so flippant Jason. I'm talking about trying to find out who murdered Hal Mulberry.'

'I know what you were talking about Amita, and I'm ignoring it,' he stepped into a high street bakery to get away from her. 'See, this is me ignoring it.'

Amita followed him in. A long queue snaked its way past fridges and shelves stacked with rolls, sandwiches and salads. Most of the customers had ignored all of that and were drooling over the pastries, pies and doughnuts in the glass cabinet up at the counter. Jason joined them, his mother-in-law in tow.

'The way I see it, it's got to be somebody he knows,' she said. 'Otherwise how else would he have been killed so close to the event.'

'I'm not listening.'

'If he was found by Sheila, his wife, in his car with his throat cut then there's a good chance he *knew* who was behind it. I don't buy the idea of some balaclavaed assassin. This isn't James Bond stuff – this is personal. I can feel it.'

'Still not listening. The pies look good...'

'That means there can only be a small number of suspects,' she said. 'People who Hal knew, or recognised well enough, not to have a problem letting them get close enough to stick a knife in him.'

'I wonder if they have any sausage rolls left?' he asked, the queue getting closer to the counter.

'Jason, would you concentrate, please!'

'Concentrate on what? I've got baked goods to choose from here, Amita. And please, the police are trying to do their jobs. Let them and let me just report on anything they do. That way our lives will be a lot simpler.'

'But there's a killer on the loose!'

The busy shop suddenly fell quiet. Everyone was staring at them. Amita didn't budge. She was serious and she wanted him to understand. Jason looked about the place, slightly embarrassed.

'Sorry everyone,' he said. 'We're just... we're just rehearsing a play.'

Nobody looked convinced by his half-baked excuse. He didn't blame them. Rehearsing a play, what was *that* all about? Surely he could have come up with something a bit better.

'Jason,' she said to him. 'I'm serious.'

He took her arm and guided her out of the bakery and back onto the busy street. His stomach rumbled, gurgling away beneath his shirt like a dog that had been taken away from its favourite treats.

'Amita, please,' he said. 'I've got a job to do here. I've told you what I'm going to do and how I have to be very, very careful in doing it. I can't play detective with you on this one, it wouldn't be ethical and above all else, it wouldn't be legal. What else do you want from me? Blood?'

'I want you to show a bit of gumption, a bit of fight,' she said. 'Anybody can write a story about Hal Mulberry being murdered. Why don't you want to get to the juicy bits, the dirt, you know, the scandal?'

'Scandal? What scandal?'

'Exactly, what scandal? We don't even know if there is any. But it's worth asking the question surely.'

'Oh lord,' he rubbed his face. 'I don't know what you think a journalist does Amita, but we don't go raking through bins and tap phones anymore. Not that *I* did that in the first place, you understand. That was a dodgy few who gave the rest of us a bad name. You remember my old job – I was hardly an undercover investigator. It was all council shenanigans, school fetes, maybe a bit of fury parking on the high street on market day–'

'Sheila Mulberry, she's the key,' said Amita, snapping her fingers. 'She's the one who found Hal dead. She's the first place we should check.'

'A grieving widow, really?' he asked sarcastically. 'You want us to rock up to a hospital ward and start interrogating a woman who found her husband dead less than twenty-four hours ago?'

'She'll understand. We're on the side of truth and justice!'

'You make us sound like superheroes. Not busybodies. I think she'll hit the roof!' he shouted. 'And I wouldn't blame her. She's being treated for shock and goodness knows what else, Amita. If we started asking her what she knows of her husband's death it might finish *her* off. Then it's straight to the cells with us. And no bread and water.'

Amita tapped her chin. She pointed a finger at him, deep in thought. 'You might be right there,' she said. 'We would need a good excuse. Something we could dangle in front of her to ease the blow of our questioning.'

Jason threw his hands up in the air. One of the bakery customers who had given him a suspicious look inside came walking out, roll in hand. He darted another glance of utter contempt as he walked past Jason and Amita.

'I've got it,' Amita snapped her fingers.

'You've got something alright.'

'You, you're the answer Jason,' she said.

'Me?'

'Yes, you,' she continued. 'You wrote that profile about Hal last week. He trusted you, confided in you. He told you his life story and you made our local-boy-done-good a national story.'

'Or painted a target on his back,' he gulped.

'What?'

'Nothing.'

'Hal Mulberry clearly had a liking for you, he took to you straight away,' she said. 'So that's what we lead on with his wife. We tell her the truth, simple as that, that you're covering the story, and you want to see justice done as much as she does. There are no lies there, are there? You'd be telling the complete truth and nothing but the truth.'

'You're persistent, Amita Kahtri, I'll give you that.' Jason shook his head.

Amita shrugged. She could sense he was coming around to the idea. He had that inquisitive look he always had when the cogs of his brain were turning and mulling things over.

'It's just a thought,' she said, casting the hook. 'I think it would probably make for a much better story for that editor friend of yours if you had an interview with the grieving widow. It would probably be exclusive too I should think.'

She had him. He chewed on his bottom lip and nodded. 'You know, that's not half bad Amita,' he said. 'That's not half bad at all. We could give her a platform to tell her side of the story. Proper human interest stuff, not ambulance chasing. Or hearse-chasing, should I say.'

'Exactly,' she chimed.

'And if she tells us to bog off then there's no harm done.'

'She won't tell us to do that,' she said. 'She'll want to know what happened as much as we do, more so. It's her husband after all.'

He continued to nod, still thinking.

Amita did her best to contain her excitement. The challenge, the thrill of the chase, the investigation, everything that she enjoyed was flooding back into her. She did her best with just an impatient tap of her foot.

'Okay,' he said. 'Alright. But you let *me* do the talking this time. No more commandeering the conversation. This has to be strictly a professional interview, on the record, with Mrs Mulberry on board from the off.'

'Absolutely,' she held her hands up. 'I won't say a word, you won't even know I'm there.'

'Good,' he said. 'Now if I could only get that pledge from you in the rest of my life, we'd be laughing.'

'Jason, honestly,' she tutted, swiping her handbag at him.

'Right, what's the next move then,' he said, dodging her weapon of choice. 'Arendonk said she was in hospital. I suppose we should find out what–'

'Cumberland Infirmary in Carlisle, Willow D Ward, under her married name of Sheila Hyacinth Mulberry. Being treated for severe shock and dehydration.'

Jason blinked. Before he had time to think, he had already said another stupid thing. 'How did you...'

'Connections,' said Amita, producing her phone and waving it at him. 'Powerful connections Jason. If there's one thing a network of pensioners knows, it's every hospital, every ward nurse and every available bed in the county. Just ask me what gossip I heard from Edith who runs the League of Friends stall in the lobby. It'd make your hair curl...'

He clamped his hands to his ears and headed towards the car park. 'I don't want to know Amita,' he called back. 'I just don't want to know.'

Chapter 9

THE SNAIL

The hospital didn't look very friendly. Then again, Amita didn't suppose it had to. This was a place of function, of practicality. A place where only the desperate and needy would visit when it was absolutely necessary. That was, after all, why they were here now.

'I don't like this,' mumbled Jason as they walked across the car park.

'I wish you wouldn't mumble,' she said. 'I hate having to ask you to repeat yourself.'

'I said, I don't like this.'

'You were fine with it all the way up from Penrith!'

'Yes, well, that was then. This is now. I don't feel very good about it is all I'm saying. It just feels, I don't know, a bit dirty.'

Amita had to admit she wasn't feeling quite as confident about her plan as she had done before. Now that they were here, in Carlisle, with the hospital looming over them, everything was altogether more *real*. She had to carry on though, they both did. The stakes were already sky high.

'We just keep our cool, that's all,' she tried to assure herself as much as Jason. 'We go in, ask some questions and then leave again. Hal was good to you Jason, don't forget that. In the short time you knew him he confided in you, trusted you, brought you into his circle. He doesn't deserve to have died the way he did. No one does. And we can help.'

'Yeah, I know,' he didn't sound very convinced. 'It's just... she's in the hospital Amita. She's just lost her husband. Isn't this a bit, well, you know, scurrilous.'

Amita took a hard line. She thought it might be best, given the circumstances. 'Tell that to your editor friend,' she said sharply.

The mention of an editor made Jason jolt. He nodded and reluctantly conceded. 'I know, I know,' he said, drawing a long breath in. 'Okay, fine. Let's get this over and done with then as quickly and cleanly as possible.'

They walked around the outer perimeter of the hospital, searching for a side entrance. If Edith on the charity stall in the lobby spotted them, then any hope of getting in without the pensioner telegraph sounding would be nil. That, plus the fact that they'd be rinsed for the price of two books of raffle tickets, a knitted tea cosy and set of notecards. Each.

The place was busy for an early afternoon. Amita didn't suppose hospitals were ever quiet. They were hardly supermarkets or shopping centres.

They eventually found what looked like an old doorway, stairwells inside that led to the wards. Following the signs, and keeping their heads down when they passed anyone, they made their way to Willow D Ward.

When they reached the entrance to the ward, Jason stopped. Amita skidded to a halt too, her trainers squeaking on the polished linoleum of the hospital floor.

'What's wrong?' she asked.

'Are we really doing this?' he asked. 'Are we really going in there to interview a woman whose husband has just been killed?'

'Jason...'

'I mean, you read about the types of journalists who do this sort of thing, don't you. They're the ones that get hauled into public inquiries, hung, drawn and quartered and for very good reason. Just being here is breaking about a dozen rules when it comes to the editor's code. Amita, I... I don't think I can...'

'Jason,' she grabbed his shoulders. 'Remember that line you put in your report – about him hating violence. Despite his bluster, you said he was a gentle man. Whatever's behind this, he shouldn't have gone that way. Hal Mulberry was murdered. You know what that means, don't you? You and I *both* know all too well what that means. There's a killer, on the loose, out there somewhere. He was your friend. We owe it to him to do our best by him, for him, to make sure the killer is brought to justice. And if that means that we break a couple of rules along the way, well, that's how it is I'm afraid.'

Jason nodded solemnly. He looked defeated. Amita's heart broke for him. After everything they had been through before, she hadn't ever dreamed of it happening again. Madeline Frobisher's murder was supposed to be a one-off, a cruel twist of fate they had found themselves caught up in quite by accident. From that horrible death something good had come – a fresh start, a new career for Jason. And more importantly, an actually (occasionally) harmonious relationship between the two of them.

Now here they were, stood outside a hospital ward, hunting another violent killer with Jason's professional morals pushed to their absolute limit. Amita understood what he was going through. She sympathised with him completely. But they had a job to do. They had done it before, successfully. She couldn't pass up another chance to do some good. It was her duty.

'I'll be with you every step of the way,' she said, squeezing his arm. 'We have to do this Jason. We have to.'

'I know,' he sighed. 'It's just, well, I didn't quite fancy myself as *that* kind of journalist, you know? Five-star Caribbean resort reviews and trips to Broadway are more where I'd like my reporting to be headed.'

Amita laughed. 'Sounds wonderful,' she said. 'Maybe next year.'

'Yeah.' He laughed too. 'Maybe next year.'

With that, he squared his shoulders. Flattening the unruly tufts of hair that poked out from the side of his head and wiping the crumbs from his fleece, he stepped forward into the ward. Amita followed closely behind.

A small, friendly-faced nurse was standing at a desk just inside. She was busy with a stack of files Jason was certain had been made from a large chunk of the Amazonian Rainforest. She was motoring through the seemingly endless bureaucracy when she caught sight of Jason and Amita approaching her station.

'Hi there,' she said, 'can I help you with anything?'

Jason froze. Amita could almost feel the frost spreading in a haze around him. She had to do something and quickly, otherwise this was a lost cause even before it had begun.

'I'm–'

'We're here to see Sheila Mulberry,' Jason blurted out suddenly, interrupting his mother-in-law.

The nurse's friendly expression faltered, as if the mere mention of Hal's wife was enough to turn the atmosphere toxic. She quietly and deliberately closed the latest file in front of her and stood up. Hurrying around from behind the desk, she leaned conspiratorially towards the others.

'Oh, I see,' she said, eyeing them up and down. 'And you are?'

'Edgars,' said Jason.

Amita gulped. She looked at her son-in-law, wondering just what he was going on about.

'I'm John Edgars, I work for Mr Mulberry's firm. And this is my colleague… Doris.'

The nurse didn't say anything. Amita did her best not to clap her hand to her face in embarrassment.

'We're here from the communications department, PR,' Jason went on. 'It's important that we put out a statement as a business – and of course, who better to lead the tributes than her. We wondered if we could speak with her briefly to put together something formal – something that will stop the vultures of the press circling. Would that be okay, do you think?'

Amita's panic eased a little. She would have believed that story. She was more surprised Jason had thought of it so quickly.

'PR you said?' asked the nurse. 'You know, I always wanted to do something like that. Working with the stars, getting all the inside scoops, telling their stories. It must be fascinating.'

'Never a dull moment,' said Jason with forced chirpiness.

'I'll bet. Okay, come with me please, she's just down here, out of the way, especially given everything that's been going on.'

They did as they were told. Amita let the nurse go ahead a few steps then tugged on Jason's arm.

'Do I look like a Doris to you?'

'Sorry,' he whispered back. 'It was the first name I could think of that wasn't yours. And John Edgars *does* work for the PR team. He was the one who paid my expenses.'

The nurse took them back out of the ward. They walked down to a small section of the corridor that was lined with doors. The nurse stopped at the first one and knocked. She waited for a moment before opening the door.

'Mrs Mulberry,' she said quietly. 'You have some visitors.'

Amita couldn't quite believe their luck. There had been no excuses, no reasoning, no bargaining or even bribery. She was amazed that Jason's dissembling had worked. And the name Doris didn't sound so bad. It almost suited her, she thought. There was a rehearsed, well-practised manner about the nurse as she stood to one side, like she'd been taking people to see Sheila all day.

Amita wasn't quite sure how she should feel about it all. On the one hand this had been a massive security breach. On the other they were getting exactly what they wanted without any fuss.

'She's still a little groggy but you'll be able to see her now,' said the nurse. 'The poor cock has been through so much, she's had visitors all day. There have been so many police and what have you here, all day and night.'

'We won't be long,' said Amita. 'Just a quick hello and we'll be gone. Isn't that right?'

'Yes, certainly, absolutely,' said Jason, agreeing.

Amita pushed him into the private suite. She closed the door behind them before the nurse's better judgement kicked in. For a moment they stood in silence, watching Sheila Mulberry lying motionless on the bed in front of them. Dappled sunlight was coming in through the blinds that were old and didn't quite close properly. If it weren't for the streaks of brightness filtering through those holes then the room would have been in near darkness.

Mrs Mulberry didn't need any medical attention, not from machines, tubes and pipes. There was no ventilator, no IV drip. She looked, for all intents and purposes, like a healthy woman tucked up in bed.

Amita nudged her son-in-law. He jumped a little, as if surprised. When he didn't move again, she drew him an expectant look.

'Eh... hello Mrs Mulberry,' Jason started. 'I was wondering if we, I, could talk to you?'

'Doctor,' came a hoarse, muffled voice.

'Excuse me? Do you need me to call someone?'

'Doctor,' said Sheila again, her face turned away from them. 'I'm a doctor. I didn't spend seven years at university studying veterinary medicine to be called Mrs Mulberry. I wish those idiot medics would get the memo.'

'Eh...' Jason stammered, looking to Amita for help. On the night of the unveiling, it had been Mr & Mrs Mulberry in all the speeches, no mention of her as a doctor. Now it seemed perhaps she hadn't been quite so keen on playing second fiddle to her husband.

'I'll have to wipe him from my life, erase him,' said Sheila. 'Everything will have to go, the mortgage, the bank accounts, the credit cards. Everything. I'll have to change it all, change my name back on the voting register. Everything. Everything will have to change.'

She started to sob. There was a weariness there, a tiredness.

Amita surged forward. She was by Sheila's bedside before Jason even knew what was going on. She took the newly widowed Mrs, or rather Doctor, Mulberry's hand and hushed her down.

'It's okay Sheila, it's alright,' she said, sounding every bit motherly. 'You don't need to worry about these things, not just now. You need to get better, get well. You've had a terrible shock, a really awful, dreadful shock. And you need to look after yourself and get yourself well before you worry about all of those trivial things. The world won't end if you don't change some silly bank account.'

Amita continued to rub Sheila's hand. It seemed to work. She stopped crying and turned to face them. Sniffing, she sat up a little, confused.

'Who are you?' she asked.

Amita looked over at her son-in-law. She was about to answer for him but he stepped forward, clasping his hands together in piety.

'My name is Jason Brazel, Doctor, or can I call you Sheila? I was a friend of your husband's,' he said, sounding like a priest delivering mass. 'I was wondering if you'd be happy to answer a few questions.'

'A friend of Hal, I'll bet you are,' she snorted. 'He had lots of friends. Lots of "good friends", some better than others.'

There was a sinister edge to her tone. Amita was about to pounce when Sheila turned on them.

'Questions? A friend of Hal's?' she repeated in reverse order. 'I... I don't understand. Are you with the police?'

'No, we're not,' said Amita.

'Then what the hell kind of questions are you wanting to ask?'

Her sadness had very quickly turned to anger. The croakiness of her voice was gone. And with it the fragility of a woman pushed to her absolute limit. She pulled her hand away from Amita and kicked back the sheets.

'Who are you?' she shouted. 'Who the hell do you think you are barging in like this?'

'Sheila, please, we just want to help,' said Jason, pleading. 'I'm a reporter, I went down to London with Hal when he bought *Buttermere at Dawn* and–'

'A reporter?' she squealed. 'You're a bloody journalist?'

'Yes, but I felt like Hal was a friend–'

'A journalist, coming in here, to a hospital ward, trying to ask questions about Hal and his affairs.'

'It's not like that Sheila, honestly it's not,' Amita tried to play peacemaker. 'We're just trying to get some infor- mation and–'

'You'll get nothing from me! Do you understand? Nothing! You'll be hearing from my lawyers about this! I've just lost my husband!' She was out of bed now. Her feet slapped on the floor as she grabbed Amita and hauled her towards the door. Jason caught his mother-in-law before she was wrestled to the ground by the rapidly recovering Sheila Mulberry.

'I'll have you both in court for this!' she shouted at them, pulling the door open. 'I found my husband with his throat cut in our car and you think it's acceptable to come in here, break in, and start asking me questions?'

'Technically we didn't break in,' said Amita feebly. 'The nurse just led us to your room. She said you've had visitors all day.'

'And technically I haven't asked you any questions,' said Jason, equally feeble.

'Get out of here!' Sheila screamed at the top of her voice. 'Nurse! Security! Someone! Anyone! Help! Help me! There are intruders in my room. Help me, somebody.'

Neither Jason nor Amita liked the sound of that. Sensing that their attempts to reason with the grieving widow were falling short of their target, they hastily beated a retreat. First they walked quickly, then they trotted, finally settling on a full-blown sprint down the corridor as the sound of commotion and raised voices followed them. Banking a swift left into a stairwell, they hurried down the steps, three at a time, before breaking out into the car park and a dash to the car.

Jason unlocked the doors long before they arrived and they scrambled into their seats with minimum fuss. The rubber burned and squealed as he put his foot down. They barrelled out of the car park and didn't look back. Only when they were convinced they were clear of being followed did Amita start to breathe again.

'Well,' she said, gasping for air. 'That went as well as could be expected, don't you think?'

'A stonking success,' Jason panted. 'I'm just glad you paid the parking before we went in.'

'I did what now?' asked Amita.

Jason looked at her briefly before turning back towards the road. Pestering a new widow, intruding on grief, impersonating relatives, loved ones and friends, and now not paying for parking. It was, by some standards, Jason Brazel's finest day as a journalist.

Chapter 10

THE JAPANESE BRIDGE

The smoke billowed out of the vent. Amita watched it go as she always did; waiting – willing it to vanish in front of her eyes. She was thinking. She always smoked when she was thinking. She *only* smoked when she was thinking. Although she wasn't sure just how much it helped her think. Or, indeed, which had come first. Maybe it was the solitude, the brief moment on her own when she knew nobody would burst in and disturb her. That was the key to her secret cigarette every now and then. Absolute confidence that she would never be found out.

All of the usual checks were in place. She was tucked away in her favourite corner of the attic, a clear view of the street below. She would see anyone coming home early, Jason, Radha, the kids – even the postie could be spotted well in advance. She had a rolled up magazine nearby to waft away any lingering smoke.

The front door was locked. The back door was locked. Everything was secure, safe. There was no chance Amita

Khatri's secret shame was ever going to be found out. Unless she let her guard down. And she knew that would *never* happen.

That's why she was deep in thought now. Her guard had served her well over the years, decades even. It had helped her juggle the trials of a successful husband dedicated to his work, toiling away eight days a week, leaving her raising a family. All of her children were grown up now and they were successful, or what *she* thought successful was: happy, hard-working, building families of their own. She was immensely proud of them and their partners. Even Jason.

She had earned this secret, she thought, watching another puff escape through the slats of the attic window. Her one vice, her solitary confinement to think and plan ahead. It had helped catch Madeline Frobisher's killer. Amita was hoping it would work again.

'Sally Arendonk,' she said, her voice low enough that only she could hear it, even if there had been anyone else around. 'I wonder what her game is.'

The new DI was a welcome change from Frank Alby. The man was a philistine, a dinosaur from a bygone age. And now he was retired and put out to pasture. For the better. His replacement already felt like she was a breath of fresh air. In the hour Amita had spent in her company she had a newfound respect for the local constabulary. If they were promoting and procuring young, sharp and enthusiastic officers like Sally Arendonk then perhaps her own crime fighting days would be numbered. She could stick to bingo and watching crime dramas on TV like people assumed people of her age should be doing – rather than confronting witnesses and hoodwinking ward sisters.

So why could she not shake this horrible feeling of dread about Hal Mulberry's murder? Why had the late tycoon's wife been so angry, so defensive around them? Was it shock? Was she still reeling from the effects of finding her husband dead in their car, minutes before his finest moment? All of those factors were *more* than enough justification of course. Amita couldn't really imagine what Sheila Mulberry was going through. Nobody could.

Yet there was something off about her, something that didn't quite sit right in Amita's mind. She couldn't quite place where her discomfort, her distrust, was coming from. It all just felt off, like facing a jigsaw puzzle with no picture to guide you. Amita took a long, hard, final draw of her cigarette and crushed it under her slipper. She blew out the smoke and used her trusty magazine, an *Anglers Monthly* from six years ago, to blow away any lingering traces of her guilt. Although she supposed there were worse vices. She reached up to close the window when a knock came from the front door downstairs.

Amita froze. She hadn't seen anyone coming up the path, or even down the street. So much for her all-encompassing view and early warning system. She hurried down the ladders of the attic. Almost tripping over a stray toy car left dangerously close to the stairs, she composed herself as she opened the door, only to be greeted by a dishevelled, sobbing Georgie Littlejohn.

'Oh Amita,' she said, throwing up her arms.

Georgie lunged forward, grabbing Amita in a bear hug before she could take evasive action. She was sobbing loudly and theatrically in a way that only Georgie Littlejohn could.

'Georgie...' Amita stammered. 'Are you, are you okay?'

'Oh Amita. No, no I'm not. It's so sad. So sad,' she wailed into Amita's shoulder.

'What is? What's happened?'

'It's just so, so sad. I had nobody else to turn to. It's just so sad.'

'So you keep saying. What's happened Georgie?'

'It's terrible. Just terrible.'

Georgie went on and on. Amita should have felt bad, but her friend, if Georgie Littlejohn was friends with anyone, was beginning to annoy her. There was nothing worse than self pity for self pity's sake. She decided to take action, her head still spinning from thoughts about Sheila Mulberry.

'Would you like a cup of tea?' she asked.

Georgie pulled herself away from Amita. Her normally pristine makeup was crumpled and cracked around her forehead and jowls. Thick lines of black eyeliner were running down her cheeks. Her eyes were like two balls of red wool and her bottom lip was trembling. Amita reached out and took her hand. It was ice cold.

'Come on,' she said, ushering her inside. 'I'll put the kettle on.'

Georgie duly did as she was bid, perhaps for the first time in their long relationship. Amita showed her into the living room and quickly retired to the kitchen to fetch the tea. She let out a long sigh, the faint sobs of Georgie wafting in from the other room. This was really the last thing she needed. There was bad business afoot, something rotten again at the heart of Penrith and she needed to investigate. Not play nursemaid to her fiercest bingo rival.

The kettle boiled, the tea brewed, and Amita sucked it all up. She moved as elegantly as her tracksuit would let her as she delivered the tray, biscuits and all, to Georgie who was sitting miserably in *her* chair.

'Get that down your neck,' she said, offering a mug.

Georgie took it. Even in her malaise she couldn't resist a slight pause to consider the fact it wasn't fine china. Amita let it slide as she sat down on the sofa opposite.

'Okay,' she said. 'Start at the very beginning Georgie. Just what has got you into such a state?' Amita sipped at her tea, hoping Georgie would get the hint.

She didn't. Instead, she sat across from Amita looking and feeling sorry for herself.

'You think you have time, don't you? You really think you've got all the time in the world and suddenly it's all snatched away from you.'

'Georgie, I can't help if you don't tell me what's wrong or what's happened. I'm not psychic.'

'One moment you're going about your business, thinking everything is fine and then suddenly, bang, out of nowhere, *this* happens. It's taken the stuffing right out of me Amita, it really has.'

'What, Georgie? What's taken the stuffing out of you?'

The bingo club's resident doyen was staring blankly ahead, somewhere between the spider plant and the faded picture of Radha and her siblings which sat pride of place on the mantle. Georgie took a long, deliberate breath.

'I don't think I'll ever recover from this Amita, I don't mind telling you this,' she said softly. 'And after all those horrible things I said about him the other night...'

Amita's interest suddenly perked up. She straightened her back, ears pricked like a meerkat in the wild at the first hint of danger. 'Georgie?' she asked with trepidation. 'Is there something I should know?'

Her taste for tea suddenly vanished. She placed the mug down on the floor beside her feet and leaned a little further forward on the edge of the sofa. Georgie stopped her aimless staring. She looked across at Amita.

'I said some horrible things about him Amita. Some dreadful things. And look what's happened now. It's my fault, all my fault. I had nobody else to turn to, you understand, don't you?'

Amita needed a moment to compute what she was hearing. She had to stall for time. Was this really happening? Had Hal Mulberry's killer just landed in her lap? Was she really sitting here, in her own living room, about to hear a confession? And what's more, not just any old confession, a confession from the legendary Georgie Littlejohn – the pillar of the community's pillar of the community.

She needed to gather her thoughts, and quickly. She eased forward on the sofa again. Any more, and she'd be on the floor. She rubbed her forehead and then pointed at Georgie.

'Just for argument's sake Georgie,' she started, thinking all the while. 'Just to be clear. You're racked with guilt over a death, that's right?'

Georgie nodded solemnly.

'And you feel bad because you were *responsible* for this death? Correct.'

'Yes, I was,' she said, tears starting again.

'Now you feel compelled to tell me about it because you feel guilty, because of the way you spoke to your victim, if we can call him that. Have I got it about right here Georgie?'

'You're spot on Amita,' she said. 'I knew I was right to confide in you. I just knew it. You're a good friend, a supportive friend. I thought, if there was anyone in the world who I could turn to in a crisis like this, it would be you.'

Amita puffed out her cheeks. Her knees and thighs were beginning to hurt from all the edge of sofa leaning she was doing. She slid back and shook her head.

'Georgie, I'm stunned,' she said. 'I'm actually shocked that this is happening. If I wasn't seeing it and hearing it with my own eyes and ears I don't think I would believe it.'

'It's true,' she said, blowing loudly into her handker-chief. 'All of it, I'm sorry to say.'

'I mean, I knew you didn't like him, you'd made that clear,' said Amita. 'But I never thought you would... you would... you know.' She nodded sideways, as if mimicking some sort of throwing overboard motion. Georgie just sat there looking sad and pathetic, her mouth curled perma-nently downwards, dragging the rest of her face with it.

'I said some terrible things before it all Amita. And then... then it just happened. Just like that, I can't really explain it. I think they call it the red mist or something. Julia Colvil's grandson's boyfriend said that expression to me once. I think I've got it right.'

'You've got it right,' said Amita with a dry gulp. 'But... why Georgie? Why would you do something so terrible? What could have made you so angry? There are serious implications for something like this. The police, they're involved. You must have known something like this would change your life completely.'

Georgie shrugged. She wiped her nose and took a sip of her tea, deliberately wincing before she could get a proper taste.

'I think it was a catalogue of events Amita,' she said. 'It just all built up and built up to this moment. His face, that horrible, ruddy face of his, looking back at me every time I saw him. It was daily Amita, every single day. I couldn't avoid it. Always staring at me before I saw him. Always with that doe-eyed, sycophantic smile on his lips. It was like he was laughing at some joke I didn't know about. In-jokes aren't funny Amita. They're hurtful and people should be more careful and kind to each other. I don't need to tell you that.'

'No,' said Amita, not really listening, she was already planning how she was going to keep Georgie here until she called Jason or DI Arendonk. 'Wait, what?'

'I didn't think I was capable of something like this, I really didn't,' Georgie went on. 'But you don't, not until you're faced with the choice head on. Do I, or don't I? It was as simple as that. Do I strike now and live with it, or do I move on and put up with another day of him lording it over the rest of us? I must be mad Amita.'

Amita felt a sudden compulsion to be kind. She got up and offered Georgie a hug. Her bingo rival looked a little pensive at first but then accepted. The two women just sat there for a moment, together, alone, with just their words hanging in the air between them. Amita had no real quarrel with Georgie Littlejohn – it was nothing but a friendly rivalry between two women who shared more in common than either was willing to admit. This, however, set them both apart. And there would have to be consequences.

'We need to go to the police,' she said softly. 'This is too important to stay unknown to the proper authorities.'

Georgie nodded in silent agreement.

'I'll come down to the police station with you, I'll make sure you speak to the correct people, that you're not messed around. There's a new detective inspector in charge of the case. Sally, Sally Arendonk. She's lovely Georgie, really nice, nothing like that bulldog she replaced. I'll come down with you and we'll speak with her, and this can all get resolved. Does that sound okay?'

'Yes,' said Georgie. 'Yes, that sounds wonderful Amita. I knew I was right to come to you. You're so level-headed and calm with these kinds of things. And I feel a little better having it all off my chest. It feels like the guilt is easing a little, you know?'

She didn't know. She didn't want to know. The full scale of everything that had happened, not just in the past few moments, but the last day or so, hadn't quite sunk in for Amita yet. She was just ploughing on, moving from one task to the next in a sort of daydream.

'Would you like to see it?' said Georgie as Amita got up.

'See it? See what Georgie?'

'The head.'

Amita froze. Had she heard Georgie correctly? Or was her mind just playing tricks on her? She wouldn't blame it if it was. Things had been a little stressful lately. She was long overdue a holiday somewhere warm, with golden sandy beaches and absolutely *no* murders whatsoever.

She very slowly turned around to face her bingo club colleague. Standing over her, Georgie was already reaching for her handbag.

'Georgie...' she started. 'What do you mean, the head?'

'I've got it right here, stupid bloody thing,' she sniffed. 'I don't know, I think I thought I should keep it as some sort of memento. You don't get the chance to do what

I've done very often in your life. It just felt, I don't know, right, is all.'

'Georgie,' Amita could feel her heart racing. 'Please, for the love of all that's good and righteous in this world, tell me you are pulling my leg.'

'No, no, I've got it right here,' she said, unzipping her bag. 'I just took it, after the deed was done, just like that. I don't know why, it's not like I could put it on display or anything. I assume the police will want to take a look. Do you have a plastic bag or something to wrap it in?'

Amita could only watch on in horror. The world seemed to have vanished all around them. It was like they were in a vacuum, the air suddenly vanished. She stared down at Georgie Littlejohn as she reached into her handbag, rummaged around and eventually produced The Head.

'Here we are,' she said, staring down at it in her lap sadly. 'What a terrible mistake. What have I done Amita?'

'What... what... what is that?'

She could barely get the words out. She was still living in that vacuum and was desperately short of air. Not even the sudden shock of seeing the decapitated head of a giant garden gnome could jolt her back to normality.

'Colonel Mustard,' said Georgie, staring into the dead eyes in front of her. 'This not-so-little bugger was the pride of next door's garden, if you can call it that. Every morning I wake up to look at my prize geraniums and his leering, creepy smirk is staring back at me from their rockery, which, I may add, directly contradicts *several* council bylaws, not to mention the tenants' association's own rules.'

'Colonel Mustard,' said Amita. 'You've killed a gnome?'

'He was almost four feet tall Amita,' said Georgie. 'That's how big he is – was, even. That's hardly a gnome. I mean, I don't have an issue with people enjoying their gardens, I know I like to sip a little gin and tonic when the weather is nice. But would *you* do it with *this* hideous thing watching your every move? He was like the *Mona Lisa* – his eyes used to follow me wherever I looked.' She held up the head and bobbed it towards Amita.

The smile was, indeed, smug and eerie. Although she didn't know what was worse, the beheaded gnome or the relief that Georgie Littlejohn was, in fact, not Hal Mulberry's killer.

'Georgie,' she said with a deflated sigh. 'I think you're on your own with this one.'

'What? But you said you'd come with me to the police station.'

'I know I did. But that was when I thought you'd killed–' She stopped herself. As relieved as she was, there was still a killer on the loose. And while this may have been some light relief, she needed to get back to business. 'You're on your own Georgie,' she said flatly.

'I'm on my *own*?' she asked. 'I'm on my *own*. Well, that's charming, isn't it? I come around here, asking a friend for help, get offered it and now you're taking it away! I knew I shouldn't have come here. I knew I couldn't rely on you when the crisis levels were raised. And I was right Amita, I was right all along.'

She shoved the head of Colonel Mustard back into her handbag and zipped it closed around him. The point of his hat jutted out through the leather, giving it a distinctly conical shape as Georgie stormed out of the living room.

'Georgie, come on, don't be like that,' Amita called after her.

'No, no, you've made it quite clear where you stand on this matter Amita,' Georgie waved her away. 'You're washing your hands of the whole affair. I thought a friend in need was a friend indeed but clearly I got my wires crossed somewhere down the line. I'll deal with this on my own, DI Arendonk need not know you were involved in this ghastly business. While my reputation goes down the tubes, you'll be perfectly protected Amita. I hope you're happy.'

She was down the end of the garden path and was still ranting as Amita watched her go. She thought about following her and trying to make amends but there was no point. Georgie Littlejohn, in times of crisis, only ever listened to the sound of her own voice.

A car pulled up close to the front gate, instantly distracting Amita. Jason climbed out and looked flushed as he ran up to the front door.

'Tie,' he said. 'I need a tie.'

'A tie? You?' asked Amita. 'What on earth would you need a tie for? You're self-employed. Has somebody else died?'

'No,' he shouted back, halfway up the stairs.

'Do you even own any ties, Jason?' she asked him.

'I can't remember. But I need one, and fast.'

Amita felt a tingle of nerves make her skin creep. She stepped back into the house and leaned on the bannister, staring up the stairs.

'Is everything alright Jason?' she asked, nervous.

'No, it's not,' he shouted back, joined by the sound of slamming drawers and cupboard doors. 'It's Sheila Mulberry.'

'What about her?'

'She's holding a press conference,' he yelled back. 'And I need to be there.'

'Are you sure that's wise?'

'No,' he said, appearing at the top of the stairs, tie slung about his shoulders. 'I think it's about as unwise a thing anyone in the world has ever thought of doing. But it's a must. If I'm not there then my editor will, quite literally, have my guts for garters.'

'Blimey,' she said. 'That's not good. What's she talking about?'

'I don't know,' he said. 'But I'm late as it is, so I need to get moving. If I'm not home for dinner then you'll know I've been arrested and I'm rotting away in jail.'

'Every mother-in-law on the planet's dream,' she said with a smile.

Chapter 11

IMPRESSION, SUNRISE

Jason hated press conferences. He had always hated them. Not that he'd been to many in recent years. Thankfully his career had taken as divergent a path as possible to mean he almost forgot how they worked.

This press conference in particular was going to be hell. Yes, he had been pestering the person speaking. And yes, he'd probably stand out like a sore thumb among other, so-called 'proper' journalists. Such was the life of a free-lancer, you were always the imposter as there was no taskmaster cracking the whip from afar.

Only this time, there *was*. He hadn't told Amita when he returned home, but the venerable Arnold Beeston had torn more than a few strips off him during their now daily lunchtime phone call. To call it a conversation would have been unfair. Jason had noted that conversations usually involved at least two people. Not one angry middle-aged man screaming down a mobile to a reporter three-hundred miles away. Such was life at the big title though. Jason had thick enough skin to put up with it. What had bothered him the most was how right Beeston had been.

There was no story here. At least, there was no story that could be used. Jason had half expected the usual diatribe and a lecture on press ethics when he'd told Beeston about the little trip to see Sheila Mulberry. He'd also kind of hoped for a pat on the back, a severely unethical well done for trying to get a scoop. In the end, it had been nothing more than a lecture on how to be a journalist. Find stories, fact check stories and write said stories.

Jason hadn't even got past the first hurdle. What was the story here? Hal Mulberry was dead, murdered, according to the police and Sheila, although he couldn't say that yet. That was like reporting the sky was blue. Everyone and their granny knew Hal Mulberry had been killed.

From what little Jason had gleaned from Sheila Mulberry, there wasn't much more to report there either. A grieving widow was so sad she was in hospital. Again, nothing new. He had no idea where to start looking for something that might not otherwise be there. In a desperate ten minutes on the drive home he'd thought about going back on his word and calling in his favourite family amateur detective. Would a first-person piece from his mother-in-law work at all? Maybe Amita could do all the press and podcasts. Maybe even get her own show – *How I caught a killer with Amita Khatri.*

No, that was absurd. It sounded absurd, even in his head. And he knew he would be laughed right out of journalism if he even suggested it to Beeston. Instead, as was the custom for every journalist being chewed out by an overworked, over-sozzled editor, on most of the calls he kept his mouth firmly shut and thought of England.

Maybe it was pity or perhaps spite, but at least today Beeston had thrown him the lifeline of the press conference. The editor expected Jason to be there, front and centre, and to be asking some questions. The only problem with a press conference was: other journos in the room heard the answers too. There was nothing exclusive about them. And Jason needed something exclusive.

The room in the police station was hot and stuffy. A row of windows ran along the top of the far wall but none of them were open for some reason. Jason suspected it was to make the gathered press pack as uncomfortable as possible. He could hardly blame the police. Reporters didn't deserve to be made comfortable. This was a place of work, not a leisure club, as one editor had so famously told him many moons ago in a newsroom so clouded with smoke you couldn't see the ceiling.

A small table with glasses and jugs of water had been set up at the front of the room. Behind them were huge posters emblazoned with the Cumbria Police logo and whatever tagline they were currently using. It was all very no-frills, a classic police appeal set-up for the cameras, of which there was a small gaggle at the opposite side of the room. Jason sat with his head down, pretending to be occupied with his notes. He could hear his kith and kin, his fellow journalists around him talking shop. Some things never changed, like the fact they all seemed to know each other, and he was alone. He speculated just how closed a shop journalism could be.

A door opened to distract him. No sooner had Sally Arendonk stepped out, than the cameras started flashing. They clapped and clicked as the new DI in town led a small entourage to the table. Everyone in the room seemed to lean forward a little more as they took their seats. The grieving Dr Mulberry was helped into a chair by a uniformed officer. Jason remained firmly close to the back, making sure Sheila didn't spot him right away and stop the whole thing short there and then.

When she was settled, DI Arendonk nodded to the gathered press and took her own seat beside Dr Mulberry. 'Good evening ladies and gentlemen, thank you very much for coming at such short notice,' she said, smooth and confident. 'As you can see, we have Sheila Mulberry here today. The usual caveats apply when it comes to questions as she's actually come straight from the hospital. Anything she can't answer I'll be glad to help with. But before we get to that, I have a short statement I'd like to read, on the record, if that's okay.'

The DI tapped her phone, gave one quick glance about the room, then read her statement.

'Cumbria Police would like to confirm that the death of Hal Mulberry is being treated as murder. Forensic officers currently remain at the scene of the local village hall and surrounding area close to Penrith Castle. The general public are warned they will likely see an increased police presence in the town throughout the rest of the investigation. At this time we are appealing for any further witnesses to come forward and present information to myself or my team, quoting the incident number online. This was a brutal, heinous crime committed to one of the town and area's most well-known public figures. Myself and the rest of Cumbria Police will not stop until the culprit or culprits are brought to justice. I will now take any questions.'

No sooner had she finished and the hands and voices were raised.

'Mrs Mulberry, Dave Kelbie, *Times*,' said the loudest voice, the others hushing down. 'Do you have any words you'd like to say in tribute to your husband?'

Sheila Mulberry looked awful. Jason peered at her through the gaggling press pack. She was small, miniscule, like a mouse caught in somebody's hand. Every cough, every scratch of a pen on a pad seemed to make her wince or twitch. She looked out at everyone through deeply burrowed eyes that seemed to suspect everything she saw.

'Hal was a kind man, a generous man,' she said, her voice equally mousy. 'You would be hard pressed to find somebody within five hundred miles of here who would have a bad word to say about him.'

Jason was confused. Not only did he know a few people, namely members of the Penrith Bingo Club, who didn't like Hal (but he supposed that many people wouldn't consider those people as 'somebodies' – the pensioners of Penrith were used to being overlooked, that was how all the trouble started last time). But more disconcerting was the fact that Sheila's tone was drastically different to the frothing woman he had pestered in hospital only a short while ago.

'Hal Mulberry did more for this town and county in his few short years than most of us can dream of in a lifetime,' Sheila went on. 'He'll always be remembered as a kind soul who selflessly gave back to the community that adored him. That's about as fitting a tribute as he could have wished for. And no horrific act of violence will ever take away from his legacy.'

Dave Kelbie didn't have a follow-up. So Monica Dewsbury from one of the Scottish papers took up the mantle.

'A question for DI Arendonk if you don't mind ma'am,' she said in a luxurious Scottish brogue that made Jason melt a little. 'Do you have any positive lines of inquiry? And if so, should the public be alarmed that there's a killer, or killers, on the loose in the area?'

That was a good question. Jason liked the cut of Monica Dewsbury's jib. If he could be a proper journalist, it would probably be her, he decided on a whim.

'Firstly, that's a bit of a ridiculous question Monica,' Arendonk cut through the compliments in a hurry. 'If there was any wider danger to the public then myself and my colleagues wouldn't be sitting here speaking with you right now. We believe that this was a targeted attack on Mr Mulberry, that the killer or killers may have possibly known him and his wife. And that I can, for the record, assure the wider public that there's no greater threat.'

Jason wanted Monica Dewsbury to fight back, to wave the banner about the free press and the importance of the fourth estate. Instead, she sat down, probably already planning her trip home over the border and battling the rush hour traffic.

The questions kept coming. Sheila and Arendonk seemed to bat them off casually. There was nothing remotely out of the ordinary about what was being asked. All the usual bases were being covered and covered again – who, what, where, why and when. Jason had made some meagre notes that he'd try to fashion into a summary, but his head just wasn't in it. He wanted out of this room, out of the police station and as far from Sheila Mulberry as he could get.

'If that's all there is, I can only thank you for your time,' said the DI.

She motioned to get up, but Sheila stopped her. Confused, Arendonk looked at her as the press pack gathered up their things.

'I think there might be one more question,' said Sheila.

'I think they might have everything they need, Dr Mulberry,' said Arendonk.

'No, definitely one more question,' said Sheila.

Jason had heard her but he didn't look up. He was untying his shoelace and redoing it, hoping the crowd of journalists in front of him would hurry up and go so he could slink away in their numbers. They had stopped now though and he began to panic. Very slowly, he peered through the chairs.

Sheila Mulberry was staring right at him. Sally Arendonk looked confused beside her. The widow then pointed and, like the parting Red Sea, the press corps all turned to look at Jason.

'Mr Brazel,' said Sheila, rising to her feet. 'Don't you have something to ask me?'

'Eh...' was all he managed, a nasty habit developing.

'Dr Mulberry, please, I think the reporters have asked everything they want and–'

'You've nothing to ask me then Jason Brazel?' Sheila's voice was rising.

'No, no I think we're all good,' he said. 'The rest of the journalists in here did a pretty good job I reckon.'

'Oh, come along Jason,' said Sheila, goading him. 'You seemed to have plenty of questions when you turned up at my bedside this afternoon. You know, in hospital, where I was being treated for shock after the murder of my husband.'

There was a noticeable hush around the room now. Every set of eyes was on Jason. He'd never been a big believer in the afterlife and all that. But if there *was* a set of Pearly Gates and he had to atone for his sins on Earth, he reckoned this moment might be played back and he'd be asked to explain himself.

'I… eh…' was all he could push out of his agog mouth.

He started to hear whispers from the other journalists. He couldn't make out what they were but he could imagine. This wasn't the time for him to get on his moral high horse with them and to accuse them of doing the same if they had a lead. If he was lucky, he'd get to the door without Sheila Mulberry tearing him limb from limb.

'Nothing to say Jason?' she laughed at him. 'That's a real shame. You seemed so enthusiastic, so very keen to get to the bottom of what happened to Hal for your precious story earlier. Well, here I am Jason, parading in front of you vultures for your benefit. Ask me what you want. What was Hal's shoe size? Or did he have any allergies?'

'Okay, that's enough,' said Arendonk kindly but firmly. 'I think we should go and have a nice cup of tea.'

'Maybe what side of the bed he slept on? Or what kind of aftershave he used the evening he was murdered right in front of me. Would that make you happy Jason? Would it?'

The DI put a friendly arm around Sheila Mulberry and guided her towards the door as she started to sob. A pair of uniformed officers took her out of sight as the press pack collectively regathered its breath. Jason could only stand there, feeling small, feeling humiliated, but most of all, feeling utterly remorseful. This whole story had been a nightmare from the moment he'd agreed to cover it. He deserved Sheila Mulberry's tongue lashing. He probably deserved more.

The room began to empty. Jason kept his head down and waited until most of the crowd had dispersed before hurrying out of the front door. It was getting dark and he'd parked the car down the street a little further away. He climbed in and let his head tip back onto the rest. Closing his eyes, he wanted to scream or punch something really hard. But he didn't have the energy. Instead, all he could do was just sit there, like a great, big forty-some-thing year-old lump and feel rotten.

His malaise was suddenly interrupted by a rattle at the window. Jason jumped with fright and looked to his right. Arendonk was leaning down looking at him, her friendly face etched with concern. Jason rolled down the window.

'Good evening officer,' he said nervously. 'What can I do for you?'

'Is she right?' asked the DI.

Jason thought quickly about playing dumb. He didn't have to play very hard, not judging by his actions of the day. Instead he sighed loudly and nodded.

'Jason,' Arendonk groaned. 'Do you know what this could mean if she decided to take it further? You could be looking at a fine, maybe even jail time.'

'I just wanted to know what was going on,' he said, electing not to throw Amita under the bus. 'I'd spend time with Hal, I liked him. Plus, I'm a journalist. I've got a big gig with a national down in London. You know what they're like down there Sally, they're parasites.'

'And you wanted to fit right in?'

'No. I wanted to get paid.'

'That's even worse!' Arendonk shouted.

'Well if it helps I'm feeling pretty awful about it.'

'And would you be feeling just as bad if you hadn't been called out in front of your colleagues?'

'Yes, I would be, as it happens,' he said. 'And they're not my colleagues. They're the big league guys. I mainly just write about cute dogs and giant marrows.'

That drew a muted laugh from Arendonk. Jason felt a little bit better. It helped that she wasn't screaming her head off at him. Or putting him in cuffs.

'Leave Sheila Mulberry to me,' she said. 'God knows why, but I believe you Jason. I believe that you weren't meaning any harm by going to see her. And I also suspect it wasn't quite as black and white as she was making it out to be.'

'Here's the thing,' he said, snapping his fingers. 'The nurse on the ward, she just let us, me, breeze in there without asking for any ID or anything. No police guard on the door so, you know, I think if someone had tried to stop me I... maybe wouldn't have...'

He trailed off as Arendonk shot him a displeased look. He bit his lip and mouthed his apologies.

'Like I said,' she started, 'I'll do my best with Dr Mulberry. I can't promise she won't want to take it further. But as far as I'm concerned, she shouldn't be using press conferences as ways of shaming reporters. It's a two-way system and I doubt the political powerbrokers above me want the police force going to war with the newspapers over dodgy, if slightly well intended, actions of one rogue reporter.'

'Thank you,' he said.

'You have to promise me one thing though,' she said, staring at him intensely. 'No more amateur investigations. I know you're covering for that mother-in-law of yours and that's your business, your prerogative even. But I don't want civilians getting mixed up with murderers and villains. It gets messy Jason, real messy, no matter what you two have done in the past. Keep your heads down and out of trouble. I won't be this generous next time and I doubt my superiors will be either. Got that?'

Jason could feel a little lump forming in his throat. He liked Sally Arendonk. She was fair and level-headed. She seemed to care about her job and she could see the bigger picture, a much bigger picture than he could even imagine. She was smart and to the point, everything a good copper should be; a good professional could be. He could learn a lot from the new DI.

'Loud and clear,' he said.

'Good,' she straightened up. 'Now go sling your hook and don't come back here again.'

'Yes, ma'am,' he said, starting the engine.

'Oh and one more thing Jason,' she said, pointing at his neck. 'Next time you go to a press conference, don't wear one of your kids' ties. Ducks with gawky looks on their faces playing trumpets isn't a good look for you.'

Jason looked down at his tie. In a rush he'd grabbed something from the kids' dress-up box and had wrapped it around his neck. He nodded and feigned a smile before driving off, ready to be gobbled up by the ground and never to be seen again.

Chapter 12

TWO WOMEN IN A ROWBOAT

There was a strange energy about the bingo hall tonight. There was an electricity in the air, an almost nervous excitement that had everyone that little bit more edgy. With everything that had been going on, Amita had completely forgotten about the monthly rollover jackpot. It was up around the hundred pounds mark, if rumour and conjecture were to be believed. Whispers had been circulating all week but Amita hadn't been paying attention. As soon as she sat down though she was reminded that this was a big deal.

'Are you ready for the feeding frenzy tonight?' asked Judy Moskowitz, twirling her dabber around her finger like an old west sharpshooter.

'Don't be so dramatic,' said her companion, Violet. 'You always have to make things sound so much more overblown than they actually are.'

'And a hundred and fifty big ones for the rollover isn't dramatic to you Vi?'

'Hundred and fifty?' Sandy coughed, leaning into the conversation. 'Is it as high as that now?'

'Why, what have *you* heard?' Judy pressed.

'I heard a hundred and twenty plus change. But that was on Sunday, could be more by now I guess.'

Amita hadn't seen everyone this excited since the new tea caddy had been introduced. At least then they had reason to be cheerful. No more cups swimming with ancient tea leaves that probably outdated most of the club members.

'A hundred and fifty is what I was told this afternoon,' Judy went on. 'That nice woman who lives above the butchers, what's her name?'

'Flo,' said Amita, still looking for her glasses. 'She's a retired school teacher, I think. Or school nurse, something to do with a school.'

'That's her,' said Judy, clicking her fingers. 'She has a permanent scowl on her face that makes her look like a burst couch. Anyway, she said she'd heard from someone who had overheard Father Ford talking about keeping so much money tucked up in the vestry and how he was terrified it would get stolen.'

'Father Ford is terrified of everything,' sniffed Violet. 'The man would jump at his own shadow if he didn't know what it was.'

'Would you listen to this?' Judy scoffed, thumbing at her friend. 'We've got a regular Clint Eastwood here dishing out the insults now.'

'I'm only saying is all,' she shrugged.

Amita couldn't argue. Father Ford was rather timid. She wondered if he would have a heart attack or something before he was fifty. He seemed the nervous type who wouldn't cope well with having the added pressure of lots of hard cash lying around to look after.

'Anyway, this Flo woman, she says he's even more nervous than usual. And it's because of the jackpot. Now I'm not one to listen to a load of old gossips...'

Violet did a bad job of concealing a snort.

'But I figure if the old misery knows something, it's probably spot on,' Judy nodded.

Amita had to agree. She found her glasses and pen and sat waiting patiently for everyone to take their seats. It was only then she realised there was a noticeable voice missing from all the hubbub and buzz.

'I see the village hall brigade are pulling ranks,' said Judy.

'Stop it Judy,' said Violet. 'You're making something out of nothing.'

Judy nodded over to the table beside the door. Barbara McLemore and Albert Chamberlain were deep in conversation. A few others were gathered around them, everyone looking very conspiratorial.

'I wonder what they're talking about?' asked Judy.

'Probably the game tonight and the jackpot, a bit like us,' said Amita.

'Nonsense,' she said. 'They'll be carving up this here hall's weekly timetable, seeing what they can bump off and claim for their own when the village hall is renovated and they're out on their ear.'

'Will the renovation still go ahead?' asked Violet.

'I imagine so,' said Amita. 'It was always meant to be Hal Mulberry's legacy, wasn't it.'

'I'd put a lot of money on it still going ahead,' said Judy bitterly. 'And that village hall lot over there, they'll be coming after us next. They'll start with this hall, slowly make suggestions, take over from behind the scenes, whispering in Father Ford's ear. Next, they'll be turning some of our regulars over to their side, promises of the grass being greener. You couldn't script it better. We'll be the last ones standing, mark my words. Well, I tell you something, they're not getting bingo, that's for certain. I'll die on that hill if I have to.'

'It won't come to that, surely,' said Violet. 'You don't think they'd take away our bingo, do you?'

'They're ruthless, that lot over there, the village hallers, ruthless,' said Judy. 'They've only started coming to the bingo since the news Mulberry bought over the village hall. They're brazen, got brass necks on them.!

'Then why are they here enjoying our bingo too?' asked Amita. 'If they replaced it with one of their classes or clubs, they'd be missing out.!

'That's what they want you to think,' Judy tapped her temple with her dabber. 'I've got the measure of them Amita, I know how they think. You, me, Georgie and Vi over there, we go to the village hall for the WI. We're the best of both worlds, we don't need one hall to be the best. But *them*, they're a different kettle of fish. When was the last time you saw Barbara McLemore here at bingo? Yet she's been here every week since that bloody Hal Mulberry swept in and bought her den up. He's stuck his nose in where it doesn't belong.'

'We shouldn't speak ill of the dead,' chimed Ethel from the end of the table.

'No, we shouldn't,' agreed Violet. 'Everything will work out in the end, you'll see. The village hall will be replaced or renovated or whatever it is, with its big fancy art centrepiece, and we'll all have plenty of space. It'll be harmony.'

'Rubbish,' said Judy. 'Glass half-full stuff and nonsense. They're coming for us ladies and gents, and they won't stop until they've taken everything from this place.'

Her words lingered a little longer than they ought to. Amita hadn't been feeling very chirpy in the first place. Now she was borderline depressed.

'Hold on a minute,' she said, speaking to the others. 'Has anyone seen Georgie?'

Sandy, Violet, Judy, old Ethel down the end of the table and a few others dotted around all looked about them. Georgie was nowhere to be seen.

'Nobody?' asked Amita, suddenly feeling a little concerned.

Everyone shrugged. Was it just that easy? Decades of loyal community service, every Wednesday night for countless more years on top, and the club hadn't even noticed she wasn't there.

'Has anyone heard from her at least?' she asked. 'Is she ill? Has she had an accident or something?'

'You seem awfully concerned Amita,' Violet said. 'Is there anything wrong?'

Amita came out in a cold sweat. She shook her head. 'No, absolutely not,' she said. 'I just figure that it's not really the bingo club without Georgie. She's been coming here longer than most of us and nobody knows why she's not sat in that seat opposite me lecturing us all on how much money is in the jackpot. That's all. Has nobody heard from her? Nobody had a call?'

'She'll be with a man,' Ethel wheezed from her chair. 'Sex-daft that one. Believe me. She's got the look in her eyes. Man-eater I'll bet.'

Nobody quite knew how to answer that. Sandy was the only one brave enough to have a go.

'Alright, settle down Ethel,' he patted her hand. 'I'll go and give her a call.'

'No!' Amita shouted, sliding out from her chair with an awkward screech. 'I'll do it Sandy. Don't trouble yourself.' She was up and out from the table before the big fellow could even stand up. His moustache twitched as Amita raced towards the door, mobile in hand, number already ringing.

This wasn't good. Georgie *never* missed bingo, not for plague, pestilence, famine or even death. Her life revolved around the club and Wednesday nights. She might never admit it, but Amita knew she thrived on the company, the gossip, and the status it afforded her being Queen Bee there. If she was missing out tonight and, more importantly, nobody knew why, then there was something very wrong.

Amita couldn't help but feel guilty. She had effectively thrown Georgie out on her ear when their crossed wires had been untangled. After all, it wasn't Georgie's fault that she was trying to solve *another* murder case. And it wasn't Georgie's fault she wasn't interested in the decapitation of what Amita acknowledged was a pretty creepy garden gnome.

The phone rang and rang until it reached the answer machine. She stood at the main doors of the hall as Father Ford, sweat lashing down his brow, welcomed the last of the players. Amita hung up and dialled again. Biting her lip, the nervous pastor began to hover around her.

'I'll be in in a moment Father,' she snapped at him.

He leapt back a little, feigning a smile as he waved his hands.

'Father, you haven't seen or heard from Georgie Littlejohn have you?' she asked him.

Father Ford thought for a moment. Then he shook his head. 'No, nothing I'm afraid Amita,' he said. 'Is everything alright? Gosh, there's nothing the matter with her is there?'

'I hope not,' she said as the answerphone message played in her ear again. She thought about heading straight over to Georgie's house. She thought about all the possible things that could have gone wrong, that could have happened to her. Had she slipped in the bath? Had she fallen down the stairs? Was Hal Mulberry's killer not satisfied with bumping off the local tycoon and they were turning their attention to the pensioner community? Again.

Then she thought about what Jason had said to her before – how she had a terrible habit of jumping to the worst conclusions. But when you'd lived a life as eventful as hers, you got used to expecting the unexpected. Still, this time Jason was right of course. He usually was. He was a good man, a good father and a great son-in-law. Although she made sure not to tell him that too often. She knew she should listen to him more often than she did.

Amita took the phone from her ear and hung up. She stared down at the screen for a moment, at the picture of Radha and the kids all smiling, enjoying ice cream on the Ullswater Steamer. Then she held firm against her paranoia.

'Did you reach her?' asked the pastor.

'No,' she said. 'But I'll drop her a message. I'm sure she's fine.'

Father Ford looked relieved – more so because he had only had two expressions – anxious, or relieved when the expected calamity he was usually braced for didn't happen. He ushered Amita in and closed the door behind them. She walked down the aisles and back to her table.

'Well?' asked Judy. 'Did you get a hold of Georgie?'

'No,' said Amita, unlocking her phone. 'It went straight to answerphone twice. I'll drop a message into a mutual group chat and make sure everyone is keeping an eye out for her.'

Amita rattled the message out quickly. She hit send and a chorus of chimes, buzzes and whistles went up around the bingo hall. The Sheriff of Penrith was well connected – well connected to a bunch of eager jackpot hopefuls. Amita stifled a groan – she needed someone outside of this hall to be keeping an eye out for Georgie.

'I wonder if whoever wins tonight will donate the money to charity,' asked Violet.

'Eh?' snorted Judy. 'Why the hell would they do that?'

'After everything that happened with Mr Mulberry,' she said. 'Don't you think it's a bit, you know, off that someone would take home all of that money just after a man has been... you know, murdered. Shouldn't we put towards a wreath for the funeral or something?'

'You can do what you like with the dough if you win it, Violet,' said Judy. 'If it's mine it's going straight into my holiday fund. I've got two weeks in Lanzarote booked for the end of the month and I'm planning on getting proper sozzled every day that I'm away. Besides, Mulberry was a millionaire *many* times over. He wouldn't begrudge a couple of hundred quid in his honour.'

'True,' said Violet, twisting her thumbs over themselves. 'And he did do a lot of charity work for the area. Still, absolutely terrible what happened to him, isn't it?'

'Terrible business. And I saw your Jason in the crowd at the press conference, Amita...' said Sandy.

Amita nodded politely. 'Yes,' she said. 'That was my Jason.'

'How exciting,' Judy smiled. 'To think, I kind of, sort of know a journalist in a murder case. You think all that bloody awful stuff happens in big cities and in far off places. But just look at what we've all been through in the past little while. Makes you think, doesn't it.'

Amita didn't answer that. Sandy remained silent too. Violet was trying to busy herself rearranging her bingo books for the thousandth time in front of her. Everyone knew and liked Judy Moskowitz's forthright manner, but sometimes she hit the nail *too* hard on the head for comfort. The only one still smiling was Ethel down the end.

'It's always the one you least suspect,' she said, flashing a devilish smile.

'What's that Eth?' asked Judy.

'It's always the one you least suspect,' she said again. 'You know what I mean, don't you Amita?'

Amita stared down the table at her. She felt a strange reassurance that had been missing for the last few days wash over her. She smiled back at Ethel who was nodding at her.

'Yes,' she said. 'I think I do Ethel.'

'Columbo!' Ethel exclaimed.

'Perry Mason!'

'That's enough for just now,' she tried to hush her down.

'TJ Hooker. He used to be Captain Kirk from *Star Trek*!'

'Good evening ladies and gentlemen,' Father Ford's dulcet, if slightly nasal, tones were finally enough to silence her.

He introduced himself and the rules of the game, as he had done every Wednesday since he'd taken over the weekly bingo. It was almost as if he didn't quite trust their memories… despite the fact that the folk there before him, in truth, held the most accurate and detailed history of pretty much anything that had happened – or had been rumoured to have happened – in Penrith since the last war.

'It's a very exciting evening for me,' he continued, 'as it is a *record* rollover monthly jackpot tonight. I'm delighted to say that there has been a pile of cash to the tune of one hundred and seventy pounds and ten pence burning a figurative hole in my mattress for the past week or so.'

The club murmured their collective approval.

'Yes, I was just saying to a few of you earlier this week about how I would be Cumbria's most wanted man if I took off to the Seychelles with the jackpot money and–'

'Get on with it!' somebody shouted.

Father Ford knew when he was beaten. He excused himself and started up the machine. Amita uncapped her dabber, but she was miles away, thinking, planning, plotting. Jackpot or no jackpot, she had an idea.

'Violet,' she said as the numbers started to appear on the projector behind the pastor.

'Yes,' she looked terrified of missing something.

'You said Hal Mulberry donated a lot of money to charity. Did he ever give anything to the WI?'

'Belt up you two,' Judy lambasted them. 'I'm on for a line here already.'

Several other voices of consternation were voiced around them. Amita didn't care.

'He did,' said Violet, haplessly flapping between her card and Amita.

'Do you know how much and how often?' she asked.

'I don't,' she answered. 'Not off the top of my head. Amita, I'm trying to play the game here and–'

'Is there any way of finding out?'

'Yes, I suppose so,' she said. 'We'll have a list of records somewhere in the office. It might be computerised or in a filing cabinet or something. It's all got to be recorded for tax purposes and–'

'Violet Heatherington and Amita Khatri!' Judy bellowed. 'If you two don't shut up right now I'm going to–'

'House!'

Albert Chamberlain was waving his card about maniacally as the rest of the village hall collective smiled around him. The jackpot was claimed to the sound of rapturous applause from the opposite side of the hall. Judy slammed a big, heavy fist onto the table, cursing. She sank back into her seat and shook her head, darting daggers at Amita and Violet to her side.

'You two muppets,' she said, her mouth scrunched up. 'Unbelievable.'

'Best to come around tomorrow, Amita,' said Violet. 'I'll take you through the records then.'

Chapter 13

SUNDAY AFTERNOON ON THE ISLAND OF LA GRANDE JATTE

As a career journalist, Jason had seen some pretty messy rooms down the years. His own desk at the *Penrith Chronicle* had been, at best, a disaster. The mountains of old papers, dog-eared notepads, press releases and every other bit of rubbish under the sun had become a staple, not just of his own workstation, but the rest of the office. The cleaners had given up long ago and he had learned a system, a unique navigation to be able to successfully sit down, work and get away again without disturbing the clutter.

The headquarters of Penrith's branch of the Women's Institute was on a whole new level of chaos. HQ was pushing it though. A long, draughty shed that looked more like an Anderson Shelter stretched out into the woodlands at the back of Violet Heatherington's garden. She had welcomed Jason and Amita first thing in the morning, honouring her word. If Jason had thought the overgrown garden and its razor-sharp rose bushes were bad, he hadn't anticipated the shed.

'She can't be serious,' he whispered to Amita as he followed Violet through the hotchpotch of strange and wonderful items and paraphernalia that dominated the place. 'She runs the WI from in *here*?'

'Ours is not to reason why,' said Amita smartly. 'Just keep your hands in your pockets and try not to knock anything over. Knowing Violet, some of this stuff is a thousand years old and worth a small fortune.'

'Really?' he sniffed. 'That decaying washing machine over there is worth its weight in gold, is it? And what about that upturned table with the broken legs, an antique I take it, belonged to Napoleon? How about this lovely contraption?' He bent down and picked up a broken toilet seat coated in decades worth of cobwebs and dust.

'You'll be telling me this is the loo that Elvis died on in a minute,' he said.

'Put that down,' said Amita. 'Come on.'

Jason dropped the toilet seat. It landed with a loud clack that disturbed a couple of pigeons hiding in the rafters above their heads. They flapped their wings and disappeared through a gap in the corrugated iron roof.

'You got lucky,' he said under his breath.

'Come along you two,' Violet shouted at them from up ahead. 'The office is in the back here. Don't mind the digger, it's getting picked up next week by the council.'

Jason and Amita ambled through the clutter that seemed to get bigger, heavier and more pointless the further they went into the shed. Violet stayed on the outskirts of Penrith, where the town vanished quickly and the countryside took over. She had acres of room behind her cottage, a place she'd lived for as long as Amita could remember. There had been some snafu with the council a few years ago about building another road behind the property, but Violet had fought it, and won.

She was a dogged woman, and fiercely loyal. Amita had always admired Violet in the way she went about her business. She could be quiet and innocuous but she was always reliable. Her time as the leader of the local WI had brought great success, both for the group and the local community. Best scones in the Lakes some said. Amita would be sad to see her go.

'Here we are,' she shouted.

She fiddled with the handle of the door. The rear of the shed had been built up into two separate rooms, an office and a little meeting area. There was a knack to opening the doors. Amita had grown to be patient with Violet as she worked it out.

'It usually... goes on the... third time of... asking.'

The door opened and she stumbled inside. Jason looked at his mother-in-law. She didn't look back.

Inside was a small round table with six chairs dotted about it. A kettle and some mugs and glasses sat in the rear corner.

'So this is where the action takes place,' said Jason sarcastically.

'What's that dear?' asked Violet, flipping the switch on the kettle.

'I said this is where the action–'

'Don't listen to him Violet, he's in one of his moods this morning,' said Amita. 'Don't worry, it usually passes around lunchtime.'

'Oh right,' she smiled. 'I see. Please, take a seat you two. Let's have some tea before we start raking through the records.'

Amita ushered Jason into a chair. She sat down beside him, making herself at home. Jason picked another stray cobweb off the arm of his seat and dropped it on the floor.

'It's not how I pictured this place, I'll happily admit that,' he said.

'And how exactly did you picture *this* place, Jason?' asked Amita.

'I don't know,' he said. 'A little office at the back of the Area 51 warehouse isn't exactly the first thing that comes to mind when you think of the Women's Institute. It's more doilies and stained glass windows is it not?'

'This isn't the usual meeting place Jason,' Amita corrected him. 'That's in the village hall, next to the station, the one Mr Mulberry was renovating. This is just the nerve centre for admin purposes and committee meetings.'

'Although, I don't know what we'll do now that the hall is being renovated,' said Violet, looking worried. 'This place was left behind after my Charles passed away, God rest his soul. He was a bit of an antiques buff actually, not that he ever found anything valuable. Every weekend we used to drive about Cumbria, Northumberland, Durham, Lancashire, everywhere picking up bits and bobs. At first it was just little things like teapots and Toby jugs, you know the sort of thing, like you see on the *Antiques Roadshow*. But when he retired it all stepped up in scale. Suddenly he was coming back with cannons and chests of drawers from Louis XIV's court. Or so he claimed.'

'He always spoke very highly of those weekends treasure-hunting,' said Amita, sipping her tea. 'He used to get very excited. I remember I used to see you both driving through town after a haul, some great contraption poking out from under a cover in a trailer. He always had a big beaming smile on his face.'

'He did,' laughed Violet.. 'Spent a bloody fortune though. I always used to tell him that if he'd saved the money he'd spent buying all that junk out there then we'd have a nice little retirement pot on top of our pensions. He was always very cautious, was Charles. Except when it came to his antiques. He could just see something, buy it and then try to sell it on, even though he had no real idea what he was doing. Bless him.'

She looked fondly up at a framed, faded engagement announcement. Charles' spirit felt like it was everywhere around them in this place.

'Why don't you get rid of it now?' asked Jason.

'I couldn't do that,' said Violet with a sharp intake of breath. 'That junk out there is all I've got to remind me of him, the soft-headed dolt. No, no, if I emptied this place then I'd lose something of him, forever. It's silly, I know it is, but when I look at some crooked standard lamp or a bath with three legs, then it feels like he's still here.'

Amita felt a lump forming in her throat. 'That's not silly at all,' she said. 'We miss them all, those who aren't with us anymore. Don't listen to Jason, he's just a big sourpuss.'

'Meow,' he said.

Violet smiled. She drained her cup. 'Shall we get to business then,' she said. 'No use sitting around here moping about the past. That, and I don't like to be out here too long, what with the asbestos and all.'

'Asbestos!' Jason shouted, standing up quickly.

'She's joking Jason, relax,' said Amita.

The two pensioners shared a little giggle between them.

Violet flipped on the light. Jason was sure he saw something scurry beneath the desk but decided not to investigate further. The office was dismal and dreary, a bare bulb offering the only light. Shoulder-height filing cabinets clung to the perimeter, their tops littered with trophies and old certificates granted to the Penrith WI from decades long forgotten.

'Charles had this place built about twenty-years ago,' said Violet, examining the cabinets. 'He said he wanted to have a record and certification of everything in the shed, should any of it be valuable one day. I think he just liked to tinker. He spent more time building that little room next door and this office than he did creating a filing system. Still, it's served the WI well over the years, hasn't it Amita?'

'Oh yes,' she agreed. 'I thoroughly enjoy coming here every month. It's nice and cosy. Makes a pleasant change from the village hall.'

Jason noticed that she had crossed her fingers behind her back.

'Now what was it you were looking for again?' asked Violet, pushing her steel-rimmed glasses back onto her nose.

'Hal Mulberry made a lot of donations to the WI over the years,' said Amita. 'You said there would be records of just how much he'd given and when.'

'That's right,' she said. 'It'll all be here. We had to keep it all above board should the authorities come asking why we were all off to Torquay for the summer outing instead of hosting events and fundraisers. But what use is it to you?'

Amita hadn't told anyone about her investigations. She was always a little wary. The last thing they needed were copycat amateur sleuths running around town making life harder for them and the police. This time, however, it seemed like she had no choice.

'I'll be honest with you Violet, you might not want to know the answer,' she sighed.

'Go on,' said Violet.

'We're looking into Hal's murder,' said Jason curtly.

'Oh my,' said Violet, reaching for her pearls. 'That's... surprising.'

'You'd think so, wouldn't you,' said Jason. 'But it appears that the Sheriff of Penrith here just loves the thrill of the chase.'

'Sheriff of Penrith?'

'Ignore him,' said Amita. 'Like I said, he's in one of his moods.'

Violet began pacing back and forth in front of them. 'Oh my, I'm... I'm not sure I like the sound of this,' she said. 'I mean, when I said you could look at the files, I thought... well, I don't know what I thought, maybe that you were just curious or something. People get their thrills from odd and strange places these days.'

'Violet, calm down,' said Amita, reaching out to her. 'It's alright. We're not going to take the files or the information anywhere. Nobody will even know we were here for them. Isn't that right Jason?'

'Yeah, sure,' he shrugged. 'I mean, I'm not entirely sure why we *are* here. But hey, what do I know, right?'

Amita tutted loudly. Violet's eyebrows arched in the middle. Amita stared into her glassy grey eyes and tried to assure her that all was going to be okay.

'We just want to see what kind of a man Hal Mulberry really was,' she said. 'If all the bluster and bravado and young local lad done well was genuine or just an act. I mean donating to the local branch of the WI isn't something you'd do for fame and accolades. So maybe he did have a heart of gold. But whether he did or not, somebody had an axe to grind.'

'Possibly quite literally,' said Jason.

Violet winced.

'And we just need to see what all the fuss was about. If there even *was* any fuss. That's all Violet. I promise you.' Amita sounded at her most convincing.

She held her stare for a moment. Violet shook her head.

'I don't know,' she said. 'It's all these confidentiality rules and the like Amita. PDGR or whatnot. It's not like it used to be in the old days where you could just thank someone for their donation. Especially not the numbers Mr Mulberry gave to us. It's all tax-deductible this and Gift Aid that. I don't even know if I should be showing you the files now you've said it's to do with – well, his unfortunate end.'

'He was murdered Violet,' said Amita, releasing the big guns. 'In cold blood. It was not "unfortunate", it was a crime. Somebody out there is walking around with a killing on their conscience.'

'What about the police though, they're all over this, aren't they?' she said. 'I mean, I saw his wife on television last night. She's appealing for witnesses to come forward.'

'The police don't know the underside of this community like we do,' Amita thumbed to Jason. 'We know people. And people are what counts in situations like this. Believe us, we know.'

'Yes, that's true,' said Violet. 'Sometimes I think the world has just gone completely mad. Did you know I walked past a young couple the other day outside Tesco kissing. And not just kissing, *French* kissing. Whatever happened to this place Amita? Did we just get too old or something?'

Amita didn't answer her.

Jason was about to say something sarcastic but thought better of it.

'Please Violet,' she said. 'Just a very quick look at the log books. Then we'll be gone. If nothing else, Jason here needs to know if the jolly entrepreneur turned philanthropist he felt he interviewed was the real deal.'

Violet thought it over for a moment. She looked at Jason and then back to Amita.

'I'm going to regret this,' she said, and stepped out of the way.

'In there?' asked Jason, pointing to the nearest cabinet.

Violet nodded, her head bowed. Amita was over like a whippet up a drainpipe. She pulled open the top drawer and immediately found a large brown folder marked with Hal Mulberry's name stencilled across the front. She began leafing through the invoices and receipts inside, handing them over her shoulder to Jason.

'You know, he was ever so hands-on,' said Violet.

'Who's that now?' asked Jason, marvelling at all the ones and zeros flashing in front of him.

'Hal,' said Violet. 'He always gave us tremendous support. Not just with all the money down the years, but with events and publicity. You remember Amita, how that fun run about ten years ago when that woman turned up, what was her name, she won that talent show on TV.'

'I remember,' said Amita, engrossed in the paperwork.

'That was all of his doing. He said it would triple, if not quadruple the donations to the charity that year if he got us a big name attendee. He always said the WI had been close to his heart, after they had been his mother's lifeline when she was ill and he was growing up. The group had brought her shopping, veg, fruit, that sort of thing, to keep the family going until she found her feet again. He always used to say that charity had stuck with him all these years, even when he was making multi-million-pound deals and jetting off all over the world. He was a saint, really. No matter what people might say about him now, or whatever comes out. Hal Mulberry was and always will be a saint in my eyes.'

Amita paused for a moment, looking like she was about to say something, then thought better of it and instead set her stack of files and paperwork down on the desk. She pointed at the handwritten notes and old typed receipts.

'Ten thousand here,' she said. 'Another five grand there. He was throwing money at the WI for years.'

'Some of these go back as far as twenty years,' said Jason, offering his own stack. 'A couple of hundreds, the odd thousand. There was one here for eight and a bit grand.'

'Ah yes, I remember that,' said Violet, looking at the note. 'There was a women's refuge in Keswick that had been badly damaged by some awful weather. You know what it can be like around these parts when there's a bad winter. Mr Mulberry very kindly handed us a huge cheque to help with the relief effort and to make sure there was a safe place for those women and children to go to while the repairs were carried out. I think we ended up spending the money on hotels for the residents or something.'

'Painting a picture, isn't it Amita,' said Jason.

She looked across at the scattered notes and paperwork in front of her. There was nothing there to suggest that Hal Mulberry had been anything other than a generous, kind and willing patron of the organisation. So why would anyone murder the patron of the WI?

'It just doesn't add up,' she said. 'I just can't understand it. Nobody has a bad word to say about him. And if these notes and *Buttermere at Dawn* saga prove anything, it's that he seemed to genuinely care about the community.'

'That's what I've been trying to tell you all along,' said Jason.

'I can't think of him ever making enemies, Amita,' said Violet. 'I know a few of us weren't very happy with his plans for the village hall, but as far as I'm concerned it was the first dirty mark on his record. He was a friend of the WI and me too for that matter. I'm shocked, devastated even, as to what's happened to him. And I can't think of anyone who would wish any harm on him. Well... not any real harm anyway.'

'Real harm?' asked Amita, sensing a shift in Violet's tone.

'It's just well... no, it's nothing.'

'No, no, go on Violet,' said Amita. 'Anything you think of, anything at all, could be vital in catching Hal Mulberry's killer. What were you going to say?'

She looked worried now, the wrinkles deepening across her forehead and around her pale eyes.

'It's probably nothing,' she said, almost whispering. 'But Judy was very aggressive towards him before, you know, the unpleasantness. I don't like to talk ill of my friend Amita, and I know how much you like and respect Judy.'

'Judy?' Amita asked. 'Judy Moskowitz?'

'Who's Judy?' asked Jason.

'Yes,' said Violet, speaking low. 'Don't you think she was a bit, you know, angry with Mr Mulberry when he revealed the plans for the village hall?'

'Who's Judy?' Jason asked again.

'Are you trying to say Judy had something to do with this?' Amita asked.

'Am I a mirage or something? A spectre? Would somebody please tell me who Judy Moskowitz is.'

'Oh be quiet Jason!' Amita shouted. 'Violet, please, if you know something about Judy and Mulberry then you need to tell us.'

Violet shook her head. 'I don't know anything,' she said. 'I've already blabbed too much as it is. This was a bad idea Amita, a really bad idea. You should both go. I need to tidy away these files and there's a nineteenth century ship anchor out there I have to drag back out to the front of the cottage.'

'Violet,' she pressed.

'I shouldn't have said anything. I'm sorry,' she said. 'Now please, both of you go. I don't want anything more to do with this whole sorry affair.' She was on the edge of tears.

Amita was about to press her, but Jason sensed it was a lost cause. He took his mother-in-law by the arm and guided her out of the office.

'What are you doing? She knows something,' she said. 'We have to find out what she means by implicating Judy like that.'

'She doesn't know anything Amita, it sounds like Judy was just another one of your set who was worried about what was going to become of the WI when Hal gussied up the village hall,' he said as they walked back through the myriad of junk.

'Then why would she say that about Judy?'

'She's upset,' he said. 'Believe me, I know when somebody is desperate and hurting. Usually I'm looking in the mirror. She doesn't know anything, she's just clutching at straws. You heard how she spoke about Hal. If we'd stayed any longer she would have set up a shrine there and then to her hero.'

They cleared the shed, the bright sunlight warm and gentle on their faces. The smell of the countryside was a pleasant replacement for the oil and stale air. Amita scratched her head.

'I'm going back in there,' she said.

Jason still had a hold of her arm, stopping her before she could head back into the shed. 'Drop it Amita,' he said. 'Please. Violet is upset. The last thing she needs is to be given both barrels from you right now. I think perhaps we've caused enough trouble.'

'But it could be a lead Jason,' she said. 'We can't just leave it hanging like this.'

'There's no lead here, trust me,' he tried to assure her. 'She's upset by everything that's happened. I don't know who this Judy Moskowitz woman is, but if she's another pensioner, from the bingo club and everything else, do you really think she's capable of murder?'

Amita stopped struggling. She stared a little into the distance, thinking.

'Could Judy really murder somebody, let alone a man thirty years her junior?' asked Jason. 'Is she even up to the physical challenge, let alone the psychological one? And what's her motive, that Hal bought Penrith Village Hall? Come on Amita, I know we like to hit and hope sometimes but this is stretching it even by our admittedly low standards.'

Amita reluctantly nodded. She sighed, her shoulders slumping. 'You're right,' she said. 'I just… I just thought we might be getting somewhere, you know? It's been one dead end after another with this case Jason. I'm getting tired, frustrated and… and, and I don't know what else. It's infuriating.'

'I know,' he said, smiling at his mother-in-law. 'But on the other hand, you just admitted that I was right. That's a pretty big milestone in our relationship, is it not?'

Amita puckered her lips. She snorted a little laugh and they started for the main road on the other side of Violet's cottage.

'I just thought we might have found something in those records,' she said. 'Something that showed Hal Mulberry wasn't this pitch perfect philanthropist with the community at the front of his mind.'

'I know what you mean,' he said, reaching the car. 'Too good to be true springs to mind.'

'Exactly,' she said, climbing in.

Amita buckled her seatbelt and stared up the road. Jason started the engine and pulled out.

'Wait a minute,' she said, nudging him. 'Do you remember what Sheila said to us in the hospital?'

'I'm trying to erase that whole episode from my memory, if you don't mind,' he said. 'Especially after she called me out in front of the rest of my profession and I was effectively given a verbal warning by the police.'

'She said something about Hal and his affairs.'

'Vaguely,' he said, thinking. 'So what?'

'Affairs, that's a funny word, don't you think?'

'She wasn't in the best of mindsets Amita, the woman had found her husband with his throat cut a matter of hours earlier.'

'No, I mean affairs, that word, it's ambiguous at best.'

'It has multiple meanings, yes,' he agreed. 'What are you saying?'

'When she said it, I just assumed she meant Hal Mulberry's business, his work.'

'Yes, me too.'

'Well, what if she *didn't* mean that?'

Jason stared ahead, watching the road with a hard look on his face. 'You mean affair as in extra-marital?' he asked.

'It's possible, isn't it?' asked Amita.

'It's possible I suppose,' he agreed. 'Like I said though, Sheila was hardly in the best frame of mind when we saw her. She could have said anything then and not really known what she was talking about.'

'But by the same token, she might have known *exactly* what she was saying.'

Jason drummed his fingers on the steering wheel. It was an interesting thought. Very interesting.

'It's just a thought,' said Amita, folding her arms and sniffing. 'It doesn't change the fact that there is somebody walking the streets who killed Hal Mulberry and we're no closer to finding out who they are and why they did it.'

'No, we're not,' he said. 'And that's as it should be. This is the police's case, not ours.'

A loud rattle gave them both a fright. Jason looked down at the cup holder beneath the radio as his phone screen lit up. Even a quick glance was enough to make his skin crawl.

'Bugger,' he said. 'I thought I had more time.'

'Who is it?' asked Amita.

'It's Beeston the Barbarian,' he said. 'Calling for his daily update. And guess what, I have nothing to give him.'

Chapter 14

THE SCREAM

'You're just taking the biscuit now Brazel, aren't you?'

It was more a statement than a question. And Jason had a feeling there was no answer he could give that would satisfy Arnold Beeston's thirst for his blood.

'You've had days to give me something, something juicy, something important, somebody bloody readable on this story and I've had nothing from you. Diddly squat in fact!'

'Yes, technically true but–'

'But nothing! I'm sitting here with a two page spread waiting to be filled and I've got the sum total of hee haw to fill it with.' Beeston's voice was cracking as he shouted down the phone. 'It's the biggest manhunt in the region in the last decade, a local philanthropist, barrow-boy turned millionaire, murdered, the whole country up in arms about it. I could write it all myself but instead I've got you floating around your hometown like a fart in a trance and filing expenses and invoices.'

'Ah yes, I'm glad you mentioned that Arnold,' said Jason, feeling suddenly brave. 'I haven't been paid yet and I don't know who to bill. Is it you or is it the paper?'

He was sure he heard something smash on the other end of the line. It could have been a coffee mug. Or knowing Arnold Beeston, the skull of an unwitting reporter who walked past him just at that moment. Jason took a gulp of warm air and waited for the punishment.

'You know fine well where you can stick your invoices Brazel!' he blasted.

'I thought you might say that,' Jason said, nodding.

Fearing the wrath that awaited him on the other end of the phone, Jason had pulled over as soon as he could. Making a newspaper editor like Beeston wait was, in his experience, a terrible life choice. They had found a quiet spot at the side of a country road a few miles from Violet Heatherington's cottage. Amita was standing at the front of the car, face turned towards the sun, enjoying the peace and quiet. Jason was at the rear of the car, enjoying nothing.

'So what have you got for me today Brazel?' said Beeston, recomposing himself. 'And whatever you do, don't say nothing. I can't handle nothing. *Something* is better than nothing. *Anything* is better than nothing. I'm giving you fair warning.'

Jason had been mulling over whether he was fit for this job. In the months since the Madeleine Frobisher story, his reputation had somewhat bloomed. Suddenly there were editors from John O'Groats to Land's End that knew who Jason Brazel was. He was grateful for the job offers, he really was, but in this case it had all started to feel a little dangerous, a little out of his league.

He had even thought about telling Arnold Beeston that fact, that he might not be up to the challenge. Beeston was a busy man. As he had said already and on numerous occasions since they'd known each other, he had a newspaper to fill, each and every day. This might be the biggest story in the country. Readers, however, wanted gory details and salacious material to mull over their breakfast cereal and morning Alka-Seltzer. Was Jason really the reporter to deliver that sort of news to them? He hadn't been sure in the first place. And he certainly wasn't now, a few days into the job.

Then there was the Hal Mulberry factor. Jason was pretty sure he should be mourning the tycoon's death a little more than he had been. In the few short days and weeks he had known Hal, he had grown quite fond of him. He even considered him a friend, especially after the generosity he'd been shown. How many other jobs had he worked on that included first-class tickets to and from London with all the champagne he could drink? Or the fact he had rubbed shoulders with Cumbria's great and good before the murder. Shouldn't he be a bit more loyal to Hal in the immediate aftermath than to be raking through his past looking for a story, for gossip?

In the end though, Jason couldn't think fast enough. Beeston was breathing heavily down the line. And even at three-hundred miles away, he was sure he could feel the heat coming from the editor's flames.

'Well, there's his charity work,' Jason offered.

'Charity work?' Beeston repeated. 'Are you for real?'

Jason had a sudden rush of blood to the head. 'Yes, his charity work,' he said, sounding strangely confident. 'A source has told me that he must have donated almost a hundred grand over twenty years to the local Women's Institute here in Penrith. And that's just local, there's no telling how much he gave away across Cumbria, maybe even the whole UK.'

A strange, subsonic rumble came down the line. Jason wasn't sure if it was Beeston or the start of an earthquake. The blood had now firmly rushed away from his head again and he was regretting every one of the last twenty seconds.

'Brazel,' started the weary newspaper editor. 'I've been in this game for a very long time. So long, in fact, that my first job was reporting on the chariot races.'

Jason let out a little snigger.

'That wasn't a joke,' said Beeston.

'Oh right, sorry,' said Jason.

'And in those many centuries of being at the cutting edge of the news agenda, I can honestly say that I don't think I've ever heard such absolute tosh from a reporter.'

'Right,' said Jason. 'It's a first I suppose. That's something right?'

Another low rumbling gurgle from the other end of the phone.

'What about the painting?' asked the editor.

'What *about* the painting?'

'Is it valuable? Is there anything in that we could salvage? Mulberry bought the painting for a couple of million did he not? Is it by somebody famous?'

'Elvira,' said Jason.

'Elv-who?'

'Elvira,' he said again, thinking if Beeston had really been around as long as he said that he should have recognised the name – from his research he knew her fame was at its height in the late 1970s. But he supposed Beeston was more actual vulture than culture vulture. 'She's dead, passed away in 2018, I think it was. She was a prolific artist, Arnold, her paintings have gone for a fortune over the decades. She was part of a movement in the seventies and all the yuppies bought up her work in the eighties. But she was a recluse in her later years, people barely saw her. She's a local Cumbrian lass. Mulberry had a thing about the painting and–'

'Right, good, excellent, that's what I want then,' said Beeston. 'The painting, give me a feature on the painting, its history, when Elvis painted it, you know the stuff.'

'Elvira,' Jason corrected him.

'That's what I said. That'll plug a gap for now, but I'm warning you Brazel, you need to start coming up with something, anything that's better than how charitable the man was. Nobody cares about that. The readers want to know about his dirty laundry.'

'What? His pants and socks and things?' Jason poked his tongue firmly in his cheek and waited for the inevitable diatribe.

'Very good,' Beeston breathed down the line. 'Hang on, wait a minute.'

There was a shuffling of papers from Beeston's end. Jason had that strange rollercoaster feeling in his gut that all journalists got when dealing with angry editors. Their bosses, who were under great strain, could be their worst enemy but also their best friends – usually in the same breath. It was a strange relationship. Both depended greatly on the other doing their jobs to the best of their ability. Any let off on either side and the whole figurative pack of cards would come crashing down. Then there would be no news.

'Here,' Beeston barked. 'I knew I'd seen something. The research team came up with a list of names to do with Mulberry when he died. Which is a real shame as I've been looking to trim the budget and could have shown them the door if they hadn't produced the goods.'

'Lovely,' said Jason sarcastically.

'Doige, Arthur Doige,' said Beeston. 'You ever heard of him?'

'The name rings a bell. I don't know him personally, I've never spoken to him,' replied Jason.

'Says here he's an art dealer. Been in Penrith since the ark was launched. He has a shop in town. Go there, get as much info on this painting and Elvis Presley painter you can and send me the words before seven pm. Actually, make it six, the sub-editors had a nightmare untangling that absolute mess you filed yesterday.'

'Oh.'

'Oh, is right. Typo. And a type O blood transfusion is what you'll need after I've finished with you if you bother my subs with that rubbish again.'

'Right, I see,' said Jason. 'It's just, well, no editor in my past has had a problem with the way I file stories and–'

'Address should be with you now,' Beeston barked. 'Get to work Brazel. And don't mention charity work around me again, it brings me out in hives. I've got enough problems with my gout and back acne, I don't need you making me nervous to boot.'

Beeston hung up. Jason's phone vibrated and a text message delivered the address of Arthur Doige's gallery. He knew the street but couldn't picture the shop. Taking a long, strained breath, he tucked his phone into his pocket and turned back to the car.

'That didn't sound very productive,' called Amita, still basking in the sunshine.

'I wouldn't say that,' said Jason, strolling up beside her. 'I've got to do a piece about *Buttermere at Dawn*, there are worse assignments, especially given I've already researched the bloody thing, seen the thing and it shouldn't anger our chum Arendonk if I'm playing art critic rather than sleuth.'

'You sound deflated,' she said to him.

'Is it that obvious?'

'The Jason is feeling sorry for himself tone isn't exactly difficult to detect,' she said. 'It's usually followed by great bouts of television watching and procrastination. But we haven't got time for that. There's a murderer on the loose out there and we need to catch them. I don't trust the police to get there fast enough, quite frankly. They'll be caught up in red tape while a killer is still on the loose, endangering all of us for all we know. We're in a much better position to find this killer. Our ears are closer to the ground. And then there's your work, your story. Just think about how wonderful it would be to crack this case, have a ringside seat at it all unfurling. What a story *that* would make. Again!'

'I guess I had it in my head that this whole working on retainer for a national newspaper might be a bit more, you know, glamorous,' he said. 'Instead, I've had nothing but day after day lectures from Arnold Beeston on how to be a reporter, that my copy is garbage and that I give him hives. Oh, and then there's the being called out in front of the police by the grieving widow of the man who's murder we're investigating. It's just all one big pile of sh–'

'Language Jason,' Amita tutted.

He puffed out his cheeks. Staring up at the clear blue sky, he felt the warmth on his face. He could see why Amita enjoyed basking in it. There was something oddly comforting about that feeling, knowing it came from a burning star ninety-three million miles away.

'I heard you talking about Doige,' she said.

'Arthur Doige, do you know him?' he asked.

'I know of him,' said Amita. 'Isn't that what you think I'm always busy doing at bingo? Knowing the business of every senior citizen between here and Windemere?'

'You don't sound very convinced,' he said.

Amita shifted a little, her trainers crunching on the grit of the path at the side of the road.

'He's a bit... eccentric, shall we say,' she said.

'Eccentric, in Penrtih? Sounds like he fits right in?'

'You'll see what I mean when we go and chat to him,' she said, pushing herself up from the car.

'We?' Jason asked.

'Yes, *we*,' Amita said. 'I'm coming with you.'

'You are?'

'Yes, of course I am. If this has any bearing on catching Mulberry's killer then I should be there. You know the deal, Jason.'

'Ah yes,' he clicked his fingers. 'This fictional deal we have when we're hunting murderers. The one that seems to change at the drop of a hat to make sure you're in the centre of the action.'

'That's the one, yes,' she smiled.

'Right,' he nodded. 'Gotcha. Come on then, we should get moving. I'm on deadline... *again*.'

'We can swing by Georgie Littlejohn's house on the way home after Doige's.'

'Georgie?' he asked. 'At her house? Why the hell would you want to do that?'

Amita didn't answer him. She climbed into the passenger seat and closed the door with a harder thump than usual.

'Amita?' he asked, getting in. 'Is everything alright?'

'Yes, it's fine,' she said, her mouth tight, arms folded across her chest.

'Are you sure?'

'Yes. Now come on, drive,' she pointed down the country road. 'You're on deadline and I happen to know that Arthur Doige is an old gossip who loves nothing more than the sound of his own voice.'

'Sounds like someone I know.' He started the engine before Amita could reply.

Chapter 15

WILD RABBIT

Whatever Jason had been expecting of Arthur Doige's art gallery and dealership, he was in for a *very* big surprise. His own experiences in the art world were limited, he was happy to admit that. And up until an hour ago he had no idea this place even existed in his hometown. The facade was sleek, anonymous. Only a small plaque on the door made any indication as to what lay behind the walls and windows. The gallery was the kind of place that could pass for a dreary business unless you were in the know, somewhere that could just sit there, forever, and never bother anyone. Its understatement oozed an arrogance, one that implied it didn't need any passing trade. It was just for the invited. Jason had always been wary of places like this. That didn't stop him from picking his jaw up when it hit the floor as he stepped into the gallery.

Everything was white. So white, in fact, that it hurt Jason's eyes a little. The walls, the floor, the ceiling, even the bare lightbulbs that were suspended by long cables from the roof were a strange, almost heavenly white. And as bright as those bulbs were, there was a distinct lack of anything in the gallery to illuminate. The walls were bare, there was no furniture, everything looked brand new and not lived in yet.

'Is this the right place?' asked Amita, whispering in case she disturbed the eerie quiet.

'Right address,' said Jason. 'Doige's name is above the door outside. This is it.'

'There's nothing here,' she said. 'I mean, has he moved and not told anyone? Maybe that newspaper of yours should update their records.'

'Maybe this is art,' said Jason.

'Art? Seriously Jason? An empty room and lights with no shades? That's art these days?'

'I know, it's over my head too, but sometimes you've just got to go along to get along.'

'Can I help you?' A voice sliced through the chilling silence of the gallery. The click-clack of footsteps on the well-polished floor followed.

Jason sidled a little closer to Amita as a tall, lean figure emerged from behind a partition at the rear of the room. Dressed head-to-toe in black, he moved like a living shadow as he stalked towards them.

'Eh... hello,' said Jason. 'Mr Doige?'

'Yes,' said the art dealer, his voice wispy and hissing. 'And who might *you* be?'

'I told you,' whispered Amita. 'Eccentric.'

Doige came to a stop a few feet from them. He was thin, almost skeletal, his old, wrinkled skin practically hanging off his high cheekbones. A ring of brilliant white hair was closely cropped around the back of his head, the rest of it bald and covered in sun spots. Two sharp eyes peered over an oddly round nose. He wore a pencil-thin moustache above his puckered lips, the hair just as black as the turtleneck, blazer and frightfully skinny drainpipe trousers of his outfit designed for men forty years his junior.

Doige cocked an eyebrow and positioned an accusatory finger beneath his chin. 'I'll have you know that I do *not* repeat myself,' he said with a sneer. 'So please, politely and kindly, answer my question or I'll direct you to the door.'

Jason wasn't quite sure what was being asked of him here. He went to answer but Amita beat him to it.

'Hello Mr Doige,' she said, stepping forward and offering her hand. 'I'm sure you don't remember me, my name is Amita Khatri.'

Doige didn't budge. Instead he offered a look of utter contempt at Amita's hand. She deliberately left it hanging in the space between them for an awkward moment longer than she needed to. Then she let it drop.

'I can't say I have the pleasure of remembering you,' said Doige.

'Really,' she laughed. 'You were at that coffee morning at the church hall a few years back. What was it for again, it slips my mind. You must know the one I mean, it was a meet and greet for all the old age pensioners in the area. We were putting it on to avoid loneliness and make sure everyone in the community knew each other. You know, the old age pensioner community here in Penrith. OAPs.' Amita stressed the age part of her point over and over again, hoping to get a rise out of Doige. Instead the dealer's insulted expression deepened as he cocked one eyebrow after another at every mention of the word pensioner.

'And are you here to invite me to another one of those ghastly gatherings Ms Khatri?' he sniped.

'No, I'm afraid not,' she batted her eyelashes at him. 'Today it's strictly business. And it's Mrs Khatri. I'm a widow.'

'How unfortunate for you,' said Doige, his eyes closing to slits. 'Please accept my deepest condolences.'

There was a moment of unsettled silence between the three of them. Amita couldn't help but feel Doige was examining every inch of her and Jason – their clothes, their posture. Thankfully she never left the house unless she was immaculate. Although there *were* some rogue grass scuffs on her trainers she was sure Doige would pick up on. Thankfully Jason was just as scruffy as usual. He would deflect from her own inadequacies.

'Is there a reason you two *people* have graced my gallery with your presence?' asked the dealer. 'Or are you just looking for somewhere to get out of the sun for two minutes?'

'You people?' Jason snorted. 'You *people*? Just what is that supposed to mean?' He stepped forward aggressively, although clearly without any clue what his next move would be. Doige didn't budge. Amita grabbed her son-in-law by the elbow just enough to stop him.

'I'm sorry about Jason,' she said with a fake smile. 'He's under a lot of stress at work at the moment, he has a tendency to fly off the handle at the mere mention of something that irritates him. Isn't that right Jason?'

Stopping short of frothing at the mouth, Jason seemed to come to his senses when he caught Amita glaring at him.

'Yes, I'm sure,' said Doige.

Amita looked around the gallery. 'It's a lovely place you have here Mr Doige. Very… minimalist.'

'Yes, well, the art world moves at such a breakneck speed, one can't be left behind with last season's colours and works, otherwise one looks rather old-hat,' he said.

'And one wouldn't want that, would one?' replied Jason.

Doige sensed he was being mocked but remained stoic. He repositioned himself from one foot to the other, switching the hand that was resting beneath his chin.

'Are you in the market for a new piece?' he asked bluntly. 'I should warn you that everything I have at the moment starts from a hundred.'

'That seems very reasonable,' said Amita.

'Thousand,' said Doige. 'A hundred *thousand*.'

Jason knew people like Arthur Doige – he'd come across them before in his time at the *Penrith Standard*. Artsy types who liked to pretend and give off the air of wealthy superiority, only to have next to nothing in their bank accounts. He reckoned, behind that partition in the back of the gallery, there was a dank, draughty and decidedly ramshackle set of rooms with a filthy mattress and a black and white television. This was all for show.

'I think that's a little out of our market, don't you Jason?' asked Amita.

'I should say so,' he agreed. 'Sell a lot of hundred grand paintings here in Penrith, do you Mr Doige?'

There was the faintest twitch in the dealer's right eye. He quickly composed himself. Jason had touched a nerve there, he thought.

'I have… an exclusive market,' said Doige. 'Not that it's much business of yours Mr…'

'Brazel,' said Jason. 'I'm a journalist.'

'Yes, I thought as much,' said Doige. 'You're here about *Buttermere at Dawn* I take it.'

'We are,' said Jason. 'And how did you know that?'

Doige moved for the first time since he had appeared from behind the partition. Jason half expected him to creak like old door hinges. But he was silent. He walked over to the wall closest to them and slid his hand across a concealed panel. A little dark box appeared in the brilliant white and the dealer reached in. He produced a large bottle of opened whisky and a single glass. Pouring himself a measure, he tipped it down his throat and shuddered a little.

All Jason and Amita could do was watch on as this bizarre little ceremony played out in front of them. Doige paused for a moment, seemingly in a trance. Then he blinked and he was back in the room. He cleared his throat, tidied away the whisky and glass and replaced the panel in the wall.

'It has been a trying morning so far,' said Doige, walking back towards them. 'In my profession, discretion is one of the key attributes that sets elite level dealers, such as myself, apart from those rag-tag shysters who are solely out to make money.'

'I see,' said Jason. Although he wasn't sure what he was supposed to be seeing. 'We'd like to know a little bit more about Elvira if you have the time Mr Doige.'

'Such as?' he cocked an eyebrow.

'Well, a little bit of her background, maybe something that some of the media and researchers have missed down the years. She was, after all, a local celebrity, arguably Penrith's most famous artist. You must have some insight into her life, being an expert and all.'

Doige gave a disgruntled sigh. He walked past them and stopped just short of the windows that looked out onto the street. He began to gently caress his cheek with the back of his hand, muscles in the back of his neck tense. Amita was strangely engrossed by him. She didn't understand a thing he was saying or what he was doing, but she found it almost impossible to take her eyes off him. There was a magnetism, a fascination about Arthur Doige. Even if he was a frightful snob.

'I'm not a public library service, Mr Brazel,' said the dealer at length. 'I really do wish you and your professional colleagues could come up with better ways to use my time.'

'So there have been others in, asking about Elvira and *Buttermere at Dawn*?' asked Amita.

'As I've already mentioned,' he said, 'I've spent the morning dealing with comment requests and my expertise to be quoted by a bunch of low-brow troglodytes who wouldn't know a Rubens from a rubella inoculation.' Doige spun around quickly. His eyes were wide and wild. He suddenly broke into a loud, shrill laugh. He guffawed over and over, clutching at his sides. Jason and Amita didn't know what to do. The previously stoic art dealer was now bent double in front of them, as tears rolled down his cheeks. His laughter bounced off the bare walls, echoing all around them.

'Mr Doige,' Amita started, but he wasn't listening, just laughing and laughing.

'Doige, listen here,' said Jason, trying his best.

The dealer waved them away, his face now bright red from extreme merriment. Eventually he began to recompose himself. The laughter turned to chuckles and then little more than the odd bob of his shoulders. He wiped away the tears with a silk handkerchief, black of course. Doige cleared his throat again and looked at them both with bloodshot eyes.

'Glad you found your own joke so funny,' said Jason.

'I am easily amused,' said Doige, his voice like concrete. 'You were saying?'

Of all the strange behaviour Doige had displayed in front of her, the laughter was what Amita found the most disturbing. It was natural, yet unnatural, normal but distinctly strange. This was a man clearly from another world than the one she was used to.

'You've been helping out the press,' she said. 'Giving them information about Elvira and the painting. It's Elvira we're here to learn more about – the artist that inspired Hal Mulberry's final great act of philanthropy.'

'If you're looking for information about Hal Mulberry then I'm afraid you've come to the wrong place,' said Doige flatly. 'The man was an imbecile, a buffoon. He knew almost as little about fine art and the behaviour of a collector as the journalists who have been traipsing in here all morning with their cheap shoes and bad haircuts.'

'Oh,' said Jason. 'And why would you say something like that Mr Doige?'

'I say it because I'm sick of seeing the same non-branded, nondescript brogue or half-heel stiletto coming into my studio and marking my floor.'

'No!' Amita shouted. 'Not the fashion choices of the journalists. Hal Mulberry. He's talking about Hal Mulberry.'

Doige's face soured, if that was at all possible. His cheeks flexed as he gritted his teeth. 'Mr Mulberry was what we call in the industry "new money",' he said. 'It's become more and more common these past few decades for men like Mulberry to buy their way into the inner circles of the art world, simply by flashing their enormous chequebooks and very little else.'

'And what's wrong with that?' asked Jason. 'Surely art, especially the art of Elvira and her contemporaries, is there to be enjoyed by everyone, from all backgrounds, races, creeds.'

Doige snorted in disdain. 'There's a reason the work I sell in my studio has such a high price tag Mr Brazel,' he said. 'It's an insurance policy, to protect the work.'

'Protect it from what?'

'From ever appearing in a newspaper or magazine photoshoot with some brainless celebrity who can't walk and talk at the same time.'

Amita was disgusted. She should have known better. From the few times she'd been in the dealer's company, she distinctly remembered him being unpleasant and aloof, judgemental and arrogant. And this encounter was no different. Not for him the Wednesday night bingo, he had always made sure he was distant from the elderly community. Nothing, she had always felt, was ever good enough for him.

'That's quite a statement Mr Doige,' said Jason.

'Hal Mulberry knew nothing about art,' the dealer went on. 'Only how much it cost. This whole charade with *Buttermere at Dawn*, it's pageantry, sheer pageantry.'

'That painting meant a lot to him,' said Amita. 'He'd known about it since he was a boy.'

'How very heart-warming,' Doige feigned sympathy. 'That doesn't give him the right to swan around town like he's some well-read expert on Elvira and her work.'

'And you *are* a well-read expert on Elvira and her work, Mr Doige?' Jason asked pointedly.

The dealer drew him a long, irritated look. 'What I am, and I am not an expert in, Mr Brazel, is none of your concern,' he said. 'But know this, Hal Mulberry only knew how to spend money. His taste in art was about as limited as his taste in women – bland and uninteresting, if Mrs Mulberry is anything to go by. While he's gone to his grave with everyone round here thinking he's something of a local hero, bringing *Buttermere at Dawn* back to its spiritual home, he's just one in a long line of owners who thought themselves equally important to the work.'

Jason's chest was tight. He was getting angrier and angrier. The only thing stopping him from exploding in Arthur Doige's face was the knowledge he had a job to do.

'What does that mean exactly Mr Doige?' he asked, swallowing some of the anger.

'It means, Mr Brazel, that *Buttermere at Dawn* has passed through more hands than is normal for a piece of its age and pedigree. I, myself, have sold the piece on at least three non-consecutive occasions. And it wouldn't be an exaggeration, as vulgar as it will appear, to say that almost every high-end dealer between here and Southampton will have had it in their catalogue at some point since it was created.'

'That can't be true,' said Amita. 'Isn't it supposed to be a treasure of Cumbria? Surely something with such high regard can't have been passed from pillar to post like that.'

'Of course, forgive me Mrs Khatri,' Doige held a limp hand to his forehead. 'I forgot for a moment that *you* were, in fact, Penrith's leading art dealer and not me. Being this close to your genius has clearly dulled one's sensibilities to the point of idiocy.'

Amita's cheeks flushed. She was embarrassed and angry all at once. 'All I'm trying to say,' she managed through gritted teeth, 'is that the painting is very highly regarded Mr Doige. Personal opinions aside, *Buttermere at Dawn* is held by most Cumbrians as something to be very proud of and part of this country's national art institution.'

'Meaningless phrases and slogans,' he waved her away. 'What counts in this industry, Mrs Khatri, is pounds and pence. When a painting has been around the course as much as *that* one, prestige is little more than a distant memory.'

'And that's all that counts then?' asked Jason angrily. 'How much something is worth? No sentimentality, no personal meaning? It's all just capitalism to you?'

Doige's eyes went wide. He stepped forward, almost goading Jason. 'Of *course* it is,' he said. 'You don't think I'm in this for the good of my health, do you? Even someone like *you*, who couldn't point out a Titian from a line up of children's drawings, must understand that. Do you think I want to be answering questions about the work of a hack that's been bought and sold more times than anyone can really remember? That's not art, Mr Brazel, it's supermarket shopping.'

Jason wanted to argue. Amita wanted to argue too. But neither of them had enough brain capacity or time to say anything.

'Now, if you'll excuse me,' said Doige, ushering them towards the door. 'I have a migraine coming on and one

174

will no doubt be bombarded with more knuckle-dragging questions from reporters later today. So, if you would see yourselves out.'

He practically pushed Jason and Amita until they were out of the door.

'Doige!' he shouted.

'Goodbye,' said the dealer.

'I'm not finished!'

'Good. Bye!'

The door slammed closed in Jason's face. Doige pulled the blind down over the window and the sound of his pointy shoes clicking on the floor faded on the other side. Jason, wanting to at least do *something*, rapped his knuckles on the door. A few thumps and there was no answer, as he had expected.

'What a complete and utter arse—'

'Jason,' Amita snapped. 'Watch your language.'

'Well, he is, isn't he,' he said. 'What a total snob. A stuffed shirt, having the cheek to talk down to us like we were dirt on his shoe. And for what, so he could lecture us on how he was little more than a grab-the-money-and-run merchant. Where do these guys get off Amita? Who wakes up every morning and thinks it's acceptable to speak to other human beings like that?' He started shouting at the door. 'Eh?' he yelled. 'A little human decency goes a long way you know!' He realised he was quite enjoying the moral high ground for once – it wasn't a place he often had cause to visit. He thumped the door again. There was, of course, no answer from within.

'Are you quite finished?' asked Amita.

Jason turned to his mother-in-law, almost remembering that she was still there.

'Yes,' he said. 'I probably should be. Otherwise I'll get arrested or something stupid like that. And it's not worth it over the head of that pompous idiot inside.'

'Good, I'm glad you can see some sense,' she said. 'And while I don't agree with you shouting and bawling like this in public. For what it's worth, I agree with you.' Amita turned him away from the door.

They began walking down the street away from the gallery. Jason's head was pounding as much as he had been on Doige's door. He was a little breathless. He couldn't remember the last time he'd been so angry. He'd never been some great champion of the socialist cause, but he detested snobs and arrogance when it was misplaced. Arthur Doige was the epitome of all of that. And it had rubbed him up the wrong way.

'What a horrible man,' he said, catching his breath. 'And he certainly didn't like Hal Mulberry.'

'I don't think there's *anyone* Arthur Doige *does* like,' she said.

'There are plenty of people I don't like Amita, but I don't speak like that about them to strangers.' He thumbed back into the shop.

'What are you getting at?' she asked.

'I don't know,' he said. 'Makes you think he had an axe to grind. Or a knife to sharpen.'

'Doige?' she asked. 'You think Doige could be the killer... or knows who is?'

'I don't know,' said Jason, shrugging. 'I don't know anything at this point. That's the problem.'

'I know. Could he have really killed Hal though? I don't know.'

'It's always the person you least suspect. Didn't we agree on this earlier?'

'This is real life, not some American detective show off the television,' she tutted. 'You know that all too well.'

'I do. Still, anything is possible with these sorts of things, as we know too. I also know that he is one of the most unpleasant human beings I think I've ever had the misfortune of spending time with.'

'Yes, he is,' agreed Amita. 'But not entirely unhelpful.'

It took a moment to process what his mother-in-law had said. Then he stopped, scratching his head. 'No?' he asked.

Amita drew him a smile. 'No,' she said, and walked on.

Chapter 16

THE SWING

'There's no such thing as a curse,' said Jason.

The way he was gulping down tea and mouthfuls of cheese roll, it was going to take a miracle to stop him from choking to death there and then in the middle of Murphy's.

'Would you please take sensible bites and sips,' Amita pleaded with him. 'My heart is in my mouth here watching you wolf down that lunch.'

'Sorry,' said Jason, licking his lips. 'I'm starving.'

'It'll be your last supper if you carry on at this rate. I don't have to tell the bairns to eat sensibly, you're a fully grown man Jason.'

'Fine,' he said, draining his mug. He sat back in the booth, the old worn leather of the seat groaning as he did so.

Murphy's was its usual busy self. A long queue was stretching down past the refrigerated cabinets and snaking out of the door. The lucky customers still in the sunshine were enjoying the heat as they waited to collect their lunches before heading back to work. Jason and Amita had beaten the rush by a matter of seconds. Now they were holding court in their usual spot near the back of the cafe, close to the deli counter.

'And again, for the record, curses don't exist,' he said.

'So how do you explain what has happened to the owners of *Buttermere at Dawn* then?' asked Amita. 'How do you explain the fact there have been so many and that a lot of them, most of them, have come to some sticky sort of end – including Hal Mulberry.'

'You really shouldn't believe everything you read on the internet,' said Jason. 'It's a dangerous game and usually ends in tragedy.'

'We've already had a tragedy,' she said. 'I'm trying to get to the bottom of it. Which is more than you're doing.'

Jason rolled his eyes. 'Alright,' he said. 'Say, just for a moment, I've taken leave of my senses and what you're saying is true. Where are you getting this information?'

'It's online, look,' she waved her phone at him.

'Okay. What website is that exactly?'

'What do you mean what website?'

'What site are you getting this info about a curse surrounding the painting? Who exactly is saying a curse exists? Is it a university professor in parapsychology? A sociology expert perhaps? Elvira herself? Who?'

Amita looked blank. She glanced down at her phone. Then shrugged. 'It's just a site,' she said. 'It's run by someone called Barry apparently. And this Barry says that there have been owners of *Buttermere at Dawn* who have actually died because they owned it. Other folk have been left bankrupt, their lives ruined. That's serious stuff Jason, this *is* serious, especially when you think Hal Mulberry had his throat cut. I mean, how can so many tragedies *not* be linked to the painting when it's the common factor.'

Jason clapped his hand to his forehead. 'Of course,' he said. 'No accreditation, no providence to go along with the outlandish and possibly unfounded statements. And let's not forget Barry, how could we? He's the best read, most famous fact finder in the history of the planet. Everyone knows Barry, good old Barry, he'll tell us what we need to know.'

Amita's face was blank. 'You're mocking me Jason, it doesn't suit you,' she said.

Reaching for her phone, Jason scrolled through the website she'd spent the whole time in the diner examining. He had seen a lot of conspiracy theory forums and pages online before. As a journalist, he never let himself be sucked down the inevitable rabbit hole of the most outlandish theories that were held by members of the general public. If he had read about aliens assassinating JFK once, he had read it a million times.

Even by the fairly low standards of internet conspiracies, this website was particularly bad. There didn't appear to be anything remotely modern or up to date on it. Not that Jason knew much about embedding social media posts and video content or anything like that. No matter how limited his knowledge was, however, he could at least say with some confidence that view counters at the bottom of pages were *so* early 2000s.

'I don't think this Barry character has heard of spell-check,' he said. 'And he seems to be making numerous threats to the Inland Revenue.' He handed the phone to his mother-in-law. Amita snatched it back.

'Never mind all of that,' she said.

'What? The grammar or the less than veiled hatred for taxes?'

'This Barry reckons the painting has some strong supernatural links,' she said. 'Did Hal ever mention something like that to you?'

'No,' Jason laughed. 'Of course he didn't.'

'Are you sure?'

'I'm sure,' he said. 'I don't imagine Hal Mulberry had much time for ghosts and ghouls Amita. He was a businessman, a commodities market tycoon. Hard facts, times, dates, pounds and pence were the order of the day. He didn't have a dream catcher above his bed either, before you ask.'

'I wasn't going to ask,' she said. 'This website says that there have been at least twenty-two owners of *Buttermere at Dawn* in the years since it was painted. And of those twenty-two, fifteen of them were forced to sell the painting for financial gain.'

'So what?' he poured more tea from the little pot between them. 'Selling a commodity for money isn't a crime, nor is it the result of witches and wizards. Who says they were "forced"? Choosing to make a quick buck by selling a picture is a very different matter to being driven bankrupt by ghoulish curse or whatnot. "Art investor sells art" is hardly news.'

'No, but don't you think that's a high proportion,' said Amita. 'That's most of the owners, Jason. It's not like it's a hundred years old either, it was finished in the seventies. Many hands, that's what Doige said, wasn't it?'

'He did.'

'What's more disturbing are these reports of owners or people associated with the picture coming to a sticky end,' she said, pointing at the screen. 'According to this website, half of those who were in ownership of the painting either died in and around buying, selling or being in possession of it. That's staggering.'

'It's also hardly a surprise. People die, it's a fact of life. And don't take this the wrong way, but people who are rich enough to afford to buy famous pieces of art have a greater chance of being in their – shall we say, twilight years? And so a greater chance of...'

'Death,' she said.

Jason stared into his tea, the milk swirling around. He had lots of patience for Amita, more than he ever had in all the years he had known her. But this felt like she was clutching at straws. If there was wickedness in the world, he tended to think it was down to mankind, not curses and incantations.

'And what about Elvira herself,' Amita asked.

'What about her?'

Amita slid around the booth so she was beside Jason. She scrolled down the page until she reached a black and white picture of the artist. Shy and meek, she looked uncomfortable being photographed, dark hair draped over her face like a set of drawn curtains.

'It says here that she bought the painting back not long before she died in 2018,' Amita went on. 'And the rumours that abounded at the time were that she was so mortified, so heartbroken by all the trouble it had caused, she didn't want anyone else to suffer more bad luck and become a victim of the curse.'

Jason snorted.

'Look, here,' Amita pointed at the screen. 'There's a link here to an interview she gave with the BBC around the time.' She clicked on the link.

A video appeared on the screen and Jason squinted, trying to focus. Elvira was sat in a tall armchair, her hair a little greyer than the picture on the site. The camera zoomed in a little as a man's voice asked her a question.

'Would you consider *Buttermere at Dawn* to be your finest work?'

Elvira looked uncomfortable. She squirmed in the seat, her fingers knotted as they poked out from the ends of the sleeves of her tatty jumper. She mulled the question over, moving to answer several times before stopping herself. Each time she appeared to be about to speak, the camera zoomed in. By the time she *was* ready to answer, her face took up the whole screen.

'I painted it when I was very young,' she said, her accent thick Cumbrian, eyes a little glassy and distant. 'I had this odd energy inside of me back in those days. I never used to sleep, I'd stay up all night and day and watch the darkness turn into the light. Buttermere is a mysterious place, the whole Lakes are like that. But Buttermere is special. It has all of those wonderful folklore tales surrounding it. And I used to take great comfort in just watching the stillness of the water, with the moon shining down on the surface and reflecting back. It was like a mirror, a mirror into my soul, no matter how I felt, happy or sad.'

'But is it your *greatest* painting? The work you're most proud of?' asked the interviewer off camera.

'Yes,' Elvira shrugged. 'If you want to put it like that, I suppose it is. It's my little way of capturing some of that magic, some of that mystery, some of the fairy dust that hangs in the air above the water that you can only see if you look hard enough and really, truly believe.'

The clip ended and the screen went black. Jason sat back up.

'Mad as a box of frogs comes to mind,' he said.

'That's not very funny,' Amita tutted. 'Eccentric, maybe.'

'The same way you said Arthur Doige was eccentric?'

'No,' she said flatly. 'He's just a bitter old man who has spent too long in his own company believing himself better than everyone else. Elvira is, was, an artist – a true artist in that she wanted to paint something that not only captured something – but she wanted to share that something with the people. And this website says that she was so worried about the perceived curse of the painting that she wanted it for herself again to keep the wider public out of harm's way.'

Jason groaned loudly. He thought he might have a Doige-esque migraine coming on. 'Amita, this doesn't make sense,' he said. 'There's no mention of a curse in that interview clip. In fact, I doubt you'll find any mention of a curse anywhere other than your pal Barry's overactive imagination. And I think you're looking for something that's just not there. As for my story tonight, I'm not going to file something saying the painting was cursed.'

'Why not?' she asked. 'Isn't that salacious? Isn't that what your editor is looking for?'

'It's barmy!' he shouted. 'Just barmy. And I'm already on thin ice when it comes to my integrity in the eyes of Beeston. This would probably see me exiled from journalism for the next thousand years, with no chance of an appeal. Not that I would deserve an appeal for filing rubbish based on the unchecked, unsubstantiated ravings of an internet loony.' He pointed down at the screen angrily.

'So you knew that Elvira was the last owner before Hal Mulberry bought it?' Amita asked him.

'No, I didn't,' he said. 'The painting was in an auction. Hal never mentioned where it had come from.'

'So Barry's website *does* have some uses then?'

Jason wagged a finger at her. 'I know what you're trying to do here Amita and it won't work,' he said. 'One fact that can be easily checked does not mean that everything else on that web page is correct. If anything, it means it's all probably a load of cobblers. Getting the simple stuff is easy, it's the more complicated that you have to worry about and question. And I question whether this Barry person, whoever he or she is, is legitimate or just another troll spreading nonsense on the internet.'

Amita tutted loudly. 'I'm only trying to help,' she said, locking her phone. 'I'm only trying to find us a lead... and something you can write about. You don't have to be so nasty about it all.'

Jason instantly felt that horrible pang of guilt in his gut. Amita was tight-lipped. He gave her a moment to see if she was just feigning offence or she was, in fact, put out. She shoved her phone into her pocket and folded her arms, staring off through the windows of the diner at the long queue of customers outside.

He felt bad. 'Look, Amita...'

'No, no, don't look Amita me, Jason,' she said. 'I've heard enough. You don't want my help, that's abundantly clear. You're shooting down every little idea I have and it's perfectly obvious that you think I'm a crank.'

'I don't think you're a crank,' he said. 'I think this Barry person is a crank. I think their website could do with an update. And I think, no, I *know*, that you always have to double check and verify your facts before you go off and make assumptions. If everyone did that a little bit more then maybe the world wouldn't be the steaming mess it is right now.'

She looked at him like she didn't trust him.

He opened his hands, trying to make peace. 'And thank you, as always,' he said.

'For what?'

'For having faith in me. For being the only one in the room who has faith in me. It's a depressing trend of my recent career that I've had to prove myself time and time again. But one thing has remained constant. You, Amita, you have been by my side for the whole time and believed that I might actually be the one to get to the bottom of a story – with your help of course. And I appreciate that.'

It was Amita's turn to feel a pang of guilt. She felt her throat closing a little and she did her very best to keep a trickle of tears back behind her nose. 'Nonsense,' she waved him off. 'Radha and the kids have *always* got your back, Jason.'

'I know,' he smiled. 'But I don't go running around Cumbria with them in tow, do I? I don't break into hospitals, fight farmers and bricklayers and solve murders with Radha and the children. I do all of that with *you*.'

He reached over and clasped her hand, squeezing it tight. She hesitated a moment before squeezing back.

'I just want you to do well,' she said. 'That's all. Not just for the money, but for your reputation, for your career. You did such a wonderful job with Madeleine. And this is a really good opportunity for you to show that wasn't a one-off, and to do something of note, something worthy.

How many journalists can say they've caught two murderers, eh? I don't know any.'

'You don't know any other journalists Amita,' he said, laughing.

'Of course I do!' she shouted. 'There's... the man, off the news at ten. And that young woman, what's her name, the one who looks like she has someone else's teeth in her mouth.'

He rolled his eyes.

'I just want you to be the best you can be, Jason,' she said to him. 'And if that means trawling the darkest corners of the internet for information and leads, then, well, that's just what we have to do.'

Jason nodded. He appreciated the pep talk. He'd been feeling rather low the last few days. His stint with the big London press wasn't quite what he had hoped it would be. Not just from his lack of stories, but from the way he was treated, the way he was expected to behave. Having Amita on his side was an asset, a bonus. She'd spent a lifetime being overlooked – discounted as a woman, a mother and now a pensioner. And she was quietly proving everyone who underestimated her that were very wrong indeed.

'Okay,' he said. 'Time for a conference.'

'Conference?' asked Amita. 'What are you talking about?'

'A conference, it's what we used to have at the paper,' he explained. 'The department heads would all congregate in the one room and discuss what was going into the paper the next day. News, features, politics, sport, everyone. It was a way of getting a handle on what was on the schedule and the radar, to get everyone's heads in the game and on the same wavelength.'

187

'Ah, I see,' she said. 'A conference. Sounds like a good idea.'

'So, to that end, let's look at what we've got here,' he said. 'Local tycoon Hal Mulberry is dead, murdered. We know he was a philanthropist, a very generous one at that, and regularly donated to local good causes and charities. He buys *Buttermere at Dawn*, which, according to our art dealer friend, has a potted history of lots of owners, including the late artist herself.'

'Sheila Mulberry found him,' Amita added. 'And is in a state of shock.'

'Yes I was just coming to her,' Jason said. 'Despite our rather brazen efforts, she seems to be on the road to recovery and has appealed to the public for help in catching her husband's killer. The police.'

'Led by that lovely DI Arendonk.'

'The lovely DI Arendonk, yes, who hasn't got a chief suspect, otherwise they'd have somebody arrested by now,' said Jason. 'So. What does that leave us with?'

He stared at Amita. She stared back at him.

'A mess,' she said. 'And not just any old mess. A pretty horrible, unending one that doesn't seem to add up anyway you look at it.'

'I agree,' he sighed. 'I don't know Amita. This all stinks. A wealthy man is murdered. The obvious reason would be money. He was rich and people don't like that.'

'Or they want it,' nodded Amita.

'It's strong enough a reason to kill someone, even Hal Mulberry. He had more dough than anyone else around. But why now? Why at the unveiling of *Buttermere at Dawn*?'

'Unless it's the curse, again,' she said. 'But we won't go into that again.'

'It's strange,' he said. 'Hal seemed so full of life, like he couldn't wait to wake up tomorrow and take everything on again. He was enjoying every moment and looked like he had a bright future. The whole town did too, despite what some of your colleagues in the elderly community thought.'

'Change isn't the best antidote Jason,' she said. 'I can't say I was impressed with Mr Mulberry's flash the cash attitude. And there were plenty who agreed with me.'

'Agree enough to kill him?'

The question felt like it weighed as much as a battleship. Amita thought carefully before answering. 'No,' she said. 'No, I don't think so. We're pensioners Jason, we care about the community, about the town. We don't like change, I grant you that. But there's nobody at the club, in the WI or anywhere else who would cut a man's throat over it.'

He nodded in agreement. 'I'm just playing devil's advocate,' he said. 'I mean, can you see Ethel taking her fish skillet to Hal Mulberry? Conjures quite an image, doesn't it?'

Amita stifled a laugh. 'Jason,' she said. 'A man is dead and Ethel isn't well.'

'No, you're right,' he said. 'But it is funny though.'

'Amita?'

She was distracted by the sudden appearance of Father Ford. He hovered around the edge of the booth, clutching a brown paper bag in his hands, the creases tightening as he held it up like a shield.

'What a lovely surprise,' he said with a nervous smile. 'And Jason too, how lovely.'

'Good afternoon Father,' said Amita, nodding.

'Yeah, hi Father,' said Jason.

'Would you like to join us for a cup of tea?' Amita asked.

Jason darted her a silent look of disdain. She fired one back, urging him telepathically to behave.

'No, I can't stay, unfortunately,' he said, waving his bag. 'Just grabbing a spot of lunch before I head back to the hall. Mr Jones says we have a small flock of bats nesting in the eves and he's wanting to show me them and the mess they've made before calling in the exterminators. So I've had to pop out to get something, otherwise I'll pass out.'

'Not an animal fan then Father?' asked Jason.

'No, I mean yes, absolutely,' he said. 'I just don't care much for heights and, well, the only way up there is with Mr Jones' ladder. It's a bit like Ship of Theseus I'm afraid.'

'Ship of Theseus?' asked Jason.

'The famous ship of the Greek hero,' said Amita. 'Legend has it that it was kept in a harbour and every part was replaced over time. The question raised was whether it was the same ship at all. Isn't that right Father?'

'Spot on,' he said with a giddy giggle.

'Blimey,' said Jason. 'I'm really glad I got you that cryptic crossword book for your Christmas.'

'Jason,' she tutted.

'Actually, I'm rather glad I ran into you Amita,' laughed Father Ford. 'I wanted to ask a very small favour ahead of bingo tomorrow night.'

'Of course,' said Amita. 'What can I do for you?'

'Well, you see, it's rather awkward,' said the pastor. 'Georgie, that's Goergie Littlejohn, she was supposed to be organising a little sponsorship collection for the Scouts' charity fun run and–'

'Georgie!' Amita shot up from the table.

The whole of Murphy's came to a standstill as everyone turned to look at her. Her face was etched in sheer fright as she stood perfectly still for a split second before reaching for Jason.

'We have to go!' she shouted.

'Amita!' he gasped, being hauled past Father Ford. 'What's gotten into you?'

'Georgie Littlejohn!' she shouted. 'We were supposed to go around to her house. And I completely forgot! Sorry Father, we have to dash, speak to you tomorrow!'

They raced through the diner and off out into Market Square, Jason being hauled behind his mother-in-law like a dog on a leash.

'What was that all about then?' asked a waitress, sidling up beside Father Ford.

'I have no idea,' he said, still clutching his paper bag. 'I only asked about the fun run.'

The waitress shrugged then began clearing the table. She tapped Father Ford on the shoulder as he was about to leave.

'Hey,' she said. 'Are you picking up their bill? They didn't pay.'

The colour drained from the vicar's face. 'Oh dear,' he said. 'Oh dear, oh dear.'

Chapter 17

INTERIOR WITH A DOG

'Georgie! Georgie! Are you there? It's Amita! If you're there please come to the door. Georgie?'

Jason had never seen his mother-in-law so rattled. She was furiously pounding on the front door, her hand clapping against the immaculately polished wood-effect plastic. She had already tried the knocker but had gotten nowhere. Now she'd moved onto pounding with her bare hands.

'Georgie?' she shouted, desperate.

'Maybe she's out,' offered Jason.

She took no notice of him. Instead, she bowed down and opened the letterbox. Peering inside, she could see nothing. So she started shouting.

'Georgie, can you hear me? It's Amita and Jason. Are you alright in there? We've come around to check that you're okay. Can you hear me? Georgie? Say something, please, for god sake let us know that you're okay.'

There was no reply from inside. Jason took a step back. He looked up at the miniature mock Georgian townhouse for any signs of life. All the curtains were closed and there were no cars in the driveway. He shook his head.

'Amita, there's nobody in,' he said. 'Stop shouting, you're going to wake up the neighbours from their twenty-three hours of sleep a day.'

'Georgie?' she shouted again. 'I don't understand Jason, I don't get it. Georgie never goes away, and I mean *never*, without telling somebody. When she went to Tenerife for three weeks last Easter we were all treated to a full itinerary and breakdown of each day *months* in advance. Georgie Littlejohn isn't someone who likes to let a good holiday go to waste when it comes to showing off.'

'So, maybe she's lightening up in her old age,' he said.

Amita cast him a dirty look. 'Are you serious? You've met the woman, do you think she's the mellowing type?'

Jason was about to argue. Then he remembered who they were talking about. 'Okay, fair point,' he said. 'But I still think you're overreacting.'

'Overreacting? In what way?'

'Oh, I don't know Amita, the banging on the door, the screaming, the fact we practically flew over here and I'm sure I'll be getting at least three speeding fines and a ticket for running a red light. Something about those things might lead anyone who doesn't know you to think you were overreacting.'

'I'm just... concerned, that's all.'

'Concerned?' he yelped. 'For Georgie Littlejohn? Now I know there is something *deeply* wrong. Do you want to fess up before I get the local psychiatric ward on the phone and have you assessed?'

Amita let out a long, deflated sigh. She lifted the letterbox flap again and looked inside. There was nothing there, only the hallway stretching out into the house. No sign of life, no sign of movement and certainly no sign of Georgie. She sagged her shoulders and closed the flap.

'I'm sorry,' she said sadly. 'I'm sorry for not telling you the whole truth. The fact is, I think something might have happened to Georgie and it may be my fault.' She stepped away from the front door, trudging up the driveway towards their car.

Jason followed her, sensing that there was something amiss, something strangely serious about her. 'Amita,' he said, reaching out for her. 'What's going on?'

She stopped. She shook her head, not looking at him. 'I made a terrible mistake Jason,' she said. 'I... I thought I was on to something with Hal Mulberry's death. I thought I might have cracked the case, but it was just my imagination getting the better of me.'

'Amita,' he said, turning her to face him. 'What's happened? What have you done?'

Her eyes were glassy, tears getting ready to trickle down her face. 'I... I all but accused Georgie Littlejohn of killing Hal Mulberry,' she said. 'Now she's vanished and it's all my fault. I made light of something that was bothering her because I was all wrapped with investigating Mulberry, and now I've driven her away and something dreadful might have happened to her. I forgot all about her Jason, earlier, when I said we'd call around to see her. I just completely forgot about her, like she was something off the shopping list. And after I accused her of those terrible things. It's awful Jason, I'm awful. And there's nothing I can do.' She began to sob.

Jason pulled her in close. He felt the shoulder of his shirt moisten as his mother-in-law cried into it. He patted her back.

'Come on now,' he said. 'There's no use in getting upset, it can't be as bad as all that.'

'No, it is,' she said, pulling away from him. 'It is. She came around to the house the other day there, in a complete state. She kept talking about Hal Mulberry and how nobody at the bingo club or the WI cared much for him. Then she said she'd done something terrible Jason, something awful that she couldn't live with herself for doing. She wanted to confess to the police, asked me to take her in. That's when I thought she had murdered Hal. I actually thought for the briefest of moments that Georgie Littlejohn was sitting there, in our living room, confessing to the murder. Only...'

'Only what?' he asked.

'Only it wasn't that at all,' she said. 'She's smashed up some garden gnome of her neighbours, Colonel Mustard I think she called him. She said she'd chopped its head off and now felt dreadfully guilty about the whole thing.'

'She beheaded a garden gnome?' Jason wasn't sure he should be appalled or in fits of laughter. Amita wasn't in the laughing mood. So he kept it to himself.

'I told her she had to go,' she went on. 'Told her that I didn't have time for these silly things and that there was serious work I had to get on with. She looked devastated and angry. I should have been more concerned for her, more sympathetic. It was just, it was just this case Jason,

Hal Mulberry. We're not closer to catching the killer and I let my emotions get the better of me. Georgie didn't need to be shot down like that. She needed help from a friend. And now she's vanished, nobody has seen her. She won't answer my calls. Father Ford can't reach her. I'm terrified that something has happened to her.' She was starting to hyperventilate. Jason rubbed her shoulders, trying to calm down.

'Alright, take it easy,' he said. 'Let's just think about this logically, okay? There's no use getting upset about something that might turn out to be nothing. When was the last time you heard from her?'

'When I marched her out of the house,' said Amita. 'A few days ago.'

'Okay,' he said, thinking fast. 'And nobody has seen or heard from her since then?'

'I don't know,' she said. 'Father Ford says she's not helped with the charity collection, you heard him back at the diner. That's not like her, you know it's not.'

'You're right,' he said. 'Sorry, but it's true. Georgie Littlejohn prides herself on her reliability, especially when it comes to the community. No, let me be more accurate, when it comes to her *reputation* in the community.'

'You see, I'm not just being paranoid,' she said. 'I've been stupid Jason, really stupid. I could have raised the alarm days ago when I thought there was something wrong. But I didn't, I didn't. I bloody well talked myself out of it because you said I was far too quick to assume the worst. Now look at what's happened.'

'If I didn't know better, I'd say you were blaming this on me!' he said.

'I should stick with my gut,' she said. 'I should *always* stick with my gut. It's never done me any harm or led me up the garden path before.'

'We don't know anything has gone wrong here Amita,' he said. 'We have to be pragmatic, use our logic. Like I said before, maybe she's lying low for a few days, gone off to see relatives, that kind of thing. Is it so unreasonable to think that Georgie Littlejohn, the most well connected person in Cumbria, if not the UK, has a bolt-hole somewhere she can go to let the heat cool off? And if the neighbours are out for garden-gnome blood money, she'll not want to be knocking around this menagerie, will she?'

Amita bit her lip. She was worried, really worried. 'For all we know, I could be the last person who saw Georgie alive,' she said, her voice filled with dread. 'There is a killer on the loose Jason. Who's to say they haven't done something to her?'

The thought made Jason shudder a little. He managed to shake it off quickly, hopefully without Amita noticing.

'Come on Amita,' he said. 'We've got one body already. We don't need to be speculating about another. And besides, what's the connection between the two of them? For all her pillar of the community bit, Georgie Littlejohn is hardly the same kind of big-time-charity-donor that Hal was. You said a minute ago you thought Georgie might have been the killer *herself*. Now you're telling me you think there's a double murderer on the loose whose offed the town's biggest gossip. This time you *are* letting your imagination get the better of you.'

Amita wasn't convinced. She had a terrible nagging feeling in the pit of her stomach that something very strange was going on here.

'Look, we can't do anything at the moment,' he said. 'There have been no missing person reports, you've heard or seen nothing in all the groups you're a member of. If Georgie *was* missing then surely somebody closer to her would have noticed and done something by now.'

'Like who?' she snorted.

That made Jason's left eye twitch a little. Only the cold, hard, unforgiving grip of logic was stopping him from kicking the front door down and searching every room for a corpse. That was if he could kick the door down in the first place. It looked pretty robust and he was hardly in prime condition.

'I have a story to file,' he said, opting for a different tack.

If reality wasn't enough to shock them both out of their imagination, he wasn't sure anything would. Especially a reality with Arnold Beeston on the other end of it.

'I need to get back to the laptop and file it for the sub-editors. And time is marching on. There's nothing we can do here if nobody answers the door. I'm not breaking in.'

'But–'

'No breaking and entering Amita,' he said firmly.

'Fine,' she sounded disappointed. 'I'm going to ask around to see if anyone has heard from her. But I think we should give serious consideration to letting the police know. I'd hate to think that nobody would alert them if I was the one who had vanished.'

'Georgie hasn't vanished Amita,' he said, opening the car door. 'We just can't raise her, there's a difference.'

'Not knowing where someone is, especially if they are upset, is vanishing in my book Jason.'

They climbed in. Jason felt a cold sweat on the back of his neck. He looked up at Georgie Littlejohn's house and started the car. There were enough fires he had to put out. A pensioner not answering her phone wasn't something he could afford to spend time on right now. Not with his journalistic integrity and a much needed pay cheque at risk.

Amita, on the other hand, could barely think of anything else. They pulled out of the driveway and she watched the house the whole way down the street. She didn't say it aloud but she wished, prayed that everything would be alright. She didn't know what she would do without Georgie. Especially if she had caused her harm in the first place.

Chapter 18

A FRIEND IN NEED

Jason didn't feel much like eating. He pushed a ball of rice around the plate in front of him, watching it gather sauce and bits of veg like a snowball down a mountain. Across from him Amita was doing the same. Neither of them spoke, happy just to let Radha and the kids lead the conversation around them. The kids were busy tucking into their own dinners, unaware of the tension, the dead weight, hanging over the pair.

'Well, I must say, this is one of the very best conversations we've ever had at this table,' said Radha, reaching for the wine. 'I can't think of another time where it's been such a stimulating cut and thrust, back and forth kind of debate about the day's big talking points. Can you?'

The question seemed to jolt Jason from his slump.

'What's that, love?' he asked.

'I said...' she trailed off. 'Never mind. What's the point. You two have been in your own little worlds all night.

And I doubt I have the brain space or the inclination to want to know what's making your faces trip over themselves.'

Jason straightened a little. He lifted the rice ball up to his mouth, thought about it and then decided he had better eat it, his wife watching his every move.

'Delicious,' he said. 'Really tasty Radha, lovely. Beef is it?'

'Chicken,' she said.

'Of course,' he said. 'Is that a Thai sauce?'

'Indian,' she replied.

'Oh yes, that's right. Really good though. Tasty.' He tipped her a wink and gave her the thumbs up of approval.

Radha sipped at her wine before turning her ire towards Amita. 'And what about you mum?' she asked. 'Care to try and keep digging the massive hole Jason has started?'

'What's that, darling?' she said, waking from a trance.

'For god sake,' said Radha, throwing her hands up in the air. 'Not you too? I might as well be having a conversation with myself here!'

'Mummy, can we watch cartoons?' asked Josh.

'Can we mummy? Please?' chimed his sister.

Radha sighed. 'Now I really am being left on my own with you two,' she said. 'Go on then, go before I change my mind.'

The children hurried away from the table and disappeared into the house, screaming and jumping with joy. That left the adults sitting in an awkward silence.

'Right,' said Radha, after a moment and realising that her family weren't coming forth with any answers. 'Do you two want to clear the air and tell me what's going on? Or will I just sit here and drink myself into a stupor with the rest of this plonk from the supermarket. Because, quite frankly, I think I'm better than that.'

Jason laughed at that. Amita was still miles away.

'Sorry Radha,' he said. 'There's just been some heavy duty stuff going on the past day or so. I guess it's catching up with both of us.'

'And do you want to let me know what this "heavy duty stuff" is?'

Jason stopped himself. He was hit with a sudden sense of place. Namely that it wasn't his to start blabbing about Georgie Littlejohn vanishing and how Amita felt responsible. Radha didn't need to hear about his own problems, his feelings of inadequacy and the constant pressure from London. She was a lawyer, she had enough to deal with. That and she was a brilliant mother, wife and daughter too.

'It's fine,' he said, forcing a smile. 'Really, it's okay. Your mother and I, we've just been running around the place and sort of banging our heads together. No big deal. Isn't that right Amita?'

At the sound of her name, his mother-in-law looked up, her concentration and malaise broken. 'Yes, yes, that's right,' she said, not committing.

'There, you see?' he said. 'Everything's fine.'

Radha twirled her fork around between her fingers. She poked her tongue into the side of her cheek and nodded. 'Alright,' she said. 'There was me thinking that a problem shared was a problem solved. How silly of me.'

'Radha, that's not what I meant,' he pleaded.

'No, no, it's just the last time you two told everything was "fine", it turned out you were stalking a killer round the hills and tarns of the Lakes. Something which you said was a strictly never-to-be-repeated turn of events.'

'Radha,' he said. 'Amita, say something, come on, back me up here, would you?'

Again, Amita looked up, a little bewildered. She was lost in her own little world, only her name dragging her back from the brink.

'What's that?' she asked.

'It's fine,' said Radha, standing up suddenly. 'Really, it is. I know you two have this special bond, or whatever you want to call it, going on. It's fine, I'm fine about it. I just thought, you know, given who I am, where I fit into this family and all of that, I might be able to help you both. You've sat there all night like a pair of turkeys who know Christmas is just around the corner.' She took her plate and cutlery.

'Radha, please, come sit down,' said Jason, reaching out for her.

'I think I'll call it a night.'

'Radha,' Jason got up.

It was no use. She'd made up her mind. She held up a commanding hand, a gesture he knew all too well, as she turned towards the kitchen. He watched her go, knowing to follow would just cause more problems. She closed the door, leaving him alone with his mother-in-law.

Jason slumped down into his chair opposite her.

Amita offered him a sympathetic smile. 'She'll be alright,' she said. 'She's just worried for you, for us, and perhaps, I don't know, feeling a bit left out.'

'You hardly did anything to change that mentality, did you?' he said. 'I was trying to make her feel better. You just sat there and said nothing.'

'And what would you have liked me to say?' she fired back. 'Would you like me to ask her who she thinks murdered Hal Mulberry? Or what about Georgie, eh? Should I have asked her what she thinks about a missing pensioner who has vanished because of her mother? Do you think that would have helped? She's an upstanding member of the legal profession – I don't think she'd appreciate our unique approach, do you?'

Amita was right. Of course she was right. They were both on the same side, they both wanted to protect the one they loved more than anything else on the planet. Even if that meant isolating her.

He let out a frustrated groan. He rubbed his face and felt the days old stubble burn on his palms. His skin was greasy, hands rough. He was tired, stressed, falling apart. He needed a holiday. They all did. He vowed to plunge every rotten penny he made from this story into a long, luxurious trip away for the whole family.

The low rumble and rattle of his phone almost made him weep. With heavy hands, he reached into his pocket and pulled it out, not looking at the number. Amita watched him from across the table.

'Aren't you going to answer that?' she asked.

He shook his head.

'It could be something important Jason,' she continued. 'It could be Sally Arendonk with news on the murder. Or something to do with Georgie!'

'It's not,' he said with a weary sigh.

'How do you know, you didn't even look at the screen.'

'I don't have to,' he said. 'I know *exactly* who it is.'

'Well, why don't you answer it then?'

There was a simple enough answer – he didn't want to. Jason Brazel had never been much of a conversationalist. It was somewhat restrictive given his line of profession.

But he'd managed well enough up until this point. Conversation with punters, members of the public, politicians, celebrities, they were all manageable. Certainly, he preferred asking questions to answering them.

'Jason,' said Amita, 'answer the phone.'

He reached over to the mobile and saw Beeston's name on the screen. He thought about changing it to something less intimidating: Satan or Ghenghis Khan, something like that.

Jason pressed the answer button. Even before the phone was to his ear, he could feel the heat of the venom radiating from Beeston.

'Brazel!' he screamed. 'What the hell do you think you're playing at with that copy tonight?'

'Arnold,' said Jason, pinching the bridge of his nose. 'I really don't have the energy for one of your lectures tonight. It's been a really rotten day and I'm having something of a minor domestic tiff at the moment. So, if I could get to bed this side of midnight without having my ear chewed off by one of your vindictive, if creative, rants, that would be a real bonus.'

The now signature heavy breathing of Beeston met him. There was a pause before the prehistoric press man started to speak.

'Oh Jason,' he said. 'I'm very sorry to hear that, pal. Domestics aren't any fun, believe me, I've got three divorces under my belt that will testify to that.'

'Eh?' blurted Jason.

'I am, truly, sorry to hear that, Jason. Your family has to come first, it always does. This job, it gets in your head, you can't ever let it go or leave it at the office when you finish at night. It can be tough on families, young families, like yours. You've got a couple of sprogs, don't you? And your wife, she's a lawyer yeah? That's tough going mate, I feel for you.'

Jason was completely shell-shocked. His mouth was hanging open so far that Amita stood up and started around the table, fearing the worst. He quickly waved her back.

'I... I don't know what to say Arnold,' he just about managed. 'Yes, yes she's a lawyer and we have two kids. It's hard going, a tough gig alright. But that's journalism, isn't it?'

'Yeah, I hear you,' said the grizzled editor. 'That's why I'm taking you off the story.'

And there it was. The gut shot, the sucker punch, the bash around the head with a frying pan when you were least expecting it.

'You're what?' Jason asked, stunned.

'No, no, don't try and change my mind Brazel, you've said enough,' replied Beeston. 'You've got enough on your plate as it is. I don't want to be piling more stress and anxiety on there when you've got domestic matters to attend to.'

'But Arnold, I–'

'That story you filed, on the history of the painting, it makes sense now,' he said. 'I mean, what sort of journalist would think that would cut the mustard with this paper anyway, am I right? Only one that's under a lot of strain with many plates to spin yeah?'

Jason smelled a rat. Never in his association with Arnold Beeston had he displayed any sort of affection or empathy towards his fellow human beings. Now he was pouring on the marriage advice like the world's greatest Agony Aunt.

'Arnold, please,' he said. 'I can handle the pressure, believe me. I just need a bit more time.'

'Don't be daft,' Beeston laughed. 'I know you can Brazel, I believe in you. That's why I'm pulling you off the story for your own good. Sometimes you need somebody else to tell you you're not fit. And that's my job Jason, it comes with the territory.'

'But I can do this story,' he said, a hint of desperation creeping into his voice. 'I can get to the bottom of it all, trust me.'

'All in good time,' Beeston said, still sounding like a kindly uncle. 'But I'm not having the end of your marriage to Mrs Brazel on my conscience. There's enough of the bad stuff on there already without that. You get me?'

Jason didn't answer. He felt like the whole bottom half of his body had turned to lead. There was nothing, no sensation, just an emptiness, a hollow pit of failure that took up where his vital organs used to be.

'You've done well to get this far Brazel,' said the editor, his tone hardening. 'You'll get your money, there's no doubt about that. But I'm pulling you off the Mulberry story, for your own good and your own sanity. Sometimes you can get too close and you don't see the wood for the trees. Take some time off to sort things out with your missus, then maybe we'll talk again. That sound okay with you?'

There was no need to answer that. Jason knew when to keep his mouth shut. He tried to mumble something, something clever, something memorable, a last stab at dignity before he hung up the phone on Arnold Beeston, probably forever. In the end he said nothing.

'There's one last thing you can do for me though,' said the editor, snorting loudly.

'There is?' asked Jason, almost hopeful.

'Yeah. My new reporter for the case, she's on the overnight, should be rolling into your neck of the woods around six in the morning. Do me a favour and pick her up at the station and fill her in on what's been going on, there's a good chap.'

'I... I...' he stammered.

'Smiffy we call her. Ayanna Smith. Annoys the hell out of her, that nickname. Got a bit of a mouth on her, tends to talk out of turn in front of the paper's top brass, that kind of thing. But she's a good young reporter and she'll gladly take something like the Hal Mulberry murder off your hands. She might even buy you a gin to celebrate. Six am tomorrow morning, she'll recognise you.'

The line went dead. Jason held the phone to his ear for a moment, just enjoying the silence. Amita was still hovering about him, unsure whether to sit down, stay standing or call for help.

'Was that your editor friend?' she asked.

Jason nodded, finally relinquishing his phone.

'Well? Is everything alright? Has something happened?'

'No,' he said. 'Actually, yeah, it kind of sort of has actually.'

'Go on,' she said.

'It would seem that I've been fired.'

Amita stood still for a moment. Jason wasn't sure if she was about to keel over or just remain there for the rest of the evening. Then she blinked, giving him a sign that she was alright.

'Oh,' she said, then headed towards the kitchen. There were some things in life that could only be tackled in one way: by putting the kettle on.

Chapter 19

SHIP BEING SCRAPPED

'This is ridiculous, what the hell am I even doing here?'

'I told you Jason, you should have just said no,' Amita was rubbing her arms, trying to stay warm.

'I know you told me Amita,' he said through gritted teeth. 'And I know I should have said no. It's all I've been thinking about for the past eleven hours. Yet here I am.'

'Here *we* are,' she corrected him.

'You had a choice. You could have stayed in bed, where it's warm, comfortable and you don't have the humiliation of having to pick up and greet the person who can do your job better than you.'

'True,' she acknowledged the logic. 'But I couldn't very well leave you to face that indignity on your own, could I?'

It was cold outside, a light, unseasonable frost making the world sparkle a little as the early sunlight peeked over the craggy outline of Penrith Castle's ruins. Jason, however, was feeling much warmer now after his mother-in-law's admission.

The last few hours hadn't been pleasant. From his sycophantic sacking by Arnold Beeston, he had headed straight to deliver the news to Radha. All animosity from dinner evaporated immediately and she gave him her full support. In a strange turn of events, it had almost made Jason feel worse. Once again, the financial burden was back on his wife's shoulders. And all she could do was back him to the hilt.

He had retired to bed not long after. Although sleep had been something of a wish, and wish only. The hours had ticked by and he was still staring at the ceiling, wondering where it had all gone wrong. Not just with Beeston and the London tabloid, but his career in general. The closing of the local paper, the Madeline Frobisher case, Hal Mulberry buying *Buttermere at Dawn* and everything in between. There was something prophetically pathetic about being able to sum up a lifetime of work in just a few short hours. He wondered if this new reporter had moments of doubt like this. He suspected she didn't.

There had been a temptation to go online and look up her profile, to see who she was, what her background was like, where she had worked before. Even what she looked like. Then he remembered that he was about as useful with online background checks as a shoulder of mutton to a sick horse. Instead he lay stewing in the darkness. The alarm he had set to get up and collect Ayanna Jones had been a welcome relief in the end. A quick change from his pyjamas and a run downstairs, he was met by Amita already at the front door. He hadn't argued, it wasn't worth it and it was too early in the morning for a barney with his mother-in-law, already dressed in one of her show-stopping glittery tracksuits.

Here they were then. Sitting in the car park at the railway station, across from the ruins of the castle and the village hall, waiting on a train to deliver a new reporter. Jason had had many, many other mornings that had been better than this. And he couldn't wait for it to end.

'It was just over there, wasn't it?' Amita asked.

The question seemed to wake him from his internal monologue. He sucked in the brisk air of the car through his nose and peered out of the windscreen.

'What was?' he asked.

'Where Mr Mulberry was discovered. His car was just over there, by the ramp to the ticket office. All of the police tape is gone now.'

'It is,' he agreed. 'I guess it's all bagged and filed now. Everything was contained in his car anyway wasn't it, blood, that sort of thing.'

'And just over there, on the road, that's where Sheila had her turn.'

'I wouldn't call it a turn Amita,' he said, laughing a little. 'The woman had just discovered her husband murdered in their car, moments after leaving him. A turn is something you have at bingo when you miss out on the Brucey Bonus or whatever it is you call it.'

'Jason,' she tutted. 'Please, show some respect.'

He gazed out at the car park. It was a strange place, it always had been. The railway station had always felt like an escape route, or a safe haven, depending on your viewpoint. Either a way out of Penrith or a way in from other, bigger, badder places. For a station that served such high through-traffic, it was relatively small and unassuming. And the competition for parking spaces in the mornings was fierce. The idea that someone had been murdered here, the beating heart of the town's commuter culture, was as bizarre as it was almost poetic.

'Hiding in plain sight,' he said.

'What's that?' asked Amita, still rubbing her arms.

'I was just thinking there, about Hal's untimely death and the fact it happened here, in the car park. How many people do you think were here the night of the gala? Hundreds?'

'At least,' said Amita. 'The great and the good.'

'Not to mention that randy old soldier who took a fancy to you,' he laughed.

'Don't remind me,' she said.

'Hundreds of people – the great and the good as you say, all here, yards from a brutal murder of one of their own.'

'What's your point?'

'My point, Amita, is that if you were going to kill somebody, ordinarily you would try to do it in a secluded, quiet place. So why does our killer decide to bump off Hal Mulberry when there's a greater, maybe the *greatest*, chance of getting caught here. I mean, his wife was in the car with him only moments earlier. She'd only just stepped out a minute before it happened.'

'Or so she says,' said Amita.

'Indeed.'

'You think she might be involved?'

'It had crossed my mind,' he said. 'Although we're at such a dead end that I'm willing to listen to *any* theories at this stage. Well, any theories not on your pal Barry's website.'

'I must admit, she was the first person I thought of,' said Amita. 'Statistics don't lie do they? The majority of murder victims know who their killer is. And she *was* at the scene, probably as close to Hal as anyone was likely to get at that stage.'

'All good points. But she's walking around free as a bird,' he said. 'If it was cut and dried, Arendonk would have her banged up and charged by now. Now, admittedly, we don't know our new resident super cop all that well, but from what we *do* know about her, she doesn't strike me as the type of bobby who would miss something as obvious as that.'

'Stranger things have happened,' she said. 'Although I do agree with you. Sally Arendonk seems sharp as a tack.'

'Of course, it doesn't mean that Sheila Mulberry *isn't* involved in some way,' said Jason. 'She just might not be the one who cut Hal's throat.'

Amita's head was starting to hurt again.

As was Jason's. He leaned against the window, hoping the coolness of the glass would help. He stared blankly over at the village hall, the sun getting ever higher above the horizon behind the dilapidated building. The outline of the temporary gazebo outside the village hall across from them stood out like spindly, black bones against the brightening sky.

As he looked out of the window, something stirred inside of him. He pushed himself off the glass and squinted, peering harder at the village hall.

'What time is it?' he asked, not turning to Amita.

'Quarter to six,' she yawned.

Jason pursed his lips. He sat still for a moment, just looking out across the road at the ruins and the gazebo. He thought about what he was about to do. Then he heard Arnold Beeston's faux sympathetic voice in his head.

And his mind was made up. He unfastened his seatbelt and climbed out of the car.

'Jason?' asked Amita. 'Where on earth are you going?'

She got out and hurried after him as he crossed the road. He skipped quickly down the pavement to the make-shift security entranceway that had been erected at the car park of the village hall. There was nobody about now, just the guard rails waiting to be stacked and collected. Long shadows from their bars and spokes were cast across the tarmac.

'Jason!' Amita called after him, not daring to shout too loudly for fear of sparking suspicion. 'Do you want to tell me what you're up to? The train is on its way, you have to meet this Smith woman.'

'It won't take a minute,' said Jason.

'What won't?'

'Just something that's been bothering me,' he said. 'It's probably nothing. I just need... a moment of inspiration.'

'Inspiration?' she gasped, putting her long-distance running training to good use. 'We're a little late for that, are we not?'

The temporary gazebo was ahead of them now. Everything looked exactly as it had done when they'd all heard Sheila Mulberry scream a few nights ago. The lighting was dormant and the inside of the structure completely dark. Where everything had been so full of life before, now it all felt empty and alone. Jason walked across to the door of the gazebo, his feet crunching over the frosty dew on the grass. The hall was towering over them now, looking down like an inquisitive but silent observer. He tried not to let his imagination get the best of him and he reached for the door.

'Jason,' Amita whispered. 'What are you doing? It'll be locked, the place is empty, this is a waste of our time.'

He grasped the handle of the main doors. Looking back at Amita, he smiled. The door clicked open, and he let out a little bit of a yelp.

'Blimey,' he said. 'I wasn't expecting that to work.'

'Jason,' said Amita. 'Would you tell me what we're doing here? You've got somewhere to be, somebody to meet. We can't be skulking about in here, it's probably against the law.'

'So was impersonating family members to visit people in hospital,' he said, stepping inside.

'We didn't say we were relatives,' she said. 'That nurse just assumed we were visitors. Which we were.'

'Tell that to the judge.'

The inside of the gazebo was still dark. Towards the far end of the giant room, some light was filtering in through the ceiling-to-floor windows. Row after row of chairs had been set up for the homecoming unveiling of *Buttermere at Dawn* – Hal Mulberry's crowning achievement and his finest hour. A moment that nobody ever got to see, least of all him.

Jason walked down the centre aisle, Amita by his side. He peered around the desolate room, looking for something, anything that might justify why he was here. He didn't know exactly what he was looking for, just that he should be there, just now, when nobody was looking. It was an instinct, a gut feeling. He'd spent too long recently ignoring it. It felt good to be back in the zone.

'Good grief,' whispered Amita.

'What? What is it?' he asked, on edge.

She grabbed his elbow and pointed ahead, towards the top of the aisle. The seats came to an abrupt halt at what was clearly supposed to be the presentation area. A glass plinth was catching the faint light coming through the tinted windows. And behind it, a large, dark mass. Jason stepped forward.

'Surely not,' he said. 'It can't be.'

'I think it is,' whispered Amita.

They looked at each other and then rushed to the top of the aisle. The large lump of darkness was a thick velvet covering that reached down to the floor. Jason took a hold of an edge and pulled hard. It dropped with a surprisingly heavy thud, revealing *Buttermere at Dawn* beneath.

There it was, in all of its glory, staring back at them both. It was unassuming, unmoving, neat and tidy in its frame. Two million pounds worth of a national treasure left hidden beneath a velvet blanket in a draughty gazebo outside an old village hall. Hardly the fitting epitaph Hal Mulberry had hoped for it, Jason thought.

'Crumbs,' said Amita. 'There it is. It's just there.'

'Yeah, just sitting here, waiting.'

'Waiting for what?'

'For the unveiling that's never going to happen,' said Jason morbidly.

'How much did you say it was worth again?' Amita asked.

'Two mill is what Mulberry paid for it,' he said flatly, still looking at the painting. 'It's probably worth double that now, given the recent history.'

'I'll bet. And yet nobody thought to put it into storage or take it away.'

It dawned on Jason then what he had been looking for when he came in here. He snapped his fingers and smiled. 'Right,' he said. 'I get it now.'

'Get what?' she asked, reaching out and touching the frame.

A cloudy veil, as thick as the velvet blanket, seemed to lift from Jason then. He took a step back and took in the whole painting.

'This thing,' he said. 'The painting, *Buttermere at Dawn*, it's not about the painting at all.'

'What isn't?' Amita wrinkled her nose as she examined the dust that came away from the frame when she ran her finger along the edge.

'Hal Mulberry's murder,' he said. 'He wasn't killed for the painting. Don't you see?'

'I don't,' she said. 'All I see is a dusty old picture that's caused trouble wherever it's gone. Curse or no curse, this thing is a bad penny.'

'And that's just it,' said Jason. 'We've been running around thinking the painting was the motive, or at least *a* motive. But it's not, it's got nothing to do with Mulberry's death. It can't do.'

'And why's that? It's worth a fortune, you just said it yourself.'

'It's still here Amita, here, in this place. Look around you, it's an empty gazebo you can probably buy from B&Q. And we literally just walked through the door. What's stopping us taking it home with us and putting it above the mantelpiece?'

'I wouldn't have it there in a million years,' said Amita stuffily. 'It clashes with the carpet.'

'Amita,' he said.

'Yes, yes, I know what you're saying,' she waved him away. 'It makes sense though. If the killer wanted the painting so badly then why has it been forgotten about and left here? I don't rate the security firm they hired.'

'No, nor do I,' he said. 'And the fact the painting is still here changes the complexion of the whole investigation. Unless…'

Amita shuddered. She stepped in closer to her son-in-law. 'What are you saying Jason?'

'Unless it's a fake. What if this is a decoy? Some worthless copy?' Jason was about to deliver his new theory when a clank from the back of the room sent them both into a panic. They spun around to see a dark figure run across towards the door, their silhouette clear against the growing sunlight.

'What the?'

'Run Jason!' shouted Amita, giving chase.

'What?' he blurted.

'Run, come on!' she called over her shoulder, bolting towards the door. 'We've got to catch them!'

Jason didn't know what to do. He spent a split second trying to think of excuses not to start running. He was not built for speed. It didn't take long, however, for him to realise there was no way out of this. Not this time. And he had to help his annoyingly fit mother-in-law.

'They had to start running didn't they,' he said, forcing his legs into action. 'They just had to start running.'

Chapter 20

COMPOSITION VIII

One foot after the other. One foot after the other. That's all Amita had to do. Keep up the pace, just keep going. She'd catch up, she *had* to catch up. Never, in all of her life, had she been so grateful for staying fit. Although the rattle in her chest was starting to worry her. If this all went to plan she vowed to cut back on the secret cigarettes.

She could better see the figure she was chasing now, the morning sun brightening the streets. It was a man who had fled from the gazebo at the hall and was bolting down Ullswater Road. The houses were still quiet, curtains drawn, everyone tucked up in bed. The sound of running wouldn't disturb them. Amita wished it would.

The man occasionally looked back over his shoulder. She didn't recognise him, not from this distance. He was young though, fit, healthy. If he decided to turn on the rockets she had no doubt she'd be left in his dust. Only he hadn't, not yet. Amita, between gulps of air, wondered why.

He took a sharp left, crossing the empty street. He hopped over the small wall that led to a supermarket car park and made off towards the building.

'Bloody hell,' she wheezed.

Running was hard enough. Now she was going to have to be a hurdler. She thought better of it and ran a little further down the road, skipping into the car park at the main entrance. The man had gained ground. Amita picked up her pace.

She sprinted as best she could across the empty car park. Her target vanished down the side of the big industrial building. Amita continued her pursuit, zooming around the corner with an elegance she didn't know she still had. Her knees were aching now, hips burning, calf muscles taut like fists. The blisters were congregating on her toes and heels. She would pay for this dearly. But it would be worth it to find out who this man was. And what he was doing near the prized painting so early in the morning.

An alleyway opened up in front of her. To her surprise, she had her prey cornered. The far end of the lane was blocked off by a ten foot high chain-link fence. The man was trying to climb it, but his shoes couldn't catch a grip. Sensing her presence behind him, he gave up climbing and turned to face Amita.

She got a good look at him now as she stopped, blocking his escape. Her lungs were heaving as much oxygen in as they could. She thought she might pass out at one point. Ironic as it would be that she had finally caught up only to let him go by collapsing.

'I didn't do anything,' he said.

'I never said you did,' she replied.

He was young, in his late twenties maybe. He looked dishevelled, a thin growth across his cheeks, hair unusually unkempt for the style, Amita thought. His clothes were filthy too. He held up his hands, close to tears.

'I didn't do anything wrong,' he pleaded with her. 'I was just... I just wanted to see the painting.'

'Then why did you run?' she asked him.

Amita was surprised that instead of protesting, he sniffed gently. Tears rolled down his dirty cheeks.

'You have to believe me,' he said. 'I didn't do anything wrong. I didn't kill him.'

'Kill who?' she asked, already knowing the answer.

'Hal!' he shouted, his sadness tipping over into anger. 'Hal Mulberry.' He clenched his fists. His chest was heaving up and down and his cheeks were getting red.

Amita had a sudden realisation of the danger she might be in. She didn't know this young man, certainly didn't know if she could trust him. He was jumping to fast conclusions and was clearly emotional. She'd been so hell-bent on catching up with this person she'd given no thought to what she would actually do if and when she did. She might, in fact, be facing off against Hal Mulberry's killer. And she was all alone. Where was Jason for that matter?

'Just try to calm down.' It seemed like as good advice as any to proffer.

'No! I didn't do anything! You have to believe me. You *must*! I'm innocent, I'm as much a victim as his wife is, as he was. I'm not going to prison for this. Not me, I won't be the scapegoat!'

'Nobody is trying to blame you for anything,' she said. 'You just need to take some deep breaths and calm down so we can talk. Okay?'

The young man looked suspicious. He was flexing his hands, tightening them into little balls as he stared at her from the top of the alleyway.

'My name is Amita,' she said. 'I only want to talk to you, okay? What's yours?'

'No, I'm not saying anything,' he said. 'Not without a lawyer.'

'Okay,' she held up her hands. 'That's fair enough. I'm not a lawyer. But I'm also not a police officer.'

'Then who the hell are you?'

'I'm just a concerned local who doesn't like to see people murdered around my town,' she said flatly. 'But let me just say, I have my reasons for doing some investigations of my own into Hal Mulberry's death. Now, you said you didn't murder him, that's okay, I believe you. But I'm wondering, why would you just say that to me, a perfect stranger? Why would you just come out with something as random as that?'

The man looked confused, like there was too much going on for him to understand. Then he smiled.

'I know what you're trying to do,' he said. 'You're trying to trick me into giving a false confession. You're probably wired up, I've seen how these things work on TV. You'll be an agent, or a copper, or both. Did Sheila put you up to this? Did she give you my name?'

'Sheila Mulberry has said nothing,' said Amita calmly. 'I don't know your name, that's why I asked.'

'I'll believe that when I see it,' he scoffed. 'She's always had it in for me, all along. She couldn't stand to see me happy.'

'And how do you know Sheila?'

'*Everyone* knows Sheila,' said the man.

He began to pace back and forth, rubbing at the back of his head. Amita couldn't tell if he was anxious or ill. This could be dangerous, she thought, but she had to keep going.

'Would you like to sit down?' she asked. 'You've given me quite the run around here.'

'What? No,' he said. 'No, I'm not sitting down. I have to get out of here, I have to leave town. I'll never clear my name, not while that cow is out there spreading rumours about me, telling everyone that I murdered her husband.' He stopped and stared right at her. 'I didn't kill Hal,' he said, beating his chest, teeth gritted. 'I'd *never* do anything to hurt him. He was... he was–'

Something barrelled into Amita from behind. She felt her legs being kicked away from beneath her and she landed hard on her backside in what appeared to be a shopping trolley. It skidded to a halt as Jason tumbled on top of her.

'Jason!' she shouted. 'Get off of me!'

'What are you doing here?' he said, voice muffled by her shell suit jacket. 'I thought you were the man we were chasing.'

'Since when did a shopping cart become a weapon of choice!' She pushed him off her.

As they composed themselves, the man darted past.

'Get after him!' she shouted, her legs poking up like two polyester clad broom handles. 'Quickly!'

Jason helped his mother-in-law back to her feet. They hurried out of the alleyway in time to see the young man duck into the supermarket. They gave chase, skidding on the freshly polished floors of the shop. The aisles opened up in front them like a giant maze.

'Where'd he go?' asked Jason, still out of breath. 'And who is he anyway?'

'I don't know, on both counts Jason,' she answered him. 'But he has to be in here somewhere. Come on, let's try over–'

'Amita!'

They both turned in unison to face the door. Amita thought her heart was going to explode as she set eyes on the person who had just called her name.

'Georgie?' she asked. 'Is that… is that you?'

Georgie Littlejohn bathed in the light of the early morning, came striding towards her. She was imperious in the way she carried herself, her white blouse and matching travel slacks catching the early rays and leaving her glowing like a renaissance cherub.

'I thought it was you,' she said, striding through the main doors, bags-for-life elegantly draped over each cocked elbow. 'I thought, there's Amita Khatri, out at this ungodly hour, running – literally running – in to get the family supplies before everyone else. It's a good ploy to grab a bargain, Amita, that's why I'm here too. I'm being treated to a day at the races by my eldest Derek and if you want to take a decent picnic, well the early bird catches the–'

'Georgie,' said Amita again, stepping towards her. 'I… I can't believe it's you.'

She grabbed Georgie by the shoulders and pulled her in closely. Prodding her back and tightening her grip, Amita wanted to make sure that the woman in front of her was actually real and not some terrible figment of her imagination.

'I was so worried,' she said. 'I couldn't reach you. We went around to your house and there was no answer. I thought... I thought you'd been kidnapped or had a turn or something. And I'm so sorry Georgie for the way I treated you and the gnome. I'm so, so sorry. I wouldn't forgive myself if something had happened. But where were you? You missed bingo...' Amita stepped back, tears pooling in her eyes.

Georgie was dumbfounded. She just stood there, looking a little non-plussed. 'Yes, well, it's all water under the bridge now Amita,' she said. 'Let bygones be bygones, that's my motto, as you know.'

'Yes,' said Amita, smiling now, their usual rivalry far from her mind. 'I'm so happy to see you, Georgie. Really I am. Jason and I were just here to—'

She spun around quickly, remembering why she was there. Jason was standing behind her, leaning on the wall.

'Where is he?' she asked.

'Save your breath,' said Jason. 'He's gone.'

'Gone? How could he be gone?'

'He's gone, Amita, because you got distracted by Mrs Littlejohn's enigmatic arrival. And while you were blubbering away over her nice Marks & Spencer blouse, I was trying to find our mystery man. In the process of my forensic search, I discovered this place has *another* door. Using all of my decades of journalistic know-how and intuition, I deduce that he has legged it and left us standing here like a couple of kippers.'

Amita felt like she had been cored. She turned around aimlessly for a moment, not sure where to go, or what to say or do.

'Is everything alright there, Amita?' asked Georgie. 'You look like you've been pulled through a mill backwards.'

'Yes Georgie, everything is fine,' she said. 'I... I think I need to sit down for a moment, that's all. It's been a bit of a strange morning.'

She wandered past Georgie and out into the fresh morning air of the car park, unsure whether it was the world that gone mad or her.

Chapter 21

THE MADONNA OF PORT LLIGAT

Sally Arendonk was about to take a bite of her giant sandwich when the door buzzer went. She'd barely lifted the mammoth lunch she'd prepared the night before to her mouth when the inevitable had happened. Since she'd moved to Penrith there hadn't been a spare ten minutes in the day. It wasn't just in the office either. Everywhere seemed to be open season for disturbing the new detective inspector.

This time, though, she was determined to enjoy some private time. She was the only person in the squad room, a rarity that should have merited a big red circle on the calendar. Sally thought she was on to a winner when she sat down at her desk moments earlier. A peaceful environment free of her new colleagues. No pressing phone calls, Zoom meetings or emails to answer. It was supposed to be a blissful pocket of serenity before the madness cranked back into gear.

The buzzer went again. She remained defiant. This was no ordinary sandwich. It was handcrafted, homemade, from the remnants of a delicious roast dinner that her husband had made the night before. Succulent chicken, crisp, fresh lettuce and tomatoes and a healthy dollop of light mayonnaise to make sure everything went down without question. The coffee on her desk may be ice cold and the can of juice in her handbag roasting warm, but that didn't matter. She was going to enjoy this sandwich, the anticipation had got her through the day. No buzzers, no breaking incidents or major crimes were going to ruin this. This was just for her.

But her best efforts to have five minutes peace were no match for the front desk sergeant, who pushed the door of the squad room open. 'Somebody to see you ma'am.'

She stepped to one side. Sally didn't budge. Her sandwich was still hovering in front of her mouth, held up like a meat and bread trombone. But as two familiar people entered past the sergeant, Arendonk finally conceded defeat, she lowered the sandwich and placed it back on her desk in its tinfoil wrapping.

'Lovely,' she said. 'Just the company I was looking for at lunchtime. Cagney and Lacey come to brighten my day.'

'Cagney and who?' asked Amita.

'Lacey, Amita, Lacey.'

'Who?'

'It was a TV show, a pair of female detectives in New York. It ran for years.'

'Never heard of it.'

'You've never heard of *Cagney & Lacey*?' the police-woman yelped.

228

'I've never heard of the programme,' said Amita. 'I had three children to raise and a house to maintain. I didn't have time for Jimmy Cagney and frilly, lacey what-have-yous.'

The pair pulled out the chairs on the other side of Arendonk's desk and sat down. She laughed a little. Lunchtime was most definitely over.

'I'm glad that burning issue has been settled,' she said. 'To what do I owe the pleasure of your company? Decided to break any more confidentiality and privacy laws have you? Or is this a social call?'

'I wish it was a social call,' said Jason. 'That sarnie looks delicious.' He eyed up the DI's lunch.

She snatched it away from him and put it in a drawer.

'You keep your mitts to yourself Brazel,' she said

Jason held up his hands in respectful defeat.

'Are you two finished talking about strange television shows and lunch?' asked Amita. 'Because I really think you'll want to hear what Jason and I have discovered, Detective Inspector.'

Sally nodded. She clasped her hands on her desk and tried to pull as serious a face as she could. One of the unexpected turns of her move to a more rural jurisdiction had been the cast of do-gooders who seemed adamant they wanted to help. Although at least Jason and Amita were a cut above the average she had met in her short time in Penrith. They had a file and, by all accounts, had been very successful with their last venture.

The others, however, weren't quite as professional, thorough or indeed accurate with their investigations. If Sally had been given a tip-off about illicit dog fouling or encroaching fences and overgrown hedgerows, she had been given them all.

'We need to talk about the Mulberry murder case,' said Jason.

'Jason,' she said, leaning forward.

'Look, I know what you're about to say.'

'Do you?' she asked. 'If you know what I'm going to say then why are we having this conversation in the first place? Need I remind you that I was near enough sweating bullets to convince Sheila Mulberry not to press charges on you. On *both* of you as it happens.'

'I know, *we* know,' said Jason.

'And we appreciate it greatly, Detective Inspector,' Amita chimed in.

'It's just, we think we might be on to something.'

Sally gave him a long, hard stare. She liked Brazel, they had hit it off immediately. But she wasn't going to let personal judgement get in the way of her job. Especially when there was an unsolved murder on her patch.

Next, she turned to Amita. On a cursory glance there was nothing out of the ordinary about her. She was seemingly a kindly, likeable, if slightly eccentric old dear with striking taste in leisure wear. A well-known face around the town and beyond, Amita Khatri ticked all the boxes of what people in the later stages of their lives should be like. Only most OAPs hadn't been held hostage by a violent killer. The same killer that she and Jason had helped to uncover. Sally had read their files from back to front. They were a formidable duo, all the more so because they looked like the last people on earth that would solve a crime. And it was the only thing keeping them sat across from her when she could be tucking into her lunch.

'You've got fifteen seconds,' she said, glancing at her watch. 'Fifteen seconds to convince me that you two shouldn't be locked up for your own good and my sanity.'

'We only need five of those seconds,' said Amita. 'Tell her Jason.'

'We might have found the killer,' he said.

Sally blinked. Jason had paused for dramatic effect.

'Right,' she said. 'And your point is?'

'What? That's not impressive enough for you?'

'It might be when you provide me with a name.'

'We don't know his name,' said Amita.

'Alright, what about an address?'

'Nope, no address either,' Jason said.

'A location then, where this mystery man is right now.'

'Sorry,' Amita shrugged.

'Right, I see,' Sally drummed her fingers on her desk. 'So what you're telling me, both of you, is that you've got no name, no address, no current whereabouts of a man you believe is the murderer of Hal Mulberry.'

'That's it,' said Amita.

'Spot on,' agreed Jason.

This was skirting dangerously close to the realms of satire. Sally's patience was wearing thin. 'Do you at least have a motive? Some sort of evidence that this guy is our man?' she asked.

'Not as such, no,' said Jason.

'Of course you don't, how silly of me,' said the police-woman. 'There was me thinking you did. There was me thinking that you came in here, disturbed my lunchtime and had a credible outlet for these outlandish claims you're making. They should call me *Silly* Arendonk, right?'

Neither Jason nor Amita laughed. They were stoney-faced.

'I'm sorry guys,' she said. 'Unless you've got something tangible, I don't really think there's anything I can do.'

'We met him, this morning,' said Amita. 'At the make-shift display centre outside the village hall.'

'Met who?' asked the detective.

'Our mystery man,' said Jason. 'We just happened to be down there this morning at the crack of dawn and went in to take a look around.'

'I'll pretend I didn't hear that,' she said.

'And out of nowhere comes this man, a young man,' said Amita. 'He scared the living daylights out of us, didn't he Jason?'

'He did,' he agreed.

'Anyway, he makes off out of the door and we chased him, all the way down the road. I had him cornered down the little lane that runs beside the supermarket.'

'You?' asked Sally. 'You had this guy cornered?'

'Yes, I did,' said Amita defiantly. 'Is there a problem with that?'

'No,' she said. 'Carry on.'

'So I had him cornered and he was getting agitated, really very upset,' she continued. 'He starts going on about how he wasn't going to be blamed for Hal Mulberry's murder, how he refused to be made a scapegoat. Then he starts talking about Sheila Mulberry.'

'The wife?' asked Sally. 'What about her?'

'He says that she had been spreading stories, lies, about him,' Amita went on. 'He said that he wasn't going to be left with the blame for Hal's death. And that it was dreadfully unfair how he had been treated.'

Sally admitted that she was intrigued. She pulled out a notepad and a pen from a drawer. 'What did this guy look like?' she asked.

'He was sort of plain looking, wasn't he Jason?' said Amita. 'Dark blond hair that looked like it needed a good wash. In fact, everything about him needed a good wash.'

'He looked like he had been sleeping rough,' said Jason.

'I see. Age?'

'No older than thirty,' said Amita. 'He was lean built, fast. I kept thinking he would take off and leave me behind but he never did. He just took a wrong turn.'

Sally made careful notes of the man's description.

'So what happened to him?' she asked. 'Why didn't you call us?'

'I thought I could reason with him,' said Amita. 'I thought I could get to the bottom of what he was talking about. But we lost him, didn't we.'

'You lost him,' said Jason. 'I was all ready to continue the foot chase when Georgie Littlejohn showed up, back from the dead.'

'A miracle,' said Amita.

'Who's Georgie Littlejohn?' asked Sally.

'If you don't know her already, then you soon will,' said Jason. 'She makes the Sheriff of Penrith here look like a hermit.'

'Jason,' Amita tutted.

'What makes you think this could be Mulberry's killer?' asked Sally.

'He was pretty antsy,' said Amita. 'And he made all of these wild statements without prompting. I never once mentioned Hal's name or why we were looking at *Buttermere at Dawn*.'

'Which is still unguarded by the way,' interrupted Jason. 'I want that on the record that I've done my part for local culture. Any old Tom, Dick or Harry could waltz in there.'

'We did,' said Amita.

He pinched her under the desk.

'Alright,' said Sally, tapping her pad with the end of her pen and looking over her notes. 'This is potentially very useful. I'll put out a general call to officers across the county to keep their eyes peeled for this guy. Make him a person of interest. Where did you last see him?'

'In the supermarket off Ullswater Road,' said Jason. 'He's quick on his feet.'

'Not quick enough,' winked Amita.

'Alright. What time?' asked the detective.

'Must have been just after six am,' she said. 'We would have been here sooner only you wouldn't believe the red tape it takes to come speak with you Detective Inspector. You really should take a look into that when things quieten down. We have vital information on an important case. You shouldn't have us waiting around in a draughty lobby.'

'Amita, zip it,' said Jason, stepping in. 'Sally knows what she's doing.'

'It's Sally now, is it?' Amita raised an eyebrow.

'It's Detective Inspector,' said the officer, 'and neither of you should forget that.'

She stood up from behind her desk. Jason and Amita did the same. The policewoman headed for the door, her notebook in hand.

'What's the next move then?' asked Amita.

'Next move?' smiled Sally. 'The next move is you two let the professionals do their jobs. You don't do a thing.

You head home, lock the door and watch for the arrest on the news. That goes for you too Jason.'

'Fine by me,' he said as they were ushered out of the door. 'I'm not working on the story anymore anyway. Whatever happens is the responsibility of my replacement...' He trailed off. A dreadful realisation set in, and he could feel his bones turning to lead.

'Jason?' asked Amita, concerned. 'What's the matter?'

'Smiffy,' he said. 'I forgot all about Smiffy. She was coming on the next train and then I got distracted by the picture.'

'Oh no,' said Amita. 'I completely forgot too. But why didn't she call you, surely she had your number?'

Jason scrambled for his phone. He pulled it out and saw a number with thirteen missed calls on the screen.

'Why didn't it ring?' he asked. 'Why didn't the stupid thing ring?'

'You've got it on silent mode,' said Amita, snatching it from him.

'Right, that's quite enough from both of you,' said Sally, marching them to the front door. 'Thank you for your help, we'll be in touch if we need anything else from you. Goodbye.'

The heavy doors of Penrith Police Station closed with a thud. Jason trotted down the steps and started on up the road. Amita followed him, keeping a safe distance.

'This is all we need,' he said. 'Beeston will have my guts for garters. In fact, he'll probably feed them to his bulldog Smiffy when he gets the chance.'

'It's for the greater good Jason,' Amita tried to console him. 'We might have just managed to catch Hal Mulberry's killer, quite by chance. That's worth more than kowtowing to that awful newspaper editor.'

Jason slowed down. She was right. They had done good work this morning, really good work. Whether this guy was their culprit or not, he was officially a person of interest, they had started the wheels of justice. And he had only been meeting Smiffy out of courtesy, out of some outdated notion that it was the right thing to do. He owed Beeston nothing and had been shown very little in return. He turned back to face Amita and smiled at her.

'Home?' he asked her, offering his arm.

'Home,' she agreed, and took it.

Chapter 22

WOMAN WITH UMBRELLA

Amita was looking forward to bingo tonight. It had been far too long since she'd been able to say that with any real conviction and honesty. The last few weeks and months had been a real strain on her. They'd been a real strain on everyone associated with the club. Ever since Madeline Frobisher's untimely demise, the club had been trying to pick itself up again, dust off and get on with things.

Things had settled down of course. Christmas had helped, when everyone was playing for charity and they could all rally around a common cause. Then into the new year there was the inevitable lull in play. People got sick or just couldn't be bothered bracing the bitter Cumbrian winter. It took a lot of dedication to traipse to the old church hall when the sleet and snow were hitting you at right angles.

Amita had been there every week of course. As long as she could draw breath she would be there for the opening game. And still there at the bitter end. Only Georgie Littlejohn had an equally perfect attendance record. Perfect until a week ago.

The news of Hal Mulberry's death had brought up all the old fears the club members were just getting over. Another murder, another set of suspicious circumstances. And the threat of yet more danger stalking the streets of their beloved town. Amita had felt those pressures more than most as she had tried to get to the bottom of things. She had always disliked the Sheriff of Penrith nickname – Jason's smart, journalistic quick-thinking at its best. But this time, with everything that had been going on, Amita had felt like she was wearing the badge and Stetson more than ever.

Not now. Not tonight. Tonight was different. She walked along the street, her head held high and filled with nothing but focus and concentration on the game ahead. There was no mind map pulling clues and suspicions together. No great masterplan to catch a brutal killer and trick them into confessing. The universe had thrown her a bone, and with DI Arendonk seeming to take her and Jason seriously, maybe for once she could actually let them get on with it and act on their tip-off.

And then there was Georgie Littlejohn. Not only was she alive and well, she seemed to be forgiving Amita for her shortness. For the first time in what had felt like an eternity, she could just go to the bingo, say hello to everyone, and head home again afterwards without a care in the world.

Father Ford and Mr Jones the janitor were waiting at the door for her as she climbed the stairs.

'Good evening gentlemen, how lovely to see you both,' she said, shaking both their hands.

Jones gave a sullen grunt. Father Ford looked terrified at the positivity.

'Oh, my, you're in a good mood this evening, Amita,' he said.

'I am, Father, I really am,' she said. 'The sun is in the sky, it's warm enough not to have to wear six layers of clothing and I'm feeling lucky. I hope you've warmed up the bonus numbers for me, said a little prayer.'

The meek pastor's cheeks turned scarlet. 'Amita,' he leaned forward, speaking conspiratorially, 'I couldn't possibly ask God to do something like that.'

Amita waited for the punchline. When one wasn't forthcoming, she narrowed her brow. 'I know that Father,' she said. 'It was a joke.'

The realisation that he had been a complete imbecile was swift and hard on the young vicar. He let out a noise somewhere between a sob and a laugh and clapped a hand to his head.

'Of course, yes, sorry,' he said. 'A joke, yes, that's right, just a joke. Wonderful.'

He let out the worst fake laughter Amita had ever heard. She nodded and excused herself politely, deciding to let him off the hook easily.

She wandered over to her usual table. Sandy was settling Ethel at the far end, Violet and Judy were bickering about something or other. Everyone was there, except Georgie. For a brief moment Amita panicked. She cast a long, swooping gaze around the hall and spied her best friend and nemesis by the huge urns of tea in the corner close to the door that led to the vestry.

She was cleaning up, assuming the role of mistress of ceremonies as she always did. Even from here Amita could hear her tutting at the state the tables, and cups and saucers had been left in. She decided to go over and give Georgie a hand.

'People need to learn to pick up after themselves, am I right?' she said, diving straight in.

'Amita Khatri, if I had more people like you on my team, this place would be run like the QE II.'

Her team, Amita thought. She let it slide. She was in too good a mood to let something like Georgie's relentless god complex get the better of her.

'How was your day out at the races Georgie?' she asked.

'It was wonderful, it really was. My son Derek, I told you he's a big city banker in London, didn't I?'

'Several times.'

'He gets us into all the exclusive lounges and clubs when he's up here. He knows how to look after his family that boy. I'm immensely proud of him.'

'I'll bet,' said Amita, clearing away some used cups.

'Is everything alright with you,' asked Georgie. 'You seemed a little... overwhelmed when I saw you yesterday morning.'

A lump was forming in Amita's throat. She wanted to tell Georgie how guilty she had felt, how she had panicked and thought she was in mortal danger. She wanted to tell her that in her darkest moments she had pictured her lying in a ditch somewhere, her throat cut, a victim of a serial killer she hadn't been able to catch. She wanted to tell Georgie that down the decades they had known each other, she had actually grown quite fond of her, as a companion, as a constant in an ever changing world she understood less and less. And how if anything were to happen to her, she would be devastated beyond words.

'Georgie,' she started. The lump was there now. Only something was stopping her – an invisible, unspoken barrier that she couldn't climb and couldn't conquer. Everything she wanted to say was locked away again, deep down and out of the way, as it always had been. 'Where have you been for the past week?' she asked. 'Father Ford was asking me to organise the whip-round for the Scouts' charity fun run.'

'All in hand my dear,' Georgie flashed one of her typically false smiles. 'I had a bit of a social blackout last week. Nothing serious of course, just a little "me time". You know how it can get around here Amita, what with all my responsibilities at the bingo and WI and beyond.'

She thumbed at the gathering crowd. Placing her freshly polished stack of saucers down close to the tea urn, she leaned in closer to Amita. 'But enough about me. Have you heard about Judy?' she said quietly.

'Judy? Moskowitz?'

'The one and the same,' she said.

'What about her?'

'Seems she has been given the bad news that she *won't* be welcome back at WI board meetings in the future.'

'Why not?'

Georgie looked around to make sure nobody could hear anything she said.

'It seems she's a little bit too handy with her fists, if you know what I mean,' she nodded.

'Judy?' Amita blurted, looking over at the other pensioner across the hall. 'I can't believe it. She hit someone?'

'I don't know the details,' said Georgie. 'When I was away last week, I heard, through mutual friends that she used to have a bit of a temper on her when she was younger and even used to give her husband a bit of a hard time.'

'Judy? Really?' asked Amita.

'Apparently so,' said Georgie. 'you have to admit, she does fly off the handle every now and then. And poor Violet gets it in the neck more than anyone else. Just look at how the pair behave here at bingo.'

Amita looked over at the two women. They were in another heated debate. Even from this distance it was clear to see who was winning. Judy, with her bravado and confidence, seemed to dwarf poor Violet who was sat beside her. Amita knew they had a strange co-dependency, but the idea that Judy would have raised her hand in anger in her past was quite a revelation. It seemed hard to credit, but it must be serious for someone like Violet to have kicked her off the committee.

'You know what this means though, don't you?' asked Georgie.

'What's that?' asked Amita.

'Well, I don't like to talk about these sorts of matters, not in the position I'm in. But if Judy is being excluded from board meetings, I imagine there will be an opening in the not too distant future.' She reached out and touched Amita's elbow.

'Me?' she blurted.

'Keep it down a bit Amita, blimey,' said Georgie. 'I shouldn't even be talking about this to you. We don't want the likes of those village hall lot getting wind of this. Barbara McLemore would be all over it like a rash. And we don't want her sort in the WI committee. But yes, in short, you would stand a very good chance of being elected onto the WI's governors, maybe even as president when Violet steps down. Judy won't be considered for the role, even if she does decide to run, not with her temper. I know she said she wasn't throwing her hat in the ring, but you can't trust a word that woman says. I'd be happy to speak for you of course. And without blowing my own trumpet, a word from me can go a *very* long way with these sorts of things.'

Amita was flattered. She had always harboured mild ambitions of board level roles with her various clubs and societies. Only she always seemed to miss out at the last minute – either through commitments to Radha and the children or just plain bad luck. Now, it would seem, she was standing on the precipice of a great seat of office. Relatively speaking.

'I can't thank you enough Georgie,' she said. 'Especially after our... unpleasantness over your gnome situation.'

'Don't be ridiculous,' said Georgie, flashing that all-too-perfect smile again. 'Water under the bridge my dear. All forgotten about and all resolved in the end, which is the main thing, am I right?'

'You are,' said Amita.

'Now come on, we should take our seats before that bumbling fool Father Ford starts up with his usual patter before the game.' She linked her arm in Amita's and they walked in tandem over to their seats.

'How the hell can you still be standing up for that idiot, Violet!' Judy was shouting as they arrived at the table. 'The man was an insufferable snob and an oaf too. He flashed money around like it was going out of business.'

'He was generous to the last, Judy,' said Violet adamantly. 'I don't care what you say, Hal Mulberry was a good man and he didn't deserve what happened to him.'

'He had it coming and you know it,' said Judy in a huff. 'He might have been generous in public but I've heard rumours, *lots* of rumours that he was a rascal behind closed doors. And that wife of his was standing by him for the money and the attention.'

'Please, Judy, stop with all of this,' her friend pleaded. 'You're hurting my head, not to mention making a scene.'

'Hal Mulberry, again,' said Sandy quietly as Amita and Georgie sat down.

'I had a feeling,' said Georgie.

Amita took her seat. She dug around in her bag for her bingo pen and made a conscious decision not to listen to Judy and Violet arguing. She had heard every word, of course, but that was okay. She was finished with the murder investigation. It was out of her hands now. The police would get their man and everything would be alright. What was it Jason always used to tell her – this wasn't her fight.

'All I'm saying is that people are different in public than when they're in their own houses, that's all,' Judy went on.

Georgie nudged Amita in the ribs. 'Pot calling kettle,' she whispered under her breath.

'Hal Mulberry liked the sound of his own voice too much to be genuine,' Judy continued. 'Somebody like that is always hiding something. And the fact he was bumped off doesn't surprise me in the least.'

There was a nervous moment at the table. Amita said nothing. She had her pens out and was cleaning her glasses. This wasn't her fight, she kept saying to herself. It was over. Cut and dry.

'Hopefully this will be the end of it all,' she said. 'And that monstrosity of a structure up at the village hall will be taken down and the place left as it is, how it *should* be.'

Still Amita said and did nothing. She polished her spectacles, then polished them again, hoping, praying that Judy would shut up before she said anything else.

'I heard that someone was sleeping in that gazebo,' said Violet quietly. 'That a local homeless person had already called squatter's rights.'

'I'd heard that too,' agreed Sandy. 'They'll be taking over the hall itself soon at this rate.'

'There are shelters already for these poor folk,' said Judy snobbishly. 'They don't need another one at a place we use day in, day out, no matter how tired and falling to bits it is. And that's before we think about the tourist trade. Can you imagine visitors coming from across the country to visit the town and seeing a load of tramps trapsing around close to the castle? I think not.'

Amita's eyebrows shot up in appalled surprise at Judy's lack of feeling for those less fortunate. But at that moment, the lens popped out of Amita's frames and rattled on the table, cutting the conversation short. The distraction was enough to let her swallow her anger, and stopped her utter contempt for Judy Moskowitz turning to the kind of words you couldn't take back. She composed herself and reached for the lens, ready to pop it back into her spectacles.

'Sorry,' she said. 'That always happens.'

Father Ford took to the stage. He gave his usual greetings as the hall prepared to knuckle down for another game of cut-throat, high-stakes bingo.

Amita tried to focus. Still, there was something gnawing away at the back of her mind. Snippets of conversations, words here and there that had never added up. The numbers started to flash on the screen as the game rolled on. Amita couldn't concentrate, not until she checked. She slipped her hand into her pocket and pulled out her phone, unlocking the screen. She scrolled through her notifications, searching for the news channels.

There was nothing. No arrest, no charge, not even an appeal yet. That's when she started to panic.

Chapter 23

GARCON A LA PIPE

It wasn't that Jason was trying to avoid Ayanna Smith. It was more that he didn't want to bump into her on the off chance. Ever since he had realised he was supposed to pick her up from the station, he had been trying not to think about the whole sorry affair. There had, after all, been very good reasons for it to slip his mind. That and he had been in no way obliged to carry out any extra duties for Arnold Beeston. The man had sacked him a matter of seconds before having the brass neck to ask him to be a chauffeur for his new pet.

Round and around these ideas went. One feeding into the other, over and over again. Jason was getting sick of the sound of his own voice prattling about inside his head. The worst-case scenario would have been to run into Smiffy accidentally. With no prep of an excuse and nothing really to go on, he might make a complete fool of himself. Again, he wondered why he should care. She was his replacement, another news reporter sent up from London to stomp around his patch and get the names of streets and people wrong. He owed her just as little as he did Beeston.

So why had he been hiding in the house for the past thirty-six hours with the door locked? Why had he stayed away from all windows during the day and insisted the curtains be drawn at six on the button? Why was he now sitting watching his knee bob up and down, biting his fingernails to the bone and nervously awaiting *another* phone call from Ms Smith?

He had no idea. Maybe it was the sense of letting someone down. Jason had, at heart, always striven to be a crowd pleaser. That's why he was a journalist. There was nothing more satisfying than having his name on a piece of work that some people found wonderful. You couldn't please everyone. That didn't matter. He was happy with those who *were* satisfied.

Now he'd let Smiffy down. He'd let Beeston down too in a roundabout sort of way. And most of all, he felt like he'd let himself down. Jason Brazel always carried through when he gave his word and promise. Well, most of the time.

'Mum's late tonight,' yawned Radha, curled up on the sofa beside him.

'What's that, love?' he asked, not paying attention.

'It's gone ten and she's still not home.'

The news was just beginning on the TV. It wasn't helping matters inside Jason's head. He was half expecting to see Ayanna Smith on there reporting from a crime scene with Sally Arendonk beside her. They'd be discussing how Hal Mulberry's murderer had been caught after an anonymous tip-off. And how Smiffy, less than a day on the scene, had the world exclusive.

Jason wasn't sure how he should feel about that happening. On the one hand, Hal's murderer had been caught. That was a good thing of course. And he had played a hand in catching him. On the other, his replacement had come up with a much better story in few hours than he had in weeks. Once again, the crowd pleaser.

'She's probably gabbing away with the others, right?' asked Radha.

'Yeah, yeah, I'm sure she is,' Jason offered.

'Did you notice anything different about her tonight when she left?'

Jason hadn't even realised Amita was gone until just then when Radha brought it up.

'I can't say I did, love,' he said.

'I don't know,' she said, sitting up. 'She just seemed a bit more bubbly, enthusiastic or something. Like she was really looking forward to going to the bingo.'

'She always looks forward to going to the bingo,' said Jason. 'It's the highlight of her week.'

'I know that,' she said. 'It was just something about her demeanour tonight. She seemed really up for it, happy, you know?'

'Maybe she was seeing The Ghost afterwards and they were, you know...' He winked and cocked an eyebrow.

Radha wrinkled her nose in disgust.

'Jason Brazel,' she said, hitting him with a cushion. 'If my mother was here she'd make you wash your mouth out with soap and water.'

'She's not here, is she?' he laughed. 'She's out there, somewhere, staying late with a man that could be your new daddy.'

'Jason!' she shouted, trying to muffle a laugh. 'Irvine Carruthers is a very kind, very gentlemanly old man who looks after my mother when they go out. It's just a bit of company for them both, nothing more.'

'That's how it starts though, isn't it. First they're going out for tea, then it's the football and wham, the wedding is booked for next summer and you're giving Amita away at the ceremony.'

'Stop it!'

'I'm The Ghost's best man, everyone else is scared of him.'

'Jason!'

'That little dog of his is the ringbearer. He brings them in on a cushion that's strapped to his back, tail wagging, the lot. It'll make for wonderful photos Radha, I can see them already.'

'Right, that's it!' she said, getting up. 'You're sleeping on the sofa tonight Brazel.'

'That's a bit harsh!' he laughed. 'I'll have to have a word with Irvine, tell him to bring his daughter into line a little bit.'

She threw another cushion at him. They were both laughing. He reached up and pulled her down onto the couch by the hips. Radha sat on his lap and clasped his cheeks in her hands. She kissed him warmly and he wrapped his arms around her.

'You know,' she said. 'I can't remember the last time we had the house to ourselves like this.'

'Mrs Brazel, you're not suggesting what I think you're suggesting?'

She kissed him again. All thoughts of Smiffy, Beeston, Hal Mulberry's murder and everything else went out of

Jason's mind. It was the first time in a long while where he was living in the moment. He was happy here, at home with his wife, their children asleep upstairs. He vowed to savour these little moments more. They were preciously fleeting and all too rare.

He leaned in to kiss Radha again but was stopped by a sound upstairs. First it was a creaking floorboard, then a faint thump. They both sat perfectly still, trying to make as little noise as possible, staring up at the ceiling. Then it came – the crying.

'Rats,' said Radha. 'They've always got perfect timing.'

'Ain't that the truth,' droned Jason. He sat back and released his grip around Radha's shoulders. She gave him a sympathetic smile as the crying grew louder.

Rubbing his stubbly cheek, she sighed. 'I'll put them back down again,' she said. 'You come to bed when you're ready. Leave the door off the latch for mum coming home. Whenever that is.'

'It might not be until the morning–'

Radha climbed off him and held up a stern finger. 'Don't, Brazel,' she said. 'Just don't. For that you can take out the bins, it'll save you doing it at the crack of dawn tomorrow.'

'Oh the glamorous life of a professional journalist.'

She took his hand and kissed it before heading out of the living room. Jason sat there for a minute, basking in the warmth of the moment. Even the prospect of having to drag the wheelie bins out to the pavement couldn't spoil his mood now.

He got up and went out of the back door to the garden. Using the age-old logic of the man who doesn't know the collection schedule, he peered over the fence into next door to see which bins they had left behind. He thanked the universe for providing people much more au fait with the council's rota. One week next door had gone on holiday and the whole street had been thrown into chaos. There were bins of all colours dotted up and down the pavement in the strangest game of Russian roulette Jason had ever witnessed.

He dragged the bins around from the back and down the path towards the gate. He even whistled while he went and instantly regretted it. Dragging the wheelie bins onto the pavement outside his gate, he was about to head back inside when a voice made him jump out of his skin.

'You Brazel?'

A short woman with a fierce face was staring up at him. Her hair was pulled so tightly back across her skull that her forehead looked like the surface of a bowling ball. Two focussed eyes were locked on him like guided missiles.

'Eh... yeah.'

She took a step forward. Jason stepped back and bumped into his bins.

'You were supposed to pick me up from the train,' she said.

'Oh, god, Smiffy?'

Somewhere, in the distance, he could hear Arnold Beeston laughing from his corner office overlooking the centre of London. The focussed eyes of Ayanna Smith burned with a new fire now, like they had focussed to laser beams. Her little mouth curled into a snarl.

'I don't like that nickname Brazel,' she said. 'Did Beeston put you up to all of this? Eh? Calling me Smiffy? Leaving me standing at the railway station until eight in the morning? All of that? Well I'm telling you right now, I'm not going to stand for it. If this is some sort of test to see if I have the minerals to cut it as a crime reporter then you can bet your bottom dollar that I have them.'

She was poking him in the chest now, standing on her tiptoes. All Jason could do was stand there and take the assault.

'I'm going to be the best crime journalist this country has ever seen,' said Smiffy. 'And mopping up the mess you've left me here with Hal Mulberry's death is just the start of that. I was going to thank you for cocking it up Brazel, for giving me the chance to prove myself. But I don't think I'll bother now, seeing as you've ignored *all* of my calls and haven't had the decency to call me back with a handover.'

Jason was speechless. This was the nightmare he'd been hiding from for the past day and a half. Oddly, the worst part about it was the fact he was being accosted on his doorstep, in his pyjamas.

'Eh... how did you know where I live?' he asked.

'Hello? Weren't you listening to what I just said?' she wrapped her knuckles on his forehead. 'I'm a crime reporter, finding out where an out-of-shape former local hack lives on his own patch is child's play.'

'Right,' he said. 'Very clever. Although I notice that you left out any and every detail that would properly answer that question, Ayanna.'

'Ms Smith to you, Brazel,' she backed off away from him.

'Sorry,' he said. 'Ms Smith. And for what it's worth, I'm sorry about yesterday morning too. Something came up, something a bit on the big side. And, quite frankly, I completely forgot about meeting you off the train.'

Smiffy folded her arms across her chest. Her face was still full of scorn. But her eyes had at least cooled.

'What do I need to know, then?' she asked him. 'About this story? What am I walking into here? Gangsters? The Russian Mob maybe? International art thieves who suddenly think Penrith is the cultural centre of Europe? Come on, give me the gossip.'

'Gangsters?' he asked. 'International art thieves? This is Penrith, not *Ocean's Eleven*.'

'Then what the hell has been happening here Brazel? What's the story? I've not been sent up here rattling around in that tin can of an overnight train for nothing. The cops are nowhere to be seen today, I can't get a hold of the local press office and nobody in town wants to talk about this Mulberry dude for love nor money.'

She rattled off her questions like a machine gun. Jason had known eager, young journalists who were super-keen to make impressions on their superiors. Some of them tried this by diving straight into all the worst jobs news-papers and reporters could do.

Others, like Smiffy, were of a different breed – head-strong, ambitious and above all else, capable of achieving every dream she wanted. People like that scared Jason as much as he disliked them. But he did feel like he owed Smiffy something.

'You better come in,' he sighed. 'But take off your shoes and keep your voice down. My kids are trying to sleep.'

'Blimey, you have kids?' she said, looking him up and down. 'You don't look like you could mind yourself, let alone offspring.'

'Charm gets you everywhere in this world, Smith. But you already knew that, didn't you?'

She snorted and followed him up to the front door. Jason let them in quietly and showed her into the kitchen. He flipped on the kettle without bothering to ask her what she wanted.

'Nice place,' said Smiffy, looking about. 'If I ever have to visit the frontline of a conflict I'll know what to expect.'

'How old are you?' Jason asked, pouring the tea.

'Not that it's any of your business, I'm twenty-three.'

'Twenty-three, bloody Nora,' he said. 'I hope I wasn't anywhere near as gobby as you are when I was your age.'

'Did people even speak English when you were twenty-three?' she asked with a smirk. 'I didn't think humanity had developed verbal communication a million years ago.'

'A comedian too, you'll go far.'

He offered her a mug. Smiffy took it, examined the rim for any lingering dirt, then took a very small sip. She didn't hide her disgust well.

'It's true what they say then,' she said. 'You really can't get a decent cuppa north of the M25.'

'Who exactly says that?' Jason sniped.

She ignored him. Jason sipped at his own mug. He secretly admitted it wasn't his best effort. His head was a little scrambled from being jumped outside his own house by his replacement.

'You're covering the murder case then,' he said, changing the subject quickly.

'Bravo,' droned Smiffy. 'I can see you're one of the sharper ones up here. You'll be mayor soon enough.'

'I should warn you now, I don't think there'll be much left to go on.'

'And why's that?' she asked, casting her mug to one side, the smell of blood in her nostrils.

'I have it on very good authority that the police have their man,' he said, taking another sip.

'What authority is that then?'

'Journalism one-oh-one, Ms Smith. Always protect your sources.'

'So you think there's going to be an arrest? How come?' she asked, fidgeting by the fridge.

'I don't know what Arnold Beeston has told you about me,' he said. 'But I can take a pretty accurate guess that it involved the terms incompetent and time wasting.'

Smiffy shrugged, not committing or arguing. 'Your words, not mine,' she said.

'Yes, well, whatever it is he's said to you, I'm still a journalist and I still know how to hunt out a story.'

'Brazel, I'm not here for *your* life story. I'm here to cover the Mulberry murder. Now you either have a lead or you don't. Either way I don't really want to be wasting my evening drinking rotten tea and listening to an old man talking about his waning relevance.'

The laser eyes were back again. She stood with her hands on her hips, waiting for Jason to do some party trick like a prizewinning dog owner. He couldn't help but feel a little intimidated by her.

'There's a man,' he said. 'Out there, just now, god knows where.'

'A man? So what. There are plenty of men out there. It's practically raining them.'

'Very good,' he smiled. 'This man, don't ask how I know, but he's the police's number one suspect. DI Arendonk is leading the case, she's got her best men out searching for him just now.'

'And women too presumably?' she pointedly asked.

'Of course,' he said. 'This guy, he's young, a bit nervy. I don't know how he knew Hal. I don't know his name, I don't know anything about him. What I *do* know is that the police are on the hunt. And they'll find him, sooner or later.'

Smiffy closed her eyes until they were almost shut. 'Are you having me on Brazel?' she asked. 'Is this some sort of Northern initiation or something? Because I don't have the time nor the patience to be messed around like this.'

'Listen, you wanted my help didn't you?' he said. 'Take it or leave it, this is what I'm telling you is going on.'

'I don't recall asking for your help. I asked you to pick me up at the station.'

'Fine,' he folded his arms.

'Fine,' she did the same, huffing.

They stood in silence in the kitchen, the ticking clock the only thing breaking the monotony. Jason was determined not to be the first to speak or break the ceasefire. Even if that meant Smiffy spending the night pouting in his house.

'Listen,' said Smiffy, the first to crack. 'I'm not trying to be a cow or anything. It's just, this is a really big opportunity for me and I don't want to blow it. You know what Beeston is like, he doesn't take prisoners, you're evidence of that.'

'You sound almost human,' he said.

'I just don't want to leave here with some cock-and-bull story about the cops on a manhunt when I could be filing something worthwhile.'

Jason felt a sudden professional compassion. Maybe he had been too hard on Smiffy in the thirty minutes he'd known her. Maybe he was just jaded, bitter and more than a little tired from running the rat race. Or perhaps it was just the rotten tea making his brain itch.

'Look, if you don't want to chase up my lead, fine, I'm not going to lose any sleep over it,' he said, sounding much more fatherly than he thought was possible. 'But there's a life lesson to be learned here Ms Smith. When another journalist throws you a bone, you should rip their arm off and run to the hills. It doesn't happen that often, believe me.'

Her laser beam eyes cooled down again. Instead she drew him an earnest, believable look that cracked the hardened, hard-nosed reporter shell she'd been wearing since he met her.

'Take the bone,' he said, and instantly regretted it.

'Take your bone?' she snorted. 'Is that some sort of eighties slang or something?'

Jason let out a sigh, his shoulders slumping. 'It's too late, I'm too tired and far too old to be having this conversation,' he said. 'It's your call Ms Smith. You know where the door is.' He pushed past her and made for the stairs.

'Wait. That's it?' she followed him. 'That mumbled, muddled piece of tinpot philosophy is my handover? You've got to be kidding Brazel.'

'I gave you a lead,' he said. 'It's more than I was handed on my first gig. Think yourself lucky that there are still human beings like me left in this industry.'

The front door burst open. Amita stood in the doorway, out of breath. Her eyes were wild as she darted between Smiffy and Jason halfway up the stairs.

'Is there any news?' she asked. 'Do they have him yet?'

Smiffy laughed. 'Now I know you're having me on,' she said to Jason. 'Who's this, the Fairy Godmother?'

'Oi!' Jason shouted. 'That's the Sheriff of Penrith you're talking about.'

'Jason!' Amita.

'Amita!'

'Both of you!' Smiffy shouted.

She held up her hands to hush them both down. When silence was restored, she stomped down the hallway, barging past Amita on her way out. 'I'm done with this town already,' she said. 'And this stupid bloody story. Good. Night!'

Amita rubbed her forehead. 'Should I know who that strange young woman was?' she asked.

'Probably,' said Jason, climbing the stairs. 'But I'm too knackered to explain.'

'Wonderful,' said Amita, left alone in the hallway. 'I'll just lock up then shall I, to make sure we're not invaded by more young women desperate for your company.'

'That would be lovely Amita,' he called down to her. 'Thank you.'

Amita muttered something under her breath that she was glad nobody could hear.

Chapter 24

CHARING CROSS BRIDGE 9

'Anything?' asked Amita.

'Amita, I'm only awake three minutes, give me a second to pull myself together, would you?' answered Jason, rubbing his eyes.

He staggered into the kitchen and reached to touch the teapot. He pulled his hand back immediately as the porcelain scalded his fingers.

'Bloody hell,' he said. 'That's roasting.'

'It would be, I've just made a fresh pot,' said Radha, rushing about him.

'You're up early,' said Jason.

'We've got a call with a client in Singapore,' she said. 'I need you to get the kids ready and take them to school. They're still in bed.'

'Of course,' he said, grabbing a mug from the cupboard. 'This an important meeting then?'

'They're *all* important, Jason,' said Radha, stressed. 'If we lose these accounts then people have to be laid off.

And as I'm not a partner then I'll potentially be in the firing line. With you out of work at the minute, we can't afford that right now. So yes, it's pretty important that I'm there and don't look like a scarecrow's stylist.' She hurried out of the kitchen.

Jason bit his lip, sitting down at the table. Amita kept her mouth closed, stirring her own tea.

'What?' he asked her.

'Pardon me?' she asked back.

'You're sitting there desperate to say something aren't you?'

'I have no idea what you're talking about,' she answered him. 'You could be offering her some support though. Instead of inviting strange women who are half your age into the house when your wife is asleep.'

'That was Smiffy!' said Jason. 'Ayanna Smith, from London. You know, the reporter we were supposed to collect at the station the other morning there.'

'You can't blame me,' she said. 'I come home, late at night, and find a stranger waiting in the hall, speaking to you in your pyjamas. What am I supposed to think?'

'You're not supposed to think anything until you have the full facts,' he said. 'I've told you that before, that's how you get into trouble – jumping the gun. And another thing, while we're talking about late nights. Just where were *you* until that time? Bingo finishes at nine, right on the button. I know that because old Mr Jones the janitor doesn't dally when it comes to throwing you out. Father Ford would descend into a fit of apoplexy if he was up any later too.'

Amita stopped stirring her tea. She looked into the milk swirling around. It was hypnotic. Meditative. It gave shape to her day and often was when she did her best thinking. But not today.

'Do you think we have the right man?' she asked, not looking up.

Jason almost fell off his chair. He found himself frowning, quite by accident. 'Amita, are we really doing this?' he asked. 'That mystery man, he admitted Sheila thought he killed Hal, even if he protested his innocence. Whatever the truth of the matter, he's got something important to say. We lost him, sure, we shouldn't have done that. But Arendonk is on the case now.'

'She's not found him though, has she?' she asked. 'That's been two days and nights now Jason and still nothing. No press release, no news report, nothing about the police catching this man and charging him with murder.'

'These things take time,' he said.

'You saw the young man, you saw what he was like. He wasn't some survival expert who could last days and days in the wilderness. He was scared, upset. And besides, like you just said he insisted he *didn't* kill Hal. He was adamant about that.'

'That's not what you said the other day there,' said Jason, laughing. 'You were quite convinced we had found our man. You told me he mentioned Hal's murder before you talked about it. And why was he hiding out in the village hall with the painting? Closer you are to danger, the further you are from harm, right?'

'Hiding in plain sight,' said Amita.

'Exactly. And look, it's been proven to be correct. We've pointed the police in the right direction. Our part in all of this is over. We can move on.' Jason was breathing a little heavier now. He wasn't so sure he was convincing Amita. He wasn't so sure he had convinced *himself*.

'I just can't get over what Georgie was talking about last night,' Amita went on. 'What she said about Judy. And then there was everything Judy herself was saying. It was horrible Jason, really horrible. You would have thought that *she* had ordered the hit on Hal Mulberry herself. Or at least wanted to.'

'And what gossip was Georgie spreading now?' he asked. 'That Judy doesn't tip her binmen at Christmas? That she has six toes on her feet, all of them webbed. Come on Amita, you know better than to trust Georgie Littlejohn. So what if Judy is brassed off about the late Mr Mulberry buying her beloved village hall. She doesn't strike me as the type to have a handy list of assassin's phone numbers on her mobile.'

'She said she used to be violent Jason, to her husband.'

'How could Georgie possibly know that?'

'They have mutual friends in Kendall.'

'Of course they do,' he rolled his eyes. 'There's always a mutual friend in Kendall. I sometimes wonder if there's anyone left in Kendall who isn't friends with everyone else.'

'I trust her Jason, I trust her sources,' said Amita, seriously.

'So what does this all mean anyway?' he asked. 'You really think that Judy had something to do with the murder? You think that *she* might even have killed Hal herself? Come on, Amita, do you know how ridiculous that sounds? What are you suggesting we do? Check if she's missing a carving knife from her Sunday dinner set?'

Amita was trying her very best to think clearly and logically. She kept hearing the spite and the venom in Judy's voice. On and on she had gone about how horrible Hal Mulberry apparently was.

'I don't know,' she said, sinking into her chair. 'I just don't know anymore, Jason. This whole thing has been one dead end after another. It's like we've been running through treacle the whole time and have gotten nowhere. And then, just as I think we might have made a breakthrough with our mystery man, something like this comes along.'

'It's not a thing Amita, believe me,' he said. 'I know how you feel. Do you know, I was almost relieved when that Smiffy woman appeared last night. I've been hiding out here for the past few days hoping to avoid her. Now that she's been here, I've told her all I need to and she's gone, forever, I feel much better. I feel like the elephant that's been sitting on my chest for the duration of this rotten affair has finally gone.'

'I was the same Jason,' she said. 'I couldn't wait to get to the bingo last night, to see everyone. I thought that things were over, that the mystery man would be caught and he'd be charged with the murder. That would be that and we could all move on.'

'So why are we having this conversation then?' he asked. 'Why are we trying to talk ourselves into feeling bad again when we know we've done our bit. It's sick.'

Amita nodded. She was staring across the kitchen at the fridge. A picture Josh had drawn when he first started school was lovingly stuck to the top door with magnets. It showed the whole family wearing gold medals and smiling. Underneath the teacher had written, 'I love my family as they are the best at everything they do' – Josh scribbling in crayon underneath the marker. She could feel the tears welling up in her eyes. The nasty sting behind her face got stronger as she tried not to burst into tears in front of Jason. Taking a moment to compose herself, she sniffed and got up from the kitchen table.

'It's not sick,' she said. 'It's the right thing to do. And you know it Jason, you know it because we hold ourselves to the very best standards, especially with these sorts of things. You always talk about gut instinct, well mine is playing up just now. I'm not convinced that our mystery man is the killer. I'm not convinced Judy Moskowitz is the killer either. All I *am* convinced of is that there could still be a murderer out there and I, *we*, can't stop until they're behind bars.'

'Amita,' he said, but she'd headed out the door. 'Amita wait.' Jason chased after her. She was already pulling on her trainers, getting ready to leave, when he caught up with her.

'Where are you going?' he asked.

'Out,' she said. 'I need to do something, anything. I can't just sit about all day when I'm feeling like this. The police could be making a terrible mistake.'

'Or they could be doing absolutely the right thing,' he said. 'Please don't interfere with Arendonk's business Amita. We're on her good side, in the good books. That's where I'd like to stay for as long as possible, indefinitely even. She did me a big favour with Sheila Mulberry and the hospital incident. I don't want to anger her by wading in when we're not needed.'

'Daddy?' A little voice drifted down from the top of the staircase. Clara was staring down at them, rubbing her eyes and yawning.

'Morning darling,' he said. 'Daddy and gran are just having a little talk. I'll get your breakfast now.' He turned back to his mother-in-law. 'Amita, I don't have time for this just now,' he said. 'I have to get the kids washed and dressed and off to school. Would you please just come back in and think about this for a second?'

'I've been thinking all night Jason,' she said. 'It's all I've been doing. You don't have to worry, I'll keep you out of it.'

'Keep me out of what?'

Amita stood up straight. She thought about not telling her son-in-law what she planned on doing. Maybe that would be for the best. He was right about Arendonk, she didn't want to push the DI's good favour. Not at the moment anyway. She was a good detective. But she might be chasing nothing. Amita couldn't sit around and let that happen.

'I'm going to find our mystery man before the police do – whether it rules him in or out, it will save time,' she said.

'You're *what*?' he asked.

'Daddy.'

'I'll be right there Clara, hold on,' he said. 'Amita, please. You have to let the police do their thing. It's over, let it go.'

'I can't Jason, I really can't. And if I can get to this man before they do then I can find out either way.'

She was right, Jason knew that. He let out a sigh. If he was being completely honest, he couldn't deny that no small part of him believed Amita. The longer it took for the police to catch up with their mystery man, the less convinced he was that they had their culprit. Surely it couldn't take *this* long to find him.

'If Arendonk can't trace him, what makes you think you can?' he asked, a last stab at trying to stop her.

'What's that name you always call me?' she asked, pulling out her phone.

'The Sheriff of Penrith,' he said. 'And you think your network of contacts and busybodies will be able to find him.'

'Maybe not find him,' she said. 'But give us a pointer in the right direction. Odd behaviour and unfamiliar folk are something of a speciality of the bingo club and beyond. Plus we don't trust anyone under forty, you know that.'

'I'll say,' he said.

Amita started furiously typing and swiping on her phone screen. It was quite a vision, Jason thought, to see the inner workings of Penrith's elderly social scene come together so quickly. He still didn't really know how it all worked – something about Facebook pages and group chats. In a way he didn't want to know. It would be like learning how magicians cut their assistants in half then pieced them back together.

'I'm coming with you,' he said.

Amita looked up. 'You are?' she asked.

'Yes. I am.'

'What's changed your mind?'

'Nothing,' he said. 'I'm just chasing after my vulnerable mother-in-law to make sure she's safe. Or at least that's the official line if I'm thrown in a cell for yet more police investigation tampering.'

'Vulnerable?' Amita looked she might lose her glasses lens again but Jason interjected.

'What I will say though is that I think you're right too.'

'You do?' she seemed surprised.

'Yeah. I don't know what the odds are of us finding him first, there's a good chance he's legged it out of Cumbria, even out of the country by now. But I *am* convinced that if anyone could track him down, it's you and the cronies.'

'There's a compliment somewhere in there Jason,' she smiled.

The children began bickering upstairs. Jason laughed.

'You've got an hour to do your stuff,' he said to Amita. 'Then we hit the road, Khatri.'

Chapter 25

FOREST

'Hold on, this could be something,' said Amita, scrolling through the messages on her phone.

'You said that about the last three somethings, Amita, we've been driving about for hours now and aren't any closer to finding our man,' said Jason. 'What we *have* found out from your network is that half of the new estate haven't had their bins collected, someone's scam-selling double glazing in town and that the local supermarket is doing a great deal on fig rolls. Not exactly the kind of laser-sharp intelligence I was hoping for.'

Jason's back was sore and his stomach was grumbling from a lack of breakfast. Those weren't excuses though. He shouldn't be so grumpy given he'd agreed to this magical mystery tour. At least they were getting to see all the nooks and crannies of Penrith. There were worse ways to spend a morning and they had some sightings – just not useful ones – so far.

Amita's contact network of nosey pensioners and do-gooders was throwing tips and leads at them non-stop. Barely five minutes had passed since she put out the call-to-arms and they had their first potential sighting of the mystery man. A distant second cousin of Blair Lightfoot, a casual bingo player from the south side of the town, had noticed some of his clothes had vanished from the line. And there had been rumours abounding on his street about a vagrant sleeping in the communal bin shed. Nobody had been gutsy enough to check it out, so Amita and Jason sped over there immediately.

They didn't find their fugitive in the bin store of Blair Lightfoot's second cousin's flat. Instead it was a pile of old, mouldy clothes that hadn't been collected for years, judging by the smell. The first tip had been a bust, the mystery of Blair's missing clobber would have to wait to be solved another time.

Amita, however, was very positive about the next one. Ethel's home help had apparently been complaining about a strange man hanging around outside the pensioner's cottage to the west of Penrith. As with everything related to Ethel, Amita wanted it checked, double- then triple-checked it was true. According to the group it was all legitimate, Francine, the carer, had been scared stiff to see a face at the window just two nights ago.

What the tipster had failed to mention, however, was her eleven-year-old son who had a penchant for practical jokes. After a quick trip around to Ethel's to speak with the woman herself, Jason and Amita had learned that Francine's panic at the face was in fact nothing more than her son getting bored in the car waiting for his mother. He had crept up to the window as Francine tucked Ethel into bed and scared her witless by standing at the window and tapping ever so lightly.

There had been more tips filtering through but nothing of any great substance. Amita had worried this would be the case. Her extensive network of Cumbrian pensioners were very helpful and their intentions were honest. But a scent of a bit of gossip, a little taste that there could be wrongdoing afoot and they became trigger-happy with what was considered a lead.

That was until the most recent lead. Violet Heatherington had messaged twenty minutes previous to say she'd seen something strange just last night. While Jason had joked that it may have been an uncluttered square foot in that shed of hers, Amita had been more intrigued. Violet's house looked out across the countryside. On a clear day there were miles and miles of uninterrupted rolling hills and dramatic skies. It was the kind of view that showed just why visitors flocked to the Lakes – a quiet grandeur, the type of landscape that made you feel small yet rooted at the same time. Humbling and amazing all in one breath. Violet's view of Cumbria at its finest was one many would pay a fortune to have. And it was all hers. Amita had always been envious.

'You think this is a goer then?' asked Jason.

'She was going to bed and saw something on the horizon last night,' said Amita. 'She said that there's never anything to see up her way, there's nothing around her, full stop. We've seen that for ourselves.'

'What was it she saw again?' he asked.

'Hold on, I'll get the message here,' she flicked back through the chat. 'Something orange and gold, like a fire, that's what she said.'

'A campfire maybe?' he asked. 'There's nothing out that way except the Long Meg and Her Daughters. I can't think of anywhere else anyone would go.'

'If Violet says it's unusual to see something then I'm inclined to believe her,' said Amita. 'She's not given to contributing much to these sorts of things without good reason. And she's the world's biggest doormat. If she says she's seen something then she's seen something. And that stone circle is our best bet.'

Jason agreed. The hedgerows and trees were in full bloom, glossy green leaves shimmering in the morning sunshine.

'Why is it we only get to see the countryside when there's trouble afoot?' he asked, minding the road. 'How come you and I are never just out for a drive to take in the splendour of wild Cumbria?'

'Focus, Jason,' she said. 'If our man is up at the stone circle then we have to be sharp, have to stay in the zone. We can't be filling our heads with your lyrical nonsense just now.'

'It's true though,' he said. 'I can't remember you, me, Radha and the kids just going for a drive in the country. We're always dashing about, running here and there, on the trail of some terrible people, and it's all just here on our doorstep. It's a great shame.'

'Then you can organise the next bank holiday activity, would that make you happy?'

'It wouldn't Amita, you know it wouldn't. I'm all about the here and now. I'm a journalist, news never sleeps.'

'Unlike you.'

'Touche,' he clapped the steering wheel.

They rounded a tight bend in the road as the land around them began to grow a little steeper. Over the crest of the hills, they could just about make out the tips of the neolithic stone circle known as Long Meg and Her Daughters. Jason slowed down as the road got progressively worse. Crawling along the path, the circle opened up in front of them, the road cutting right through the centre.

There was nobody else about. Jason had never been up here before. He'd heard of tourists making the trek from Penrith but he didn't see what the fuss was about.

'It's just a load of old rocks, isn't it?' he said, getting out of the car.

'I never saw the attraction myself, either' said Amita. 'Though there are lots of stories about this place of course, local folklore and the like.'

'I'm not one for myth and legend, Amita. I prefer a cold, hard fact.'

'That's as maybe,' she said as they walked into the centre of the circle. 'Still, I quite liked the one about the stones being witches that were punished by a wizard. And if you can count the uncountable stones twice then the curse will be lifted and it's bad luck for everyone involved.'

'Great,' said Jason, looking about. 'Count the uncountable, makes perfect sense. You should get on to your friend Barry with the website about the cursed painting. Sounds just up his street.' He shaded his eyes from the sunshine. The rocks were all arranged about them, save for the road. He couldn't see anything that immediately pointed to there being anyone here.

'I'm no survival expert,' he said. 'But I reckon it would be pretty exposed and cold up here at night, even in the summer.'

'I agree,' said Amita, looking around too. 'There's that little bit of woodland we drove through to get here but that wouldn't match with Violet's description. It's too far away.'

'Yeah,' said Jason. He took a long, deep breath of the morning air. It was pleasant here, quiet. While camping wasn't quite Jason's scene, he could see why the solitude and the peace would be appealing. 'I think we're on to a hiding to nothing here,' he said. 'There's nothing up here and, more importantly, nobody either.'

Amita reluctantly agreed. She took a long look back around the wide circle of stones. She was about to concede defeat when she decided to do a recce of the largest of the rocks standing outside of the circle. It was tall and jagged, like a shark's tooth protruding from the grass. Amita stepped out of the stone circle and walked over to it. As she drew nearer, she heard something flapping in the breeze. It sounded unnatural, like plastic, completely out of place for the moment.

She reached the tall stone, its peak looming over her, and she peered behind it. A tiny tent was pinned to the ground, the front door unzipped, flap wide open. What looked like the remains of a rudimentary fire were close by, along with empty crisp packets and crushed cans of lager.

'Jason! I've found something!' she shouted.

He joined her. 'Blimey,' he said. 'Somebody had a good time of it.' He reached down and lifted a can. It was premium lager, super strength. The smell almost knocked him on his back and the can was empty.

'Somebody yes,' she said. 'But who?'

They were both startled as the sound of coughing drifted towards them. Amita grabbed Jason and pulled him behind the giant stone. They peered around the edge as a dishevelled figure stumbled up the pathway towards the circle.

'It's him,' whispered Amita.

'Are you sure?' asked Jason.

Amita was certain. She'd spent enough time chasing him to recognise his gait immediately. The mystery man walked with his head bowed. He was wearing the same clothes from the other day, only now they were much filthier. Now he looked rough and tired.

He walked up the path, Jason and Amita watching every step. He passed through the edge of the circle and was about to make for the giant stone when he stopped.

'Oh no,' said Amita.

'What?' whispered Jason.

'He's spotted the car.'

As if hearing Amita's revelation, the man immediately looked up towards the large rock. He quickly turned and tried to run but stumbled, tripping over his own feet and landing hard on the gravel path.

'Get him!' Amita shouted, sprinting off after him.

'Not again,' moaned Jason, following her.

Before the mystery man could get back on his feet, Amita was on him. She jumped on his back and he let out a wheeze, a plume of gravel and dust kicked up from his breath.

'Stay where you are!' she said. 'This is a citizen's arrest.'

'What are you talking about? Get off me!' he demanded.

'You have the right to remain silent. You have the right to... eh, how does it go again? A solicitor, you have the right to a solicitor, I think that's it.'

'Get off me!'

The mystery man wriggled about beneath Amita but she had him pinned down tight. Jason came lugging up behind them, out of breath and sweating.

'Alright Amita, let him up, you've made your point,' he said.

'It's a citizen's arrest Jason, I don't want him taking off like he did before, especially if it's for his own good.'

'Get off me!' he shouted.

'Get off him Amita.'

She thought about staying put. Then conceded. She climbed off. He rolled over, his face covered in grit, clothes even filthier. He coughed and spluttered, the smell of booze reeking off him.

'Are you alright, mate?' asked Jason, helping him to sit up.

'Yes, I'm fine,' he said. 'No thanks to you two.'

'Just doing my duty,' said Amita. 'Now you have to promise me that you're not going to run away this time. We're here to help you.'

'Help me?' he gave a disgusted laugh. 'Nobody can help me now. If I could be helped I wouldn't be camping out in the middle of nowhere drinking myself to death.' He slumped his shoulders.

'You're going to be okay,' she said. 'We're here to help, regardless of what you've done.'

'Or not done,' added Jason.

'I haven't done anything,' he said. 'That's the point. My life has been snatched away from me, ripped up and put in the bin without as much as a so long, good luck. Look at me, I'm a mess. I stink, I haven't had a shower in days and I'm living like a... like a... like god knows what. I'm a professional, an accountant. I have a flat, a life, I make good money. It's all gone. Just like that, all away.' He snapped his fingers.

Amita looked up at Jason. He wasn't sure what to think or say. The mystery man seemed genuine enough. Why would he make all of that up? Unless he had a murder charge he wanted to dodge. It was very confusing.

'Come on, let's get you indoors for a minute,' he said, offering the mystery man his hand. 'I think there's a flask of something warm in the car.'

'Glad I brought that,' said Amita, also helping him.

The mystery man nodded. He got to his feet and they walked over to the parked car. Climbing in, Amita poured some tea from the Thermos and gave it to him.

'Now I want you to get some of this into your system,' she said. 'It's not rocket fuel or any of that other ghastly stuff we found at your campsite. It's good, old fashioned tea and it'll warm you up a treat.'

'Thank you,' said the mystery man sadly, taking the cup. 'I've been desperate for a cuppa for days. I was starting to think I wouldn't ever get one again.' He slurped the tea down in one gulp then stared at the empty cup. Tears rolled down his filthy cheeks and he sniffed. 'I'm sorry,' he said. 'I just... I just don't think I can cope.'

'That's what we're here for,' said Amita.

'You are?' he asked.

'We'll try, won't we Jason,' she said.

'Oh yeah, we'll try alright,' said Jason. 'It might not come to much but we always give it a try.'

The mystery man smiled at that. He sniffed again and wiped his nose. 'Thank you,' he said.

'That's quite alright,' said Amita. 'I want you to take a long, deep breath and calm yourself down. Then I want you to tell us everything you know about Hal Mulberry and what happened to him. But first, before any of that, I would very much like to know your name.'

The mystery man nodded. He took a moment as Amita had instructed him, wiping his face and taking long breaths that made his chest puff out. When he was ready, he looked at both Amita and Jason, his mind beginning to make sense of everything he was about to say. Then he started.

'Okay,' he said. 'It's Gill. My name is Martin Gill. And I was Hal Mulberry's lover.'

Chapter 26

UNTITLED (1952)

Martin sat with his hands clasped, staring off out of the windscreen at the stone circles and countryside beyond. The tea he had just drunk could do little to assuage what he'd been through. His head was aching, his tongue furry, the remnants of the awful lager he'd poured into his body the last two nights.

As painful as the fallout of his hangover was, it didn't compare to that of losing Hal. Every time he closed his eyes he could see his face staring back at him, smiling. There had been no final arguments, no cross words exchanged when they had last seen each other. If anything it had been perfect, beautiful even, a moment that they'd both remember for the rest of their lives. That much was true for Martin at least. It would be forever the final memory he had of the man he loved.

'You have to believe me that I had nothing to do with Hal's murder,' said Martin. 'I was just as shocked as everyone else when I found out what happened. It's not the sort of thing you expect to wake up to after you've left your beloved to have a night that was meant to be the culmination of a lifelong dream.'

'How long had you two been together?' asked Jason. 'And I take it nobody knew about it?'

'No, nobody knew, nobody publicly at least,' Martin continued. 'We'd been seeing each other discreetly for about a year when Sheila found out.'

'His wife knew then?' said Amita.

'Oh yes, she knew, she knew all about it,' said Martin.

'And she was okay with it?' asked Jason.

'I wouldn't say that,' he went on. 'But I wasn't the first person Hal had been in a relationship with while married to her. He wasn't happy with her, you have to understand that. But he is, was, a man of a certain generation that always worried about his public reputation. That's why he kept his "other side" – as he liked to call it – quiet.'

'But it's the twenty-first century,' said Jason. 'Surely a prominent businessman, a potential role model like Hal wouldn't have anything to fear. If anything, he could set a good example for others.'

'You're very sweet, Jason,' said Martin, smiling a sad smile. 'In a perfect world, maybe that's how it works. We don't live in a perfect world I'm afraid. And our relationship was a victim of that.'

'A dreadful shame,' said Amita, shaking her head. 'How did you meet him?'

'I work for him,' said Martin. 'Or at least I did. I don't know what they'd say at the office if I turned up looking like this.' He surveyed his filthy, torn clothes. 'I'm an accountant, like I said. I worked in the finance department of his exports business. It was the usual sort of thing, an office Christmas party. I'd love to say there was some universal force that pulled us together, a regular Romeo and Juliet, but in the end it was just opportunity. Well that and some Bollinger. There were always whispers about Hal and his extra-marital affairs, but nothing concrete. However, when the boss of the company invites you onto the roof with champagne, you get lost in the moment.'

'You said it was more than just a fling though,' said Jason. 'You were in a relationship.'

Martin shifted uncomfortably. He rubbed his eyes, face etched in pain. 'I thought it was just a casual thing at first,' he said. 'But Hal kept calling me. We went out, I suppose you could call them dates, I don't know if that word is what I'd call them. You didn't date Hal Mulberry, you just went along for the ride while he threw money at anything and everything that moved. He was speaking at an international trade conference in Oslo, just before Christmas, and wangled a ticket for me. It was a wonderful few days, just the two of us. He dropped the act, the big business macho stuff when we were alone. It changed everything. I loved him. I knew it then and I know it now. I loved him more than I've ever loved anyone or anything before.'

He started to cry. Amita reached to console him but he waved her away. 'No, no, I'm fine,' he said. 'I'm okay. I have to get this off my chest, I have to tell someone. It's been eating me up ever since Hal died. I can't keep living like this, living in secret.'

'You said that Sheila knew,' said Jason. 'And you told Amita that you thought she was trying to blame you for Hal's murder. Why would she do something like that? And forgive me Martin, she's not exactly been throwing you under the bus in public. You've not been named, and the police didn't know anything about you.'

'Sheila is a clever woman,' Martin said. 'She knows that she can't just name someone random and not expect questions. The last thing she wants is for it all to come out about Hal's affairs. Especially when she's eyeing a run at parliament.'

'She's what?' asked Jason. 'She wants to be an MP?'

Martin nodded. He smiled, bitterly and looked out of the rear window. 'She wants to rule the world,' he said. 'Sheila Mulberry is one of the most manipulative, vindictive women I've ever had the misfortune of meeting. The way she speaks to people in private, the way she treats them, it's disgusting. I could tell you stories about her cruelty to the men and women who worked for Hal. I've known colleagues who have lost their jobs because they didn't hold a lift door for Her Majesty when she was making one of her rare visits to the offices.'

'We had a suspicion she was a bit like that,' said Amita.

'Let's not deal in speculation here,' said Jason. 'Things are serious enough Martin, the police are after you on the suspicion you're Hal's murderer.'

'I know,' he said. 'I know that. That's why I've been hiding since it happened. A friend of a friend told me that Sheila has been talking about me to the police, spreading rumours about my background. I don't have a background, you have to believe me. I grew up in Watford, I went to a normal school. I didn't smoke pot at university and I pay all my taxes. Why the hell would I murder a man that I wanted to spend the rest of my life with?'

'Do the police know about your affair and Hal's private life?' asked Jason.

'I don't know,' said Martin. 'I don't know. I just needed to get out of here, leave Penrith, start somewhere new.'

'So why didn't you go?' asked Amita. 'You can't be short of money, you're a young professional. Why not jump on a plane and never look back?'

Martin's face went blank. He stared off into the distance, not looking at anything.

'I couldn't bring myself to leave not knowing who did that to him,' he said. 'The thought of not being near Hal, even though he was… he was dead, it made me feel sick. I just had to be close to him, I had to know there was going to be justice served. I didn't want to lose him any more than he was already gone. That sounds silly, I know how mad that sounds. But I couldn't go, I just couldn't. That's why I've been living like this these past few days, weeks too maybe, I've lost track of time.'

'Oh Martin,' she took his hand.

This time Martin let her touch him. He broke down as she squeezed his hand. 'I'd been lying low. But I had to see the painting,' he said. 'Hal had talked about it so often, he was obsessed with it. He used to get so giddy when he was talking about it. I only went in on a whim – I assumed it would have been whisked away the night it all happened. He was such a kind and generous man. The world only knew a fraction of that. But I got to see that side of him almost every day. Just little moments when we were together, little gestures or a word here and there. All of that is gone now. When I saw the painting it brought it all back. This was everything to him. I couldn't even bring myself to leave that hall. That's when you two arrived. I had to run, I couldn't think of anything else. I panicked, just seeing other people. That's what this has done to me, it's made me so paranoid that I don't know what I'm doing anymore. I need help.' He sat back in the seat and held his hands to his face, crying.

Amita could only look on, helpless.

After a moment of gentle crying, Martin rubbed his face. 'I need a cigarette,' he said sniffing. 'Can you both give me a minute, just to get my head together.'

'Of course,' said Amita.

'Don't go too far,' said Jason, but Martin was already out the door.

He circled around the back of the car. Jason watched him in the rear-view mirror the whole time.

'He didn't murder Hal,' Amita whispered.

'We don't know that,' said Jason. 'We've only heard his side of the story.'

'And it's a pretty compelling story, Jason. Do *you* think he killed Hal or had anything to do with it?'

'No, but that's not the point,' he said. 'It doesn't matter what I think or what you think. There's a murder investigation ongoing and this guy has been acting suspiciously. He's also a secret lover of the victim, that means the police need to know. And we can't just leave him like this. It wouldn't be safe for any of us.'

Amita agreed.

The back door of the car opened. Martin climbed back in, the smell of smoke drifting in with him. He looked miserable, fatigued, great bags under his bloodshot eyes and a layer of grime coating every inch of him.

'Martin, you're going to be okay,' she said. 'Now I don't want you to panic. But we're going to take you to the police.'

'No!' he said, sitting forward suddenly. 'No, I can't go to the police. They'll throw away the key.'

'We'll speak for you, mate,' said Jason. 'We'll explain how we found you, how we came across you. All you have to do is tell them the truth.'

'The easiest thing in the world is to tell the truth,' said Amita.

Martin looked devastated and weary, like the fight had left him.

'You just need to let the police know everything you know,' she said. 'If you're innocent then you have nothing to worry about. But the longer you're on the run, the longer you stay living in the wilderness, the more it'll look like you've got something to hide.'

'She's right,' chimed Jason. 'You don't want to make yourself look like you've done something when it's the opposite. We know the investigating officer, she's fair and a decent person too. She got me off with a little run-in I had with Sheila Mulberry, so she knows what she's like.'

Martin nodded. Amita offered her hand again.

'I'm sorry all of this has happened,' she said. 'Losing somebody you love is one of the worst feelings anyone can ever go through. Believe me Martin, I know, I've been through it too many times. It never stops hurting – but you do get better at living with it, things always get better.'

'Yeah, that's what I tell myself,' he laughed bitterly. 'It doesn't feel that way to me right now though. It feels like my soul was killed the same way Hal was. And it hurts *so* much that I wish it would all just go away.'

'You'll be okay,' said Amita. 'And it sounds like Hal wouldn't want you to do anything stupid. He'd want you to take care of yourself, now he's not around to.'

She nodded at Jason to start the car.

'What about Hal's reputation, his legacy? Won't all of this ruin that?' he asked.

'That's not for us to decide, I'm afraid,' said Jason, looking at him in the rear-view mirror. 'People will think what they want to, you can't control that. I know, I'm a journalist. What they make of Hal Mulberry because of your relationship and everything else is entirely up to them. You have to do what you feel is the right thing, Martin. We all do.'

'I know,' he said sadly. 'I know.'

Jason turned the car around and started on the road back to Penrith. They left Long Meg and Her Daughters behind as the day started to wear on. The stones stood firm in his rear-view mirror, as they had for centuries. The thirty great lumps of rock had doubtless borne witness to stranger things than this sorry affair since they began their watch, thought Jason. He wasn't sorry to see their silhouettes vanish from view.

Chapter 27

THE SEED OF THE AREOI

Neither Jason nor Amita spoke much very much on the drive back to town. They didn't need to. They both knew what the other was thinking and how they didn't want to say it out loud.

The case was wide open again and their investigations had been a bust. The only positive lead they had had was now sat in the back of their car. And they were convinced that he wasn't the man who murdered Hal Mulberry.

Martin hadn't spoken a word either since they left the countryside. Jason kept checking on him, making sure he was still alive at least. All the young man did was stare out of the window at the world zipping past.

He had a great deal of sympathy for Martin Gill. Sure, he didn't trust him, not fully. That was just part of his job as a journalist. However, he understood the plight that Martin was facing. His world had been completely ripped apart in one small moment. Jason couldn't really imagine being put in a similar position with Radha, the kids and Amita. The thought alone made him a little queasy.

All he could do for Martin was take him to the authorities and let them sort it all out. If that saw the young man let off or thrown in jail, it really wasn't up to him.

He swung the car around. The road outside Penrith Police Station was unusually busy. A number of patrol cars were parked up on the street and there were other motors packing the spaces. Across the road from the main entrance was a van with a satellite dish perched on the top. Jason's stomach churned.

'What's all this about?' asked Amita. 'Why is it so busy?'

'I don't know,' said Jason. 'But if I didn't know better, I'd say the press pack was on the prowl.'

'Press? Journalists?' Martin leaned forward, peering between the two. 'What do you mean press? I don't want them to see me, not like this, not at all.'

'He's right Jason. It wouldn't be fair. You know what your colleagues are like, they take one little thing and run a mile with it. If we march him through the front door of the station his face will be on every newspaper and bulletin by teatime,' said Amita.

'Would you two just calm down,' he said, parking up. 'We don't know this is press. It could be anything, a training day, some sort of police summit.'

'In Penrith?' Amita and Martin said together.

Jason switched off the engine. They sat staring up the street at the police station for a moment. Jason had a bad feeling about this. He'd seen these sorts of scenes before. He could play devil's advocate all he wanted. But this smelled of a press feeding frenzy.

'Go in and find out what's happening,' said Amita.

'What? Me?' he asked.

'Yes you,' she said. 'You can go in and see what's going on and report back to us. Or give us a signal if the coast is clear and all of these cars have nothing to do with anything.'

'Why me? Why don't you go?'

'Because I'm not a journalist, Jason. If this is some sort of media event, you can at least make your excuses and leave. We can't just throw poor Martin out of the car like that. He deserves confidentiality.'

'If he's innocent.'

'You should know better than to say something like that, Jason. We are *all* innocent until proven guilty,' Amita huffed.

'I *am* innocent,' Martin said angrily.

Jason drummed his fingers on the steering wheel. He didn't like this at all. The prospect of stumbling into a press pack in his current state didn't appeal to him. The word would be out by now that he'd been dropped by the London tabloid. He didn't need sympathetic pats on the back and questions on his welfare. Or worse, he didn't want the judgemental stares and sly remarks. Smiffy would surely be there too. The less time he spent in the company of that jumped-up little know-it-all was a blessing.

'Bloody hell,' he said. 'Is there really no other way around this? Couldn't we come back later?'

'You know we can't do that,' said Amita. 'Time is of the essence in an investigation like this. Go on, we'll wait right here.'

Jason cursed under his breath. He opened the door and looked up and down the street. As he walked towards the station, he really wished he'd worn something a bit smarter than a washed-out T-shirt and battered old jeans and trainers. He hadn't quite expected to be making the leap back into journalism so quickly. Who was he kidding, he'd dress like this every hour of every day if he could.

Trudging up the steps, he paused and looked back up the road at his car. Amita was shooing him in from the passenger seat, Martin cowering in the back.

'Bloody hell,' he said again. 'What an absolute shamble–'

Jason was cut off by the door of the station swinging open. It bashed him in the face, mashing his nose. He stumbled back, foot slipping on the well-trodden step. Losing his balance, he flailed around wildly before hopping, skipping and finally jumping back down onto the pavement.

A gaggle of news reporters flooded out from the police station, washing past him like he wasn't there. A cameraman barged past, shouldering him out of the way as he tried to get his bearings back. Touching his nose and top lip, he tasted blood. Although none of his professional brethren seemed to care. None of them, except Ayanna Smith.

'Jesus Brazel, what happened to you?' she asked, swaggering down the steps. 'You look like you've had a fight with a revolving door. You still not got the hang of those things yet?'

'Smiffy,' he said. 'I'm really not in the mood for your effervescent humour right now.'

'Oi!' she shouted. 'What did I tell you about calling me Smiffy? It makes me sound like a football pundit.' She jabbed him in the chest with her pen.

Jason winced. He blinked, rubbing his nose. 'I think I've lost a tooth!' he said.

'Let me see,' said Smiffy, standing on her tiptoes.

Jason leaned down and opened his mouth. Smiffy stared for a moment at him, then grabbed his nose between her thumb and forefinger. She cranked it upwards and he let out a loud shriek of pain.

'What was that for?' he said, pulling free and cupping his nose in his hands. 'Are you insane?'

'That's for calling me Smiffy,' she said. 'And for being such a big wet blanket. There's nothing wrong with your teeth. When I was twelve, a girl in my school bit a boy's lip so hard that she went right through the skin. Now *that* is pain.'

Jason didn't know where to start with that one. He rubbed his nose and top lip until the pain started to subside. When it did, he was able to think straight again.

'What are you doing here anyway? This press conference was just for real reporters,' said Smiffy.

'I *am* a real reporter,' he fired back. 'And have been since you were hanging around with cannibals.'

'You didn't answer my question,' she said.

'Why I'm here is none of your business,' he said. 'But given I have seniority in both experience and years as a journalist, you can tell me what the press conference was all about.'

'You don't know?' she gave him an odd look.

'If I knew I wouldn't be stooping to the indignity of asking you, would I?'

'Are you serious? You don't know what's going on? I thought you said you used to be an actual reporter.'

'Smith, I'm not in the mood to play these juvenile games,' he said, going into full dad-mode. 'Either tell me or I'll find somebody who will.'

'Sheila Mulberry has been arrested,' said Smiffy.

'What?' Any lingering pain had now gone. Replacing it was a state of disbelief.

'Yeah,' said Smiffy. 'She's been held on suspicion of Hal Mulberry's murder.'

'I don't believe it,' he said. 'I mean, I can't believe it. She's not been charged yet?'

'No, not yet,' said the young reporter. 'Can't say I'm all that surprised. These things are usually the scorned wife or husband. I would have thought even you bumpkins up here in Cumbria would have been able to work that one out.'

'Sheila Mulberry has been arrested.' Jason repeated as if we was reading the headlines on the local news. But he supposed she had always been a prime suspect. The fact she was the last person to see Hal alive. The dramatic breakdown at the scene. Even the police appeal where she'd called out Jason all seemed forced, as if to take the scrutiny off her. And if Martin Gill was telling the truth about her spreading lies and rumours about him, it made sense she would try to deflect from her own guilt.

'Blimey,' he said. 'What are the police saying? Have they given you any off the record guidance on how they caught her?'

'As if I would tell you that,' snorted Smiffy.

'You've been told nothing then,' said Jason.

She didn't reply. She nudged past him, pulling out her phone. Jason was going to say something bitter, something smart, but he dallied too long. He would have to settle for taking the moral high ground instead.

The last of the press pack had gone now, roaring away in their cars and vans to all file the same story. Their hands would be tied behind their backs now that there had been an arrest. Nobody wanted to risk being held in contempt, or prejudicing the case by spilling any juicy details they'd learned on the side. That wasn't going to stop Jason though, he had to know.

He marched up the steps to the front doors and gave them an extra hard shove – revenge for the earlier confrontation. His momentum took him into the lobby where the same desk sergeant was still sitting, wrestling with her computer.

'DI Arendonk please,' said Jason.

'She's just busy with the press at the moment, sir,' said the policewoman. 'If you'd like to take a seat I'm sure she'll–'

'Brazel!'

Jason swung around. Sally Arendonk was in full flight, papers and files in hand, making her look even more dynamic than usual. Jason was caught up in the wake of her force as she swept through the lobby.

'Sally, you've arrested Sheila Mulberry,' he said, trying to keep up with her.

'Yes, we have,' she said. 'I thought you would have been at the press conference.'

'No, I didn't know there was one. I mean, my hands were full with something else.'

They pushed through a set of doors. Jason probably wasn't allowed to be in here but nobody was stopping him. Arendonk was busy signing forms as she moved.

'Life moves fast, you know that,' she said. 'One minute you're on the hunt for a mystery man that a couple of concerned local citizens have brought to your attention, the next you're finding a bloody knife in the recycling of a murdered tycoon's mansion. Funny old world, isn't it?'

'Is that what happened?' asked Jason. 'You raided the Mulberry place.'

'Didn't have to,' said the DI. 'We got a tip-off around three this morning saying that something dodgy had been found at the rear of the property. Local squad car takes a swing by, finds the murder weapon wrapped up in newspaper from the day of the murder. I think it had one of your bylines in it actually.'

Jason wasn't sure if he should be happy or mortified.

'I get my warrant, we knock on the door and grab Dr Mulberry and boom, we have an arrest. Simple as that.'

'Yeah,' said Jason. 'That does sound simple when you think about it. So that's it then?'

They came to a stop outside the security door of the CID squad room. Jason was relieved, he didn't think he could keep up with Arendonk for much further.

'You know how this works Jason,' she said, sighing. 'We've still got to put a credible case together to charge Sheila with Hal's murder. A bloody knife among the Waitrose flyers doesn't immediately point to guilt. But it's safe to say it's the breakthrough we've been looking for all this time. And about time too, my superiors were starting to get squeaky bums. Not exactly the best look for a new DI on her first big murder case, you'll agree.'

'No, I know what you mean,' he said. 'What's your feeling on Sheila being the killer though? You must have a theory Sally, otherwise you wouldn't be this happy.'

'I don't get happy at murder cases Jason,' she smiled. 'But I do get happy when I've got somebody sitting waiting to be interviewed who fits the profile of a potential killer. Hal Mulberry was a saint to some, but he was also a sinner. We know about his affairs and we know that things weren't too hot between him and his wife behind closed doors. But she's got ambitions, Jason, big ones. And it wouldn't fit the public optics if she was fresh from a lucrative divorce from her philanthropist husband, would it?'

'No, it wouldn't,' he agreed. 'But you must know Sally, you must *know* if there's enough to charge her.'

Arendonk sighed again. 'Strictly off the record, we'll have to wait and see,' she said. 'I might not be in this job very long, but I've seen enough cases fall through right at the last hurdle over a lack of credible evidence. It's rotten luck and even worse for wider society to see bad guys and girls walk free, especially when you know they did it.'

'And you think Sheila Mulberry did it?' he asked. 'You think she killed Hal?'

Arendonk swiped her security card on the scanner beside the door. The little light turned from red to green and she stepped inside.

'You won't catch me out like that Brazel. It doesn't matter what I think,' she said. 'It's what the truth is that matters. My job is to find out what that is. You know it yourself, sometimes it doesn't present itself in a nice, easy, ready to wrap up with a bow manner, it takes digging. A bloody knife in a bin is a pretty good start though, right?'

'Right,' he said.

She gave him a cordial smile and closed the door. It locked firmly and he was left alone in the draughty corridor of the police station. He shoved his hands in his pockets and started walking back towards the lobby, hoping he was going the right way.

Sheila Mulberry had been arrested, a knife found in her rubbish. If all the forensics reports checked out, it would be confirmed as the murder weapon. Jason was certain that would be the case. Yet something still didn't feel right, it didn't feel *real*. If Sheila Mulberry had been putting up with multiple affairs just to keep up appearances so she could make a Westminster bid, why would she suddenly bump him off? And a woman like that, clever enough to play the long game, would she discard the murder weapon outside her own house?

Arendonk's lack of confidence and glib ambiguity weren't helping him either. Much as he desperately wanted somebody to tell him that this whole incident was over, that the killer was caught and rotting away in jail, catching the wrong person was worse than catching no one at all. He had a terrible sense about what he had to do next, so he could move on, mourn for Hal and try to put it all behind him. He knew Amita felt the same. Still, he wasn't looking forward to explaining all of this to her.

To Jason's surprise, as he gingerly exited a pair of swinging doors, wary of getting another blow, there was his mother-in-law standing at the front desk with Martin Gill, the pair of them looking about like lost children in a museum.

'Oh good, there you are,' she shouted. 'I'm trying to explain to the lovely policewoman behind the desk who Mr Gill is and how they've made a desperate mistake in trying to pin Hal Mulberry's murder on him.'

'She has been,' agreed Martin. 'And been saying some lovely things about me too. Thank you, Amita.'

'A pleasure Martin.'

'It's okay,' said Jason. 'That ship has sailed, they won't be searching for you anymore.'

Amita and Martin looked a little surprised. Then they looked at each other.

'Are you alright?' asked Amita. 'I saw you get bashed in the face by the door. Has it given you a concussion or something?'

'What? No, I'm fine,' he said. 'I've just spoken to DI Arendonk there, she's the one leading the investigation. You're not going to believe what's happened.'

'Try us,' said Amita.

He took a deep breath. 'Sheila Mulberry has been arrested for Hal's murder,' he said.

At first neither Amita nor Martin said anything. They needed a moment to process the bombshell, just like Jason. He was only glad there was still somebody left to tell.

'Is this true?' she asked the desk sergeant.

The policewoman politely nodded. Amita patted her chest.

'Looks like you're in the clear Martin.'

The young accountant stood perfectly still. His eyes had filled with tears, his mouth trembling. Eventually he couldn't hold his grief in any longer. He bowed his head and began to cry. Amita wrapped her arms around him and brought him in close for a hug.

'It's okay Martin,' she said. 'Everything's going to be alright now. What did I tell you, the darkest hour is always just before the dawn. Things always get better.'

Chapter 28

FIRE IN THE EVENING

Amita didn't feel much like celebrating. There was no glory to be had in someone's gruesome death, an arrest didn't bring them back. She had thought twice about joining Jason and Radha on their night out, but they had both insisted she needed a break. A break from the kids, a break from bingo, a break from her investigations.

So here she was. Sat in a pub where the music was too loud, the lights were too dim and the smell of drink and bad cooking almost knocked her on her back as soon as she set foot in the place. If Radha hadn't suggested the impromptu evening out, she most likely would have never set foot in the place. But Amita thought they might deserve some relief after the past few weeks.

Jason wasn't helping the frivolities much. He had sat across from her at their table all night looking worn out and miserable. In many ways she couldn't blame him. The last few weeks had taken their toll on both of them. Everything about the Mulberry case had felt like it was designed to pull the rug from under their feet. Every answer they found only pointed to more questions. Even now they hung heavy in the air – why had Sheila wielded the knife? Was the curse of the painting back to prove them wrong for doubting it? And what really was going to happen to the village hall now its new benefactor was dead and his estate in the hands of someone on a murder charge?

'There we are,' said Radha, arriving with a tray of fresh drinks. 'Large red for me, a gin and tonic for you mum and a pint of bitter for the man of the house.'

'Thanks love,' said Jason, taking his drink.

'I think it was my round Radha,' said Amita.

'It's alright, I've got a tab open,' she said, sitting down.

'Blimey, get the drinks in fast Radha, before your mother backs down from actually paying for a round.'

'I'd consider it an act of charity buying a drink for the unemployed and down on their luck, Jason,' Amita responded.

'Could you two calm down please,' said Radha, sitting between them. 'This is my first night out without the kids in about a zillion years. And it's my first night out with just you two in even longer. Could we keep the comedy lessons to ourselves please.'

Jason nodded. Amita did the same.

'Thank you,' she said, sipping at her wine. 'Did Irvine not want to join us tonight mum?'

Jason sniggered into his pint. They both darted him a quick disapproving look.

'No, I didn't think to invite him,' said Amita.

'That's a shame. Are you two still getting on?'

'Oh yes, splendidly,' said Amita.

'Then why not bring him along?'

'I guess there's been an awful lot going on recently.'

'There's no time for romance when you're Cumbria's answer to Miss Marple is there?' chuckled Jason.

'Oh would you look at that,' said Radha. 'My drink's finished. Would you go up and get us another round in Jason?'

He looked at her glass. 'But it's full.'

Radha tipped her head back and downed the wine in one gulp. She slammed it back on the table, winced as she swallowed and slid it over to him.

'There, satisfied?' she asked.

Jason wandered up to the bar. He lazily looked about the room, hoping that Smiffy wouldn't be in. He wondered if she was headed back down to London now that there had been an arrest. All of the colour surrounding the story would have to wait until the trial, if Sheila was in fact charged. Dealing with the young reporter had been one of the contributors to his fatigue. It wasn't that he disliked the youthful exuberance of new journalists. He just found them all a little intimidating. That's why he'd never considered teaching. Being in a room full of student hacks all eager to make names for themselves was about as bad a nightmare as they came for Jason.

The drinks arrived and he put them on the tab. He was about to start back to the table when a heavy clap on his shoulder stopped him.

'Large brandy please barman,' came a familiar voice from behind. 'And stick it on this one's slate, would you? He owes me one.'

Jason didn't need to turn around to know who it was. The stench of the Brylcreem that kept Frank Alby's combover in place was an immediate giveaway. The retired detective inspector sidled up beside Jason and gave him a disconcerting smile, his broken capillary-marked face looking like a clown's mask.

'Frank, hello,' he said politely. 'You're looking ... well.'

'You're a liar Brazel, always have been, always will be,' said the former cop. 'Still, it's nice to see you actually putting your hand in your pocket for a change. I always had you down as a skinflint.'

'Just one of the many infamous misconceptions about me DI Alby. Although it only ever seems to be fake facts you catch on to about me, not the truth. Funny that.'

'Isn't it?' Alby laughed.

The barman delivered the ex-detective his drink. DI Alby pursed his lips and sipped at it almost delicately.

'How have you been then? Keeping out of trouble?' he asked Jason.

'I'm sorry, who are you and what have you done with the real Frank Alby?' asked Jason. 'Since when did you give a hoot as to how I was and whether I was keeping out of trouble or not. In fact, I seem to recall you went out of your way to make sure I was *in* some sort of bother towards the end of your career. Isn't that right?'

'I'm a changed man now Brazel, completely changed,' he puffed out his chest, belt straining under the pressure of his gut. 'Since retirement I've learned to let go of all of my anger and rage. I just coast on through life now, always searching the horizon for a new tomorrow.'

'Wow,' said Jason. 'That was almost poetic.'

'I know, what a load of cobblers, eh?' said Alby. 'The wife enrolled me in an online anger management class. She said I was carrying too much rage with me. And that if I let go of it now then I might live long enough to enjoy my retirement, grandkids, great grandkids, you know the script. My god but it's a load of old tosh, Brazel. Not as bad as the kind of stuff you write, right enough. But not far off it.'

Jason kind of took that as a compliment. Although he wasn't sure he was supposed to. Frank Alby was probably one of the angriest men he had ever met. That included an endless list of newspaper editors who were stressed from the moment they got up to when they didn't go to bed the next night. He suddenly thought of putting Alby in touch with Arnold Beeston. They would be united by a hatred of him and they could set the record straight in a way only men with a common enemy could.

'Well it's been nice seeing you and all Frank, but my family is waiting,' said Jason, keen to not be in the former DI's company for too long.

'Family? Here?' sniffed Alby. 'That mother-in-law of yours with you then?'

'Amita, yes, she's over there,' he nodded.

'Oh aye, I heard about your antics,' Alby nodded. 'Couple of old friends still behind the desk told me you'd been sticking your nose into this Mulberry murder. You were mates with him, weren't you?'

Before Jason answered he had to remind himself that Alby was retired. He held no special sway, no influence, not even a whisper of an ability to fit him up with something he wasn't guilty of. He was safe.

'Not that it's any of your business Frank, but yes, I considered him a friend,' he said. 'And he'll be a huge loss to the charity sector of Penrith now that he's gone.'

'I'll bet,' he said. 'Who's going to pay for the WI's trips to Monaco and the Seychelles now, eh?' The old policeman laughed. He swirled his brandy glass then took another delicate sip. 'What do you think of it all then?' he asked.

'What do I think of all what?' asked Jason pointedly.

'Mulberry's murder. The wife being nicked. What's your thoughts?'

Jason didn't answer straight away. He wanted to try and outsmart Alby at whatever game it was he was playing. He replaced the tray with the drinks and took up his own pint. Stalling for time, he sipped from his second fresh pint in ten minutes.

'I think that your replacement is a fair and honest copper and I trust her to have made the right call.'

Alby's moustache twitched a little and Jason could see his already ruddy face reddening further.

'Was that what you wanted to hear?' he asked.

'You're on the wind up Brazel, and I'm not going to rise to it. Calm blue ocean and all that jazz.'

'Quite right too,' said Jason, taking another sip.

If he was being honest, this conversation wasn't as bad as he had expected. Alby was like a bulldog with its teeth removed. He posed no real threat anymore and without the long arm of the law behind him, he was little more than another angry little man in the pub.

'Arendonk is fine, if that's the sort of thing you're after in a DI,' Alby continued.

'What sort of thing?' asked Jason.

'She's thorough, I'll give her that. But it wouldn't take much for a skirt to walk into a job like mine these days.'

'Ah, I see,' Jason said. 'I'm going to pretend you didn't just say something abysmally sexist and instead what you meant to say was that she's an intelligent, diligent, educated woman who has progressive attitudes and opinions that are in-line with the rest of twenty-first century thinking. I bet she's never even *heard* of *The Sweeney*, Frank.'

That touched a nerve. Jason could see Alby's hands flexing into little fists beside him. The tendons in his cheeks were doing the same. Suddenly the thought that a rabid bulldog, even without teeth, could still be something unpleasant. He decided to cool his tactics.

'Like I said, she's a good copper and she appears to have the right person locked up.'

Alby seemed to calm down at that. He leaned on the bar and rolled something around with his tongue. 'You're not convinced, are you?' he said.

Jason wasn't sure if it was the implication or the words the former detective had used. Regardless, he felt like he'd been punched square between the eyes. Hearing his worst, suppressed fears spoken out loud was enough to make Jason feel a little queasy. Again.

'What do you mean?' was all Jason was able to manage.

Alby smelled blood, like a shark with a rumbling stomach.

'You don't, do you?' he asked. 'You don't think Arendonk has the right killer. The wife, Sheila Mulberry. You think it sort of makes sense but it won't hold up in court. Hell, I don't even think they've charged her yet.'

'They haven't,' said Jason, counting the hours since the arrest in his head.

'Wasn't like that in my day,' Alby whistled. 'The whole force is getting panicky Brazel, jumping to half-baked conclusions for the sake of a nick. Pressure from the powers that be to have someone in custody when they should be out finding who really did it. It won't do. And your precious Arendonk is going to feel it from up on high when Mulberry's lawyers prove she's got nothing to do with old Hal's murder.'

'Why are you telling me all of this?' asked Jason. 'What do you care?'

'Hey, I was a copper for most of my life,' he said, slamming his hand down on the bar. 'I still care about what's right and what's wrong. And I don't like the thought there's still some bloody maniac out there.'

Jason couldn't argue with that. So he didn't.

'The spurned wife and husband routine is as old as the ark,' said Alby. 'But it's too neat. Sheila Mulberry might spend tonight and tomorrow in the cells but there'll be something to get her off, something won't add up. And that's when Arendonk has a problem on her hands. She's nicked a political hopeful, weeks after her husband's murder *and* the killer is still at large. I wouldn't like to be in her size sevens when that happens.' He swirled his brandy, drained the glass and then clapped Jason on the shoulder. 'Anyway, can't say it was pleasant seeing you again Brazel,' said Alby. 'I've had better nights after a spicy ruby murray. Still, always nice to talk shop with somebody I suppose. See you around.'

He left the bar, Jason himself was a little speechless. Everything the former cop had said made perfect sense. It all hinged on the evidence of the bloody knife but that could easily be planted.

'Hold on, Frank!' he called after him.

Alby stopped just outside the door. Jason pushed his way through the gathered smokers catching the last of the summer sunshine.

'What would you do?' he asked him.

'Eh?' asked Alby.

'What would *you* do if you were heading up this case?'

Alby's face stretched into the smuggest grin that Jason had ever seen. He instantly regretted asking the former detective for *anything*.

'Sorry, I don't think I heard you right there Brazel?' he said.

'Frank, come on.'

'No, no, it must be my old age, my hearing isn't what it used to be.'

'Alby.'

'I thought you just asked me for my opinion on something. Is that right?'

'Why do you have to make everything so difficult?' Jason asked.

'I'm a copper,' said Alby, bursting with pride. 'What would I do if I was heading up this investigation, that's what you asked?'

'You know it is. Just answer me or sod off home.'

Alby tucked his hands into his ironed denims and rocked back and forward on his heels. From a distance he must have looked like a medicine ball on legs.

'It's a good question,' he said. 'And about time somebody asked it, quite frankly.'

'Come on Frank, this is important. I don't have time for showboating. What would you do?'

Alby rubbed the side of his nose then wagged the finger at Jason.

'I think Arendonk and her team have been looking at the wrong part of the puzzle,' he said. 'And, knowing you and that mother-in-law of yours, you have been too.'

'What do you mean?' asked Jason, stepping forward.

'Hal Mulberry was a local legend, right?' he said. 'Nobody had a bad word to say about him, nobody that really knew him that was. And all the folk that knew what he was really like still couldn't deny he gave a hell of a lot of dough to charity and good causes. When somebody like that winds up with a cut throat and no suspects, you've got to look at the whole picture, not just the victim.'

'And what's the whole picture here?' asked Jason.

Alby snapped his fingers and smiled at him. It took Jason a moment, then it dawned on him.

'Big picture,' he said. 'The painting? *Buttermere at Dawn?*'

'New factors in the victim's life,' said Alby. 'You look at what's going on in and around the victim, see what they've done out of the ordinary, what they've been up to, who they've been seeing, who they've not been seeing. Arendonk is a good detective, you're right about that Brazel, as much as it pains me, but she's been looking in the wrong place. If it's not a crime of passion, then cash is king. And in this case, the first thing I'd do – after releasing Doc Mulberry – would be to take a good, hard look at that pretty picture he spent all his cash on.'

'It's cursed,' said Jason. 'Or so they say.'

Alby let out a loud, rasping laugh. It led to a coughing fit and he wiped away a tear before it rolled into his moustache.

'Good one Brazel, really good,' he said. 'I knew you were gullible but I didn't think you were that bad. You'll be putting it down to alien abductions next.'

'Get lost,' said Jason with a sneer.

'There's no such thing as curses, believe me,' wheezed the former DI. 'What there *is* is a lot of money to be made in the art world, especially with dodgy deals and backhanders happening all over the shop. Dealers turning blind eyes here and there can cause rifts, rivalries, vendettas even. I'd wager that painting has a history that goes beyond what the fancy Sotheby's catalogue had written in it when Mulberry bought the bloody thing. A golden rule of detective work Brazel, always, and I mean *always* follow the money. Where there's cash to be made, there's cash to be stolen. And if somebody feels like they've been conned out of readies then there's no stopping what they'd do to get it back.'

'But no one's made any money out of the painting – in fact, until we reported it, the blooming thing was just left under its little velvet curtain,' Jason protested. 'And if you're asking who stands to gain from Hal's death, then it's his wife who inherits – and you've just ruled her out!'

Alby checked his watch. He gave Jason a sycophantic smile. 'Well, I'm sure you'll work it out. It's been lovely catching up but I've got a wife to go home to,' he said. 'And an hour of meditation before an early night.'

'Yeah, okay,' said Jason, lost in a bit of a daze.

'Think about what I said,' said the former DI. 'You never know, there might be a story in it.'

He crossed the road and didn't look back. Jason watched him until he had vanished further up the high street. He turned to the pub and walked back to the table, his head swimming with everything that Alby had just told him. When he plonked himself down at the table, Amita and Radha were staring at him.

'Jason,' said Amita, sensing there was something afoot. 'Is everything alright? Who were you talking to?'

'Frank Alby,' he said.

'Alby!' Amita yelped. 'The policeman? He was here? Just now?'

'He's just left,' said Jason. 'And he had some very choice words to say about the Mulberry investigation.'

At the mention of the case, Amita's eyes widened. 'What... what did he say?' she asked, trying not to look too eager.

Jason took a sip from his first unfinished pint, the lager already flat. It didn't matter, he just needed something normal before he ruined their night.

'I think Sheila Mulberry is innocent,' he said. 'And the killer is still on the loose.'

Chapter 29

NOTRE-DAME, UNE FIN D'APRÈS-MIDI

'Alby said he would look at the history of the painting, not Mulberry,' said Jason. 'So that seems like a logical place to start again.'

'Yes, I know he said that,' replied Amita. 'I'm just not sure you should be trusting that man. He's had it in for you ever since our paths crossed. Why the sudden change of heart now?'

Jason had been pondering that notion too. It wasn't that he didn't trust Frank Alby – the man had been a police officer his whole adult life. Amita was right though. They hadn't enjoyed the best of relationships. And now it seemed that the former DI was bending over backwards to help them out.

'We can worry about that when this is all over and done with,' he said, remaining tight-lipped about his own fears. 'What matters now is that we press on and try to get to the bottom of this.'

'And how many times have we said that over the past few weeks?' asked Amita. 'How many times have we thought we were onto the right line of investigation only for it to blow up in our faces. We thought it was Martin Gill, we were convinced of it. We had our suspicions about Sheila Mulberry, now we're not so sure. I'm certain we even considered Arthur Doige at one point too. When will it end Jason?'

'I know,' he said. 'After what happened with the Frobisher case, we were feted as super sleuths. But I'm starting to think that was a one-off.'

'As do I, Jason,' Amita sighed. 'That's why I'm wondering if any of this is worth it. Chasing up another lead, maybe for nothing at all. We're back where we started – researching the painting – we're going in circles.'

Jason nodded solemnly. 'The curse of *Buttermere at Dawn*,' he said.

'What?' she asked.

'The curse. You said the painting was cursed, so did Doige. I didn't believe you, Alby doesn't believe in it either. But maybe the curse isn't just limited to those who own the painting. Maybe the picture is just a magnet for trouble and everyone involved with it gets dragged down too.'

'I thought you didn't believe in curses,' she said with a fond smile.

'I don't,' he smiled back. 'I'm just hypothesising. You know how philosophical I get when I'm hypothesising.'

That made his mother-in-law laugh. She let out another sigh, her shoulders sagging.

'I'm tired Jason, really very tired,' she said. 'The person who murdered Hal Mulberry in cold blood should be caught. But maybe it's not our place to do it, not this time. Maybe we're out of our depth with this one.'

Again, Jason couldn't argue with her. He looked up the street, the white façade of Arthur Doige's gallery only a few shops away.

'Look, it's ultimatum time,' he said. 'We've come this far today, the gallery is just up ahead. Why don't we at least go shakedown Doige one last time to see if he'll give us anything useful. If he does, great, we can take it from there. If he doesn't then even better, we call it quits and go home. Arendonk and the police can have their red faces if and when Shelia Mulberry is released without charge, Alby will be pleased, but it's nothing to do with us. It's the last roll of the dice Amita, then we're out.'

They walked side by side up the pavement, nearing the dealer's shop. Amita felt a little better, a bit more energised. Now that there was a tangible end in sight, she could focus on that.

'What the hell?' gasped Jason.

As they neared the gallery, they both came to a standstill. The normally immaculate front of Arthur Doige's gallery had been smeared with black paint. Written in huge letters across the windows was the word 'snitch'.

'Good grief,' said Amita. 'Who would do such a thing?'

'I don't know,' said Jason. 'I mean, he's not the nicest of people, is he?'

'Jason,' she said, heading for the door. 'You know you said it was our last roll of the dice? Well, I think we just rolled a six.'

She knocked on the door. It moved, unlocked, one pane broken where the vandals had broken in. Amita pushed it and stepped inside, her feet crunching on broken glass. Inside the gallery had been trashed. More black spray paint covered the walls, the same word over and over again. All of the lights had been broken, the floor awash with debris.

'Hello?' Amita called out. 'Mr Doige? Are you there? Are you okay?'

'It's us Mr Doige. Your favourite customers!'

'Jason,' Amita hushed him down.

'Mr Doige? Are you here? Is everything alright? We've come to speak with you.'

Doige appeared from the back of the shop. Clad in his trademark black outfit, the bright yellow Marigold rubber gloves and matching brush and dustpan a strange addition. He already looked enraged, his pointed eyebrows even more daggered than usual. When he spotted Amita and Jason, his mood soured further.

'Get out of here,' he rasped. 'Can't you see I've got all of this to deal with. I don't need you two busybodies poking around and revelling in my misfortune.'

'We're not revelling in anything Mr Doige,' said Amita. 'We wanted to make sure you were alright? Have you been hurt, has anything been stolen?'

'Only my dignity and my pride,' he said bitterly. 'Do you know how long it's taken for me to build up this business? I'm the premier art dealer in the north of England, you know. That's a title I wear with pride. But when you deal with the kind of exclusive collectors I do, it's all about discretion. My buyers need to know that what they buy or sell through me will go to grave with me. What are my clients or, god forbid, the rest of the art community going to say when they hear about this?'

'You've been burgled Doige, not outed as some kind of fraudster,' said Jason. 'The police will catch whoever did this.'

'And I'm supposed to take great comfort in that, am I?' he marched over to Jason. 'I'm supposed to throw myself at the mercy of John Law and hope that my rivals don't sneer, my customers don't abandon me and my reputation isn't sunk like the Lusitania.'

Jason backed off from him. There was clearly no getting through to him like this.

'Look, we just swung by to ask some questions, that's all,' he said. 'But you're clearly busy with all of this so we'll leave you to it. Amita, are you coming?'

'Good riddance to bad rubbish,' snapped Doige. 'The best news I've heard all day.'

Jason pulled the door open. He was about to step outside when he realised Amita was further into the gallery, staring at the graffiti on the walls.

'Why have you been called a snitch, Mr Doige?' she asked.

'What are you babbling about?' the art dealer hissed. 'What does it matter what I've been called, the whole gallery is ruined.'

'I know that,' she said, pointing to the black spray paint. 'But why a snitch? That's a very specific word to use, it means a certain thing. Why would anyone want to break in here, smash up the gallery and call you something like that?'

Doige's face contorted. Jason thought he might be having a medical emergency. When he started speaking those fears were well put to rest.

'The graffiti is aimed at me speaking to all of you people,' he barked. 'Talking to ignorant cretins who don't know the first thing about the art world. Opening my door to all and sundry to come poking around business that they can't even begin to understand. Hacks like you and your son-in-law, Mrs Khatri, nosey parkers who can't help but feel they need to get their hands dirty in other people's affairs.'

'Hey, calm down Doige,' said Jason.

'Calm down? Are you serious?' he marched up to him again. 'You're telling me to calm down when it was all your fault in the first place? You and those tinpot journalists who came skulking around here trying to find a story that didn't exist. There's an old saying, Mr Brazel, you reap what you sow. And this place, this *mess*, that used to be my business, is evidence of that. I should never have spoken to any of you. I should have kept my door shut and my mouth closed. And now look what's happened. I'm ruined.'

He held his furious stare a little longer after his rant. Jason wasn't sure what he was supposed to do. Doige retreated first, kneeling down and starting to sweep up broken glass and debris into his dustpan.

Amita looked over at her son-in-law. Jason shrugged, still unsure as to what exactly he was supposed to have done. She decided to try a different approach as a last resort. She kneeled down and took the dustpan from Doige. He let it go easily, his head dropping, veins still bulging.

'I'm sorry this has happened Arthur,' she said, calmly and softly. 'There's absolutely no reason you should have been targeted like this. Or called that awful name. The police will catch whoever did it, trust me.'

'Trust you,' he laughed mockingly. 'I shouldn't have let you in.'

'We were only doing a job,' said Jason.

Amita backed him away.

'I know,' she said. 'You're a victim here Arthur. I'm truly sorry for that.'

Doige groaned loudly. He reached down and picked up a large fragment of glass. He held it up so the light refracted on its shattered edges. A little rainbow danced across his angry face.

'These lightbulbs came from Italy,' he said. 'They're handblown, of course, cost an absolute fortune. Everything had to be just right for this place when I did it up. I sank every penny I had into it, to make it just right. That's how it goes in this business, there are no half measures. You're either all in or you're all out. And if you *do* go all in, you gamble on that one sale that will secure the future for you, so you can do it all over again.'

'It sounds cut-throat,' said Amita.

'Yes, that's one way of describing it,' he said. 'And now, it appears the throat of my business has been cut permanently. Just like Hal Mulberry's.' He dropped the fragment of glass and it joined the others.

Amita had sympathy for Doige. He wasn't the easiest man in the world to get along with. If what he was saying was true, that he had been targeted by someone for helping the press, then he didn't deserve all of this. His business had been ruined because he'd opened his doors. That was vandalism of the worst kind.

'Arthur, we need your help,' she said.

Doige laughed. It was the maniacal cackle they'd heard before. When he settled down, he blinked and looked at her.

'You can't be serious? You can't seriously be asking me for something after everything that's happened. Are you trying to put me into an early grave?'

'We wouldn't be here if it wasn't serious, Doige,' said Jason. 'We think you might hold some sort of clue as to who sent Hal Mulberry to his grave.'

Doige ran his hand over his bald head. He stood up, old knees creaking.

'I think you should both leave immediately,' he said. 'Before I do something that I would later regret and probably face charges for.'

'Arthur please,' said Amita.

'Go!' he said. 'Now. I have an awful lot of work to do and you're getting in my way.'

'Arthur, please, we just need to see what records you have for *Buttermere at Dawn*.'

Doige's eyes narrowed on her. He leaned forward but Amita stood her ground, unshaken by his intimidating, skeletal presence.

'Why would I help you?' he asked in a low grumble. 'Why would I even entertain such a notion after everything that's happened here.'

'Because you've got nothing left to lose,' she said, meeting his glare. 'This place has been ruined, I'm sorry about that, truly I am. But there's a chance that somewhere in all that paperwork and information you keep in the back shop we could find the person responsible for murdering Hal Mulberry. And if we catch them then we might find out who did this to your gallery.'

'She's right Doige,' chimed Jason. 'Whoever did this, they weren't petty thugs or no-good teens. They know you've been helping the authorities throughout all of this. They're trying to intimidate you, to let you know that they're on to you. If it's not the killer then it's somebody close to them. And they want you to shut up.'

A little of the redness vanished from Doige's face. Amita reckoned he hadn't realised there was a chance of rescuing his precious reputation.

'Why wouldn't I just shut up then?' he asked. 'If what you're saying is correct then why should I try and antagonise a maniac, or maniacs, further?'

'Because it's the right thing to do,' said Amita. 'Because you shouldn't be pushed around by thugs and bullies who have ruined everything you've worked so hard to achieve. It must stand for something Arthur, your life's work. Don't let some violent yob steal that away from you when there's a chance you can bring them to order.'

Amita wasn't sure if what she was saying was having any effect on Doige. She decided to step it up a gear. 'You've dedicated your whole life to art, Arthur. And what is art if not truth? This is not the ruin of your career – it's the peak.'

Had she overdone it? Amita eyed her audience. The dealer was icy calm, his face stoic to the point of rigour mortis. Eventually he blinked, showing at least some sign of life.

'In the back, behind the partition,' he twitched his head towards the rear of the gallery. 'Everything I have on *Buttermere at Dawn* is on my computer. It's easy enough to find if you know what you're looking for. The password is *Ars Longa Vita Brevis*.'

Jason couldn't stifle a schoolboy chuckle. Doige shot him a look as sharp as the broken glass that surrounded them.

'You do know what that means, I hope?' Doige added icily. 'Art is long, life is short. Strangely appropriate, you could say. Now you've got ten minutes then I'm throwing you out.'

Amita breathed a sigh of relief. Jason clapped Doige on the shoulder.

'Thank you,' he said, hurrying around the dealer.

'We won't let you down Arthur,' said Amita. 'I promise you that.'

Clearly enjoying his new role as fount of wisdom Arthur continued, 'As Nietzsche once said, Mrs Khatri, one must have a good memory to be able to keep the promises one makes.'

For the first time Amita saw Arthur Doige smile. She smiled back at him and nodded as she waded through the broken glass and debris to join Jason in the back shop.

Chapter 30

PARIS STREET IN RAINY WEATHER

Amita knew nothing about art. She loved long walks around galleries and quiet days contemplating big, expansive paintings. But she would never claim to know anything of form, of art history, of the place these masterpieces held in the great, grand scheme of the cultural world. She was never sure if they were masterpieces in the first place. Amita Khatri appreciated art for what it was to her, not to other people: quiet company and contemplation on Sunday afternoons when the rain was pouring down outside.

Arthur Doige's back room was like a gallery that had seen much better days. Or the impound yard of a very lucrative repo team. While the front of house had been slick, sleek, shimmering and without even the most basic of accoutrements like chairs, tables and desks – the back shop was much more practical. Paintings were stacked up high on top of each other, every spare bit of floor taken up by some asset. Sculptures of all shapes and sizes, covered in paper and bubble wrap were left sitting on cabinets, desks and anywhere else that might house them.

She had almost knocked a few of them over on her way into the back. Jason hadn't fared much better, catching the odd piece before it shattered on the ground. Damage to his stock was the last thing Doige needed right now. Amita wasn't in the mood to make him angrier.

Eventually they found a small computer terminal. The screen was on and the processor fan was whirring away loudly beneath the desk.

'It sounds like it's ready to take off,' said Jason.

'I don't blame it, it's stifling in here,' said Amita, unzipping her shell suit jacket. 'It must be like a volcano at the height of summer.'

'I could see Doige living in a volcano,' he said. 'I could see him wanting to throw you and I into one too. I'm surprised he played ball.'

'He was always going to,' said Amita.

'How do you possibly know that? He was practically ready to combust out there.'

'I told you before, Jason, Arthur Doige is an inherently selfish man. His self-preservation comes before everything else. If there's even the slightest chance that his reputation can be salvaged from this whole episode, he'll snatch at it with both hands.'

'I don't know,' said Jason. 'I think he was about ready to tear us limb from limb at one point.'

'I'm sure he was. But he knows better if there's a chance he can still get out of this. And what better way than to be able to say that Hal Mulberry's killer was discovered here, in his very shop.'

Jason wasn't entirely convinced that was the case. He sat down in the old office chair that squeaked every time he blinked. He cracked and flexed his fingers, staring down at the big, chunky keyboard, the letters faded from decades of use.

'Do you know what we're looking for?' asked Amita.

'Yes,' he said. 'I want to see a full, or as close to full, history of who has owned *Buttermere at Dawn* and when. Alby said that the painting was the key to all of this. We'll take a look and see what stands out.'

'If anything.'

'If anything,' he agreed as he typed in the password and a flurry of icons filled the screen. 'Now, what button do you press to bring up the filing system?'

'Out of the way.'

Amita slid him away from the desk before he could protest. She hunched over the keyboard, pointing and clicking furiously until the screen was filled with spreadsheets, folders and files.

'You should really be more computer literate Jason,' she tutted. 'There are classes for pensioners in the village hall every Friday morning. They're very good, that Miss Wilson from the school takes them in the summer.'

'I'll pass, thanks,' said Jason.

'You shouldn't. The children will be getting taught all of this stuff, do you want them to know more than their father?'

'Now is not the time or the place for a debate on my fatherhood credentials,' he said. 'Can you just make R2-D2 there show us all the owners of *Buttermere at Dawn* before I sweat out any more body weight.'

Amita huffed. She started highlighting names and boxes across the spreadsheet. Jason leaned in closer, trying to decipher the data.

'It's not all there,' said Amita.

'How do you know?' he asked.

'Some of the years are missing, see. And what was it Barry said again, there had been twenty-two owners. There aren't twenty-two names here.'

'Ah yes, Barry the conspiracy theorist.' Jason rolled his eyes. 'I trust him about as far as I could throw him Amita, you know that.'

She highlighted the space between a few of the names. The years, months, dates, were all lined up from when the painting was first sold in 1974. From that point the decades all ticked past right up until the ownership before Hal Mulberry had bought the painting at Sotheby's.

'Hold on,' said Jason, pointing at the screen. 'It says Elvira owned this thing on at least three, non-consecutive occasions. Maybe she counts as three separate owners.'

'It would appear so,' said Amita. 'The notes here just say the painting was back in the hands of the original artist.'

'So she sold the painting way back in the seventies. Bought it again in the early nineties, sold it after a year and then bought it again before she died. That's where Hal comes in, snapping it up from her estate for the two million quid.'

'She must have been hard up to keep parting with it,' said Amita. 'But why did she want it back so badly?'

'Everything I've read about her points to her being a private person – maybe she wanted to buy a back a piece of herself with the painting – to shape her own legend.'

'Legendary status doesn't pay for your shopping at the checkout, maybe she was broke,' she said then paused. 'Scrap that, that last time she's listed as the owner, it can't be *the* Elvira, she was already dead.'

'Strange,' he nodded. 'It must have been her estate.'

They went back to checking the names and dates, running back through time through each of the boxes and entries in the database. Every name had notes typed up beside it, giving a vague description of when, where and why the painting had been sold. Most of the entries were similar – the seller wanted a quick sale for cash, no questions asked. Jason remembered what Alby had told him about art fraud and crime within that world.

'Dodgy dealings and backhanders,' he said. 'That's what Alby had called all of this. He wasn't wrong, I can see that now. So what do you think? A dead end?'

'I don't know,' she said. 'I do *The Times* crossword online every day, as you know.'

'Oh yes, I know,' he smiled.

'I'd like to think if there was a pattern or something hidden in all of this it would have jumped out at me by now,' she said. 'But I'm not seeing anything. What about you?'

'It's just data Amita, a list of names, dates and numbers,' he said. 'I don't know what we were hoping to find.'

'You'll never listen to that Frank Alby again I take it?' she smiled.

'I shouldn't have listened to him in the first place,' he said. 'Come on, let's get out of here before I'm fit to be served on a platter. You can deliver the good news that we've come up with nothing to Chuckles outside. I'm sure he'll be delighted.'

Amita shook her head. Jason got up and slid the chair back under the desk. She leaned down to close the files and folders but stopped at the master spreadsheet. Scanning all the cells once more, something struck her suddenly.

'Hang on,' she said.

'Hang on? Hang for what? Come on Amita, let's get out of here.'

'Hang on just one second.'

She expanded the spreadsheet and highlighted the last column. Jason peered at the screen and saw an ascending list of numbers.

'What's this?'

'It's the price the painting went for,' she said. 'Look, every time it's been sold, the money has increased.'

'Right, so?' he asked. 'Isn't that why people buy famous art – it's not all just for the love of it, it's an investment for lots of people like I said.' Jason looked at the numbers again.

'A steady increase in value for the near fifty years the painting has existed. All the way back to...' She scrolled through the spreadsheet. 'Blimey,' she said. 'There's a hidden row of data. Poorly hidden. Our friend Doige clearly hasn't taken advantage of Penrith's library's excellent Computing for Beginners course. I should tell him it taught me a thing or two.' She clicked purposefully at one corner of the screen. 'Look at that. We think of it as a masterpiece now, but see – it was bought for just ten pounds originally from the artist and sold the next year for only thirty to a...'

'Raymond Mulberry,' said Jason, staring at the screen.

'A relation?' asked Amita.

'I don't know,' answered Jason, his skin prickling. 'Hal never mentioned anything about the painting ever being in his family. He just said that he'd always admired it after seeing it on television. But you don't meet that many Mulberrys. It's got to be a relation.'

'What age was Hal?'

'Fifty next birthday,' said Jason.

'So conceivably, the painting was sold again before Hal ever knew it had belonged to his father or whoever this Raymond Mulberry is. The records show Mulberry sold it again after six years, to a dealer by the looks of things.'

'This is very strange,' said Jason. 'Why would Hal not know that it had already been owned by the family? And sold for much more than they bought it, what does that say?' He squinted at the screen.

'Ten thousand pounds,' said Amita. 'And do you see who the dealer was?'

Jason puffed out his cheeks.

'Arthur Doige,' he said. 'And I'm sure he spent his commission wisely. Probably on this place.' He looked about the little office. 'As for Mulberry, not a bad investment,' whistled Jason. 'That's almost ten grand in profit in half a decade. You wouldn't say no to that in *any* market, would you?'

'You're right,' said Amita, barely audible. Her hand was quivering, causing the curser on the screen to shake.

Jason felt like the room had suddenly plunged into an icy chill.

'Amita,' he said. 'Are you okay?'

She didn't answer him. She was staring, wide-eyed at the screen. She looked like she was trying to say something but the words were escaping her.

'What is it?' he asked her, grabbing her by the shoulders. 'Are you feeling okay?'

'No...' she forced out, the shock rippling through her system.

Amita had expanded the document to see all of the data. The additional information in the first data block had made her blood chill.

'Look... look at the first owner.'

She pointed a nervous finger at the screen. Jason followed it to a name next to Elvira's. He stared at it, confused at first, a name he didn't recognise. But the more he looked at it, the more pieces of this unfathomable riddle began slipping into place.

He jolted back, pushing away from the desk and computer like they were on fire. He pointed at it and then to Amita. 'Is that...'

'It is,' she said, swallowing a dry gulp.

'Are you sure?' he asked. 'You have to be sure Amita, you have to be surer now than you ever have been before.'

'I'm sure,' she said. 'I'm as sure as I can be, Jason. I'm sure.'

He was breathing heavily now, drinking in great gulps of air to stop himself from fainting. In one tiny, blink and you miss it moment, they potentially had their killer.

Chapter 31

WOMAN WITH FLOWER

The sun wasn't as strong as it had been over the previous few days. There was a milkiness to the air, clouds had also started to form high in the beautifully blue sky. The Cumbrian summer already felt like it was starting to shift away from its peak. Before long the winds of autumn would be bringing a great change across the landscape.

Amita didn't mind. She loved the Lake District in autumn. The richness of the golds and bronzes on the trees and bushes gave everything a homely glow. The brightness of summer was fine for the tourists. But to a local like her, she preferred the mellow comfort and beauty that only the latter half of the year could provide.

As they drove on through the countryside once more, she was struck by a morbid thought. Hal Mulberry would never see another autumn. His time was up. His life had been cut drastically short when he was in his prime. Fame, fortune, success, they all had prices that the eye and the bank couldn't always see or afford.

She was grateful for everything that she had. Her family, her daughter's success, her grandchildren's health. And most of all her son-in-law's solidarity. Without Jason by her side, she wasn't sure if she would have been able to cope with the pressure and responsibility she'd piled on herself. The two had grown much closer and their relationship was better than it had ever been. If any good was to come out of Hal Mulberry's death, it would be that she appreciated that more than ever. Funny how the differences that had once drove them to lock horns had somehow made them a formidable pair.

Now they had a job to do – again. Once more they were at the sharp end of justice, about to confront what could be the murderer. After everything that had happened with Madeleine Frobisher, Amita thought she might be less nervous this time. It wasn't the case, wasn't to be. Dangerous people were always dangerous, no matter how many times you confronted their type. She had to stay focussed, keep her concentration, right to the last. It had saved her before. She just hoped it would save her again if called upon.

'This is absolute madness,' said Jason, leaning over the steering wheel. 'I can't believe we're doing what we're doing.'

'You must have known it would come to this,' she said calmly.

'I don't know, maybe I did, maybe I didn't,' he shook his head. 'Maybe I thought the police would beat us to it in the end and we'd just have to read about it in the papers. Like with Sheila Mulberry.'

'We still don't know she's innocent,' she said. 'All we have is a lead, a name.'

'Yeah, a pretty distinctive name, Amita. It's not too late to tell the police and get them to check it out, you know.'

'No, Jason. This is personal. If we get this wrong – and I admit I might have jumped to conclusions in the past – it will ruin my world. I've learned from all that to-do with Georgie that you need to tread lightly when it comes to accusations of such wickedness. There may be a fine art to murder, but so is there to pointing the finger.'

'Don't you start talking in riddles, for goodness sake. That's all we both need after the few weeks we've had.' He puffed out his cheeks as the country road weaved its way through the fields and meadows.

The route was taking them north of Penrith. They'd been here already of course. Neither thought they'd be back so soon. Although that all made a strange sort of sense now.

'Hiding in plain sight,' said Jason again.

'Hiding in plain sight,' Amita agreed.

The road curved to the right sharply. Jason guided the car expertly around and they caught sight of it on the horizon: Violet Heatherington's shed. It loomed up ahead of them like a huge tombstone, low, thick, and dark, completely at odds with the rest of the rolling country. Amita gripped the handle of the passenger door that little bit tighter when she saw it.

They pulled up outside the cottage. The huge anchor they had passed only a few days before was still standing in the front yard. The hooks were dug firmly into the turf and there was a sense of permanence about it, like another headstone marking a grave. Amita tried to refocus.

'Right, are you ready?' she asked Jason.

'No,' he said. 'But then again, when are you *ever* ready for this kind of confrontation? I think I preferred it better when I didn't know the person being interviewed was a killer. You could at least enjoy the tea and biscuits more.'

'We don't know Violet has done anything yet,' said Amita. 'Let's not get ahead of ourselves.'

'True,' he said. 'But she's kept a pretty big bit of evidence quiet from us and the police. If she didn't kill him, chances are she knows who did. And that makes her dangerous Amita. Really dangerous.'

'Then we'll just have to charm her, won't we,' she said.

Amita opened the car door. A surprisingly sharp wind whipped down the road and almost knocked her over. She stalked around the front of the car and joined Jason as they walked up the garden path towards the front door of the cottage.

'Do you want to knock, or shall I?' he asked.

Amita ignored him. She rapped her knuckles against the wooden door and stood back. As she did so, something cracked beneath the heel of her trainer. She looked down and saw what looked like the discarded lid of a can, black paint pooled against the rim. She tried to swallow but her mouth was bone-dry.

'Okay. So *now* I have a terrible feeling,' she whispered to Jason.

The door opened and Violet appeared. She looked surprised to see them, but not startled. She smiled warmly.

'Amita,' she said. 'And Jason. What a lovely surprise. What are you two doing here?'

Amita took a deep breath. This was it. One more step forward and there would be no going back. If they were going to do this, now was the time.

331

'May we come in?' she asked politely.

Violet looked between them both. She was drying her hands with a dish towel, furiously rubbing at each finger. She stepped to one side.

'Of course,' she said. 'Come in, I'll put the kettle on.'

Amita went in first, Jason close behind. Violet closed the door, the snib clicking firmly shut. The cottage was cramped and as untidy as the huge shed full of junk at the bottom of the garden had been. Various odds and ends were littered along the hallway and they had to weave between them for fear of trampling on something expensive.

'You'll have to excuse this old place,' she said. 'It's rather untidy. A bit like me, wouldn't you say?' She laughed.

Amita couldn't tell if she was on to them, if she could sense something was wrong. Would it make a difference anyway? They were here now, inside the house. Violet had nowhere to run. But then, again, nor did they, she realised with a shudder.

Violet showed them into the living room. There was a dusty old couch and an armchair that had seen better days close to the window. A huge, old television took up most of the corner beside it, the flat top caked with dust. The walls were lined with old, faded photographs, the wallpaper cracked at the seams leaving ugly stripes.

'Take a seat, make yourselves at home, I'll just bring us some tea,' said Violet, leaving them to it.

When the door closed, Jason whispered to Amita. 'This feels like the land that time forgot,' he said. 'Look, there's those bits of cloth you put over the back of chairs. Are they still a thing?'

'Antimacassars,' said Amita. 'And no, I don't think they are. I haven't seen them since my mother died...'

The whole place reeked of stagnant air. Amita was tempted to open the window and let some fresh air in. But given what they were there to do, she thought that might be a bit much.

'Here we are,' said Violet, returning with a tray.

Amita and Jason took their seats, both of them remaining as close to the door as possible. Violet poured them cups from an ancient looking teapot and handed them over.

'Biscuit?' she offered them a plate of broken digestives.

'No thanks,' said Jason, politely passing. 'The tea is enough.'

The tea was pale and weak. He didn't much fancy it either so left it sitting on the arm of the sofa. Amita was much the same.

'I must say this is a surprise,' said Violet, drinking down her own cup. 'I was just about to go into the back shed and start clearing out some of the old records we've collected over the years.'

'Records?' asked Amita. 'For the WI? Are you allowed to do that Violet?'

'No, no,' she laughed. 'Vinyl records. We must have hundreds of them all piled up in there, rotting away with all the other junk. I understand they take them in charity shops these days. Who would have thought that would come back into fashion. It's funny how time is cyclical, isn't it? What goes around, comes around, eh?'

There was the faintest trace of anger in her tone. Amita felt her muscles stiffening. Jason was the same. The atmosphere had turned just a little. And they both wondered if they had been rumbled.

'Thank you for having us Violet,' said Amita. 'We won't take up a lot of time. It's just a quick couple of questions we wanted to ask you.'

'Questions?' Violet seemed confused. 'Questions about what? The WI again?'

'No, not about the WI,' said Amita.

'Because I'd heard you were eyeing up a spot on the board when it became available.'

Violet's tone had got distinctly chilly now. Amita was shocked. She had never heard Violet speak that way, let alone to her. She sat directly across from her, still sipping her tea.

'No, it's not about that,' said Amita.

'Ah, I see,' she fired back more warmly. 'You don't need to go about with the cloak and dagger approach, you know. If you wanted to be considered for the board then you should just have asked me. Judy won't be considered for the next round of elections and I'd be happy to sponsor you. As I say, all you have to do is ask.'

'Thank you, Violet, that means a lot,' she said. 'We're not here about the Women's Institute, it's something a little more sensitive than that.'

'Oh,' she said, drawing the word out. 'And what might that be?'

'Why didn't you tell us you once owned *Buttermere at Dawn*?' Jason said.

Violet's expression didn't change. If she was surprised she was hiding it very well.

'I beg your pardon Jason?' she said.

'We know you bought it from Elvira, when she was an unknown artist,' said Amita. 'We've seen the records

Violet. You weren't Heatherington back then, you used your maiden name.

'Violet Lowe,' said Jason. 'It's all there, in black and white. You were the first owner of the painting and you paid a tenner.'

'I'm not quite sure what's being implied here,' said Violet. 'You're saying that I owned that awful painting that Hal Mulberry bought for two million pounds.'

It was subtle, a tiny movement, but Amita spotted it. Violet's left cheek pinched ever so slightly at the mention of the money.

'That's what we're saying Violet,' she levelled at the pensioner. 'We're saying we've seen the official records and they name you as the first owner of *Buttermere at Dawn*. Now, we're not accusing you of anything.'

'You're bloody right you're not accusing me of anything,' Violet shouted.

'We just want to know why you didn't tell us about it, that's all,' said Jason. 'Can we assume that the police don't know either?'

Violet tapped her fingernails against the porcelain of her cup. The light tinkle was eerily loud, the whole room feeling like it had gotten that little bit darker suddenly. She sat staring at Amita across the room, unflinching, unbudging.

'Hal Mulberry was murdered, Violet,' she said.

'I know that, Amita,' Violet sneered. 'It's not been off the news, never been out of the papers. I suppose we have you to thank for that. Playing detective again so you can have something to lord over us at bingo, I'd imagine. This is all your son-in-law's influence, I bet. Guttersnipe!' She volleyed a disgusted look at Jason.

He didn't rise to it. Instead, he stayed calm and let Amita do what she did best.

'Why Violet, why the secrecy?' she said. 'Why not just come clean about it all? Why leave a degree of suspicion?'

Violet said nothing. Still she tapped her mug and stared blankly at Amita.

'I'll be perfectly honest with you,' Amita continued. 'I got the absolute shock of my life when I saw your name on the records. It took me a moment to process it at first, but I knew I recognised your maiden name. Don't you remember that talk you gave on genealogy, researching your family tree? Well it's conveniently been saved on the WI website. I checked it on the way here to make sure I wasn't making a terrible blunder.'

'Penrith WI has a website?' blurted Jason.

'Yes, it does,' said Amita. 'All of the board members' profiles are there, and yours, Violet, also happens to mention you're a keen collector of antiques. I always thought that was just something you did to feel close to the memory of your dear Charles. But I see I was wrong.'

Another tiny flinch from Violet. Amita could sense she was getting somewhere now.

'You can imagine my shock though, surely,' she said, 'to see your name on that list of owners. Not only that, the first owner, you bought it directly from Elvira. What we don't understand is why you would keep it a secret all this time. Especially when you sold the painting to a relative of Hal Mulberry's.'

'His father,' said Violet suddenly.

Amita blinked. She leaned forward on the sofa.

'They were cut from the same cloth,' said Violet, spitting the words out. 'Both of them, generous to the last penny. Too generous in fact, too generous for their own good.'

The familiar tingle of progress made the hairs on the back of Jason and Amita's necks stand on end.

'What do you mean by that?' asked Jason. 'You seem to have benefited greatly over the years from Hal's generosity. You showed us the records of how much he had donated to good causes.'

'I'm not saying he wasn't generous, Jason,' she said bitterly. 'I'm saying that his generosity was *too* much.'

'Can somebody be *too* generous?' asked Amita. 'That doesn't make a lot of sense.'

Violet grimaced. She stared down at her empty cup and began playing with the handle. Her bony shoulders were up around her ears, her whole frame taut. She looked like a spring that was ready to uncoil and leap through the ceiling.

'Charles always said we shouldn't have taken the money,' she said.

'Your husband?' asked Jason.

'He always said that the moment we sold that picture we were cursed. He always believed that it would be worth a fortune one day. He was the collector, but it turns out I was the one that had the keen eye for art. Everything else was a load of rubbish, you've seen in my shed. But he knew that *Buttermere at Dawn* would be worth something when Elvira was a name to be reckoned with, a national treasure, that's what they call her now, isn't it?'

'It is,' said Amita solemnly.

'He had a feeling in his water, as he liked to put it. Even after we'd sold it to Mulberry, he used to say to me that we'd made a mistake. It drove me nuts, made me mad as hell. We came to blows over it down the years, especially if he'd had a drink. I didn't hold back in the end, I couldn't stand him trying to lord it over me when I knew we'd made the right decision.'

'Why did you sell it in the first place?' asked Jason. 'If Charles was so adamant that you should have kept it until its value went up, why bother getting rid of it to Mulberry senior?'

Violet's mouth contorted into a bitter frown. 'Do you know what it's like to live in poverty Jason?' she asked him bluntly. 'To not be able to afford to keep the heating on *and* feed yourself? Do you have any idea what that's like?'

'No, I don't,' said Jason. 'I've been very lucky.'

'And what about you Amita? Have you ever faced that decision?'

'No,' she said. 'But it's been close. My parents knew it all too well Violet, when they first came here from India. It's a terrible decision for anyone to have to make.'

'Try making that decision when you know, you absolutely *know* that it was unavoidable in the first place,' she continued. 'Try sitting having eaten nothing for three days knowing that if your husband had just thought for a split second and not spent the last of the money in your savings on some bloody folly, some piece of junk that wasn't worth scrap, you wouldn't be in that position at all. Charles was a loving husband, a doting one. But he couldn't see the wood for the trees. And as always, I was left to deal with the consequences, forced to beg for money from my mother, from my brother, from the bank, just to make it to the next pay packet. This place, this cottage, that shed out the back, it's testimony to Charles' haphazard

338

spending and his inability to think straight when it counted. I'm still living with the consequences fifty years later!' She was angry now, her grey face flushed.

'What about the painting?' asked Amita. 'And Raymond Mulberry? They gave you thirty pounds for it, didn't they? That was a lot of money back in the seventies.'

'Hah,' Violet laughed. 'A lot of money back then. A pittance to them. Raymond Mulberry was about as rich as they came. New money too, made a fortune. And he liked to show it off, rub in everyone's faces his good fortune, the fruits of his labours. He was always throwing cash around like it was going out of fashion. And everyone loved him for it. Sounds familiar, doesn't it?'

Jason felt his hands getting sweaty. He didn't like where this was going.

'What happened Violet?' asked Amita.

'Charles knew Raymond from the pub or the golf club or something. I think it may have been the club actually, that was another waste of money. He bought clubs and a membership and I think he only ever played a handful of times during his life. The bloody fool that he was. He said he was "networking", finding customers. He probably spent more at the bar than he made on sales to that lot. All apart from Ray Mulberry.' She looked up to the mantelpiece at a photo of them on their wedding day.

There was no longing there, no great sense of loss. Amita thought, briefly, that she might actually be glad he was gone.

'He got speaking to Raymond about *Buttermere at Dawn*, talked about how Elvira was going to be a super-star and that this would be worth a fortune,' she continued. 'Somehow, I don't know, he must have mentioned that we were struggling and Mulberry offered to buy the painting for three times the amount we had paid. Charles had said no, outright, he refused. He believed his own press more than reality at times. But when he told me there was a chance for us to have some money, even thirty pounds, I knew we had to take it. So I did. I took it to Mulberry's office in town and took the offer.' Her voice began to crack a little.

'Do you know what he said to me when I shook his hand?' she asked the others. 'He said, "I hope this money does you some good Violet." Just like that, he took it off me with glee in his eyes. I can still see him now, sat behind his desk, smiling at it like he'd painted it himself. I felt sick as I left that place. I never set foot in it ever again. I still can't walk past the building it used to be in, it's far too painful. Especially when he went and sold the bloody thing a few years later for thousands.'

'Ten thousand,' said Jason quietly.

'Yes, that's right,' Violet sneered. 'Ten thousand pounds in just a few measly years. It made the papers, I remember it. Charles probably took a clipping, it'll be out there with all of his other junk.'

'And what did Charles say when he learned you'd sold the painting?' asked Amita.

'He was furious,' said Violet. 'Absolutely furious. He never acted on it of course. Charles Heatherington was many things Amita, but a man of action he most certainly wasn't. Ironic, of course, that the only time he was right about all of his little trinkets and foibles, was the time it was sold for next to nothing when we could have been millionaires if we'd hung onto for a couple more decades.'

She stood up from the couch and lifted the picture of the two of them. She stared down at it, touching the glass.

'It's consumed me, you know,' she said. 'All of these years. The thought that if we'd just kept that rotten painting, we would have been rich. The "what if" question, it's haunted me, haunted my every waking moment. I even went to get help for it about twenty years ago. Our marriage was strained, I thought I was going to kill Charles, I needed to just vent, to just talk about it. That's when I got involved with the WI and started giving back to the community. Nobody knew, after all of this time. It filled a hole, of course it did, you know what it's like trying to organise anything around here, Amita. Judy, Georgie Littlejohn, they don't make life easy.'

'No,' said Amita. 'And did it work? The distraction?'

'For a while,' Violet sighed. 'I think I was overwhelmed with everything and then I retired and it became more manageable. But I never really lost that feeling of resentment, that dreadful burning in the back of my mind, not really. It's always been there, it's still there. Whenever there was an overdue bill it would rear its ugly head again. Whenever I didn't have enough change for the bus, there it was. It became a voice, a presence, do you understand what I mean? It was constantly riding my back, always whispering in my ear – what could you have had? What kind of life could you be living now if you'd just held your nerve, just kept hold of *Buttermere at Dawn*. It sounds strange, I know. But that's how I've lived all this time.'

'It must have been awful,' said Amita. 'I can't begin to imagine how bad.'

'No, you can't,' said Violet. 'Nobody can, I don't think. How could you? How could anybody? How many people do you know sold a two-million-pound painting for thirty quid? It doesn't calculate.'

'But it's all in the past Violet,' said Amita. 'You can't undo it.'

'Don't you think I know that Amita!' she screamed. 'Don't you think I know there's nothing I could do to change it? That's the absolute worst part of the whole thing. I've been powerless. I've spent my life wondering what could have been so much so that I never really lived at all.' She hurled the picture down onto the floor. It shattered instantly, the photo tearing.

'You have to tell us what you did Violet,' said Jason. 'There's no point hiding it now.'

The pensioner nodded in agreement.

'I knew Hal through his father,' she said. 'Long before he became a friend and patron of the institute. I'd watched him grow up, watched him make his own fortune with the computers and internet and all of that. Then he eventually took over the family business and countless others in the area. He became so much more than Raymond. I never blamed him for what happened, it wasn't his fault. But, as is often the case, like father like son. Every time he donated more and more cash, I felt the cheque burn in my hands. I was right back in Raymond's office, watching him leer at *Buttermere at Dawn*, so chuffed with himself, so proud. I managed to contain it for so long, I managed to keep a lid on my anger, made sure that he never knew how I really felt. The money helped people, I can't deny that, but I was left living in this place, coming home to this dump every night surrounded by the memories of a fortune squandered. Then Elvira died, a few years ago. Again, it made all the newspapers. Everything was brought racing to the surface, I couldn't escape it. Charles and I decided to go on holiday, to Guernsey, but it followed us there too – the art world in mourning, all of that rubbish. Things eventually settled with time and I thought I was over the worst, then I heard about Hal's plans to purchase the painting and "bring it back to its spiritual home". I could have been sick there and then when I read your article Jason.'

Jason thought he should say something. But what was there to say to that?

'The anger was uncontrollable, worse than it had ever been,' she said. 'The WI, and that village hall, has been my rock and my refuge all these years. And now he was not only buying the place – but buying it to put the blasted painting at its heart, as if to taunt me. It broke me. I read the news and came home and cried myself to sleep. When I woke up, I had an epiphany, a moment of clarity that I hadn't felt in years. When you have a weed growing in your flower bed, you don't ignore it, you don't walk away and pretend it's not there. You grab it by its throat and you pull it out. So that's what I did.'

Amita felt sick. Jason didn't budge. They sat there staring at Violet as she lamented in front of them.

'I contacted Hal's office the next day to congratulate him on winning the auction,' she said. 'He got back to me right away, being an old friend and all of that. He said he was having a black-tie event at the old village hall, a final farewell to the old place before work started on the fancy new building, and how he was going to turn it into a shrine to Elvira with *Buttermere at Dawn* the centrepiece. He asked if I wanted to go. It was all too perfect really, he even offered to pick me up on his way there. So that's what happened. He and the wife, Sheila isn't it, they collected me on their way to the gala. I sat in the back of that huge car of his, I felt like royalty. They had been arguing, or something, I don't know, there was an atmosphere between them. He was jovial enough, chatting away to me like she wasn't there. When we arrived at the car park, Sheila couldn't wait to leave. I stalled for time and pulled the knife from my handbag. The last thing he said to me, the last thing he said to anyone, was, "What's that you've got there Violet?"' She started to laugh.

It was Jason's turn to feel sick.

'Can you believe that?' she asked them. 'All his great speeches, his moments in the sun, the last thing he ever said was asking me what I had in my hand. I didn't hesitate at that point, I was too far gone. I sunk the knife into his throat and that was that, done. The sad thing is, I can't say I felt any better after it, you know. The anger is still there. Only Hal Mulberry isn't.'

'But Sheila was covered in his blood when she appeared at the party,' said Amita. 'I don't understand how she didn't see you?'

'I was gone by the time she came back,' she said. 'She assumed I left with her. She was on her phone, those bloody mobile phones, as she got out of the car. I think a meteor could have landed on top of her then and she wouldn't have noticed, blabbering on about campaigns and policies and things like that. Conveniently, she even gave me an alibi without realising it. Then she made the discovery that no wife ever should have to make. And the rest, as they say, is history. I mean the police popped round and asked me a couple of questions about the evening –

turned out my story tallied with Sheila's statement: "*Mrs Heatherington and I got out of the car as soon as we parked*" it read. She thought I was so unimportant that she didn't even notice I wasn't with her. I mean, little old Vi who runs the WI – I'm used to people seeing through me. That's why me and Judy have always run the institute together. She's the fiery one and I'm the one that everyone thinks does the filing and the donkey work.'

Amita swallowed hard. She was exhausted listening to all of this. It seemed so clear now, so simple almost. If only they'd known the connection with the painting in the first place.

'You tried to frame Sheila for the murder,' said Jason. 'The police found the murder weapon in her rubbish. I assume it was you who tipped them off.'

Violet sat back down in her chair. She let her head rest against the back, a calm smile on her face. 'It was a half-baked idea,' she said. 'To be honest, I'd assumed I'd get arrested the moment I got out of the car. I wasn't trying to get away with it – it was revenge. Plain old revenge. Except poor old Hal didn't know what for. Yes, I was furious that Hal was bringing that cursed thing back into my life and making me see it week in, week out. But really, I was mad at the painting itself and letting Hal fall under its spell. And then when Sheila accidentally struck me off the suspect list with her statement, well, I thought maybe it was a sign. You see it all the time, don't you? The first suspects are always the partners, the ones who know the victim the best. It was working too, the police arrested her, didn't they.'

'Why help us?' asked Amita. 'Why go to the bother of trying to unravel all of this.'

'I'm beyond caring now,' she said honestly. 'Like I said, I didn't think it through much beyond killing Hal. I thought that might bring me some satisfaction, some closure. I thought at least I'd killed off the idea of that painting sullying our village hall along with Hal. I was ready to walk away in handcuffs. Only when that didn't happen, there was a little flicker of life about me, something within me that urged me to keep going, to keep seeing how far I could take it all, to see if I could, literally, get away with murder. The longer the police investigation went on, the longer they didn't have a suspect, the easier it became for me to pull the strings. Showing you the records was nothing. Telling you about that secret boyfriend of his up at the stones, child's play. Yes, I knew all about that lad. Hal Mulberry was a loudmouth, he couldn't keep quiet about anything, even his secret lovers. I just hoped that one of them would end up taking the blame. What did I have to lose?'

'And Doige's gallery?' asked Jason. 'You broke in and smashed the place up.'

'That was a shame,' she said regretfully. 'Arthur Doige is a gossip, he always has been, Amita you'll back me up with that one. The old blabbermouth was talking to the press, telling the town about his own plight and the painting. Maybe I was too harsh on him, he's more to be pitied I thought. I had to send him a message though, I couldn't run the risk of my connection to the painting getting out. And look, I was right, my fears were correct. You two are standing here right now because of that connection. I don't know if I should be pleased or saddened by that. Everything catches up with you in the end, doesn't it? There's no evading the piper forever.' With that, she closed her eyes. She looked peaceful and quiet.

Amita puffed out her cheeks and looked at Jason.

'You know we have to go to the police about this Violet,' she said. 'You'll have to face the consequences.'

'Not just now Amita,' she held her hand up to her. 'Not just this minute. I feel suddenly very tired. So, so tired.'

Jason stood up and took Amita by the arm. They quietly eased out of the living room and closed the door behind them. Heading down the hall, they stepped out of the front door and into the brightness. Jason pulled his phone from his pocket and found DI Arendonk's number. He hit 'call'.

'Are you okay?' he asked Amita.

'Yes,' she said, her lips tight. 'I will be. I always am.'

'Yeah,' said Jason, waiting for the policewoman to answer. 'I'm not okay too.'

Chapter 32

AT SAINT-VALERY-SUR-SOMME

'At the risk of perpetuating negative stereotypes, look what I found while raking through the bins around the back of the cottage.' Jason emerged from around the corner carrying two plastic bags.

He presented them to Amita who was sat on the front doorstep. She opened them up and was immediately hit with the pungent smell of paint. She looked inside. Six spray cans were leaking black paint into the bottom of the bags.

'What odds do you want to give me that these were used to redecorate Arthur Doige's gallery?' he asked.

'I'm not a betting woman,' she said. 'Unless you count bingo. But whatever the shortest odds are, I would wager it would be them.'

'Agreed,' he took the bags back.

'Is the back of the cottage secure?' she asked him.

'As far as I can see the front door is the only way in and out. Unless old Violet legs it out one of the windows.'

'I wouldn't put it past her,' she said.

'Come on Amita, have you seen her?'

'She was able to slash Hal's Mulberry's throat, a man at least twenty years her junior. And besides, do you not think *I* could get out of a window.'

'I wouldn't put *anything* beyond you, Amita,' he said.

Jason sat down beside her and let out a groan. They hadn't gone back into the house since he had called Arendonk. She said she was on her way and bringing the cavalry. For now all they had to do was sit and wait and make sure Violet didn't escape. Then it would be over for them. Finally.

'I still can't believe what we just heard,' he said. 'I mean, I can't say I didn't have a degree of sympathy for Violet in the end.'

'I agree,' Amita hummed. 'She's been a victim of circumstance. That doesn't give her an excuse to do what she did though.'

'Of course not,' he said. 'I just think there's no small part of me that would be just as devastated as she was if the same thing happened to me. Two million quid Amita, and she sold it for thirty. That's a sore one.'

Amita nodded. 'She always seemed like such a level-headed person too,' she said. 'At the bingo, with the WI, she was quiet, yes, of course she was. And the way some people treated her was absolutely diabolical at times. I always had a quiet respect for how she handled it all though. She never lost her temper, never had a bad word to say about anyone.'

'You called her a doormat once,' he said.

'No I didn't,' Amita sounded appalled.

'You did, you said she was the world's biggest one too. I'm not disagreeing with you, I'm just stating facts.'

Amita suddenly felt very guilty. 'Yes, well, we all say things we don't mean from time to time. I never thought she was capable of murder though.'

'Like she said, she had nothing to lose in the end. She's lived with that anger and torment for so long she was desperate to try anything for some relief. It's not how I would have handled things but again, I can sympathise with her to a degree.'

The cold wind blew up again and Amita shivered. She rubbed her arms. Her head was swimming with everything that had been going on. The confession, the anger and hatred that Violet had harboured for decades and how she'd kept it all hidden.

'There's a lesson to be learned here,' she said. 'A valuable one at that. Never, ever keep things bottled up, they'll only hurt you in the end.'

'It's okay not to be okay, that's how the phrase goes, isn't it?'

'Absolutely,' she said. 'Nothing, and I mean nothing, is worth keeping locked away inside of you for as long as Violet kept that fury at the painting. Look where it's got her, a lifetime of abject misery and the prospect of her final days being spent behind bars, her freedom revoked.'

Jason nudged Amita gently. She squeezed his arm affectionately. She was glad he was with her this time, that she wasn't on her own.

A set of blue flashing lights appeared down the country road. Jason stood up and helped Amita after him. A squad car came skidding to a stop behind their car at the end of the drive. It was followed by an unmarked vehicle, Sally Arendonk climbing out before it came to a full halt.

She was up the path and greeting Jason and Amita before they knew it.

'What the hell do you two think you're doing?' she asked. 'Do you have any idea how bloomin' dangerous something like this is? What am I saying, of course you both know. That makes it even *worse*!'

'It's alright Detective Inspector,' said Amita. 'I know Violet, I've known her for years and years. She wouldn't harm me, or Jason for that matter.'

'You don't know that Amita,' said Arendonk, two uniformed officers joining them from the squad car. 'If what you say is true, she's a killer and that makes her dangerous in my book. Neither of you should have taken the risk of confronting her, that's what we're here for.'

'We didn't know she was the killer,' he said. 'That's what we were here for, to find out.'

'Don't make this worse,' she fired back. 'Where is she?'

Jason thumbed back towards the door. 'She's inside. We left her sleeping. There's no way in or out apart from this door.'

'She's alone?' asked Arendonk.

'She is,' said Amita.

'When was the last time you checked on her?'

'I don't know,' he said. 'I called you as soon as we left.'

Arendonk pushed them both out of the way. The uniformed officers followed her, Jason and Amita bringing up the rear.

'Violet!' the DI shouted.

They all thumped up the hallway, Arendonk bursting into the living room. She called Violet's name. Jason and Amita arrived and saw her clapping the pensioner's face.

'She's taken something,' said the policewoman. 'We need to find out what she's taken.' She grabbed the empty teacup that was sat beside the chair.

Amita felt her blood run cold. 'The kitchen,' she said. 'She brought us the tea in from the kitchen.' She turned and made her way through the house.

The kitchen was just as chaotic and messy as the rest of the house. Amita spied a brown bottle tipped on its side beside the kettle. She snatched it and ran back into the living room.

'Bisoprolol!' she shouted as she came back in.

'What's that?' asked Jason.

'It's a beta blocker,' said Arendonk, getting Violet down onto the floor. 'My mum is on them. How many has she taken?'

'I don't know,' said Amita, panicking. 'But if she was putting them in the tea, I'll wager it was a lot.'

'Damn,' said Arendonk. 'Her heart rate is slowing. She knew what she was doing, that'll be why she confessed.' She kept trying to wake Violet but there was no response.

One of the officers was calling for an ambulance. All Amita and Jason could do was stand there and watch. The room was awash with a sudden flurry of action, a stark contrast to what it had been before. Amita put her hand to her mouth as Arendonk started performing CPR.

Jason realised his mother-in-law's distress. He took her hand and led her out of the cottage and into the front garden. They came to a stop at the huge anchor that was wedged in the lawn. Amita leaned against it.

'I'm okay, honestly,' she said. 'That was just... that was just all a bit too much, that's all. Violet is part of furniture round here, I knew her for a long time. I never thought she would do anything like this. It's a dreadful shock, absolutely dreadful. And I... I...' She trailed off.

Jason pulled her in close to him and hugged her tight. She hugged him back, squeezing as hard as she could. They stood there in the front garden as the ambulance arrived. The medics raced past them like they didn't exist, and that was fine. Jason and Amita were happy just to be left alone in their own little world.

Chapter 33

LAVENDER FIELDS IN OLD PROVENCE

'You didn't have to drive me to the railway station. I'm not six you know,' said Smiffy.

'I'm aware of both of those facts,' said Jason. 'Let's just call it my good deed for the day and a way of me paying you back for standing you up when you arrived.'

'Please,' she rolled her eyes.

Jason pulled into the car park next to the station. The place was busy, the commuters all gathering early for the train down to London. He parked up and smiled.

'What's so funny?' she asked him, looking up from her phone.

'Nothing,' he said.

'Come on Brazel, nobody who ever says nothing means it. You're fishing for me to ask you questions.'

'You're a journalist, or supposed to be, asking questions is part of your job. It's the *biggest* part.'

'Just tell me,' she said.

Jason continued to smile. Ever since he and Amita had uncovered the truth behind Hal Mulberry's murder, he'd felt like he was able to breathe again. He'd had at least three nights' uninterrupted sleep in the past week and he was starting to feel a little more human. It had been the same for Amita and he knew she was relieved. This had been a troublesome case but it was over, finally. Violet was recovering in hospital and charged for the murder.

'Do you remember that night you surprised me taking out the bins?' he said.

'The first time we met, how romantic that you remembered,' droned Smiffy.

'Do you remember you asked me for a handover for this story?'

'I do remember that,' she said. 'Although I shouldn't have had to ask. You should have been doing that as a fairly standard professional courtesy, when you were supposed to meet me off the train, which you didn't do. Remember?'

'I remember thinking at the time that it was probably the very lowest point of my career. I had been sacked from a job that, admittedly, I wasn't very good at or cut out for. I had forgotten to pick you up and now I was being chastised, quite rightly, by a reporter who was half my age, but it wasn't the lowest point in my not-so-glittering career,' he said. 'It probably wasn't even in the worst three.'

'No?' she feigned interest. 'Is this the moment I'm supposed to ask you what *was* the lowest point?'

'I was probably about your age when it happened,' he said, ignoring her.

'Here we go.'

'And I was sent out to interview some historical battle recreationists at Penrith Castle, just over there,' he pointed out of the window. 'I was meant to get dressed up in a suit of armour, try it all on and pretend to bash somebody else's head in for the pictures. It was all set up, ready to go, the historical society happy for it to go ahead. So I turn up, quite excited to get kitted out, when it hits me, like a mace between the eyes. It's a bank holiday and the place is awash with schoolkids out enjoying the lovely weather. There must have been hundreds of them Smith, hundreds. And I had to strip down to my boxers, pull on some smelly chainmail and a bucket for a helmet while all of these children pointed and laughed. If the heat of the suit wasn't bad enough, the rotting fruit and everything else they threw at me dragged it all down to a low I've not had before or since.'

'Great story bro,' said Smiffy. 'You want to tell me what the hell it has to do with me?'

'Nothing,' he said. 'Absolutely nothing at all, Smith. I just thought you'd like to know that, if you were harbouring any deep-seated fears that you had offended me in some way by taking over this story that you weren't to worry.'

'Seriously?' she asked. 'Have you read what I've been filing?'

'I have,' he said. 'I enjoyed it all the way up to the point where I stepped back in with an exclusive over the new arrest. I thought it all progressed really quickly from there, don't you?' He sat with a smug satisfaction.

Smiffy grinned. 'Yeah, yeah,' she said. 'You did good Brazel, bravo.'

'Did I mention how much Beeston offered me for the story?'

'Yeah you did,' she pouted. 'Did I mention the absolute roasting I was given for *not* getting that story? And how I'd filed a lovely background piece from Sheila Mulberry's neighbours on what she's *really* like, which has now been confined to the bin forever as she tries to become an MP? That was days of work totally wasted because of your exclusive. And I got shouted at. Thanks for that Brazel.'

He smiled back at her, knowing that he'd probably end up answering to her one day, begging for a job. She was going straight to the top.

'Cheer up,' he said, nudging her. 'At least you've been able to see some of the countryside, eh? That must be a plus.'

'Oh yeah, no signal and a curly old sandwich on the train. It'll be a highlight of my year.'

'What's next then?' he asked. 'Anything juicy?'

'Crime, crime and more crime.'

'Lovely.'

She checked her watch. Unfastening her seat belt, she opened the door. 'Got to run,' she said.

Jason got out and helped her with her bags. They walked to the station as the huge train pulled up next to the platform. Smiffy found her carriage and stepped onboard behind everyone else.

'Thank you,' she said, stopping in the doorway.

'Thank you?' he asked. 'For what?'

She looked down at him with her big, dark eyes. There was a humble demeanour about her and she looked, for the first time, like the junior reporter that she was.

'For putting in a good word with Beeston for me,' she said.

'I don't know what you mean,' he lied. 'I filed my own story and made a small fortune. That's all.'

'He went through me like a dose of salt, Brazel, but he didn't sack me. I've seen Beeston bin journalists for less. My feet shouldn't have touched the floor for being scooped.'

'His bark is worse than his bite,' said Jason, batting her away. 'You'll learn to handle people like Arnold Beeston, you just need to know what buttons to press.'

She nodded.

'And besides,' he said. 'Their days are numbered. It's people like you who'll be calling the shots soon enough. The generation who actually know what's happening on the street, what people want to read. Not old men in their ivory towers getting fatter and richer with every passing century. Enjoy it Ayanna. You'll do okay.'

The doors began to bleep. She took a step back as they slid closed. Jason smiled and waved. She flipped him the middle finger as the train began to move off.

'See you, Smiffy,' he called.

Chapter 34

THE ARTIST'S GARDEN AT GIVERNY

Amita sat on her own at her usual table in the bingo club. It was a nice relief to be there first. Usually she would arrive and there would be a myriad of conversations all going on at once and she'd have to play catch-up. Instead, tonight, she had made the effort to get there just that little bit earlier. Now she was reaping the benefits.

There were a few other early birds there too. Amita had given them an acknowledging nod as she took her seat. She got the same gesture back. It was as though they all knew how precious this time before bingo was. And that they shouldn't interrupt it with small talk or gossip. Mr Jones the janitor was sweeping something up in the far corner close to the stage. The back and forth swishes of his brush were rhythmical and almost hypnotic. If Amita closed her eyes she was sure she would drop off to sleep. It had been that kind of month.

It struck her then, as she stared down at her glasses, her bingo blotter and her money for tonight's game placed neatly in front of her on the table, that this was the first time she had really stopped in weeks. Ever since Jason had taken the Hal Mulberry job in London, life had moved at a million miles a minute. There had been little time for rest, little time for sleep, even her nicotine intake had been drastically reduced.

The doors of the hall swept open dramatically. A large crowd of regulars came in, the blissful silence broken. Amita didn't mind, not really. While it had been all too short and fleeting, she was just glad to be there, surrounded by friends.

'You've been at it again, haven't you?' came Ethel's unmistakable voice.

'Evening Ethel,' said Amita.

'You've been putting your nose in where it doesn't belong again, haven't you?' she said. 'You're always doing that. And one day you might get more than you bargained for.'

'Alright Ethel, that's enough now,' said Sandy, wheeling her to her usual spot at the end of the table. 'Let's just give Amita a break, eh?'

'Evening Sandy,' she said. 'How's the back?'

'It's better, Amita, thank you for asking,' said the big man. 'Although I don't know if these bloomin' plastic seats will do much for it.' He pulled a chair out with a big, bear-like paw, and sat down. Wincing, he rolled up his sleeves. 'How are you getting on anyway?' he asked. 'We heard about, you know, Violet and all of that.'

'I'm fine Sandy, really I am,' she said with a sigh. 'It was all such a terrible shock at the time. I mean, you never think you'll ever sit and spend time with a murderer, do you? Let alone it turn out to be somebody you've known for decades.'

'A crying shame that,' he shook his head. 'I mean, if anyone had asked me to pick a killer out of a line up from this place, I think Violet would have been the *last* person.'

'It's always the ones you least suspect,' cackled Ethel. 'The quiet ones too. They're the ones you have to watch the most. Like that Violet woman. Keep an eye on her, you mark my words, the woman is trouble.'

'Steady on, Ethel,' said Sandy.

Amita smiled. It was always good to talk to Sandy. He felt like the conscience of this place, of the collective group. He was level-headed enough to see the big picture. And he knew right from wrong.

'Evening folks,' said Judy Maskowitz, sitting down with a lot of movement. 'Sorry I'm late, got stuck in traffic didn't I. Then the sat nav took me the wrong way and I had to double back down the road and, well, you get the picture. I've not driven here in a very long time.'

'Hello Judy, are you alright?' asked Sandy.

'Yes, fine, why do you ask Sandy?' she said to him. 'Is it because I drove here myself? Is it because I'm sweating like a Christian in the Colosseum? Or the fact that the woman who was probably my best friend for thirty years is a homicidal maniac?'

Sandy looked a little embarrassed. Judy dumped her bag on the table and began rummaging through it for her things. She shook her head.

'I'm sorry Sandy,' she said, still out of breath. 'It's just been a challenging few days, that's all. You don't expect to get a phone call from Georgie Littlejohn telling you Violet has been arrested for the murder of Hal Mulberry every day. And when it does arrive, you kind of don't know where to put yourself. At least it explains why she started spreading those rumours that I was some kind of violent husband-beater. The moment I tried to help her with her filing, she changed. I was barred from the committee in a flash. I think she thought I was on to something. But I was only trying to help.'

'It must have come as a shock,' said Amita.

'Shock!' Judy yelped. 'Shock? I don't think I've ever been more shocked at anything in my life. And that includes when my Maurice passed away eating a brown bread turkey sandwich. He always hated brown bread, wouldn't go near the stuff. Yes, Amita, I was and am still shocked. Not least all of Violet's WI duties have fallen to me and I now have a summer fete to organise. I was supposed to be getting out!'

Amita smiled at that. She suddenly had images of the Penrith WI as a rival to the KGB. Once you joined, you could never leave. Judy settled down. The hall continued to fill up and Father Ford was on door duty welcoming everyone in as they arrived. Amita was certain he looked a little more tanned than usual. Maybe he was getting over his crippling anxiety at leading the bingo every Wednesday night. She very much doubted it though.

The colour drained from his face as she watched him talking to somebody just outside the door. Amita had her suspicions who it was. She wasn't disappointed as Georgie Littlejohn graced the hall with her presence.

'Good evening my darlings,' she said, tipping her designer sunglasses down her nose to meet them all.

'Good evening Georgie,' they all said in unison, like well-trained schoolkids.

'And how are we this lovely evening? All well I trust?'

'Can't complain,' said Sandy.

'Quite fine,' said Judy with a sneer.

'All the better for seeing you,' said Amita.

'Oh you,' she batted her away. 'See this is why we're so much better than that village hall rabble, wouldn't you agree? Comradeship, teamwork, it can't be beaten.'

'Speaking of rabble,' said Sandy. He nodded over Georgie's shoulder.

A very serious, stern looking Barbara McLemore and Albert Chamberlain were eyeing her up and down from their table by the door. One whispered something to the other then they fired another murderous look her way.

'You've done it now Littlejohn,' said Judy. 'They must have heard you.'

'What? No, surely not. Surely they know I was only joking,' said Georgie, panicking a little.

Barbara, Albert and a few of the other village hall loyalists got up. They made their way across the hall towards Amita's table. Standing at the far end, they offered meagre smiles.

'Evening,' said Barbara.

'Evening,' said Georgie, backing away from them a little and heading for her seat.

'To what do we owe your gracious company?' asked Judy sarcastically. 'Come to carve up the bingo hall's Wednesday night schedule, have we?'

'Judy,' Amita tried to call her off.

'No, actually,' said Barbara succinctly. 'We came over to offer our condolences. We heard about Violet Heatherington and knew you lot were pretty close to her. So we came to say we were sorry about what happened.'

'Oh,' said Georgie. 'Well, that's very sporting of you. Isn't it Judy?'

Judy grunted something and pretended to be searching her bag.

'And as for carving up your schedule for this place, we have no intention of doing anything of the sort,' said Barbara. 'When the village hall is back open after its renovations, we'll continue our own schedule, thank you very much. And it won't affect anything that goes on here. The WI will also be more than welcome to stay there, as it has done for years.'

'Again, very gracious of you Barbara,' said Georgie, regaining her confidence.

'So any bad blood that there might have been between us is over, right?' said Barbara said. 'Nothing to say you can't be a regular at the church hall bingo and the village hall events, is there?'

Nobody answered. They all looked to Judy and Georgie, the unofficial spokeswomen for the bingo hall faction.

'Fine,' said Judy. 'Very gracious of you.'

Barbara nodded. She looked at her posse who all stood around her, and nodded to them too. They were about to leave when Albert piped up.

'Did you ever get Colonel Mustard fixed, Georgie?' he asked, leaning on the table, a knowing look on his face.

It was Georgie's turn to go pale. Her mouth dropped open and hung there for what felt like an eternity. Amita could only sit and watch on.

'How... how did you know... about Colonel Mustard?' she just about managed eventually.

Albert straightened himself again. He tapped the side of his bulbous nose and continued to leer at her. 'You're not the only know-it-all around here Littlejohn,' he said. 'We know what you did.'

The village hall loyalists turned and went back to their own table. Georgie sat down, clutching her bag like it was a lifejacket and she'd just been thrown overboard.

'Colonel Mustard?' asked Sandy.

'Colonel Mustard?' asked Judy.

'Colonel Mustard?' asked Ethel.

Georgie didn't say anything. She just sat there, staring blankly ahead, her cheeks a dreadful grey.

'I thought I'd gotten away with it,' she whispered. 'But it's true what they say, isn't it? There's no such thing as the perfect crime and you reap what you sow.'

'I'm sorry,' said Judy, waving her hands about. 'Does somebody want to tell me what the hell you lot are babbling on about?'

Amita smiled. 'Perhaps we need a joint event to mark this new era. Anyone for a true-crime evening?'

Chapter 35

THE FRAME

The great and the good of Penrith were gathered once more in the car park outside the old village hall. While the venue had seen much better days, that was all about to change.

The renovation work had already begun in earnest. Scaffolding rigs climbed high around the walls now, hiding all the cracked paint and broken masonry. There were no workers today, of course, not for something as important as this. All work had been stopped and the red carpet rolled out, quite literally, for the local dignitaries. Even the weather had decided to behave itself, a comfortable warmth making the air shimmer a little.

Jason was sweltering. He tugged at his collar. Every time he did so, his tie grew that little bit looser. If Amita hadn't been with him it would be long gone by now. As it was, his mother-in-law was rigidly by his side, his plus one and only one.

'Would you stop fidgeting,' she said. 'And fix your tie.'

'It's a hundred degrees out here,' he said, keeping his voice low. 'I'm literally melting away inside this suit.'

'I told you to get a new one for the occasion, something light for the good weather.'

'And I told you, Amita, I wasn't forking out good money for a suit that would get worn on the three days of summer we get a year in this country.'

'You've made your bed then,' she said. 'So sleep in it.'

'It's alright for you, you've got that parasol for a hat keeping you cool. I'm burning up here.'

Amita adjusted the brim of her hat. She felt good, at peace. She just hoped, she *prayed* that today wouldn't turn out like the last time.

A waiter glided close to them and offered two flutes of champagne. Jason grabbed them in earnest and drained his glass. He felt the need to explain himself immediately.

'This suit is made from polyester,' he said. 'I'm absolutely toasted in the sunshine.'

The waiter gave a polite smile and moved off to serve others in the gathered crowd. Jason tugged at his collar again.

'I wish they would hurry up.'

He didn't have to wait long. The tall host from the unveiling ceremony took to the small stage that had been erected in front of the village hall. She still looked like a supermodel, unflinchingly and unattainably beautiful. The gathered crowd of dignitaries, business people and well-wishers all let their conversations come to a polite stop.

'Ladies and gentlemen,' she said, gazing out at the crowd. 'On behalf of everyone at the Mulberry Group, I would like to express our deepest gratitude for joining us this afternoon. As you know, this venue was a very special location for the late, departed Mr Mulberry. And we are delighted to welcome Penrith's mayor here for the unveiling of the dedication. But before we proceed with the ceremony, Dr Sheila Mulberry has asked to share a few words with you in memory of her late husband. I would like you to join me in welcoming her to the stage.'

She stood to one side as a respectful round of applause rippled around the crowd. Sheila Mulberry strode confidently across the small stage to the lectern. She gave a quick nod of acknowledgement to the tall host and stared out across the audience.

'She looks a lot better now than when we last saw her,' he whispered.

'Don't we all?' asked Amita.

'Good afternoon,' she said. 'Hal was a beloved member of this community. He was a local lad who was raised on good ethics and morals from his hard-working family. What happened to my husband was a tragedy and one that this community will feel for many years to come, I am sure of that. However, Hal wasn't one to dwell on the past. He was always looking to the future, looking towards what came next. He would often tell me that there was no use dwelling on the past as there was nothing you could do to change this. I used to say the same to him when the credit card bill arrived every month.'

Well-mannered laughter and some knowing smiles scattered through the audience.

'I will miss him more than any words can describe,' she said. 'But I know that with the full weight of justice on our side, his killer will face the justice she deserves when she reaches trial.'

Some agreements from quarters of the audience. Jason and Amita said nothing.

'It is with a bittersweetness then that I stand before you today,' Sheila went on. 'The building behind me has been a staple of this community for more years than any of us can care to remember. Much like Hal himself. He had a vision for this place, a clear idea in mind to make it the centre of Penrith's cultural heartbeat once again. A dedicated exhibition space for up-and-coming artists, an elite level conference area and of course a permanent home for Elvira's masterpiece *Buttermere at Dawn*. As you know, these plans are now in full progress and, as you can see, the work to renovate the old village hall is underway. So it is my absolute honour and privilege to stand here, at the doors, to officially dedicate the building to my late husband Hal Mulberry. His legacy will live on much longer than any of us. And I can't think of a greater tribute to a man who gave so much of his time, money and effort to this town.'

She stood to one side as the mayor made his way onstage. The gathered photographers joined them and huddled around a small curtain that had been temporarily put up in front of the scaffolding. Sheila stood on one side, the mayor on the other. They tugged at the cords and curtains parted, revealing a plaque with Hal's name on it and a likeness of him smiling back.

The audience erupted in a full applause, some whooping and cheering. Sheila stood staring at the plaque with her husband's name on it for a lingering moment. Then she turned back to the crowd, smiled, waved and made her way off stage. Amita nudged Jason and he followed her gaze to see Martin Gill across the room, smartened up and almost unrecognisable from the last time they'd seen him. He was looking up at the image of Hal, as if he were saying the farewells he never got to say in life.

'All very smoothly done,' said Jason clapping. 'A dry run for Dr Mulberry's hustings and campaign trail no doubt.'

'No doubt indeed,' said Amita. 'I don't think she would have had any problems anyway. But this ordeal won't do her ambitions any harm, even though she was arrested. It probably adds to her glamour – the innocent victim of a potential miscarriage of justice.'

'True,' he nodded.

The host took to the lectern and invited the crowd to continue enjoying the atmosphere. The audience were invited to share their pictures of the new plaque on social media but Jason headed in the other direction. He was desperate for another drink.

'A nice day out I suppose,' sighed Amita. 'It will be interesting to see what they do with this place.'

'It can't be any worse than it was already,' he said. 'Holes in the roof and a stagnant pong of wet dog didn't exactly do it for me, Amita.'

'No, nor I. Although I understand the WI are moving into the bingo hall while renovations are taking place.'

'That'll be fun,' he laughed.

'I can hear the arguments already,' she sighed.

'Jason!'

A voice called out to them. Jason was always wary of that sort of thing. He was always tempted to shout 'friend or foe' just to be sure.

Sally Arendonk eased her way through the crowd. She waved at them both and was smiling. Jason was relieved.

'I thought it was you two,' she said, arriving beside them.

'Yes, we're here,' said Amita.

'Trussed up like a pair of spare ones at a wedding,' said Jason.

'Although you're looking very smart Detective Inspector.'

Arendonk took a step back and surveyed her own outfit. She removed her hat and wiped away a little sweat from her brow.

'Yes, well, it's a special occasion and all of that, isn't it,' she said. 'Can't let the side down. That and the Police and Crime Commissioner is over there eating the venue out of house and home. I don't imagine he'd take too kindly to me rocking up in my jeans and Thrasher hoodie.'

'Thrasher hoodie?' asked Amita.

'I'll explain it later,' said Jason. 'How is the old commish, anyway? Still giving you a hard time over the future Right Honourable Dr Mulberry's arrest?'

'It'll pass,' she shrugged. 'It helped that I was able to bring in the *correct* suspect only a few days later. And for that I am truly grateful to you both.'

'Oh, stop it,' said Amita. 'You've already thanked us enough. If it hadn't been for your quick thinking Violet would be dead now and there would be no chance for justice.'

'We know how that feels,' said Jason solemnly.

'Have you seen her recently?' asked Amita.

'No, not for about two weeks now,' said the DI. 'She's being well looked after by the psych department. She's confessed and pleaded guilty at her initial hearing so it's just a case of sentencing now...'

'How do you think it'll go with the judge?' asked Jason.

'It's hard to say,' said Sally. 'Her age will be a factor, then there's her mental state. Who knows. All that matters is we caught the killer and hopefully our trust with the public isn't shaken up too much. Which reminds me.' She reached into the pocket of her jacket and produced a sealed envelope, handing it over to Jason.

'What's this?' he asked, frightened to accept it.

'A formal thank you, from the commissioner,' said Sally.

'What?' blurted Amita.

'Calm down, it's not something to get excited about,' she went on. 'It just reaffirms everything is above suspicion. As far as Cumbria Police is concerned, you two were just a pair of old friends who were confided in with Violet's confession. You had no role in the investigation and you won't be getting warned about poking your noses in where they don't belong. Although I probably shouldn't say this but I'm glad you did. We never would have put those connections together. I appreciate it, really I do.'

Jason took the letter. He smiled at the DI. 'Not a bad scalp for your first case on the patch, eh Detective Inspector?' he laughed.

'A death inspired by high art, it's a new one for me,' she smiled back. 'Let's hope it's the last time.'

'Never say never,' said Amita.

'No, that's true,' she said. 'If I've learned anything in my time being a copper, it's to expect the unexpected. Even if that comes in the shape of a dodgy journalist and his mother-in-law.' Arendonk offered them each her hand and replaced her hat.

Jason and Amita watched as Sally moved back into the crowd and disappeared.

'She's a good egg,' said Amita.

'I don't think I could agree any more with you on that front,' he said. 'Which is actually something special, given we've been agreeing an awful lot recently.'

'We have?' she asked, turning from the crowd and starting for the exit of the car park.

'Yes, don't you think so?' he said, joining her. 'I mean, it's been almost a day since we had a fight. That's got to be a new record.'

'What about your collar? Doesn't that count?'

'Oh yes, so it does, damn,' he clicked his fingers. 'Scratch that idea then. Maybe I was too hasty to think we were more and more on the same page.'

'I don't know whether to be offended by that or complimented,' she clicked her tongue.

Just then, the official photographer sidled over, camera pointed at them. 'Picture for the paper sir, madam?' he asked.

Jason grinned and threw his arm over Amita's shoulder. 'Say cheese, Amita!'

The flash fired and the photographer went to stalk his next prey.

'Don't you ever hug me like that in public again, Jason Brazel,' she shrugged his arm off of her.

'Come on, Amita. It'll be a lovely shot. You know what they say: a picture paints a thousand words.'

They walked off out of the car park, leaving the gathered audience of dignitaries behind them. The sun beat down from the clear blue sky and, in the stillness of the warm Cumbrian afternoon, everything seemed that little bit brighter, that little bit more safe.

MURDEROUS OAP JAILED
FOR BRUTAL SLAYING
OF CUMBRIA TYCOON

*By Jason Brazel and
Ayanna Smith in Penrith*

A VINDICTIVE pensioner who cut the throat of one of the UK's leading philanthropists has been jailed for life. Violet Heatherington, 72, pleaded guilty to the murder of Hal Mulberry in Carlisle County Court and has now been sentenced to life behind bars. Sending the OAP down, a judge said that while she had suffered a number of difficulties throughout her life, the brutal slaying of a prominent public figure could not go unpunished without a custodial sentence.

Heatherington, of Penrith, murdered Mr Mulberry just moments before he was due to unveil *Buttermere at Dawn* at a planned new arts centre in the town. While police had initially arrested another suspect over the killing, the pensioner was later brought in for questioning. It's understood that the culprit had previously owned the two-million-pound painting but had sold it in the 1970s for a fraction of the price.

The popular local pensioner showed no emotion as she was sentenced. However, it's thought that Heatherington, a prominent figure in the local Women's Institute, saw Mr Mulberry as a focal point for her anger and targeted him ahead of the unveiling of the Elvira masterpiece.

Mr Mulberry's estate has confirmed that his original vision for the old village hall in Penrith will proceed. Developers are already working on the multi-million-pound makeover, with new facilities expected to help local causes and support the thriving arts scene in the town and surrounding area.

A statement from Mr Mulberry's lawyer said: 'The whole family and businesses associated with Mr Mulberry are looking forward to the bright future away from this tragedy. We know that his legacy will remain as one of the most fondly remembered entrepreneurs in Cumbrian history.' The statement went on to quash reports that the artwork had been accidentally left unguarded in the grounds of the village hall on the night of the murder. 'We are delighted to confirm that a top quality reproduction has been used throughout and will remain on display until construction work is over. As custodian of the *Buttermere at Dawn*, Mr Mulberry did not want to risk it getting damaged in the renovations.'

Local art dealer, Arthur Doige, whose podcast 'Buttermere at Dawn: Curse or Crime?' which has been gathering notoriety across the internet, refused to confirm or deny whether he was providing safe storage for the original.

Heatherington was also found guilty of breaking and entering and extensive vandalism to Doige's gallery in the days leading up to her arrest.

Cumbria Police were quick to quash any rumours that their investigations had been helped by members of the public and a vigilante group.

Detective Inspector Sally Arendonk said: 'My team are pleased that Violet Heatherington will face the justice that she deserves. This was a complex and difficult case but the public can rest assured that myself and the rest of my colleagues at Cumbria Police work around the clock to ensure the safety of this county and the people who call it home. And I would take this opportunity to remind everyone – and I mean everyone – that if you witness or suspect a crime, to leave it to the proper authorities to handle.'

Acknowledgements

I'm a great believer that writing a book is a team effort. The days of scribes working furiously away by candlelight on their own are long gone. And this book, for me, is as much a tribute and testament to teamwork as I think I've ever had. To that end, I want to thank EVERYONE who has helped bring it together into what is hopefully the enjoyable story and caper you've just read.

I'll start, as always, by thanking the wonderful HarperNorth team. Genevieve Pegg is absolutely the best editor and person that any writer could ever hope to work with – from her tireless efforts to fix my (awful) spelling to sharing brilliant ideas, quirks, dialogue and everything else that makes *The Village Hall Vendetta* sparkle. I am lucky and privileged to have such support doing something that I love.

Alice Murphy-Pyle cannot be thanked enough for all of her genius in getting this book and my work into the world. Her enthusiasm, vigour, talent and verve are a constant inspiration. Again, without her, I wouldn't enjoy half as much what I'm very privileged and humbled to be able to do.

A massive thanks to the Northbank Talent Management team – Diane, Natalie and Elizabeth – for being such sterling champions of my work, not to mention me, at every turn. And to Hannah Weatherill for always believing in me.

A thank you also goes to my dear friends Chris McDonald and Steven Kedie. Their boundless support and sheer will-power to put up with me, sometimes on an hourly basis, has been the backbone of the writing of this novel. And while I'd never admit it to them in real life, their friendship has become something immeasurably special.

I'd also like to thank two art teachers who had the misfortune of having me as a pupil in school. This novel involves art of various forms and it was Mrs Brown who first sparked that interest I have in all things from that world. She taught me that Leonardo, Michelangelo, Donatello and Raphael weren't just Ninja Turtles. And that with the subtlest of brush strokes, the chaos, mayhem and magic of the world can be recaptured by the very boldest and brilliant of talents. Meanwhile Mr Brunton had that indefatigable knack for encouraging my own attempts with a down-to-earth, almost football manager-style approach to his teaching. He combined the modern world with the ancient one so deftly that I learned that time held no limit on what a masterpiece can be.

Thanks too to the brilliant booksellers who've been so enthusiastic in getting copies of my books to readers everywhere. And finally, before the hook comes to take me off the stage, I want to thank you, the reader. I love telling stories, I have done since I was in shorts. Without you, I can't to that, it's just me ranting and raving into the mirror. So thank you for being there and for listening.

PS. Let me know if you spotted the hidden link between the paintings that give the chapters their titles. Find me online at @jdwhitelaw13 if you did.